C000182135

THE SON

The Sean Rooney Psychosleuth Series

Tom O. Keenan

Published by McNidder & Grace
21 Bridge Street
Carmarthen SA31 3JS
UK

www.mcnidderandgrace.co.uk

Original paperback first published 2020

© Tom O. Keenan

All rights reserved. No part of this work may be reproduced or transmitted in any form or by any means, electronic or mechanical, including photocopy, recording, or any information storage or retrieval system, without permission in writing from the publisher.

Tom O. Keenan has asserted his right to be identified as the author of this work in accordance with the Copyright, Designs and Patents Act 1988.

A catalogue record for this work is available from the British Library.

ISBN: 9780857161994
Ebook: 9780857162007

Designed by JS Typesetting Ltd, Porthcawl
Cover design: Lara Peralta

Printed and bound in the UK by Gomer Press Ltd, Ceredigion

PROLOGUE

I will begin with the end, for everything in here, as you will see, arrives at an inevitable consequence: death.

I have emerged from the dark and I cannot return without him. He looks at my canine form silhouetted against the moonlit backdrop of the harbour and says, "I'll see you away, you stupid mutt." He reaches into his car and pulls out a heavy looking spanner. This man understands his frailty, the possibility of attack, but not from the likes of me.

I slope closer to him and expel a deep growl. "Jesus, you are a big fucking pooch." It has dawned on him I am no ordinary 'pooch'. In the dim light I see his face drain of blood, his eyes widen as he takes in my deathly shape, my eyes of fiery embers. He girds himself and takes a swipe with the spanner. It strikes my snout but it makes no difference, I feel no pain. He kicks out at me, crashing into my middle: same thing, it only defers the inevitable. I leap and batter him, knocking him to the ground next to the car.

He reaches for the frame of the door to pull himself up. A normal hound would set about him, tear at his limbs, rip at his flesh. Me, I have one destination. I wrap my jaws around his head and, with the power of a hydraulic arm, I squeeze. I hear two things together, the crushing sound as his skull gives way under the weight of my teeth and his moan, now increasing in volume to a scream. I have no wish to prolong his agony as my final embrace cracks the skull and his brain sprays out through the gaps in my teeth. It tastes good. I have not had physical matter for such a long time and I enjoy the taste. I give a hefty twist and take his head from his body, spitting it out to within a foot of it. His eyes remain wide open, as if observing me in this task.

It is now time for me to deliver the duty for which I am destined. I reach into his chest and remove his soul. It comes easily as if it is pleased to be removed from a lifeless body. In removing his head, however, I have exceeded the mandate I was given lives ago. I have become a taker of life rather than the conveyor of souls. It is clear I can no longer be what I was destined to be.

CHAPTER 1

First, though, I will take you to Lochdarrach School, the day after the Samhuinn, exactly three months before. It is the midday break when we run together, the children and I. The playground is small and we cover its length with the lightness of youth and the freedom from age or concern. I meander between them, for they do not all see me, nor are they to know I am here for one of them.

I can tell you it is not John McLeod, this lad of ten winters, who will live to take over the croft as a young man; who, like his father Iain the croft, he will be seventeen years when I come for him.

And it is not Mary McNeil, the girl of eight years of the fair skin Viking folk who settled on these shores. She is slow to cover the ground due to a fall from the cliffs at Stoer when she was six, but *ma-tha*, she will survive into adulthood and become teacher of this school.

It is not John Sinclair, the fastest of foot, out of reach of the rest. I will take him on his twenty-second year when he is washed ashore, his boat sinking off Callaness point.

It is not Angus Stuart, from the Islands. A bold lad of nine, he will see his life out to be one hundred and three years and he will chronicle the events to occur here. An inquisitive boy, he is not concerned in using his energy in the playground. He is a *taibshears* and sees those who have left their worldly form to come with me, the *taibhs*. He has *an da shealladh* and can predict a passing. He is aware of me in his midst, though avoids me, like all taibshears do.

Nor is it Andrew Dewar, a boy of nine winters, who lives down *Bótha Dubh*. I took his alcoholic father last year, when he overturned his tractor while on the drams. Andrew will come to me in six years when he takes his own life.

The lad trailing Mary McNeil is a dark, swarthy child from the lowlands. He is new to these parts, but not to me. He will be mine soon. It is for him, I am here.

The teacher, Eileen McIsaac, claps her hands to herald the end of playtime and a return to the classroom. "*Am ri teachd ann*," she calls out, for the ancient words are enjoyed here in this school.

The children filter in one by one as they march up the ramp and through the door of the schoolhouse. Each saying, "*Feasger mhath, Mrs McIsaac*," as they pass the teacher. It takes seconds for them to go inside. I hesitate, taking in the scene. You will appreciate I do not follow, but there is a fine visage for me in a highland school, a place to foresee the inevitable from the very earliest days.

It is time for the *balach*, Calum Rooney.

It is four beyond the noon and he waits for the mother to collect him from the school. She is late. He paces the entrance hall and peers out of the door checking if she has arrived to take him home. Fumbling with his backpack, tight on his back, heavy and uncomfortable, it nips the skin on his shoulders. Full of jotters and textbooks, it is his homework for the next day. With an empty lunchbox, he is anxious to get home for his tea.

The day is Tuesday, the first day of the eleventh month, sixteen years from the millennium, and three days to his eighth year. The days have turned, giving less daylight from an already darkening sky; the dark days, when the cold and mist combine in the glens and the waves crash against the rocks making foam on the beaches. Nothing fazes me. I do not feel the cold or the rain, nor fear the dark nor the task or the burdens or consequences before me. Nothing will defy my purpose: to take them away.

Befitting my presence and Samhuinn, the school is bedecked in spectres, witches, ghouls. Ghostly figures, these worldly emblems will be removed when the cleaners arrive later this evening. The souls have returned to whence they came; not, you will understand, that I have had respite; for once emerged I cannot return alone. As proper for the Cù-Sith, I give three howls to herald my arrival.

The *balach* is the one to be collected this day.

The teacher is busy writing at her desk in the classroom, confident the boy will be picked up soon. She hears a car arriving outside the school with a couple of toots on its horn. *It will be the mother arriving to take him home*, she thinks. She will finish her reports and go out to say hello to her and goodbye to the boy, but she hears him call, "*Oidhche mhath*, Mrs McIsaac," in soft, happy tones. How sweet he sounds.

She remembers the day the parents brought him to the school to meet her. It was almost Christmas of the year before. They were on a trip north to plan their move here. He impressed her as a confident child; with a police detective mother and a forensic psychologist father she thought she knew why. Previously of mixed faith, the father, a lapsed catholic and the mother, a never-practising protestant, viewed themselves to be faithless. However, the choice of the catholic gaelic medium school offered the best education for their son. They were enthusiastic about the school, and open about their previous divorce and reconciliation, which led to the adoption of the boy, and their plans for a new life in Achfara. Although they had 'history', they said, and would be older parents, they were keen to assure her, as they did the adoption agency, they were stable, *safe* parents.

The teacher calls back to the boy. "*Oidhche mhath, Calum, chì mi thu sa mhadainn.*" A few moments later, she peeks out of her window to see the rear red lights of the car heading off up Bhother Beag, the small road leading towards the coastal road. This would mean the boy would be home within ten minutes. Content all the children are home safely, she returns to her reports.

A few minutes later, she hears another car arrive. *It would be her husband for her*, she thinks, and is surprised when the mother of the boy walks into the classroom. "I'm just in for Calum, Mrs McIsaac." The mother is also surprised to find the boy is not there, nor outside in the hall waiting. She looks around the room. "Is he in the toilet again; have you ever known a child who goes as much as he does?"

The teacher rises from her desk, not concerned; another mother may have stopped by and collected the boy to drop him home. "He is just away, Jackie; I thought it was you picking him up."

"No, not me." The mother pauses only long enough to make the point.

"I wouldn't worry; it will be Mrs McAlliog who stopped by after shopping in Lochdarrach to see if anyone needed a lift home. He will be waiting for you when you get back."

"Strange, she'd normally phone or text to save me the journey." The mother checks her phone.

"Jackie, you know what the mobile reception is like around here. Get along the road a bit and a text or a call notification will pop up I'm sure. It'll be nothing to worry about." The teacher returns to her desk.

"Aye, you'll be right." The mother seeks the words which would not make the teacher think she was questioning her. She wanted to say she should know who is picking up the children, but she has been in Achfara long enough to realise no one there worries about the children. If she had still been in Glasgow she would have been more pointed, like 'now you listen to me, miss'. Well, she would have made her point, but "I'm sure you're right, he'll be making the tea with his dad by the time I get back," comes out instead. "I'll give you a ring then… just to put your mind at ease." She questions herself for saying this; the teacher's mind would not be troubled. This is Lochdarrach, and as safe as can be: the people here look out for each other, especially the children, and they did not expect me.

The teacher looks up from the depths of her work. "OK, Jackie, *oidhche mhath*."

The mother smiles at the gaelic. She enjoys the language and is a learner herself. "*Oidhche mhath*, Mrs McIsaac, I'll see you tomorrow no doubt – have a good evening."

The teacher raises her eyes to just above her glasses to see the mother leave. Ten minutes later, she would get the call to change her life.

"Calum's not here, Mrs McIsaac, he's not here." There is panic in the mother's voice.

"Jackie, don't worry, Mrs McAlliog will have taken him to her house and she'll be about to call you to pick him up there."

"I called her, he's not there either. Did you not see the car, whose car was it? I need to know who picked him up."

The teacher stops herself from saying something pointed. The mother had been a high-ranking police officer and a lowlander, both aspects which she thought might make her prone to an overreaction in this highland village, but she does not answer giving the right message.

"I'll call some of the other mothers, just in case it was one of them who picked him up." It is just as well the mother does not see the teacher shaking her head; she would have really got annoyed then.

Bloody hell, the mother thinks, *complacent or what up here*, then cautions herself against thinking those kinds of thoughts or voicing those words. She wants to make a go of it in this community and understands the sensitivity of the locals about incomers making outsider remarks.

Please understand I have known these people, their forebears, and their descendants, for ages. They are loyal to their faith and to their community, faithful to their beliefs and their highland views, but most of all protective of their culture and way of life – as am I.

I remember when they were cleared from the pastures to crofts on the seashore, to eke out a wretched existence, surviving on meagre crops and occasional fish. They are a proud and god-fearing community; always have been, even in the days of starvation, clan wars, and rebellion. They have faced me through hunger, war, disease and disaster, and met me with forbearance, coming to me as if they owed me a death for having lived.

They have particular names, made up of their forenames or what they are or where they are from. John the post, or 'Post', who followed his father and his father before him as the postman, trekking over one hundred miles a day over rough terrain to deliver the mail. Annie McDonald: '*Cailleach*', the ninety-two-year-old matriarch of the village. Douglas 'Caber', a McKinnon, who runs the post office but known more for his annual caber throwing at Achfara Highland games which he has consistently won, despite fierce competition from the young lads, since '76. Caber has a fierce tongue, notwithstanding an even fiercer right hook after a dram or few. An incomer is not accorded with such respect by being given a title, sometime only being referred to as the visitor or the lowlander, or even the *sasunnach*. There are others, however, I will introduce you to as I reveal the story of this place and the sad circumstances drawing me away from my destined duties.

I am the Cù-Sith or, as they refer to me, the 'taker of souls'.

The mother and father got out of Glasgow. They had to: murder, injury, and self-abuse had taken their toll on the both of them. It was time to retreat to a quieter place, to heal, to live the peaceful life, to come to terms with the chaos of their lives.

After the inevitable divorce, separation and living apart, they came to the one reasonable conclusion: despite their obvious problems they were better off together, but only by seeking a new life and turning their backs on their old lives as partners in the crime. They were sick of crime in the city, the mob, the police, too many psychopaths, and they were tired of the likes of me.

Remarrying and adopting the boy made their reconciliation official and gave them the family they wanted and needed. The *balach* was encouraged to come here by his love of seashells and steam trains, both of which were available in the area, a place he had holidayed in a year before arriving. A promise of a dog sealed it. They took a pup from a local farmer, a border collie they called Lass. The local authority had removed the boy from parents who had succumbed to the drams and the drugs, neglecting his needs so much so he was released for adoption.

They sold up what they had, including an art collection and antique furniture, sold to a private collector; trappings from parallel lives of crime. The crime syndicate took back his house near the long western road; it was fortunate this was the only thing they took. His mentor and crime boss once said to him, "When you chose the life of a gangster there is nowhere else to go, you will live and die in the Family." She sold her townhouse near the park by the river. All of this was enough to buy a farmhouse in the highlands.

They found the house in Achfara, this small north coast place, a few miles between the fishing village of Stoer and in the opposite direction the tourist village of Lochdarrach – my domain.

In earlier times, when they were first married, they came here on holiday and loved it. It seemed the perfect place to settle. Here, they could put the past behind them and start afresh. The mother took early retirement from the police and the father had retired from his profession years before when alcohol and mental illness took a serious hold on him. With their pensions, the mother's part-time job in the local health centre, the father's in the local bar, the Small Isles, they had enough money to live their new life.

It was a good time to move for them. In the lowlands, the father led a crime syndicate, achieving notoriety impossible to sustain, far less protect himself or his family against. The mother was involved with the Glasgow underworld, but from the opposite perspective of law-woman, to obvious risk to herself, evident by a disability sustained by a car bomb attempt on her life.

With this irregularity, the family arrived in a place where there was no such thing, no such history, and no such danger.

CHAPTER 2

Their house is not the usual welcoming place for the father as he returns home. "Is he back, Jackie, in his room?" He hangs his jacket on a door peg.

The mother rushes to meet him. "He's not here, Rooney; obviously why I called you."

This does not stop him looking in the boy's bedroom. "You know I was in Invernevis. You pick him up on a Tuesday when I'm at my meeting."

"I know, but he wasn't there when I went for him. Do you think I would lie to you?"

The father checks his phone for anything he might have missed. "But I dropped him off this morning."

"I know you did." She turns to the window.

"Where is he then?"

Her voice rises to the level of the church choir. "Rooney, he wasn't here when I came home. I wouldn't have dragged you back otherwise; I know how important it is."

"Important?"

"To the both of us."

The stop for a moment; this was part of the deal: to keep the father off the drams.

"He could have got in himself. He knows the spare key is always in the shed." He looks at her. "And aye, I've checked, the key is there."

"Why do we lock the door? This is the highlands, not Glasgow."

"We lock the door, we agreed."

"He didn't go to the beach?"

"Rooney, Mrs McIsaac said he was picked up in a car, and before you ask no one else picked him up to my knowledge."

"Calum would have never got into a car with anyone he didn't know," he says to offer reassurance and control the panic setting in. "*I* taught him."

"Aye, so you did." She paces the floor, her stick clacking on the planks, occasionally glancing out of the window. "And it's been an hour since he was picked up by someone we don't fucking know."

The mother understands whatever the circumstances, the boy should be home. She called into Mrs McAlliog's house after the school; she seemed upset the mother thought she would pick him up and not contact her.

"What about the other mothers?"

"I called them all, Rooney, even though Mrs McIsaac said she would." With twenty-six pupils from fifteen mothers, it did not take her long to get around them. "No one saw him." They offered other possibilities, like Jan Legowski the priest, or John the post, or Teenie the taxi, all popping in to see if anyone needed a lift. "I've checked them all."

"McIsaac, the guy with the bus?"

"I think she would know if it was her husband."

"This is my biggest fear." The father drops to a seat at the table.

"I'm calling the police." The mother is aware in the event something has happened to her son time is important; his time as a forensic psychologist tells him the same.

"You do that."

She calls Stoer police station. John Broomlands, *the* police officer for the area, picks up the call right away. He knows of her and the boy, after much chattering in the office over their arrival, much of it due to her being the daughter of the chief constable of Police Scotland, Hubert Kaminski.

Broomlands spells out 'Ca … lum Roo … ney', as he writes out the name. He reminds her in the vast amount of cases the child turns up within a few hours, then asks what they had tried, all the while playing down any possibility of abduction. Never in the history of the three villages had there been such an incident, he says. Nevertheless, he would contact the area office in Invernevis where the register of local child abusers is held. He declines the possibility of a local search. "It is too early for that, Mrs…"

She casts her eyes upward. "Not Mrs, just Jackie… Jackie Kaminski."

"Aye, sorry, it is just your son, Calum Rooney?"

"Kaminski's a bit of a mouthful."

Only the surname of the chief constable, the boy's adopted grandfather. "Oh, right, thank you." The father shakes his head.

The mother put him straight on the surname, just another incomer habit – surprised they managed to adopt without being married, he would have thought.

"All procedures need to be carried out, constable. You'll know protocol in these matters."

I am not sure he does, but there is an authority in the mother's voice, which tells him he should, borne from her previous status as assistant chief constable in Police Scotland. Now retired, however, he is just as aware of her lack of actual authority. He is not going to be told how to do his job by an ex-policewoman who knows nothing about policing in the highlands.

"I know, Ms… Kaminski. We've been trained in all necessary procedures." She should not worry too much, the boy will turn up, he tells her, and he would be in touch later, but she should call him back 'either way'.

Her face belies her anger over his indifference. "Listen, Broomlands, if—"

"Please, Jackie." The father rises from his seat, just in time to receive one of those stares which says 'don't Rooney, just don't'.

She ends the call there, saying, "I'll back in touch later, one way or other."

"Right, I'm going out to look for him." The father snatches his jacket from the back of the door. The mother reaches for hers. "No, you stay here by the phone," he says. "Someone may call, even Calum, and he might just walk in the door." She knows he is right. "I'll start in Lochdarrach and go to the school and take it from there." This would take him along the trunk road to Lochdarrach, onto the back road to the school, from there onto the coast road towards Achfara and on into Stoer and then back to the house. A circular course of around eight miles, it would cover all the main routes around there, apart from the dirt forest tracks and minor paths snaking out to remote areas, crofts, and bothies. "I'll take Lass. If he's out there she'll find him."

The dog leaps into the car as the father turns to look towards the house. The mother is at the kitchen window, the phone pressing against her ear. She puts her hand up against the glass, a gesture of oneness with him, but her eyes say she is scared. He knows she will be fastidious, contacting all and any friends and acquaintances, extending to just about everyone in the area. With around two hundred souls, this would take hours. She need not have worried, however, the jungle drums are beating. Teenie the taxi had been onto her extensive family and the news had spread across the village; her friends had done the same and they had been on the phone spreading the news even wider. "Wee Calum is missing," echoes across the phone lines.

The *coigreachs* arrived at the farmhouse at the end of February, in the twenty sixteen beyond the millennium. A cold and windy day, it took hours to get the AGA and the wood burning stove going enough to raise the temperature of the house. This was a far cry from Glasgow with its modern centrally heated homes. The *balach* loved it, especially the beach where he amassed a collection of seashells: queen scallop, pelican's foot, spoot and periwinkle. He ran around it and the farm courtyard as if he had been locked up for his whole life before then. Glasgow was like a prison for him in many ways.

The mother and father received threats from some of the criminal families the father had associations with, one of the reasons they spent a lot of time indoors down there. Then it was time for the boy to go to school, and they both knew this meant constant worry. The father had a mental illness too which did not help; his paranoia was crippling all of them. The authorities, MI5 and ISIS; often it was hard to separate fact from fiction.

It was clearly time to move from Glasgow and the first weeks in Achfara felt like they had been let out of jail. They spent hours on the beach, playing with the dog and paddling in the sea, even although it had only been around five degrees. They worked hard repairing and upgrading the farmhouse. The father, unaccustomed to working with his hands, developed a love of dry stone dyking, repairing old boundary walls. It was a 'metaphor' he said, for his ailing body: while repairing the walls he was repairing himself. His physical and mental health improved with the repairing of the walls around their land. The mother for her part took a UHI course in business administration with the intention of a career change towards hotel management.

The *balach* was a friendly but quiet lad, preferring a solitary life, exploring rock pools and adding to his burgeoning shell collection. He detested being pushed into groups. He could have been 'autistic' the mother thought, although he had never been tested or confirmed to be so.

It was not hard to find him earlier standing on his own against the stone wall of the school playground. He did not take part in the game of chase. He would not run the length of the schoolyard nor the beach ever again. I studied him for a minute, wondering why one so young should be taken so early in life. But it was not for me to try to understand this; I know my calling and I have to do my duty.

The father searches for the boy. He has just turned into Lochdarrach when he sees Donald McDonald, also known as Inverbeg, having come from the isolated village of the same name, some twenty miles over the hill. He stops the car and winds down the window. "Inverbeg, you OK, you seen Calum?"

"I heard about Calum from Mary, Rooney; she called me." Inverbeg enjoys his walk at half past five every evening, to be back in time for the BBC Scotland news. He had been given a diagnosis of diabetes a few weeks earlier by Richard Black, the local doctor, who put him on a strict diet with a demand he lose weight. He would be mine soon. After the walk and the news, he will spend the rest of the evening in the local hotel bar, the Small Isles.

"You'll be worried." The father grits his teeth and nods his head. "I'll look out for him and I'll ask in the bar. If anyone's seen him, I'll give you a call."

"Right, thanks. Oh, Inverbeg?"

"Aye, Rooney?"

"Could you tell Maggie or Magnus I won't be in tonight?" The father would normally start his shift behind the bar at eight.

"Of course, hope the wee man turns up soon."

The father intended going into the bar anyway, but is relieved not to; his time would be taken up with answering their questions, hearing their concerns, receiving their offers of support. Talking to them is a distraction. He just wants to get on with it, to find the boy. The bar is the centre of the community and accepted as the best place to circulate information, or obtain any, but this night Inverbeg would be happy to do spread the word. It will give him an excuse to talk to anyone approaching the bar while he is standing there. The father had worked in the Small Isles for eight months, a bit of a risk for an ex Glasgow drinking man – he understood a few drinks would take him over the edge into a binge which at best would inflame his mental illness or at worst kill him. Immersing himself in a drinking culture honed his defences against it, reminding himself of the dangerous relationship he had with the *uisge-beatha*. He knows Magnus Stuart, the owner, would not be expecting him, not this night.

He drives through the village at speed as a range of possibilities arrives in his mind, notably the boy has been taken or *they*, from Glasgow, had caught up with them. All he knows is the boy got into a car, or maybe he had not got into any car, but had decided to walk home thinking his mother would pick him up on the way. An independent boy, this was something he would have expected of him. He may have decided to cross the moors and had become lost in the dark. The teacher might have assumed he got into a car having seen one going away from the school up the road, where it may have been just passing by. He knows the car is important as the driver may have seen the boy.

The light is on as he reaches the school. He thinks about going in to talk to the teacher, but knowing the mother would have questioned her decides against it. Time is not his friend as it has been nearly two hours since the boy left there. He cannot phone the mother because of the lack of a signal there, but knows by then she would be 'pressing all the buttons'. He will continue the search on his own in the meantime. Working as a team, her inside, him out, they would find him. He parks in the school car park, lets the dog out of the car, collects a torch, and walks up the road at pace in the direction of their house, two miles away, following the route the boy would have taken to go home.

He travels along the deserted single-track road, panning the torch light from side to side. It is bright, giving a fine illumination of the countryside. There are pine martins in the area of his house and, given they have a few hens, he bought the torch, capable of covering the seven acres of their field into the trees. He hopes he would be able to see any moving creatures that could harm the hens, and scare them away.

Walking along the road like a moving lighthouse, the *athair* heads towards the shore at Claigan. It has become dark, a cloudy night with minimal moonlight and without the torch, he would not have seen a yard in front of him. He hopes the boy has not decided to walk into this darkness. He approaches the shore; the sound of the waves slapping the beach create a whoosh, whoosh sound, as the clouds part to allow the moon to give some light on the coast. He switches the torch off, trying to decide if the boy had been out there somewhere whether he would have been able to see his way home.

Just then there are books and a bag at the side of the road, a Hogwarts bag, light grey. "It's Calum's." He picks it up. "Hufflepuff, it's definitely Calum's." He looks for the dog, but she has disappeared from his side. Then he hears her barking from the beach, next to the water's edge.

It is there, rocking with the lapping waves, he sees the *balach*.

I had found him earlier. His eyes were wide open, looking up at the moonlit sky, or at something as life left them. His face was like a shiny porcelain doll, angelic, glistening from the light of the moon. His arms were stretched out like he was about to embrace someone; though his hands were clenched fist-like, like he had been in a fight in the school playground. His legs were together, bent at the knees, a ninety-degree angle, as if had you raised his body onto them he would be kneeling. With his arms splayed and his eyes looking upward, he looked like he was in church looking towards his heaven or his god.

I reached into him and felt the warmth of his life, cooling steadily with the chill of death invading him. The young soul felt good, it invigorated me, energised me. It pulsated with energy not known to me, like the heart that no longer beats. The ones I normally take are tired and done. But this one fought me, a defiance also not known to me. It confused me, it rattled me.

The father did not see me taking him, or what they describe as his soul, to what they also describe as the afterlife. But this did not happen in the way I intended. I would leave this dead boy with his soul, for the meantime. Something told me not to take him; something powerful challenged my death given duty. He would remain an undead, until I could reason why I feel this way about him, this death over the countless others. And, for the meantime, the circumstances in which the boy died will remain with me. You will understand, I have no concerns as to the means or consequences of death. It happens eventually to all. It is an inescapable occurrence: all living beings die.

I am called many things. In these parts I am the Cù Sìth, the fairy dog; in other places the Dullahan, or the Malak al-Maut, the Angel of Death, or for many the Grim Reaper. Unlike, Charon the ferryman of Hades, no one pays me to carry souls across the river of death; I do it because it is my duty. We are spirits, angels; deities in many religions, whose sole responsibility is to convey souls to where there are destined to go. Our role is neither to judge nor question, but to provide safe passage. We could be described as death, though death is the condition, and heaven, hell or wherever, the destination, where we are the escort.

Maha, where they go, is of no interest to me, you will understand. The faithful folk around here aspire to heaven, others elsewhere to nirvana or paradise. They fear the other place, mostly called hell. Some believe they will be reborn, recreated; but they are wrong, this is a one-way road and I bring no one back. Many believe death is not the end – though it is of course the end of the body, the spirit may remain, however.

I am inevitable; believe me, you too will come my way, one day. On this matter, there is nothing I have not seen, and my knowledge on the subject is infinite. The means by which you and most people die, normally by natural causes interests me less than those caused by a human hand. With a natural death, there is me and there is the deceased. With a murder, there are three of us: the deceased, the slayer, and me, an unnatural relationship not of my liking, but a death is a death, and even the murderer will be mine one day.

The boy's circumstance is of particular interest to me, however, because within it exists the possibility of more coming my way.

You will understand death by old age, illness, or accident bores me; death by one's own hand confuses me, but death caused by another's hand interests me. In my patch, death is generally by the former and increasingly the latter; but the last, before the boy, just does not happen here. So when it does, I raise my head, prick up my ears, and howl with all my might at the anticipation of it. Ha, how I relish the opportunity of murder.

The constable, John Broomlands, is home; it is beyond six. His wife, Mary, has just put out the soup when he receives the exasperated and broken phone call from the father. It suffers from the poor signal in these parts, but he catches all he needs to hear. "Calum is dead … Claigan beach." It was shortly after the mother called to say the boy remained missing.

"I'm coming," he says, immediately contacting 'control' at Invernevis, who passes the call straight through to a detective chief inspector Euan Boyd. "Protect the scene," he tells the constable. "I'll come right away."

The constable arrives at Claigan beach in minutes to find the father cradling the boy in his arms, the waves lapping his legs. "He is dead," he says. The constable crouches over him and tries to take the boy from him. The father refuses to give the boy away. The constable takes a step back. He will wait for the doctor to arrive before demanding the boy.

The constable had called the doctor, Richard Black, on route; not so much to give the boy medical help, it is too late. The the doctor needs to confirm the death as a suspicious death, so much so for him to set up a crime scene around the boy's body, as the inspector demands. The doctor arrives shortly after.

"He found his boy. I couldn't separate them," the constable says.

"He is his boy."

"He keeps saying he 'squeezed the boy, like he was trying to squeeze the death out of him'."

"People say all sorts of things, at times like this."

It takes determined persuasion from the constable to get the father to release the boy's body as he tries to carry it farther up the beach and away from the waves. "He has to stay here, Mr Rooney, it is important." The father lays him gently on the sand, the waves almost covering him. The doctor examines the body as the father moves to the top of the beach, where he sits on a rock in the machair.

His face is white as new snow, despair written all over it, as he looks out towards the west.

The inspector arrives and immediately goes to the father. "Mr Rooney, my name is Euan Boyd, Detective Chief Inspector Boyd. "I am so … atishoo," he sneezes. "Sorry, I have a terrible cold."

The father gets on his feet. "You shouldn't be out on a night like this."

The inspector looks at the father, his pained face, heavy eyes, trembling lips. "I am sorry for your loss." He goes on to say, though the father understands this, the boy has to remain there to be examined and he must ensure 'nothing is disturbed'.

The doctor confirms the boy's death as unexplained and the constable sets about securing the area, fearful of others who may tread on the sand around the boy. From what I understand this is now a 'crime scene' and the boy's body is part of an 'investigation'.

The boy is confused, as most, regarding what will happen now. He looks at me as if he knows I have to assist him. I will, but I am in no hurry with him. I need to decide *his* time.

The father arrives home and the mother is waiting outside for him. "Where have you been? I've been frantic. It's been over two hours since you left." She looks into his face, drained of blood and white with shock. "Have you found him, Rooney, where is he?" She pushes around him to see if the boy has followed him along the path.

He reaches for her, grabbing her, almost taking her breath away. "Jackie—"

"You have found him?" She seeks a 'yes, he's safe'. "Haven't you, Rooney, for god's sake tell me?" She brings her arms up inside his and tries to wrestle herself free.

"Jackie…"

"Just tell me he's OK?" She pushes him back an arm's length.

"I found him."

"If you've found him, where is he?" He does not answer, he does not need to; he is with me, of course. "I need to know where he is. I need to go to him."

"An Inspector Boyd is there. He said no one is to go near."

"I don't give a fuck what he says; I am going to my son."

"Jackie." The father grabs her once more. "You are going nowhere. I won't let you." He almost carries her inside and closes the door.

"You fucker, Rooney, you fucker." She rushes into the boy's bedroom. "He's Calum, my boy, my wee boy." She pulls the bedroom door closed behind her.

It is nearly fifteen minutes before the mother comes out of the boy's bedroom, her eyes swollen from crying. The father is sitting at the kitchen table, the telephone in front of him. "He's been murdered, hasn't he?" His empty look confirms this. "How do you know?"

"Jackie, I saw him. The constable is there, and this inspector, a DCI from Invernevis."

"Where is he, Rooney?" He looks at her dispassionately. She holds up her hands pleading. "Where the fuck is he?"

"He was on the beach, at Claigan."

"How'd you find him?"

"I found his books on the road, they went down to the sea, and there he was."

"What was he like?"

"Jesus, Jackie."

"I want to know."

"He was just lying there, his arms out."

I had not expected this, but the boy is there, as if he has just arrived in from school. Like me, he appears wherever he needs to be. I allow this; it is his home after all. He reaches for the mother as if he hopes she will reach out to him and lift him into her arms. She turns away from him. He appears upset at this, moving around her; she moves away once more. He follows her through the kitchen, she avoids him. I have seen this before in the young dead; they do not have the understanding of death. I move to him. He seems to warm to me, like I am a friendly pet. He turns to his real dog, which moves away and cowers under the table; she will have none of me. Gradually, he seems to appreciate something has changed and nothing would ever be the same.

The *máthair* drops into a seat across from him. "Was he clothed?" The boy looks down at himself.

"Jackie."

"I want to know."

The boy moves to stand in front of her, as if to say 'of course I am'.

"Yes, he was."

"Was he … did he, look … battered?"

"No, not that I could see, apart from some blood around his nose."

The boy puts his hand to his nose. His living body may have still bled, but not anymore.

The mother looks down at the floor almost looking at the boy. "My poor wee mite, what did he ever do to deserve this, apart from being adopted by us?"

"He did nothing, and he deserved none of this."

"Did you see anything … anything material?"

"Jackie, I am not a police officer."

"You said you found his books; where was his bag?"

"It wasn't there."

"It wasn't there?"

"No … I didn't see it."

"Rooney, you need to tell them everything. He was fully clothed, shod, nothing missing except his bag. Everything at the scene has a bearing on the success or otherwise of the outcome. You know that."

"Jesus, doesn't take much to trigger the copper mode does it?"

"Rooney, this is murder, our son's murder, some sick bastard's killed him." The boy turns his head to me; murder, what is murder, on his face.

I am drawn to these people, to this boy, you will understand. I do not feel emotion, but I have an interest in their circumstances. I will align myself with them. Not though I have done this before; but *maha*, would a herring fisherman refuse a salmon?

CHAPTER 3

The word is out, and by the tenth hour, Wednesday, the second day of November, everyone knows about the boy. It does not matter who started it, but information travels like a hill-fire around here. The constable, the previous evening, contacted the teacher to advise her of the child's death. She was then advised by the authorities to close the school and her husband, the driver of the school bus, was dispatched to advise the mothers.

Later this morning every bunch of flowers across the three villages has been bought and placed at the roadside adjacent to Claigan beach. The road has been closed by the police, but people walk to the edge of the crime site and place the flowers on the grass verge, covering much of the ground between the road and the Machair, something of ten square yards.

People are sobbing as they look towards the forensic tent, set up over the site of the boy's body before it was taken away. They are holding each other, comforting themselves as they head back, whether to Achfara, Stoer, or Lochdarrach. They walk along the coastal road, almost like a pilgrimage, stopping to talk to others heading to the beach. The snaking procession goes on all day, as if every one of the seven hundred or so inhabitants of the three villages will pay their respects. A procession of vehicles is also snaking along the main road from further afar as word reaches the television and radio stations, the newspapers, the 'media', I hear it called, sending dozens of reporters and 'news crews' to the area.

The parents of the boy are entrapped in their home. They are not to go to the scene while 'forensic activity' is going on. They are advised the procurator fiscal has ordained the boy's body to go to Abertay for a pathologist examination. They spend the morning wandering about the house, answering many telephone calls and drinking cups of tea. They say little to each other and only show emotion when talking to others on the telephone, until a Land

Rover turns up on the road outside of their farmhouse. The satellite dish on the vehicle's roof gives it away; a news crew has arrived to talk to them. The father has no hesitation in going down the path to shout abuse at them and to tell them to "get the fuck off my land".

Then, as the father is about to go back up the path, he hears a well-kent voice. "You tell them, Roon." The man approaches him. "Bloody parasites."

"Great, that's all we need: Bensallah." The father turns away.

"Heh, mister, remember me?" The interloper follows the father along the path.

"Aye, a so-called friend, and god do we need one of them." The father and the 'friend' go to the house, not saying any more to each other. "We have a visitor." The father opens the door, his voice reaching into the kitchen.

"Why can't we get some of the privacy we asked for?" The mother is there, sitting by the AGA knitting. She turns to see the friend standing at the door. "Jesus, Ben!"

"I came as fast as I could, Jackie. As soon as I heard; it was on the news."

The father follows him in. "National and international, child killer at large in the highlands, or murder in the machair."

The friend shakes his head. "Why can't they leave you alone?"

"Are you going to stand there or are you coming in?"

"Oh, really." The father has no say on the matter.

"How are you, Jackie?" The friend moves into the kitchen.

"Oh, just tikitiboo. As you would expect?" She lays out the boy's school clothes over a kitchen chair as she would every school night.

The friend picks up a document lying on the kitchen table. "The SOP crime investigation policy?"

She takes it from him. "The investigation needs to be followed to the letter, no fuckups."

"Still knitting I see." He picks up the half-done cardigan.

"It's for Calum, I want to finish it."

"It'll be good, to focus."

She grabs it from him. "Put it down, and don't touch anything else." She lays out the cardigan on the table. "And don't tell me what to do. I'm sick of people telling me what to do." She scowls at the father.

"I don't need to be here." The father takes his coat and hat and heads off to his shed at the end of his garden, his retreat in times of stress. In there, he would read, write, paint, think … cry. "Come on, Lass." She would get her walk on the way.

"You shouldn't have come. It's not…"

"I had to, couldn't not. It's just terrible, terrible."

"You could have called."

"I had to just come, you would've said not to."

"If I didn't *he* certainly would've."

"It's been nearly a year, Jackie, since I was here last; Calum's seventh birthday party."

She picks up the knitting and starts again. "I thought we could be friends, Ben, friends."

"I bought him a Hogwarts backpack."

"He loved the bag."

"He called me 'Big Ben', like the clock."

She looks at the knitting. "There's tea in the teapot, fresh, and biscuits in the tin over there."

He pours tea, adds milk from the fridge, and takes a biscuit. "Rooney still seems a wee bit off with me. Is he OK?"

"Oh, he's psychotic, Ben, what you want to hear? He's not doing well, what do you expect, he's just lost his son?"

He pulls up a chair close to her at the table. "The news said he found Calum."

She lifts the cardigan to the light to examine the stitching. "On the beach, just off the road."

"Is he still going to the AA meeting?"

"He was there last night, before he came up the road and found Calum."

He rests his hand on her shoulder. "I'm worried about you."

She gets up and moves away. "I don't need you to be worried."

"You needed me in Glasgow."

"I didn't need you, I wanted you. Anyway, that was Glasgow."

"I was, am your friend."

"Give *him* your support, *he's* your friend."

"I doubt if he would want it anymore."

She picks up the friend's cup and takes it to the sink. "Well, I don't want it either, so leave, I've things to do."

"Jackie, I…"

"Just go, Ben." The phone rings. "Yes… Oh, hello Dad, one minute." The mother turns to the friend. "There's nothing for you here." The friend gets up to leave. "No, not you, Dad, it's Ben." The friend takes his coat. "Where are you staying?"

"The hotel."

"Don't say anything to anybody, this is a small place."

"I wouldn't…"

"Hello, Dad?"

"I'll see you later." The friend pulls the door closed behind him.

"Aye, fine." She goes back to the call. "Dad? Tomorrow, right… Oh, Dad? Are you coming on your own? Well, don't bring her here; you got it? OK, bye."

The friend leaves the house, turning to see the mother smoothing the boy's school jacket over the back of a chair. He passes the shed on the way and opens the door. "Rooney, are you OK?"

The father is in the dark. "Ben, you're not welcome here." The boy has chosen to stay in the shed by the father, keeping well to his side while the friend is there.

"No, I guess not, but if there is anything—"

"Just go, social worker!" The friend takes his leave.

The mother goes to the shed. "Dad phoned; he's coming tomorrow."

"Oh, great, first the lover, then the father, what next, the killer?"

"I don't need your fucked-up wisecracks at a time like this." She looks around the shed. "You think you can hide yourself away here in this hovel, shutting the world out, trying to block it all, but you can't Rooney, you fucking well can't."

"Oh, go away."

"He's dead Rooney, dead." The boy looks at the father as if he wants him to correct her.

The people filter into the community hall. It is evening and there are over seventy there, yet it could have been a library, with a muffled whispering throughout the room. Far from a lack of emotion, there is an updraft of feeling. It is hard for me to describe it, but I detect the usual human characteristics: pain, anger, guilt, sadness, and confusion, but I also get others such as interest, curiosity, and even blame.

A hush arrives in the room with John McIsaac, the chairman of the community council and husband of the teacher. He arranged the meeting and is there to chair it. Euan Boyd, the inspector in charge of the investigation, is there to inform the congregation, and Jan Legowski, the local priest, there to provide spiritual support to the community at this 'difficult' time. They both join him on the stage. Richard Black, the doctor, arrives too, not like medical help would be needed, but it emphasises his status in the community. The meeting will give voice to its concerns, offer assurance, and answer questions on the investigation. It will allow the community to show unity in the face of something akin to a battle encampment which had arisen around the village. A 'media circus,' I hear it called.

The parents of the children at the school are at the front, the front rows, alongside other parents in the village.

As expected, the older folk are there, as if to take ownership of 'their village'. For them, this is a new trial, but this community's strength lies in its self-reliance. One hundred and seventy years before they had been offered thirty thousand pounds to give up Bonnie Prince Charlie and none of them succumbed to the temptation, even although it would have made them richer than they could have ever imagined. This is no different today, however, because as far as they are concerned whatever happened in their midst would remain in their midst.

The chairman opens the meeting. He welcomes them all and wishes them a 'good meeting', which would offer information and, as much as would be available, some answers. He explains the priest would begin the proceedings by giving a blessing to the *balach* and the community in this time of great loss. Then the inspector would provide an update on the investigation; after which, he would open the floor for questions. Tea and sandwiches would follow, he says, with an opportunity for the community, in an informal way, to discuss their views, fears … demands.

The doors are locked and manned by a sturdy group of men from the village. Neither press nor tourist would be allowed entry to the hall, consistent with the wishes of the community.

"I will now pass you over to—" The chairman's words are hardly out of his mouth when there is banging on the door.

The father's voice can be heard from the other side of the door. "You will let us in; it is not a meeting without us."

"Open the door," the chairman says, looking along the table to see the shocked faces there. Surely, the parents of the boy have been invited, but it is apparent they have not. It had been thought they would have been mourning and would be best left alone. Though some folk there thought it may be best for them not to be there, fearing it may hinder the meeting, people would be less inclined to talk.

The parents enter a hushed room. They stand together looking around the room. They say nothing as space is made on the row next to the wall near the door. The chairman nods in their direction. "We are pleased Sean and Jackie are here amongst us. No words are necessary from me to describe their loss, but we are heartened they are here in our midst at this terrible time, for them." There is a welcoming murmuring in the room and nodding of heads in support of the chairman's words. "I believe we should voice our thoughts over the death of a seven-year-old child in our midst which has shocked our community and it is imperative we find out what has happened. In this regard, I will now pass over to detective inspector Euan Boyd from Police Scotland's major investigation team at Invernevis."

It is obvious the parents' presence has wrong-footed the inspector. He looks uncomfortable as he prepares to describe the events. "Thank you, Mr McIsaac. I will of course limit my description of the incident itself to prevent discomfort to Calum's parents."

The mother pipes up. "We want everyone to know what happened to our son."

The father puts his arm around her, adding, "There is nothing you or anyone can say which will make it any harder for us to take. We will not have limits on anything said on our regard."

The inspector blows his nose and takes a deep breath, then goes straight into a prepared statement. "This investigation is at a very early stage and I am appealing for information in order to piece together Calum's last known movements." Some look at each other. "In particular, we wish to talk to anyone who was in the vicinity of Claigan beach and the surrounding area between 4 and 6 p.m. last night, as they may have critical information which could assist with the investigation." He pauses and looks at them. "I must reassure the public this type of incident is rare. I understand there are real concerns in the community. Please be assured a team of detectives are now allocated to this investigation to establish the circumstances leading to the death of this young child." He turns to the parents. "Specially trained officers will support the family during this difficult time."

This is news to the mother. "And where are they, these … officers?"

"They are en route as we speak."

She will have none of this. "Tell them not to bother; we will look after each other."

"Yes, thank you. Though I have to stress if anyone has any information they must contact the police. You might think it is insignificant, but please let us be the judge and contact us immediately." He scans the room to see if anyone responds, but no one does. "Due to our initial findings we feel we can treat the death of this young boy as a murder investigation." He blows his nose again, maybe to give him time to gauge the reaction of the hall. Seeing the eyes of the crowd pushes him further into the details of the death. I have no need for this information, but the people here do.

"These are the facts of the case as I know them at this time." People looking for gory details would be disappointed, but the hush deepens as he arrives at the details of the boy's death. "Calum's body has been taken to Abertay where a pathologist will conduct a post mortem. At this stage we are ruling out a natural death, such as he mistakenly wandered into the sea and somehow drowned." This sounds a stupid thing to say as he looks up to acknowledge a hushed congregation. "From Doctor Black's initial examination, the cause of death was not due to drowning; there were signs of strangulation." There is a collective gasp. What he does not mention is the force with which the boy had been dispatched, nor the strength applied to his neck that had drained his lungs of air so much so that it caused his death. Although this is known by those around the table on the stage, especially the doctor, first to examine the boy, this would not be shared at this time here in the hall. "I will, of course, keep you informed of the ongoing investigation, and if we have any significant news we will share it as soon as it is possible."

There is a long hush as people take this in. It is for Father Legowski to give some words of comfort. The priest gets to his feet;

but before he has the chance to talk, the boy's father gets in first. "I do not wish Calum to be dignified in this manner here tonight. There will be time at his funeral." Now there is an indignant silence, confirming some view this to be disrespectful and somewhat unbefitting the father of a dead child in this Roman Catholic community. "I want you to forestall the religious stuff, please."

The chairman looks to the priest who retakes his seat in deference to the father's remarks. "I will now open the meeting to questions." His initial thoughts are to turn to the parents, but he feels this would expose them unnecessarily. *Maha*, they will be happy to await their opportunity.

It is around thirty seconds before Douglas McKinnon, Caber, rises to his feet, his voice more than able to carry in this small hall. For many of the community he is their unofficial spokesperson and it is expected he would have first say. He is a forthright man not known for the diplomatic approach. "I have two questions for you, Mr McIsaac."

The chairman wonders about curtailing it to one, but he knows this man can be thrawn. "Yes, go on, Douglas," he defers.

"Thanks, this first is this. If this is a murder investigation then there must be a murderer." He looks around to see if he is correct to voice this unnecessary truism. "The inspector needs to say who might have murdered this child, here in our place?" It is clear this is on people's minds, but he risks it being viewed as brash and insensitive. "And two, what are the police doing to make sure all the children are safe from this … murderer?" A number of 'tuts' resound around the room indicating he has gone too far, but they are in the minority; the majority there, had they his courage, would have asked the same questions.

Determined to ensure a measured response, the chairman paraphrases the questions. "Thank you, Douglas. To be less pointed, you wish to know who, whom I am sure would be known to all if it were known … but more usefully, you wish to know the kind of suspect who is being pursued." Caber shakes his head at the man's verbosity. "And I must state, unless the investigation says otherwise, no fingers are being pointed at anyone in this community."

Caber's face remains stolidly vacant. "Someone from outside the area then?"

The inspector is about to thwart the chairman's response, when he is hit with a sneezing attack. "Atishoo! I would be pleased to answer this … atishoo!" he starts, with more of a wheeze than a voice. He blows his nose again and starts over. The hubbub in the room drops to a hush. "At this stage we have no leads, no information, and no idea who could have killed Calum." Caber's wife, Shelia, grips him by the arm and holds him to his seat, fearing a retort like 'so we are all suspects'. The inspector coughs. "We will, of course, in accordance with proper procedures, be conducting interviews of everyone who could have been in the area that night." The mother knows what he means by this, having been involved in many similar investigations. She understands the man would be thorough and clinical, but not as much as she would have been herself, given her son is the victim. Anticipating a "and two?" the inspector prevails through another coughing fit. "And," cough, "I can assure all here tonight and indeed the whole community we will make all efforts," cough, "to apprehend this … man, while applying maximum resources and visible," cough, "manpower to assure all of you, you and, importantly, your," cough, "children will be safe."

I must express my doubts about this.

"You said 'man'." Caber's wife, Shelia's voice cuts through the room like a scythe.

"Sorry, I meant person."

"He said man … he said man."

"I do not anticipate any more questions." The chairman knows this is not a community to descend into argument nor to express distrust or disquiet about the authorities, but it is clear what they are thinking. 'Is this … murderer in our midst, even here tonight?'

It is for the father to express this on their behalf. "I want to say, immediately, we don't think Calum was…" He should have checked this with the mother, however, appeared confident she would share this view.

Having none of it, she gets to her feet. "What my husband is saying is this." The father gives way to her and sits down. It is clear they are not of the same voice in this. "We hope to god Calum wasn't killed by someone in our midst, we just hope to god." If anything is going to stir this proud congregation, this is.

It takes the *cailleach* to voice the views of the majority there. "I want to speak." She uses both of her sticks to get to her feet. Mamie, her seventy-year-old daughter, tries to hush the mouthy mother, but when the *cailleach* wants to speak everyone there knows she will. The *cailleach* had been born and bred in this community and would come with me before the end of the year, and she would have her say. "Never in my life or in those before me has there been a murder in Stoer, Achfara, or Lochdarrach." Nods abound. "If the child was murdered it must have been someone from … the outside." What she avoids saying, however, but that which is in her, and others within the indigenous community, thoughts are, 'unless it was an incomer'. *Maha*, she will keep these words for the drams to come later within her select group over the sandwiches.

No one adds anything to these words and, for all there, they offer a way to end the formality and the tension associated with the proceedings. No one thinks, however, Annie's words would offer any of them less attention by the authorities or the media in the forthcoming days. Far less the parents, who, while trying to build relations in this community, would view anyone who could have killed their child as his potential killer. It is for the community to show their support of them and they will be surrounded by well-wishers and friends. Hugs and handshakes mix with offers of support for the difficult days ahead. They will try to avoid the invitation to stay for the sandwiches and tea, however.

The father's battle with alcohol is well known. Working in the bar, he explained it on numerous offers of a dram. He is a known teetotaller and it is understood why—a binge could kill him—although that doesn't stop Caber thrusting a large glass of whisky into his hand. The mother's liking of a drink is less well known, as she tries to take it from him. He will have none of it and downs it in one. She takes a sherry and also downs it in one. An hour or so goes by like this, one drink after another, and it is then, like a big stone has been rolled from his chest, he lets it go.

I appreciate there is never a right time or a place for this. I have seen it happen anywhere and anytime, even years after, but when it comes there can be a loss of control. For him, the sobs come from deep within and he drops to his knees in despair. "My god, Calum, my son, my son." The mother tries to get him to his feet, but he is like a sack of potatoes.

Then, the friend appears on the scene just as he had in the afternoon. "I'll get him, Jackie." He gets the father to his feet. "Come on, we'll get him home." She says nothing, knowing they could wait an hour or so for Teenie the taxi to arrive, if she is not at the church whist. They get the father into the back of his car and head along the coast road, the same fateful road the father travelled to find the boy the previous evening. They do not say anything more until the friend drops the father into his bed fully clothed.

"Will you be alright, Jackie?" The friend stands at the door, showing he intends going back to the hotel.

"I'm drunk, but I'll be fine. I'm in the spare room tonight; he snores like a pig when he's pissed."

"You've got my number, just call if…"

"Aw, Jesus, just stay, Ben; that's what you want me to say."

"I will if you want, just to be sure you'll be OK."

"You're on the couch in the sitting room, no more rooms available I'm afraid."

He nods and smiles as she goes to get him some bedding. He pulls a chair up close to the AGA. She returns with some blankets and a pillow. He looks around. This is a lonelier house than the last time he was here for the boy's birthday. Then it was full of noise, fun and colour; now it is dark, bleak, quiet.

"Do you want to talk, Jackie?"

She looks at him, wondering if this is him trying to get her into bed.

"I'm not fucking you, Ben; not like I wouldn't like to, I could do with a good fuck."

The friend looks at her as she hangs onto the rail of the AGA for support. "I'm not expecting you to, Jackie. I just wanted to offer you a chance to talk."

"I don't need to talk; I need to think." She slides a seat in close to the AGA and sits.

He moves closer to her. "Calum brought you happiness, Jackie."

"Something you couldn't have given me."

"Something you didn't have when there were the two of you."

"He brought us together."

"Even after his affair, Jean Dempsie, in Glasgow?"

"Settled before we came, promised it wouldn't happen again.

He knows if it did we would be finished."

"You said you'd never leave him as long as you had something, the togetherness Calum brought."

She gets to her feet feeling the need for some emphasis. "And now he is gone. So you think I'll leave him. Calum is dead one day, I leave Rooney the next, and you are ready to step in the day after. It's not like that, Ben."

"And what about his story?"

"His story, wow Ben, the friend, the social worker, the chancer."

"He walks along the road and finds Calum's body, just like that?"

"I'm not getting it, pal."

"It just seems a bit … coincidental."

"No coincidence – he followed the route Calum would have gone himself."

The friend moves around the table. "Jackie?"

"What?"

"I'd like Calum's bag; something to keep, as a minding of him – it was my birthday present to him."

"Rooney didn't come across it, only his books."

"No bag, only his books?"

"Yes, that's right."

The friend tightens his mouth. "If you find it—"

"If it is found, presuming it isn't evidence, we'll keep it for you, OK?"

The friend reaches for her. "Thanks, and remember I'll be here Jackie, at any time."

She allows him to kiss her. "My husband is next door, Ben." She pushes him away. "You go to sleep. I doubt if I will."

"I know it's not easy, Jackie."

"No, it's not; goodnight." She gets up to leave, but hesitates long enough to leave the impression she wants to stay.

I shake my head, not that anyone can see me. This alcohol changes people. I have never known its effect, but I see it in the living. How they do things they intend but do not intend. How they say things they do not mean, but really mean. *Maha*, the living can be … confusing. *Oidhche mhath.*

CHAPTER 4

It is early morning, the day after, and the father wakens to the sound of a car door closing. He looks out to see what he thinks to be his car driving off. He thinks it is the mother going into Stoer for fresh bread and milk for breakfast and is surprised to see her sitting at the kitchen table looking forlornly out of the window.

"I thought it was you in my car."

She points out of the window. "Your car is there. It was Ben's car."

"Ford Focus, black, like mine; couldn't see green cheese going past him. What else does he want of mine?"

"Please?"

The father fills the kettle with water and puts it on the AGA. "Have you had breakfast?"

"I don't feel like eating."

He puts bread in the toaster. "What was he doing here?"

"He brought you home last night, you were in a state. It was late, I said he could stay."

He takes a carton of orange juice from the fridge and fills a glass. "Oh, you did, and where did he sleep?"

"On the couch, and where do you think?"

"Oh, on the couch, right."

"How can your stomach cope with breakfast?"

"I didn't mean to—"

"No, you never ever mean to."

"It just happened."

"Sure, and you're a dead man if you start it again."

"Jackie?"

"What?"

"Do you think we can survive this?"

"Individually or together?"

"We have to get through this, for Calum."

"Boyd is coming to see us, tonight, so keep your head on."

For the meantime, the *balach* is mine. His body, however, is not. It is now two days since it breathed and now it is now at the Fatalities in Abertay, where, due to the Fiscal's procedure, it lies on a stainless steel tray waiting for the 'post mortem'. To them, his death remains unexplained. To me, it is not. He will pass on soon, though, when I deem it right. I grant, however, similar to many souls taken before their time in an unprecedented way, he should remain where his body was, in the proximity of those closest to him; for him, his parents. They do not know and would far less believe it, however. I will not try your patience by telling you every time the boy appears, but please just know he stays close to the mother and father, especially when they are together in the house; he holds onto his last semblance of normality, his family life with them.

The father, a failed catholic with bad experiences, believes the boy has gone. The mother, as with many of a deceased child, still searches for him. She refuses to move anything of his. His room remains the same as it was, where his everyday clothes, his jeans, jumper, shirt, socks, trainers, lie on the bed where they were waiting his return from school, his collection of sea shells in a box. She wanders the house picking up items of his, putting them where they will remain. The father supports this, believing this is part of the process towards eventual acceptance. He cannot bring himself to touch anything of the boy's. If he had known the boy was there in their midst, moving with them through the house, he would have reacted in a different way. The boy has no emotion, though, a physical characteristic, but he is locked to them. He is not ready to go, not yet.

It is already dark when the inspector arrives to interview the parents. "Thank you for seeing me, Mr and Mrs, sorry, Mr Rooney and Ms Kaminski," he says, entering the kitchen. He pulls out his handkerchief and blows his nose. "Sorry, swine of a cold."

The mother takes his coat. "Sit by the fire, and Jackie and Rooney's fine … tea?" She lifts the kettle. He nods.

"Thank you." He takes the seat and warms himself. The father takes the seat to his side. This unnerves him. "Nice place, comfortable." He looks around the lounge of the house, pausing to take in the view from the window, the light of the winter sun dropping over the islands. "Lovely view, over the sea, always wanted a place like this."

The father looks to the mother. "So did we."

"Yes, nice." The inspector catches sight of the collage of photographs on the wall of the boy, the parents, on the beach, in the water, on the boat, on the train. "I just want to say…"

She pours the tea. "Look, there's a guy out there who killed our wean. Let's get down to it. Milk?" The inspector nods.

The father adds the milk. "You wanted to see us; here, in our home."

The inspector loosens his jacket and makes himself comfortable. "It is best, with a loss such as this."

She passes him the tea. "Why, to get an idea of our environment?"

The inspector pulls out a handheld recorder, a notepad and a pen. "Well, in an initial interview, it's always best."

"Belt and braces?"

The inspector looks at her. "As you would expect, a few questions?" He just gets it out before a sneezing fit.

The father hands him a kitchen roll. "Yes, from us too, Inspector, like how confident you are in finding—"

"Are we suspects in the death of our son?"

"Why would you think that, Jackie?"

"I need to get it out of the way."

"In a murder investigation everything is an open book. But it is right we talk to the victim's, the deceased's family."

The father persists. "Will you get him?"

"All information is important, Inspector; even things that don't seem to be important, to piece events together."

"Yes, indeed, to piece together."

"How confident are you of nailing this bastard?"

The inspector buries his head into his handkerchief trying to prevent a coughing fit.

"Leave it, Rooney. Would you prefer a Lemsip?"

The inspector looks from one to the other. "No thanks, but more tea may help." She refills the kettle and puts it on the AGA.

"He was my son too."

"Fuck's sake, Rooney." She gets up and marches across the room, arms flailing. "Why don't you leave it to me?"

The inspector turns to the father. "I have to ask, sir. Do you have a … mental illness?"

The father glances at the mother. "God, doesn't word get around; why do you want to know?

"It's about questioning a vulnerable person whose ability to understand their rights might be impinged by a mental health condition. We need to ensure an appropriate adult is present."

"I don't need an appropriate adult."

"Thank you, then I'll continue."

"Good."

"Good." The mother returns to the table with more tea. "Can we get on with it?"

The inspector takes the tea and wraps both hands around the mug. "Of course; your thoughts?"

"Thoughts? I gave you my thoughts the night I found him."

"Yes, I know, Mr Rooney, but you would have had time to reflect on his death; maybe something has come to mind."

Murder *is* death, Inspector.

The father puts him right. "His murder, you mean."

"Yes, of course, and you will have a unique view, professional and familial."

"Indeed," the mother says. "Doubt you'd have had many parents of murdered children who were in the field?"

"No, exactly."

The father leans over. "This is hard for us, Inspector."

"Would you prefer…"

"No, we're happy to share our views."

The inspector's voice has now become a wheeze. "Tha … you."

"I'll go first. A local paedophile, Calum was in the wrong place at the wrong time."

"A pae …, Ja … ie?"

The father passes him a glass of water. "How do we know he was abused, before he was … murdered?"

"How do we know he wasn't, Rooney?"

The water helps, the inspector's voice returns. "We are not sure, at this stage."

"Was he harmed, physically, Inspector?"

"We can't say yet."

"Tell me?" the mother says.

"He was fully clothed when I found him."

"Thanks, Rooney. So, Inspector, you can't rule out a sex offender."

"No, of course not."

"Was he—?"

"He was fully clothed."

The mother grabs the father's arm. "Rooney, I need to bloody well do this." He pulls it away. "You would have checked the register, Boyd, brought them in?"

The inspector looks shaken at the use of his name, like he is a subordinate being debriefed by a senior officer. "Not all sex offenders are on the register, ma'am. He could have been unknown to us, as you would know."

She appears empowered by his use of 'ma'am'. "As it happens I do know. Have you checked it, Inspector, anyone between here and Invernevis, anyone visiting the area, working up here, the records? Dammit, have you checked?"

He sinks back in his seat.

The father is waiting for his wife's inevitable attack on the inspector's credibility. "The chances he's on the register are zilch, Jackie."

"Shut up, Rooney, leave this to me. Well, Inspector, have you?"

"Fucking hell, Jackie."

"Rooney, don't you fucking hell Jackie me; you know how important it is to check the fucks out early before they get a chance to settle back into normal life, while they are in remorse, guilt ridden, even ready to admit they need help, for fuck's sake." *Maha*, the mother's kettle has boiled.

"Just tell her, Inspector."

"I cannot divulge internal—"

"Oh, so you can't say, but you can tell us who they are and I'll bloody well check them out."

"Do you think that would help?"

"It would help me."

"Jackie!" The father reaches out to her to calm her. Even the boy appears startled. "I am so—"

"There's no need, Mr Rooney." The inspector gets to his feet and moves to the window. "However, do you mind if I ask…"

The mother knows something is coming. "Here we go."

The inspector turns to the father. "When you found the boy?"

"Yes?"

"He was in your arms when Broomlands arrived."

"Yes, I strangled him with one hand as I phoned him with the other."

"Sorry, not what I meant."

"No, the killer got to him before I found him."

The mother is up, her stick clacking across the floor. "Je-sus, can we keep this rational."

"Rational? There's nothing rational about this."

"The only thing about this that's irrational, is you, Rooney. Maybe if we hadn't come here. It was you who wanted it."

"Oh, Jackie, not now, not here."

The inspector notices they drop into their respective seats rather than reach out to each other in support. From his face he meant to stir up a wasp's nest. I move between them, to study theirs. Is there anything here I can learn from?

The inspector put a stick in the hive and now moves back to a safer place. "I'm sorry; was there anything, anything, about Calum or what he said, about anyone, or anything suspicious, or strange?"

The father gets up and walks to the window, turning his back on the inspector. "Nothing, Calum said nothing, before. Believe me, if he had mentioned anything of concern I would have been on to it."

"And anyway, you moved off the bloody point." The mother is still bealing from the inspector's intrusion.

"Everything to do with the boy's circumstances is *my* business, ma'am."

"I—"

"I know, you were in the field."

"Yes, in the field."

"Retired ma'am … from your respective position in criminal justice and you, Mr Rooney, you—"

"Just come out with it, Inspector."

He does. "Before you left Glasgow to come to the highlands, you both led … irregular lifestyles."

"I'm sure you'll know our previous backgrounds, Inspector, our irregular lives, as you say. Is this a factor for you?"

"You led a syndicate, a crime syndicate, Mr Rooney."

"Not something I am proud of."

"And you, ma'am?"

One 'ma'am' too many. "It's Jackie, for fuck's sake."

"Sorry, as an assistant chief constable. Heady heights, crime and terrorism; high profile position, but with exposure to—"

"Very dangerous groups, individuals, it came with the job. Now?"

"I'll be blunt."

"Yes, you will."

"You would have had your enemies."

"And these enemies followed us here to kill our son."

"It has to be considered, Mr Rooney."

"Don't you think we haven't—"

The mother is now also on her feet. "Listen, Inspector, if our enemies had killed our son, they would have been on the phone the minute after to tell us, to gloat, rub it well in, besides…"

"Besides?"

"Our enemies would not have stopped at our son; they would have killed us as well."

"I'm not so sure, an eye for an eye."

The father tops up his tea. "What *are* you saying, Inspector?"

"Some say to kill the child of a mafia boss is to kill the family."

"The mob does not touch the women or children, Inspector."

"Please, both of you, this is not the Godfather."

"This is not Glasgow, Jackie. This is the highlands," the father says.

"Look, I do appreciate—"

"No, Boyd, you don't."

A long collective silence follows.

The inspector breaks it. "We need to identify anyone from your past; we need to—"

"Rule them out from your inquiries?"

"Or rule them in."

"And you are going to plague us until we do it. And where do you want to start?"

"Top possibilities; a list of those you think would have done you harm."

She goes first. "Oh, Christ, I don't know."

The father follows up. "Top possibilities, I've got ten right off."

"Give me the top of your list."

"The McGings and the Taylors, two heavy teams from Glasgow, they would have done me in."

"Why?"

"Mick McGing was … killed; head of the McGing family, and the Taylors—"

"Why you?"

"Mick was killed by my … *the* crime bosses."

"In the syndicate you ran, the Family?"

"Yes, he and others in the McGing family; then the Taylors, another Glasgow team."

"They too were hit?"

"They were a danger—"

"To the Family?"

"They were out of control, loose cannons."

"They would have harmed you."

"Harmed me, they would have crucified me on a lamp post on Partick Cross."

"They would have harmed yours, your child, to get at you?"

The father is back at the window, looking out into the dark. "Not quite their style, Inspector, but many nights I would be here wondering if they would."

"Aye," the mother says, "with his Winchester rifle, eyes peered for Indians; give us a break."

A grin appears on the inspector's face. "You, Jackie, a few bad guys would have wanted to do you harm?"

"Aye, a few, and a few others, no doubt."

"Anyone in particular?"

"Most in jail, I think."

"Most are released, some with revenge in mind."

"Most wouldn't be daft enough to do anything to put them back in, besides…"

"Besides?"

"They would have my father to contend with."

The inspector purses his mouth as if to agree with this, curtailing this line of enquiry. "Thank you. Was there anything of interest in the boy's circumstances before he left for school that morning?"

"What, like he knew he was going to be killed?"

"Please, ma'am…"

"Jesus."

"Sorry, was there anything of interest?"

She settles down to think. "Right, well he got up, showered, got ready, had his breakfast, played with his shells, and put his books into his bag."

"His books, into his bag?"

"Yes."

"We found the books, but there was no bag. We covered the area."

"It was his Hogwarts backpack. He took it everywhere."

"It wasn't with him."

"My husband said he didn't find it."

Both of them look at the father.

"I wasn't in police mode. I didn't think to look."

"No, indeed, Mr Rooney," the inspector says, writing it down, "Backpack missing, Hogwarts. Any photographs of it?"

"Yes, I am sure there'll be some; like Jackie says, he took it everywhere."

The mother pounces on this. "Jesus, Rooney, the murderer may have it."

"He may have discarded it, Jackie, thrown it away, disposed of it."

"He might have held on to it. Weirdos do that. Keepsakes."

"We need to consider it."

"Yes, of course you do. And we'd like it back if you find it. It's kind of special."

"Yes, Jackie, I'm sure."

The father yawns, he has not slept since the boy was taken. "Is there anything else, Inspector? I have to…"

The inspector delays his response, like he was keeping this to the last. "There is one thing, Mr Rooney. Jean Dempsie, the murdered MI5 agent and your relationship with her."

"Oh, aye." The father huffs and catches the eye of the mother.

The inspector persists. "This was very controversial at the time; some would say … risky behaviour."

"Aye, I know you share information."

"Naturally, Mr Rooney, especially when she was murdered." The inspector turns to the mother, acknowledging she is aware of this.

"What has this to do with our son?"

"The inquiry into her death viewed you both as suspects."

"She had numerous enemies."

"It was understandable, Inspector. Believe me, if you had known her."

"Our son?"

"We need to consider every possibility."

"What, he was killed by MI5?"

"Your … fraught relationship with her exposed you to danger sir."

"I was aware of it at the time."

"So, your … activities and why you came here; we have a range of possibilities, both personal and official."

"It was safe here."

"Yes, was…" The inspector allows the phrase to linger as he slowly puts his notebook back into his pocket, creating enough of a pause to confirm the end of the interview. "Thank you, Mr Rooney and Ms Kaminski – I'm sure I will be in touch." He takes out his handkerchief and coughs into it.

The mother gets up and moves into the hall. "Yes, you better, Inspector, with some decent news." She comes back with his coat.

He takes his coat. "Goodnight."

"There's one last thing, Inspector?"

"What's that, Jackie?"

"I need to see him."

He looks at her a full five seconds. "I am really sorry, Jackie, he's in post mortem, pathology, it's not possible."

"Yes, just bloody evidence, but I am his mother, I want to see him."

"I am sorry, ma'am." The inspector looks at his watch. "I have to go; I have another interview."

The mother shows him out. "Yes, you would have covered enough for one day."

He leaves without saying anything else.

The parents pull their seats around the AGA. They looked

stunned and weakened by the interview, like they are bruised by their past being opened up like a can of peas.

"Rooney, do you think, your … affair with Jean Dempsie had anything to do with this?"

"For god's sake, Jackie, why would it?"

"Well, why would he mention it?"

"Why didn't he mention your affair with Ben?"

"It wasn't relevant; you know what he's doing, trying to flush out absolutely anything relevant."

"I'm not getting you."

"MI5, they don't give up."

"I didn't kill her, Jackie, we've covered that."

"Well, someone did; maybe they came for us as well. Maybe Calum was a warning, a terrible horrible message: don't mess with MI5?"

"And Ben?"

"In the overall scale of things, not important."

"No, not important."

They stop talking; exhaustion, tiredness, or fear something 'important' would come out, something too painful to contemplate or cope with then. They elect to sit looking vacantly at the AGA.

The inspector travels a mile or from the parent's house to see the teacher at her home. It is just before six when he gets there. Although she was at the school to allow him access to check it out, take pictures, carry out 'forensic procedures', she did not want to be interviewed there. For him, he had to start the investigation at the school, the last place the boy was seen alive.

They, John and Eileen McIsaac, the chairman and the teacher, live in a croft house overlooking Achfara beach. It is late evening. She had arranged to see the inspector at six after she returned from the school. Though the school will be closed for the rest of the week, she has been briefing the counselling team that arrived to provide support to the children, shocked at the loss of their friend.

The chairman has also just arrived home from his business, the local bus service, which is contracted to the local council to provide the school bus for the three villages. She agreed an hour with the inspector before she leaves to attend the vigil for the boy and then onto the Achfara Community Council meeting, where she is secretary. Her husband, the chairman, would accompany her. They would eat dinner and answer the inspector's questions at the same time.

The inspector waits outside until they arrive home in their respective cars. They see his car as they arrive, and wave for him to come in as they enter the house. He gives them a few minutes to settle before going in.

The chairman welcomes him at the door with a handshake and receives a reciprocal grip. "Please, Inspector, come on in. Jesus, it's a cold night."

"Thank you." The inspector is relieved to be inside, taking out a fresh handkerchief and blowing his nose. "Sorry, lousy cold."

The chairman shows him to a seat next to a large radiator, which throws off a welcoming heat. "I believe you're a travelling man."

"Yes, Mr McIsaac, I have a large catchment area."

The teacher has heard these Masonic greetings in the past, but is surprised to hear them in this circumstance. She studies both of them. She keeps out of her husband's activities in the local Masonic lodge, but wonders at the appropriateness of his greeting a detective chief inspector of the local police in this way. "Could I get you a cup of tea, Inspector?"

"No, I'm fine, Mrs McIsaac, thanks."

"Some dinner?" she asks, putting a fish pie in the oven. "There's plenty."

"No, thanks, I've had mine." He rubs a protruding belly. "Small Isles, fish and chips, fish like a whale on the plate."

The chairman concurs. "Straight from the sea, so fresh, flapping about on the plate, Stoer haddock, the best."

"Please … have yours." The inspector takes out a notepad and places it on the table next to his pen and glasses.

"It'll take a wee while to heat," the chairman says. "I'll get the tea."

The inspector smiles at him and casts his eyes around the room. It looks more like an office than a kitchen, covered in folders, books, a computer station next to the window.

The teacher transfers her school files to the table, to be followed by a set of buff folders. "Community council minutes," she says. "I wrote them up at the school, gave me something to do."

"Right," the inspector says.

The chairman passes his wife and the inspector a mug of tea. "We don't have much time Inspector; the vigil leaves the village at seven." He makes sure the inspector knows of the impending evening vigil for the boy.

"Oh, yes, of course. I'll be as quick as I can."

The chairman nods. "Thank you."

"OK, let's start." The inspector opens the notepad and writes and speaks: "Interview Eileen McIsaac, third of November 2016, Craigmore, Achfara." Then he goes through the usual initial interview dialogue with her, checking her full name, address, and date of birth for the benefit of the record. "OK, Mrs McIsaac, thank you."

The chairman passes her a plate of food. The inspector asks if she wants him to stop. She shakes her head and takes a forkful of fish pie.

"Did you see anything suspicious, Mrs McIsaac?"

"Sorry?"

"Anything suspicious on the day or the day before, like strange cars, men, anything?"

"No, I didn't, but I seldom leave the school during the day."

"Yes, of course."

She looks anxious, as if he had said something significant. "Do you think I should've? I feel a bit guilty I didn't see anything or wasn't more vigilant with Calum, but normally there isn't anything…"

"I'm not here to impart any blame. I'm sure you look out for the children very well."

"Yes, I do. I hope so, Inspector."

He writes a few lines into his notebook, then goes back a few pages to the parent's interview. "Did the boy have his bag?"

'Strange thing to ask,' she almost says, but, "Yes, he had it on," comes out instead.

The inspector keeps his eyes on his notepad. "Thank you, and the car?"

"The car; I thought you would come to the car. God, I wish I had seen the driver."

"Could you describe it, the car?"

"God, I wish I could. It was getting dark, dusk, all I saw was the tail lights as it moved away up Bhother Beag."

"No identifying features, make, colour, size?"

"No, sorry, only red lights."

"LED?"

"Sorry?"

The chairman clarifies. "Light-emitting diodes, dear, some new cars have LED lights, rather than the bulbs."

"Thank you, Mr McIsaac."

She looks at her husband. "Sorry, just tail lights."

The inspector flicks through his notes. "What do you think of the parents?"

This seems to throw the teacher. "The parents?" She catches the eye of her husband.

"Mr Rooney and Ms Kaminski." He notes them sharing a long look at each other.

"We don't know them well, not many people do."

"That's true, Inspector," the chairman says, "they are … private people."

"They only arrived here last February." The inspector checks his notes.

"Yes, correct," she says.

"You are not long here yourselves?"

They look at each other. "No, just three years. I'm highland, from the islands, where I got the Gaelic, and I suppose why I got the job."

"Yes, Gaelic medium school, good educational attainments. I read your profile on the council website. You moved up from London."

"I had moved to London and met John. It was a dream come true to come here, like coming home."

"Indeed."

The teacher finishes her dinner and dispatches the plate to the sink. "Why are you asking us about them, Inspector?"

"Just a generality; it's important to know about them as parents."

"Are they … under suspicion?"

"No."

"Inspector, it is not for me to cast aspersions on parents,"

"Yes, I know, I just—"

The chairman gets up and moves to the window. "Inspector, if you're looking for suspicious characters you would do worse than look at the man who lives down there, on the beach."

"John, you have no—"

"Eileen, the man is strange, he lives on a beach, he's not from these parts."

"But John, you can't—"

"It's fine, Mrs McIsaac. It's good to know of anything or anyone which prompts … suspicion." He joins the chairman at the window. Although it is too dark to see much, he can just see the outline of the coast, the moon silhouetting its shape. "Where does this man live, Mr McIsaac?"

"Just there." The chairmen points to a promontory at the far end of Achfara beach. "In a ramshackle boat house, lives there like a hermit, a strange guy, worth checking out I would think."

"Thank you, Mr McIsaac, helpful."

The chairman looks at his watch, making sure the inspector sees him doing so. The inspector ignores it and spends a few minutes filling in his notes before he gets up and takes his coat and hat, then heads out the door. "Thank you, Mrs McIsaac, Mr McIsaac, you have been helpful. I am sure we will see each other around. I'll be in touch if I need to see you again." He shakes their hands and takes his leave. The teacher and the chairman watch him disappear down the path into the dark.

The curious activity the chairman called a vigil is happening at the perimeter of the crime scene where the boy was found. The whole area had been combed for 'evidential material' and the road, closed for two days, had reopened. Some three hundred souls from the three villages stretch in a candlelight procession all the way from Lochdarrach to the beach at Claigan. As they arrive at the scene, they place their candles in rows at the side of the road. It takes over an hour for them all to reach the site. The candles lighten the sky and warm the air. They wait their spokesperson to arrive. Caber arrives with the last members of the procession. He assists the *cailleach*, who, despite her great age and a minibus being arranged for the older folk, was determined to walk all the way. The teacher and the chairman arrive. He pushes forward to speak, but the congregation crave Caber's words.

Caber raises his voice to reach the back of the crowd. "I want to thank you for coming here tonight." The chairman retreats into the crowd as Caber continues. "It's a cold night and I'll not keep you, but tonight … tonight we showed the world we are a caring community. We have gathered here to mark the passing of one of our children, Calum Rooney, and this vigil gives respect to his young life." The gathered community clap in appreciation of his words. "But also … but also, our solidarity here tonight gives out a message to the world that we are united despite this tragedy inflicted on our small community, and no one … no one, can come here and take one of our young lives, without massive, massive condemnation. Thank you." They applaud in acknowledgement and almost immediately begin filtering back to their homes, to their villages.

Inverbeg is at the back of the crowd. While out for his walk he would normally pass Claigan beach, though tonight he is late; he wants to attend the vigil. He already explained to the inspector he had passed the beach earlier on the evening of the boy's death, but had not seen anything. This evening, following the vigil, however, he has no reason not to walk through the golf course and along the forest path, his normal route. He has no fear of a killer lurking in the shadows. This is a child killer, not an adult killer. He'll cut through the golf course onto a path taking him a circuitous route through the woods back to the village.

As he passes the beach, to go to the path, he goes around the outer cordon of the crime scene, a light blue forensics tent in the middle, concealing the area where the boy was found. He recalls the numerous tents around there in the summer months and how lonely this one looks, with the waves splashing its outside walls, metal poles dug deep into the sand to prevent it being blown or washed away by the waves or the wind. He wonders whether the forensic team has finished there, trying to piece together the last movements of the boy, where he was killed, any traces of the killer.

He walks on past the beach into the dark of the path. After a short trek through the golf course, he stops on the brow of a hill to look to the sky over Stoer, where fireworks are going off. It is two days to the celebrations for the gunpowder plot, abandoned in Achfara and Lochdarrach due to the boy's death, but still continuing in Stoer. He shakes his head. Then, just as he is about to cross to the forest path, a voice from behind him startles him, "Hello, sir, it's a cold night." He turns to see a small stocky man standing with the light of the sky over the sea silhouetting him. "Do you mind if I ask you a couple of questions?" he asks. Inverbeg has no reason to believe he is being confronted by an attacker. "John Scott, freelance investigative journalist, sir." This is a hack with a Glasgow accent holding out a hand McDonald refuses.

"I thought you people were to leave us alone, you know how we feel about…"

"Indeed, my friend, but I saw you at the vigil and then you walking over here, near the scene, I just wondered."

"It's my walk. Do you think I have a perverse interest in the murder of a young child on a beach or I am the killer returning to the scene of the crime? Now if you'll—"

"Yes, of course, I didn't mean to trouble you."

"No, I'm sure you didn't."

They stare at each other for a few seconds.

"Listen, I am not part of the official media. I seek the truth not fake news and I keep my contacts anonymous." The hack is now too close to Inverbeg for comfort; he moves back. "I'll pay you."

Inverbeg turns and walks on, only to turn around a few steps along the way. "Pay me?"

"Indeed, and I'll keep it … under wraps."

Inverbeg's face indicates interest, though what would the community say if he talks about it, or them? They have a code not to talk to the media nor anyone outside the village; but money, this would help pay the bills which had built up since he retired, and it would be anonymous.

"Under wraps, anonymous?"

"Yes."

"How much?"

"Depends on what you have to say."

"What do you want to know?"

The hack moves closer to him. Inverbeg can now see him clearly. Typical west of Scotland man, he thinks; 'galus, cocky and up his own arse', comes to mind. Late fifties, maybe, though fit looking, but a bit old to do this job, he thinks, should be in a warm office at his age.

"Just some general information, nothing serious, just what the village is like, the community, the people."

The hack just said the wrong thing. "The people!"

"Sorry, not any detail, just a general overview, describing the kind of place Lochdarrach is."

"Go to the local tourist website or Visit Scotland."

"I just need a bit of a … you know, a more personal insight."

Inverbeg thinks for a bit; a personal insight means he would be named, then he spits "fuck off," into the hack's face.

The hack moves back out of reach of Inverbeg's whisky breath, but it is his eyes which unsettle him. Eyes he is well accustomed to in Glasgow within the fraternity he moves within. Inverbeg turns and moves to head up the path.

"If money won't move you, Mr McDonald, I have information on you which will."

Inverbeg turns. "Information, on me?"

"Yes, information."

"What kind of information?" This has the impact the hack intends.

"About the two boys."

Inverbeg moves forward to within reach of the hack, but he does not budge an inch. "The two boys?"

"You know what I am talking about."

"I do?"

"Of course you do." Inverbeg's silence confirms he does. "The two boys you accepted for boarding, from Glasgow, the ones you abused for four years, until the authorities got wind of it and had them removed."

Inverbeg looks stunned. "I looked after them."

"*They* looked after you, you mean."

Inverbeg reaches for the hack, to grab his lapels, but he is too fast for him. Although well shorter than Inverbeg's six two frame, and carrying more weight than he would have preferred in a brawl, the hack side-steps him and pushes him to the ground with the force of a street fighter from the pits, then delivers a sharp blow to his nose, bringing blood. Inverbeg staggers back.

"Sorry, I can't allow you to manhandle me, mister."

"I'll kill you." Inverbeg pulls out a handkerchief to stem the blood.

"You can try, but big and stupid as you are, you won't succeed. Now get to your feet and be sensible." The hack holds out his hand to help McDonald to his feet, but he refuses.

"I'll do it myself." Inverbeg gets on his knees; then, using a fence post, he gets to his feet.

"Good, so you'll help me?"

"If I don't?"

"I'll … out you." The hack pushes a card into Inverbeg's top pocket.

Inverbeg looks the hack in the face and knows he means what he says, then without saying anything more he turns sharply and hurries towards the forest path.

I give out three howls as I follow him there. He was due to come to me anyway – his health was failing. He has now paid the piper; he will be mine.

There is a heavy knocking on the parent's door. The mother opens it slowly to find her father there, Hubert Kaminski. The chief of the police force in Scotland is not used to being kept waiting at any door. "Hello, darling, for god's sake let me in, it's cold out here."

"Dad, what are you—"

"I had to come, I'm so sorry." He hardly allows her to get the words out, as he moves into the hall, taking his coat off and shaking it before hanging it on a hook. He reaches for her. "Come here you." He tries to embrace her. She pushes past him to see if he is alone. "I've just come from Calum's vigil."

"Oh, right. And where is she?"

"*She* is relaxing."

"Deirdre Hamilton-Brown is relaxing?"

"No horse trial events up here, darlin'. I just had to see you. I've brought some stuff from Pekhams. I know how hard it is to get quality up here." He drops two plastic carrier bags on the table and begins emptying them. "Decent coffee, not like the shit you get in the local Co-op; good ham, cheese, and a fantastic cheesecake."

"You should go home, Dad. You'll have a lot to do."

"I came as soon as I could." He takes a newspaper from a bag. He makes his way into the living room and right up to the fire. She follows him in. "I intended coming sooner, but I…"

"I know, you have a police force to manage. Did you get a hotel, you can't stay here?" She puts another log on the fire.

"I'm in the Lochdarrach, to be close to you at this time. You weren't at the vigil." His large frame is silhouetted by the glow of the fire at his back.

"No, Dad, no candles for us; there's work to be done, there's a killer out there."

"No, no candles." He makes himself comfortable taking out his glasses and opening the newspaper. "The Herald is carrying it. I could hardly read it, but it's important to see what is being said."

"I don't want to know what is being said, I know what has happened."

"I know but—"

The father arrives in the room before he gets the words out. "Oh, great, just what we need, the chief."

"Oh hello, Rooney, are you—"

"I'm OK, Hubert, as well as can be expected under the circumstances."

"I'm—"

"Yes, you're comfortable."

"No, I'm sorry."

"Oh, you're sorry. So is everyone."

"I was at the vigil." The chief turns to face the fire. "A cold night."

"Aye, very good." The father tightens his eyes.

"Who's the CSM?"

"A DCI, Euan Boyd. Dad?"

"The SIO?"

"I don't know. Dad?"

"You know we need good coordination here, so many cases are fucked up for the lack of it. I gave a statement to the papers; did you read it? Here." He hands the paper to the mother. She throws it on the fire.

"We don't want to know, Dad."

The father has had enough. "Hubert, we don't need to know about coordination, the CSM, the SIO. I'm off, so you'll excuse me, I've some calls to make."

"Who, Rooney?"

"Christ, he is just in the door and he is interrogating me already. Jesus, give me a break."

"I just—"

"Dad?"

"Yes, dear?"

"You can't come here and take over."

"I'm here to help." He takes his jacket off and puts it over the back of the chair, then starts to remove his shoes.

"I'll be next door, Jackie."

"I'm sorry, darlin'." The chief keeps his shoes on. "I didn't mean to—"

"Interfere, Dad, move right in? But that's what you do."

"I just wanted to give you some support."

"I don't need support."

"Together we can nail this … bastard."

"It's not your fight, Dad."

"Calum was my grandson, Jackie, my grandson."

"Adopted, dad, adopted."

"I loved him and he's dead." He gets up and shuts the sitting room door. "You know I didn't want—"

"It's fine, he knows you didn't want me to go back to him. A catholic, a drunk, and a danger, you said, in order of importance."

"I nearly lost you before. I didn't want you in harm's way again."

"You didn't want me to come here."

"I didn't want *this* to happen."

"Oh, so it wouldn't have happened if we had stayed in Glasgow."

She goes to the fire, throwing some coal on to dampen down the flames reaching up into the hearth.

"I could have supported, protected you, and Calum."

"Sure you would have, Dad, a wall of police around our house, stopped us living our lives."

"The man is a liability." He gets up and presses the coal tight in the fire with his foot. "This is what we would do, then throw on tattie peelings, make it last."

"We are not in the tenement now, Dad, and this is not Springburn in the sixties. The one thing we have here is fuel for the fire."

"You could have done better."

"Leave it Dad, he's my husband."

"He caused this. It shouldn't have happened."

"I could have happened anywhere Dad, even here."

"Wrong place and wrong time, always is."

"Right place; he was happy here."

"I am taking over the investigation."

Her scream almost blows the fire out. "No, you fucking well won't; you won't take over here. A conflict of interest it would say in the bloody papers. Calum's grandfather takes control of local investigation into the murder of his grandson."

"I'll be expecting results, watching things." He knows to back off, so he cosies up in the chair, resting his glasses on his chest, as if he is about to go to sleep.

"Aye, on you go, but don't you interfere, do you hear me?" He nods off on purpose. "There's one thing you can do, Dad – Dad!" She grabs his wrist. "Dad?"

"Yes, what?" He awakens. "Sorry, the fire; nearly fell asleep there. What, I'll do anything?"

She kneels down in front of him. "I want to see Calum."

"Darling, he's in autopsy." He grips her hand. "You'll get him back soon."

"It's his birthday tomorrow. I want to see him."

He looks into her eyes and sees the vulnerability but also the determination of his daughter. "I'll arrange it, you'll go up tomorrow."

"Rooney too."

"If he must."

"And Dad?"

"What?"

"The local register."

He sits up straight and purses his lips. "I'm way ahead on that front."

"But don't get involved, you'd be spotted."

"You leave that to me, hen." He cosies back into the chair and the inevitable snoring begins.

"Right, you have to go." She lifts his jacket. "Thanks for coming." She pushes his jacket into his chest.

"Well, I suppose." He puts his jacket on in a huff and moves to the hall where he takes his coat. "OK, Jackie. Remember I'm—"

"There for me, OK, I've got it. I'll see you."

"I'm in the hotel, just phone."

The father hears the door closing and emerges from the room. "He's away. What did he say, it shouldn't have, wouldn't have happened, etcetera, etcetera?"

"Who were you calling?"

"Bingham."

"Can you not leave your history in the past?"

"I need to know if there is a Glasgow link."

"Just don't get too close to them, Rooney. I can just see it. Calum's father brings in his old mob pals."

He moves to the window, as if something has drawn his attention. He peers into the darkness. I can see him, but he can't see me.

"I just heard the Cù-Sith." Lachie, also known as Dram from his love of the *uisge-beatha*, rushes into the Small Isles bar. "On the way back from the vigil, three howls. Someone is going off-you-pop tonight. Better get home before it gets you."

Ha, I am pleased I was heard, just as I was about to remove Inverbeg's soul.

"Too many drams, Dram." Maggie Stuart, the joint owner of the bar with her husband Magnus, laughs, thinking 'the alky's hearing things again.'

"I heard it. I'm telling you." He goes quiet, no support for him there.

Caber arrives at the bar to hear Maggie, having escorted the *cailleach* home. "Says he heard the Cù-Sith."

"I also heard it, on the night of the boy's death." Caber points towards the malt of the month.

"Je-sus." Maggie is exasperated.

"I heard it too." Billy the boat pipes up from deep within his pint.

Ha, my howl was just right. Too loud, it would be investigated: a feral being at large in these parts raises concerns for the sheep. Too quiet, it lacks authority and is ignored. Just right, prompts suspicion of a supernatural at large.

The hack approaches the bar. "What's the coo seeth?"

The locals are wary of him, but this is a matter of local folklore, something they are happy to talk about; it's good for the tourism.

Maggie wipes the bar. "Oh, nothing to concern you, sir, just an old folk's tale."

Caber points once again at the gantry. "Aye, just a big grey dug turns up when there's a death." Maggie reaches for the bottle.

The hack looks on as Dram glories in the detail of my image, not that I have seen myself you understand. "The fairy dug in Gaelic. It's the size of a coo or calf, dark green with shaggy fur—gets the green from the fairies—a curled tail, flaming eyes, and paws the width of a man's hand. A harbinger of death, it comes to bear away the soul of a person to the afterlife. Invisible most of the time until it arrives to get you. If you see it, you're deid."

Maggie pours the drink. "Massive, shaggy-haired dug, presaging death; funny how other drinkers see pink elephants."

The hack laughs.

Caber takes his dram. "Better watch yourself." Not taking his eyes off his drink. "He's out and about here, for sure."

I am for sure, and I mingle with them in here as well, not that they can see me.

Dram is away like the steam train heading over the viaduct. "Aye, but the fairy dog, like all the fairies, doesn't like salt. I've a packet in my pocket. I bought it from the Spar on the way here. I'll sprinkle it before and after me as I go up the road. I'll be alright." This man knows a lot about me. I look forward to paying him a visit someday, but not this day.

"Do you think he was there for the boy's death?" The hack has his tongue in his cheek.

Dram nods. "I wouldn't be surprised."

The hack goes to his notes. "The coo seeth. Presages death, doesn't like salt, big green dog, so the alcoholic says." He turns to Maggie. "You seem a more level-headed lady, Maggie; what do you think? I hear your son knows things." The hack looks in the Dram's direction.

"Oh, maybe you are listening too much to the stupid gabs around here, Mr Scott." She also looks towards Dram, raising her voice so as he can hear her. "Some folk around here talk too much."

"I'm sorry, Mrs Stuart, just natural curiosity."

"Seeing a way to elaborate your story?"

"Sorry, I'm not getting you."

"No, why are you here, Mr Journalist?"

"Doing my job, Mrs Stuart."

"Oh, you turn up here, in the local bar."

This interests me. I move between them, studying their faces. She is being facetious, to make a point, it is said. I've seen this before.

"Best place. You don't expect me to be out there in the media circus. More comfortable here."

"To catch the local gos."

"Of course, why not."

"Hate you fuckers." Caber spits his bile while not taking his eyes off his drink, causing the hack to spin on his seat.

Maggie smacks the tea towel onto the bar. "Caber!"

"Pardon pal?" The hack faces Caber.

"You heard me."

"Listen."

"No, you listen, we're sick of your type. We have a serious problem here. We've lost a wee boy, murdered as far as we know, and we don't need outside interference."

"I will do my job, sir, the wider public need to know what has happened here."

Caber bangs his glass down on the bar and lifts his heavy frame up to tower over the hack. "You stick your nose into our business and you'll get it cut off, you hear me?" He moves away, point made.

The hack turns his attention to Maggie. "Excitable gentleman, Mrs Stuart."

She leans over him. "Be advised he talks for many in this village, Mr Scott."

"Yeah, I'm aware of it."

"There's one thing, Mr Scott, interesting me."

"Oh, what's that?"

"Your reservation."

"Yes, single room, full-board, arrival Wednesday, departure to be advised."

"You made your reservation for the hotel last Saturday, two days before the boy was killed. You some kind of clairvoyant?"

"I wouldn't say so." The hack tears up a beer mat.

"No? Well I would, seems a bit odd to me. Is this something I should be talking to the inspector about?"

"Feel free, Mrs Stuart." The hack gets up. "I will tell you … if you keep it under your hat; things are mighty sensitive enough around here."

"Go on."

"I can confide in you?"

"I said go on."

"Right – I was coming here anyway."

"Oh?"

He looks around to ensure he isn't overheard. "I was coming here to do a story on the parents."

"Jackie and Rooney?"

"The very same."

"What kind of a story?"

"Human interest."

"Oh, human interest?"

The hack pushes the stool to the side and gets in closer to the bar. "I did a piece on them a couple of years back for the Glasgow Herald, as it was called then." He drops his voice. "Back in 2013, when Jackie Kaminski was promoted to deputy chief constable of Police Scotland and when Sean Rooney was a crime lord," Maggie carries on washing glasses at this as point if he wasn't telling her anything new, "they were two high profile characters. The Mother and Father of Crime, I called the story. I'm doing a follow up. You know, they adopt a child, move from Glasgow, settle in a remote area and start a new life. Don't you think this would be of interest to the public, and in particular the Sundays I sell my stories to?"

She puts down the tea towel. "And you had no inclination of anything about to happen?"

"Don't be daft, sweetheart. It just happened."

"Aye, to your advantage, to the benefit of your … story."

"Being in the right place at the right time is a gift for a reporter."

She leans across the bar to him, close enough for the hack to catch her perfume. Chanel No 5. "I'll be watching you, sir; if you cross a line I'll be obliged to inform Boyd. Sorry to be frank, but it's best being clear of where we stand."

"Maggie, I like you, why would I damage a developing friendship?"

She looks at him wondering if he is being serious, then sees a twinkle in his eye. *Is he flirting*, she wonders? She laughs. He smiles and returns to his beer.

I observe the boy at his home. His demeanour is different today. He refuses to leave their side, wandering alongside them, between them, with them, fearing separation from them. He would have been eight years alive the following morn and I wonder if he realises he will never achieve this, he would always be seven years alive. He would miss a confirmation, many holidays overseas, going on to high school in Invernevis, getting into University, meeting the love of his life, dying in his sixties. His look has been of a perplexed, confused, bewildered child, but now his movements are more frantic, fast and frenetic; like a scared fox at the sound of hounds approaching. The mother and father are deep in talk about him, about them, about the circumstances with which they have found themselves.

The mother is back to the knitting. "Boyd touched a lot of points."

And the father is back at the window. "Aye, like a scatter gun, trying to hit something, anything."

"He was implicating us in the murder of our son."

The boy looks at the father.

"I wouldn't say so."

"No, Rooney? Our irregular lives in crime, he meant. And he was right, we are … atypical as a couple."

"Doesn't mean he can point his finger in our direction."

"No, nothing to do with your gangland history or your tempestuous relationship with agent Jean Dempsie, who only happened to die in a mysterious way, and come away from the window, Lass is out there in the shed, she'd bark her head off if anyone was there."

He looks to the window again. "And the guys you put away?" The boy's head is moving side to side, as if he's watching a tennis match.

"Rooney, stay focused. Calum was killed here. His murderer was and is here."

"I know you Jackie, bury yourself in this. You have a target, a goal, forget everything else, just get the bastard who killed our son."

"Here comes the psychologist bit, once a shrink always a shrink."

"We have a relationship, Jackie, our needs, we have lost our son and we need to protect us."

"Oh, yeah, referral to a support group for parents of murdered children."

"That's not what I was meaning, although—"

"I don't do that."

"No, you get the bad guys."

The boy is looking even more confused now.

"It's all tied up, Rooney."

"Eh?"

"He touched on some things, Boyd, like your relationship with Jean, and her death."

"And what about your relationship, Jackie, with Ben?"

"Done and dusted."

"So was Jean, we all had needs."

She snarls at him. "Aye, so we had, pal."

This leads to a protracted and well-deserved pause. The boy does not need to hear this. He looks sad. How long can I allow him to suffer this? He needs to move on soon.

The mother drops to a seat. The father moves to her side.

"Jackie, let's not lose what we had, have. Bringing Calum into our lives brought us together, set us as a couple, made us a family; we still have us."

The mother turns to look at him and her eyes tighten. "You are right, Rooney, we need to stay together through this, but you need to know if we don't it will end us."

"I know if it ends, Jackie, it will end me."

She holds off for a couple of seconds, then hits him with the look that says 'your needs will have to wait'.

He looks at her without saying any more. Head bowed, he contemplates this thought as he wraps up and heads out along the path towards his shed, his place of refuge to think and plan. He gets into his wicker chair. There, he would prepare for all before him. The dog has followed him in knowing her evening walk is well overdue.

The father collects his stick and his torch from the shed and moves out towards the beach. There will do for the thoughts and for Lass's walk. Just as he reaches the beach path, a smell of burning distracts him from his dwam. He looks to the coastal road towards Achfara beach to see the sky lit by what he thought to be a hill fire. But it is too late in the year for that. He decides to head along the road to investigate. As he comes over the brow of the hill overlooking Achfara beach, the source of the smell and the fire becomes clear to him – a car in the car park to the north of the beach is ablaze. He grips Lass close to him as a thought arrives in his mind: has this any connection with the car that picked up the boy?

He moves closer, gathering the dog to him on the lead until he arrives to within three yards of the car. It is impossible to get any closer due to the flames and the smoke. The flames are around two yards high with embers carrying in the wind towards him and over his head. Pulling the dog close, he moves to the side away from the wind's direction to avoid the embers, and it is there he notices a man standing to the side of the car at the same distance.

He approaches the figure and points his stick at the burning wreck. "Is this your car?"

"Yes, I think so."

"What you mean you think so?"

"Well, it is where my car was earlier today."

"Then it is yours."

"I suppose it is, sir."

In the light of the fire, the father recognises him. "You're the Albanian man who lives in the old boathouse on the north end of the beach."

"Yes, I am sir."

The father pans the area with his torch. "Have you called the fire service or the police?"

"No, sir, I have not."

"Why not?"

"I do not have a telephone and it is not worth saving."

"Oh, and what happened?"

"I don't know. I looked out and it was in flames. It was a very old car. I suppose I had a fuel leak or something. It was fine when I went to the village earlier."

"You don't know. It didn't burst into flames on its own. Is there anyone else here?" The father shines the torch into the darkness and points his stick like a teacher at a blackboard. "My son was killed near here. He was picked up by a car. And your car just happens to burst into flames."

"Sir, I do not know what you are referring to, it was an old car."

Something inside the father's head says to calm down. If he is the man, he needs to do the sensible thing not the right thing.

The father calls the constable. "You should get over here, Achfara beach, a car's on fire, the Albanian." Broomlands recognises the significance of a car on fire less than a mile from Claigan beach where the boy was found after being picked up by a car. By the time the constable arrives, the flames have died and the smoke is billowing over the hill. A few folk have arrived and gather around it, mesmerised by the sight, as if they were standing gazing into a campfire.

The constable arrives. "I guess Guy Fawkes night has arrived early,"

"Aye, so it is. All we need are the candy apples."

"A fire tender is on its way."

"He's over there. Just tell me this is a coincidence."

"It's not wise to jump to conclusions, Mr Rooney."

The constable moves to the Albanian to enquire into the source and reason for the fire. He is unknowing on both counts. The father walks around the site, but there is nothing to see. The car is a burned-out wreck, unrecognisable. He heads back to the house to inform the mother. Interested in this incident, she says she will 'make enquires' about it in the morning. The father decides to stay up, torch, stick and Lass by his side, every so often going to the window. By three of the morning, the light from the burning car has gone, leaving a dark, unseeing sky.

CHAPTER 5

The following morning, the fourth of the eleventh month, Mhairi, the shepherdess, is on the hill tending her sheep. Grass is poor at this time of the year. She walks smartly, taking them hay and mix. Soon they will be tupping for the lambs to arrive in early spring to get the best price. She stops and sniffs the air, still holding the smell of the burned-out car. She had been thinking about it since she heard; what a strange thing to happen around here.

She heard me last night and is wary.

She turns towards the burn. For a couple of seconds she thinks she sees a man drinking there, as many walkers and golfers around here do. Liking a chat, she moves closer, and is about to ask "Is the water cold enough for you?" She realises there would be no reply from this man, who is on his knees, face down in the burn, hands tied behind his back. The dogs bark as if they know something is wrong. She moves back and pulls out her mobile phone and calls the constable. In the meantime, as is her nosey nature, she will try to ascertain who this man is, though she had met Inverbeg McDonald many times on this path and is confident from his frame it is him.

The constable and the doctor arrive within minutes of each other. She waits at the roadside to take them to the location. She is anxious to get the hay to her sheep, however, and is keen to get on. As she moves away, she tells them "It is Inverbeg McDonald, the Cù-Sith was about last night. I heard it." The constable hesitates then thanks her. The doctor proceeds to examine Inverbeg. Within a few minutes he arrives at an 'initial view' he died of cardiac arrest, but it doesn't need a spaewife to see his hands tied behind his back indicate his death is suspicious. The inspector arrives shortly after and orders the body to be taken to the same mortuary where the boy is, to undergo a similar analysis. Peter Campbell, the undertaker, also known as Funeral, would have another long journey to Abertay. Inverbeg has no need to remain there; I have escorted his soul to his eternity. At this stage, unless the investigation proves otherwise, the inspector says he is treating the death as 'suspicious'. Indeed it is, *maha.*

"Rooney?" The mother calls from the back room where she is sorting out the boy's clothes, as she has done every day since his death; almost as if she is preparing him for school.

"Yes?" The father answers from the kitchen and from the depths of his laptop.

"Calum's birthday, mind?"

"Not something I would forget, Jackie."

"I talked to Boyd. He phoned me."

"We saw him yesterday, has he a lead?"

"Inverbeg's been found dead. His body was found close to where Calum was found."

The father comes into the room. "Inverbeg's dead, he was there on Tuesday night."

"Black thinks his heart gave out. He had health problems."

"So he did, health problems indeed. This is important and so is the Albanian's car; they have something to work on." They move through to the kitchen. "Do you want something to eat? You haven't eaten a thing."

"No thanks. They are seeing Victor Temo this morning, but Boyd thinks the old banger just went on fire and was nothing to do with Calum."

"All a bit bloody coincidental, don't you think?"

"Well, he doesn't think so."

"Three days, three incidents, and he doesn't think so."

"In such a small place."

"I know, and talking about potential killers we are not talking about the whole country here, a population of seven hundred or so in the three villages."

"Whittle it down, adults of between twenty and seventy?"

"Three hundred or so."

"Half male."

"A hundred and fifty, I'd bring in all of the fuckers."

"And you'd wring it out of them."

"I'd start with the obvious."

"Sex abusers?"

"Checked."

"The register?"

"Well, Dad checked it, nothing, no one in the area. One or two in Invernevis, but iron clad alibi, one with a tag, confirmed never even been in the area, the second, recalled to prison, out of the game."

"Non-convicted?"

"Social work territory, I'll ask Ben."

"Yes, of course, your friend."

"He was your best friend, Rooney."

"Now, he's your—"

"In the past, Rooney, we have more going on now, just give it a rest." The father knows not to say anymore. She had been honest about her affair. It happened when they were estranged, when he was drinking and making a fool of himself, and ill with the mental illness. "There's one thing, Roon, it's important."

"What?" The father is still smarting about the friend.

"Inverbeg."

"He's dead."

"Well, Dad found out he had history; he checked him out, found out he abducted two boys, years ago."

"Jesus."

"It happened years ago, but there were no convictions, it was hushed up."

"Abuse, sexual?"

"No evidence, the boys said nothing."

"Did Boyd know this?"

"Yes."

"Inverbeg was in the area that night. I saw him out on his walk."

"Do you buy the story about his heart giving out?"

"'Cardiac arrest,' Black says. Boyd said his body showed no physical signs of assault, apart from a bleeding nose and his hands tied behind his back."

"His hands tied and a punch of the nose, no physical signs of assault?"

"Fran and Anna, our boy was killed, Inverbeg is found dead, a car is burned out, out there." The father points out of the window.

The mother smirks. "Just like Glasgow, Rooney."

"It's not funny, our son—"

"We're seeing him today. It's his birthday. Dad's arranging it. We're going up this morning."

"Why didn't you tell me?"

"Because you would have been up all night fretting about it; so get yourself ready, we're leaving soon."

The Albanian strikes a lonely figure as he moves around the rocks jutting out from the Achfara shore, occasionally venturing out to the skerries, which he reaches by his rowing boat. He collects whelks, mussels and the occasional scallop at low tide. He knows the locals view him to be a suspicious character who only ventures into the village once a week to collect his provisions from the local store and post office where he sends his letters and other packages. He picks up some sort of payment, which they think it is a pension, while doing odd jobs for those with holiday homes scattering along the shore. He minds his own business, however: better that way. He lives in an old abandoned boathouse separated by dunes at the far end of Claigan beach with no electricity or sewerage, paying a nominal rent to a local crofter. Lit with old oil lamps, he heats the place with a small wood burning stove fuelled by sticks from the wood separating the beach from the village road.

Maha, I have no interest in this man at this time, but I will soon. However, it is inevitable the inspector will pay him a visit.

He is gutting mackerel in a burn running down the side of the sand dunes sheltering the boathouse when the inspector and the constable come into view. The inspector approaches him. "For your lunch?"

If the Albanian is startled at the sight of the suited officers scrambling down the dunes he does not show it. "I have no other need for fish."

The inspector introduces himself, but has no need to explain his visit. "We haven't met, sir; but you've met my colleague here, last night, at the car."

"Yes, he was very helpful. The fire service was very prompt, though there's nothing left of it."

"Indeed. You would have heard about the child?"

"I have." The Albanian gets off an old wooden stool. "The police have been all over here, covering every metre of the dunes. Do you want to search my house?"

"Do you think I need to?"

"I am surprised you asked." The Albanian goes back to his gutting.

"We want to talk to you about the boy."

"Do you think I killed him?"

"Can we go in?"

"You can or is it you may?"

"You are learning English, Mr Temo?"

"I am trying to improve myself."

The Albanian gathers the fish into a plastic bag and goes in followed by the inspector and the constable. They strain their eyes in the dark, partially lit by parallel lines of light from the gaps between the wooden slats blocking out the front of the boathouse, where boats would have once slid out onto runners down the slip to the sea. The Albanian lights two oil lamps which offer more of the inside of the boathouse before opening the door of the wood burning stove to feed it more sticks. The inspector pans the inside of the place and to his surprise sees a tidy and ordered environment. He raises his eyebrows.

"What did you expect, a hovel befitting a gypsy?"

"What is your name, sir?" The inspector takes out a notepad and pen.

"Victor Temo. You know my name. I gave it to the police officer last night."

"Yes, but I need you to confirm it. And where are you from Victor?"

The Albanian looks up, surprised at the use of his first name. "I am from Albania, hoping to better my life, to bring my family to this beautiful country, to live in peace, and not to be any trouble."

"You live on a beach."

"I live by the sea, as in Albania; the sea is in my blood."

"You have skills." The constable is impressed at the quality of the carpentry, taking in the stained wooden flooring and walls. But what amazes him more are the framed pictures which bedeck the walls, coloured collages of sea shells, in the shape of the beach and the dunes. "You do these?"

"I sell them to the tourists in the village. Do you mind if I cook these before they go off? I do not have a refrigerator." He transfers the fish to a frying pan and places it on the stove, adding cooking oil.

"The pictures are good," the constable says.

"They keep me out of trouble."

"Yes, I hope so," the inspector says. "The boy?"

The Albanian removes the mackerel from the pan to a plate. "I was in the Small Isles from afternoon to the last orders. I was reading my English in the corner, minding my own business. When was the child—?"

"Sometime around five, did you leave the pub anytime around then?"

"Only to get bread and ham from the shop, before it shut, then back to the bar until it did." He takes a fork and eats the fish like it would squirm off the plate if he did not.

"You had your car?"

"Do you think I would drink and drive?"

"Now it is a burned-out shell."

"I only used it to go into the village for my supplies and to sell my mussels and my art in Stoer." He dips the plate and fork in a plastic basin of water and places it on the floor. "Do you mind if I wash these?"

"You can leave them for now," the inspector says. "Was it legal, the car?"

"You know it was, you can tell these days. I gave the police officer the registration document last night."

The constable runs his hand over the pictures. "You like shells?"

The Albanian nods and makes a roll-up. "Do you mind?" The inspector doesn't say anything either way. "Thanks." He lights up. "Well, there are a lot of them around here, they make good shapes."

"The boy also liked shells," the inspector says.

"Yes, he did."

"How do you know?"

The Albanian draws deeply on the cigarette, then exhales enough smoke to dim the light. "He used to wander over here, following the line of the beach. I showed him my shell art."

"So you knew the boy; he has been in here?"

"Yes sir, to both of your questions."

"Do you know the parents?" The constable coughs. "Do you mind if you don't?"

The Albanian puts the cigarette out. "I see them around and I have met them on the beach. The father was at the car last night."

"I believe you lived in Glasgow before you came here," the inspector says. "Did you know of the parents there?"

The Albanian opens the door full and ties the handle back to the wall of the boathouse with old rope. "I did not know them there. I had enough of Glasgow. I love it here."

"Did they know their son had been here?"

"No, I did not think…"

"You didn't think it important to tell them their son had been visiting a stranger in a dilapidated boat house, to ask their permission to see him? And you didn't tell the father last night you knew the child; even to say you were sorry about his death."

"It was not a suitable time to talk to him."

"An unknown car was seen taking the boy away, just before he was killed; your car was found on fire the very next evening."

The Albanian looks out of the open door. The constable and the inspector look at each other. Their faces indicate they do not intend leaving there without the Albanian. The Albanian sees this and makes a go for the door. The constable had anticipated this and blocks his way. "Don't son." The Albanian lifts his hands in the air in submission and the constable slips handcuffs on his wrists.

"Victor Temo, we are treating you as a suspect in the murder of Calum Rooney." The Albanian looks at him dispassionately. "You do not need to say anything but anything you do say will be noted and may be used in evidence. Do you understand?" Temo nods his head. "You will come with us." He tries to reach for a basin. The constable takes it from him. "No sir, I'll do it." He dowses the fire with the water and blows out the oil lamps.

"Look after the site, Constable." The inspector pulls the door over. "Make sure forensics do a good job."

"Do you need any assistance, sir?"

"I don't think he'll give me any trouble; will you Victor?" The Albanian shakes his head.

"Fine, sir."

"And ask them to give particular attention to finding the boy's bag, in here and around the house."

"Will do, sir."

"Protect the scene until they arrive."

The constable nods and the Albanian goes quietly with the inspector. He sits on the Albanian's stool, pulling his coat around him. The place becomes quiet apart from the squawking of the gulls and the sea crashing on the shore. The smell of smoke drives him outside where he sits on a rock. I study him. His mind is full of thoughts over recent events; his quiet existence as local constable dealing with everyday menial issues has been shattered. I move around him. Moving from the frantic office of Invernevis to the backwater of Stoer had obvious advantages at first, but *maha* not now!

The parents prepare for their three-hour trip to Abertay. The boy would have been eight years old this day and they dearly want to see him. They had been planning a birthday party; which, had he not been taken three days ago, they would have had on his arrival from school this evening, a Friday, with a weekend of activities planned. He would have gone pony trekking on the Saturday morning, then on a trip on the local steam train, The Highlander, in the afternoon, and later to the Mariner Cafe for his favourite fish and chips. He would have gone home for cake and to enjoy his birthday presents, his joint passions of sea shells and steam trains: *The Book of Shells: A Life-Size Guide to Identifying and Classifying Six Hundred Seashells* and a three-disc box set *The Greatest Steam Trains*, which includes his favourite, the Flying Scotsman. He is no longer to have these pleasures, of course. The mother had purchased the gifts a week before when she was in Invernevis on a shopping trip, while collecting their grocery supplies. She ordered them for the occasion and picked them up the same day. She hid them out of sight in her bedroom, planning to surprise him later this day. Today, she places them on the kitchen table.

The father lifts the DVD box. "What you going to do with them?"

"We are taking them with us, he'll get them on his birthday."

The father picks up the book. "I was looking at his shell collection this morning and I just can't believe he isn't here to add to it. He would have been down there tomorrow morning as he did every Saturday and Sunday to search for new ones."

"The weekend won't happen for him, but today is his birthday, and we'll mark it."

"He's coming home on Monday and that'll be hard enough, but today…"

She moves close to him. "We need to do this, Rooney. Today is going to be hard, but not going there would be harder." The father agrees and they head off to Abertay, a three-hour drive from Achfara.

Later this day, the area becomes awash with media, the police, and the terror tourists, as the locals are now calling them. In November, the caravans, mobile homes, and the tents are well gone, but there is a macabre interest in the area, and the guesthouses, the hotels, and the camp sites, normally winding down, are full. An incident room is set up in the local community centre and an additional ten detectives and the same amount in uniforms are sent down from the Highland HQ in Abertay.

The community is trying to get on with their normal lives, but they are hassled by journalists and mobile camera crews. "Could you tell us how you feel about the murders? What is like to live in a small remote area with the possibility of a murderer on the loose? Do you fear for your safety and the safety of your children?"

The school is closed for three days, but has now reopened with a police officer at the door; more to assure parents of the utmost safety of their children. Many of the children are taken to school and collected by car. Those without cars go by the chairman's school bus, but on the condition each day a male parent takes turns in being on it until the last child is dispatched through their front door. Angus Stuart, the young *taibshear*, however, refuses to travel by bus, forcing his parents to walk him to the school and back.

The parents arrive at the mortuary. The chief had arranged everything; including a counsellor should the parents suffer at the sight of their dead son. They are advised, before they go in, that the Home Office pathologist has just finished the post mortem and the body is yet to be prepared to be returned home on Monday. They are told they should not remove the sheet over the boy's torso, where key organs had been removed for analysis and returned.

They move into the examination room which reminds the father of the clinical, disinfected smell of an old swimming baths he used as a child, the tiled room creating an echo which unsettles him. They pathology staff have dimmed the lights to create a softer, more personal environment for the visit. All autopsy equipment has been removed and the boy moved from the necropsy table to a transportable autopsy table which is covered in a sheet to look less clinical, and raised to give a better view of him.

They move slowly into the room and to the same side of the table, the father standing to the side of the mother, she closer to the head of the boy. I follow them in; never before had I been in such a place, though I understand the need for it in determining how the body died. It may surprise you to know I have never had any interest in death or the varied means in which it happens: all before now, however. The fact that death doesn't interest me as much as the state of the soul may not surprise you. The soul is much more interesting; this is where you will find the being which inhabits the body. Some souls are sad and tired, mostly in the old, but sometimes in the young. Others are vibrant and pulsating like they are desperate to leap out of the dead flesh they inhabit, such as it was with the *balach*, refusing to accept death had invaded his body; that he has much more life to live outside of it.

But for now the parents look down on his face – his pale, waxy, grim face; lacking any sign of life, contrary to the young, vibrant, always smiling child they remembered. What they don't see is the boy standing at the head of his body looking on forlornly at this bizarre scene. He looks confused as he looks at this dead boy. *Surely this is not me*, he thinks. *I am here*. Yes, you are but not in the same way. He moves towards the mother, as if he would like her to put her arm around him and comfort him as she would in times of fear. Such as when he would wake up from nightmares associated with his having to be taken away from his 'biological parents'. He squeezes close to her, getting something from this, but not the kind of response he would have wished. The mother reaches out and fixes the hair of the boy on the table. "My boy, my wee boy," she says.

The father lifts up the Harry Potter gift bag he carries containing the birthday presents, covered in Hufflepuff gift wrap, wound in colourful bows and ribbons, which contrast starkly with this cold, clinical place. He takes out the individual packages and places them on the boy, on the sheet, noticing discolouration where the body had seeped fluid from open gaps in the boy's chest. He places the packages over the discoloration. Even though the boy has not the physical ability to open them, he studies the gifts, his eyes widening with interest.

I ponder on why I should take such a young lad, but I do not concern myself with it; it is not for me to judge such things, nor the human who took his life. The boy knows this person, but does not have the physical ability to say who this person is. I could ask him why he thinks he was taken. Would it help? No, it would not, nor would it help my task with the boy. I just have to do what is expected of me.

The boy leans into them as if he is getting something: support, comfort, closeness. He will move on soon, however, I must ensure this; he needs to make those steps all beings make towards their other place. Only some, and he would qualify, may remain, forever to wallow in their means of passing, unable to move on due to the circumstances of their death, the unnatural way of it, and he could be one of them for sure, but it's best for him to move on. I can see no benefit in his remaining. I need to help him with the journey across; like getting across a river he needs to find the narrowest point, the shallowest depth, the biggest and steadiest rocks with which to step upon until he reaches the other side. But I can see he is not ready to go, not yet.

I look at the father's face – he is holding it in. I have seen it before; as if, should he let it out, a torrent of pain and torment would flow, the despair would gush out, uncontrollable, uncontainable.

The father moves closer to the body. "Our lovely wee boy." The boy looks into his face and comes round to his side. "We need to help him find peace, to rest."

"Yes, but we need to find out who did it, Rooney; then he can rest." She reaches to move the sheet covering the body.

He stops her. "No, Jackie, what good would it do?" She moves it back anyway, revealing the neck and the shoulder, the top of the chest. "There is nothing more to see south of there, darling, no more."

She moves closer almost to examine his face, his neck, his chest in detail. "His neck is bruised; you can see where he had his hands around his throat. I think he broke his nose."

"We need to see what the pathologist report says, darling, it'll confirm all." He turns to the boy. "Happy birthday, pal." He leans over and kisses the brow of the boy. "We have done what we came here to do, darlin', we should go."

She too leans and kisses the child; little does she know the boy is pursing his lips too in the hope she would lean his way. "Goodnight, my lovely boy," she says, even though it is mid-afternoon. "We'll see you when you come home." He looks at her and then to his mortal remains.

That he should suffer this is my guilt, for it is my interest, my perverse interest, he should remain a *taibhse*.

They leave the boy there, in his earthly demise, but he will follow them, in his wistful wandering. For then, though, he appears glued to the body, as if—if he could—he would re-enter it and be placed in the ground with it. Oh, that I should allow this suffering, like a pained animal needing a kindly human to help it move on.

They thank the staff and ask them to respect their son's body until it is delivered to them on the following Monday. They reach their car and the father takes his laptop from his shoulder bag the minute he gets in. She will drive; he will add more notes from seeing the boy and update their thoughts on the investigation, to challenge the one going on.

He reaches across and takes her hand. "Do you feel any better now, now you have seen him?"

"Just more determined to get the bastard." She starts the engine. "We need to find him, because they won't." She pulls onto the trunk road south west to head home. "And if you won't help me, I'll do it myself."

A few minutes later, he says, "I'm going to Glasgow, Jackie."

"Aye, great, you fuck off to Glasgow, while all this is going on up here." She speeds up at the thought of this.

"I need to, I can't stay in Achfara. I need to do something."

"Inverbeg did it. I know he did."

"Oh, it's all tied up then."

"Come on, Rooney, he had the potential, a child abuser, in the right place at the right time."

"Why's he dead then?"

"His heart gave up."

"With his hands tied behind his back, convenient."

I was expecting the call, they were not.

The mother nods to the phone in the dashboard holder. "Take it."

"Hello." The father talks into the phone. "Yes, when? OK, keep us informed, right, tonight, right?"

"What, Rooney, what?"

"Boyd has the Albanian in custody."

"Knew it."

"Questioning, Jackie."

"Enough for me. It must have been one of them."

"Open and shut case then." He stays quiet for a minute. "Maybe for you, but I have to rule out the Glasgow dimension."

"Police Scotland, my father, and Boyd can do there."

"I have to do it, he was my son."

"And you get yourself killed at the same time; just great. I lose my son and my husband." The mother is increasing the speed of her car in line with her rising temper.

"I know there are people there who would harm me, but I also have some friends there I can rely on. Will you slow down?"

"Friends? The mob are no friends. Don't trust anyone, mind, Rooney. Bill Bingham might be Father, but you mess with him and he'll do you, he will." She presses harder on the accelerator. "No, I want to get home."

"I have to find out."

"We have two suspects. What more do we need?"

"Bloody factual evidence, Jackie, you know what."

"I'll find out – my dad."

"Oh, go ahead and steer the investigation to your own ends. But he won't let you."

"And what are you going to do, Mr Father, ex-crime lord, by going to Glasgow?"

"Let's say I need to exhaust some of my own possibilities."

"Aye, but don't expect me to support you when your arse hits the tarmac."

"I won't be just my arse hitting the tarmac if you keep driving at this speed, slow down, let me drive."

"My car, I drive, anyway you don't like automatics." The mother had taken to driving automatic cars due to the injuries she suffered in an attack in Glasgow, which left her with a disabled left leg. "Did Boyd say anything else?"

"He mentioned there's an update tonight, in the hall; Inverbeg and the Albanian."

"We need to go."

"What? We won't hear anything we don't know. And why listen to their platitudes, the moaning minnies, their community has been devastated, the incomers have bought mayhem to their village? No thanks, I'm going to the pub."

"Typical old Rooney, just so predictable."

"It's been a hard day."

"Aye, so it has."

"Slow down, for god's sake."

The inspector clears his throat and readies his papers for the public briefing. It is evening and Lochdarrach Village Hall is packed with media, journalists, community, visitors. The cameras are trained on him.

The chairman starts. "I want to thank you for coming. Can you hear me at the back?"

Caber calls out "Aye," and a number of coughs back him.

"OK, it's a cold night. I don't want you here any longer than is necessary. Detective Inspector Boyd will make the statement, then take a few questions."

The coughs subside.

The inspector starts. "Thank you, Mr McIsaac." He turns to those in the hall. "You would have heard of the death of Mr Donald McDonald. We are treating his death as … unexplained, an unexplained death."

He sees their faces, askance at the term 'unexplained death'.

"Don't you mean murder, Inspector?" The cameras swing around to train on the *cailleach*. She straightens her hair.

The inspector replies. "We have no confirmation as to the cause of death; his body is undergoing a pathologist assessment. When we are sure, we will be making a further statement, when we receive the pathology report." A number of obvious comments are thrown at him. "Could we hold discussion until the end, to allow me to get through the statement," he says, "as you'll understand?" The *cailleach* scowls in his direction. At least she said what the folk there were thinking. "We will make a further statement when we know more about the circumstances of Mr McDonald's death and we appreciate you will be shocked and upset at this." Many there cast a glance at each other.

The inspector counts a full ten seconds in his head before he reveals the next piece of information. "However, in relation to Calum, we have a man in custody." There is a palpable intake of breath, though most knew it already – the Albanian had been apprehended, something would not have gone unnoticed in this place. "But as to the circumstances of this, we have nothing further to say."

If this was going to quash questions he was wrong; they come at him thick and fast: "Is he Calum's murderer? Did he kill McDonald? Has he killed before?"

"He is with us for questioning. Although he is a suspect, he is not charged with any crime."

This did not prevent certain members of the congregation having their say. "He lived on the beach near where both of them were killed, who else could have killed them? The bastard must pay; bloody immigrants, can't trust them; an incomer, always knew it would be."

"Enough." The inspector's sharp tone brings silence to the room. "This man cannot be vilified by this community. If we hear of any aggression towards this man we will take action. I have to make myself clear on this."

It takes *Cailleach* to sum up the views of those there. "No one here will harm the man, Inspector. It is not our way, but we have had two of our community, in exceptional circumstances as you say, die; one an unexplained death and another, a child, murdered, and you have a man in custody. It cannot be unusual for a community, in this case us, to express its disquiet, which we will indeed do. Do *I* make myself clear, Inspector?"

The inspector does not answer her, she has had her say.

He continues his statement. "Over the next few days we will be making a public appeal for information." No one responds. "Calum's bag, which was with him the day he went to school and when he left, has not been recovered. We will post a description of the item. We wish to ask the public for any information as to its whereabouts."

"Check the Albanian's house, Inspector."

"We have, Annie, thank you." The inspector is pleased to conclude the proceedings. "We will keep you all appraised," The people move out, chatting and grumbling as they go.

The hack orders a whisky and a pint of Skye Gold in the Small Isles as those from the hall descend on the pub. They are full of the Albanian's arrest. It is Friday night and the pub is busier than normal for this time of year, but, failing the father's understandable leave, only Maggie is behind the bar. She is serving three drinkers at once, pouring draft beer in a multiple way. The hack is impatient, rubbing a five-pound note between his fingers, trying to catch her attention.

"Good evening, Mr Scott, I'll be with you in one second."

"Thanks, darlin'."

"Hello, Mr Scott." He turns to see the inspector standing behind him.

"Oh hello, Inspector Boyd, you in for a drink?"

"I am, but I like to buy my own."

"You not on duty, just when there's lots going on for the polis around here?"

"You're right there." The inspector pans the bar, catching some serious scowls directed his way. He shakes his head. "I thought I would see you at the briefing. It's what journalists do?"

"I know you took the Albanian guy in. I had no need to be there to hear this or the rabble squabbling amongst themselves."

"No, you'd rather come in here and hear it." The inspector looks around. "Who told you?"

"Come on, Inspector, you know how information gets out. I knew the minute he arrived in the police station in Invernevis, it's a small place."

"Indeed, can I have a word?" The inspector gestures to the hack to move away from the bar to a vacant spot by the wood burning stove. "Better over there."

"Aye, warmer, let me get my drink."

The hack takes his pint and follows the inspector.

The inspector speaks quietly in the hack's ear. "Your card was found in McDonald's pocket; you want to tell me why?"

The hack looks around to see if the inspector had been overheard. "I talked to him. I tried to get some … information."

"You tried to get information from him; nothing more?"

"Nothing more; was he murdered?"

"Died of heart failure, but something didn't appear right."

"He seemed alright to me."

"He had a bad heart and his hands were tied behind his back."

"Lovely, thanks Inspector." The hack takes out a notebook and writes. "His hands were tied behind his back."

"Surprised you didn't know, Scott, everyone knows. Mhairi told everyone."

"Aye, slipping up, Inspector." The hack puts the notepad back. "His heart gave out. What with all the walking and exertion; exercise kills people you know." He pats his tummy. "Me, I do my exercise with this." He raises the pint to his eye line.

"Where did you talk to him?"

"Near the beach."

"Oh, near the beach, just happened to be passing?"

"I followed him there."

"Why?"

"I wanted to talk to him." He finishes the whisky in one glug. "Look Inspector Boyd, we both know about McDonald and the two boys." The inspector looks at him. "McDonald had a history."

"Doesn't mean he—" Magnus pushes by with a tray of drinks. The inspector waits until he is well out of earshot before he completes his sentence, "—killed the child."

"No, well, he could have killed the boys."

"But he didn't."

"Regular beatings, starved them, neglected them."

"He didn't … abuse them."

"Abuse? Not sexually, as far as we know, the boys didn't say he did."

"No charges were made."

"No, the boys didn't say much."

"You smelled a story, Mr Scott?"

"I smell a bigger story."

"Oh."

The hack looks around the bar, then drops his voice. "They knew it was going on."

"Doesn't mean—"

"It means they could do the same, Inspector. Who else did they protect, are they protecting?"

The inspector takes in some faces in the bar. "Did you see anything?"

"When?"

"Inverbeg."

"You said he died of a heart attack."

"A cardiac arrest. His body is with pathology, an autopsy."

"Oh."

"And you were the last to see him."

"Really?"

They trade looks for a few seconds.

"Don't go far. We will want to talk to you, properly."

"Don't intend to, enjoy the beer here too much, and the talent." The hack nods towards Maggie.

"Aye, indeed." The inspector makes to move away. "Keep the McDonald stuff, the two boys, to yourself, will you?"

"My lips are sealed, but look around Inspector; lips won't stay sealed here forever."

No, they won't. This is a proud community. Saying they protected McDonald and knew the abuse was going on is a fearsome accusation to make.

The friend pushes in beside the father at the bar. "Sure beats Tennent's Bar on Byres Road, Roon." He turns around to the sound of two traditional musicians tuning up in the corner.

"Don't know. If I could, I'd be there right now."

"Thought you were on the wagon?"

"Was the other night on the wagon?" The father nods at his pint of Guinness. "I've been nursing it for over an hour. Controlled drinking it is called; don't you know this is now an accepted treatment option?"

"Yes, for those who find abstinence too—"

"Difficult, Ben; you think I am weak?"

"It's difficult here, Roon." The friend looks over to the inspector and the hack in the corner, then to a group of visitors looking their way.

"How would you know how difficult it is here? What you doing here?"

"I booked into the hotel and this is the bar."

"I know it is, but what are you doing *here*?"

"I thought we covered that the other night."

"Maybe you and Jackie did, but not me."

"I'm here to offer my support, to you both."

"I know you better than most, or I thought I did until you fucked my wife."

Maggie's eyes lift from the pint she is pulling.

"Shushed, Rooney; she wasn't your wife at the time."

"She was still mine."

"Let's not go back there." The friend creates a long enough pause to move the father off the subject. "You been interviewed yet?"

"I guess you mean the investigation, of course I have, I found him."

"I know, Rooney, and it couldn't have been easy."

"No, not easy finding your dead son, find anything else?" The father looks at him. The friend takes a big breath. "How did the AA meeting go?"

It is now for the father to demand the friend lowers his voice. "Now you shushed, Ben, people don't need to know about my meeting."

"I heard you missed it, that night?"

"Jackie phoned me to say Calum was missing. I came right back down. Why are you asking?"

"Oh, I just wondered; maybe you wouldn't have found him, if you had been at the meeting,"

"No, I might have been in 'my name is Rooney and I am an alcoholic' mode, while my son was being killed."

The father gestures to Maggie; she picks it up. "Pint of Guinness, Rooney?" He nods.

"Controlled drinking, Rooney? Jackie says the meeting is helping."

"Oh, you two have a quiet word about me the other night?"

"I was asking how you were doing."

"With the drink?" The father gazes at his Guinness settling on the bar.

"With all the things troubling you."

"Before I got pissed and you poured me into bed and spent the night in my house."

"I didn't sleep with her, Roon."

Although much quieter, Maggie's ears are well attuned to bar conversations, especially interesting ones. "Your Guinness, Rooney," she says, delivering it.

"Thanks, Maggie." He takes the stout and a large mouthful. "No, I didn't think you did," he says to the friend.

"Rooney, why are you going to Glasgow?"

"Oh, Jackie told you."

"Yes, she did, she's worried, naturally."

"It's none of your business."

"You're going tomorrow."

"I am. I'm going down in the morning, and I'll be enjoying a decent pint in Tennent's by tomorrow night." The father lifts the pint to eye level. "Better than this pish."

"Rooney," Maggie calls, "enough!"

"Sorry, Maggie."

The friend persists. "Why?"

"Why Glasgow and why Tennent's?"

"Just why?"

"I've business there."

"Rooney, I know the kind of business you do, or have done in Glasgow in the past. It'll get you in trouble."

The father shakes his head. "As I said, it's not your business."

"You are my friend."

"And I thought I told you to fuck off."

Maggie is watching the father now; she knows he is about to turn.

"Jackie wants to see me, on Sunday."

"Oh, a fuck in the offing, when the cat's away?"

Maggie's eyes lift once more.

"She wants to talk to me. I've offered her my support."

"Is *that* why you came?"

"Of course, to give my support. I'm a friend, mind?"

"Was, mind."

"Rooney, you've just lost your boy, why wouldn't I come?"

"To be with Jackie, maybe."

"We sorted it out, Rooney, like adults. You said it yourself at the time. We talked it through. It was clear you and Jackie were meant to be together. I was—"

"A fly fuck."

"Come on, Rooney, I was a mere distraction in your relationship. You guys got it together. Here, with your wee boy, a new life."

"And then you turn up, just when we needed you … not."

"I care about you guys, Rooney. You were my best friend, and Jackie—"

"Your best fuck."

Maggie has had enough. "Listen guys, there are ladies in the bar, including me, so keep the language down. You got it? Thank you!"

The father apologises and the friend is determined to make his point. "You weren't around, Rooney. You weren't together. She needed me at the time. And you needed me in a different way if I recall."

"I was ill, you were my named person, a formal role as *I* recall."

"You know I helped you."

"My guardian-bloody-angel."

The father catches Maggie's eye. "I said bloody, Maggie."

"Just remember I was and am still there for you, Rooney. Jesus, look at what we went through together with the major incident team, the bloody shitey job we had to do."

"Is it any worse here?"

"I like it here."

"I thought you might."

"The trad music, a big roaring fire, good seafood."

"You should see it in the summer, tourists everywhere, not a seat to be had in the pub, though with the media circus going on just now not much change there."

"What are you going to do, Rooney? Do you think you can you stay here after—"

"My son?"

"Yes, your son. Things will be very different now. You know, this new life and all, without the wee guy."

"This is our home. We'll have to get on with it."

"I know you, Rooney. You won't rest."

The father moves in. "Listen, I don't have the fight in me anymore. I'm not the man—"

"Who brought the Glasgow teams to book, got them together, got rid of ISIS in Glasgow?"

"I'm a different man, now."

The friend studies him. "You're cycling down, Roon. I can see it."

"Oh here we go with the shite again. You're not my named person anymore, Ben. I was discharged from the community order before I came here."

"The black dog follows wherever you go, pal."

Or maybe the green fairy dog, friend?

"I take my pills."

"Major attack on your psyche, Rooney, wouldn't surprise me if you relapse."

"I'll be fine, named person."

"Just don't get too involved. You'll know the characteristics of the guy who did this better than anyone, but leave it for them. Don't go there, you'll end up back in hospital."

"I'll do what I have to do."

"Aye, you will."

"Go home, Ben. It's time you went."

"Do you know why Jackie wants to talk to me?"

"Social work stuff, Ben, she'll tell you."

"Rooney?"

"What?"

"Calum's back pack."

"What's it got to do with you?"

"I gave it to him; I'd love it, as a wee minding of him. You obviously didn't find it … when you found him?"

The father gets up. "No, I've already explained it." He notices the inspector getting ready to leave. "Excuse me, I need to go a place." He heads for the toilet and slips out the outside door.

The father is leaning on the inspector's car as he approaches it. "Why didn't you tell us about Inverbeg, Inspector?"

"Ah, Mr Rooney. I wondered whether I might see you in there."

"Happens to be my boozer."

"Yes, of course it is."

"McDonald; you have something to tell us?"

The inspector sneezes and pulls a handkerchief from his pocket. "Sorry, bloody horrible cold." He opens his car door and is about to step in. "Of course, your wife's contacts. I guessed you would find out about the boys."

The father reaches and holds the top of the door preventing the inspector from closing it. "Yes, inevitable, Inspector. It must be uncomfortable when we find out everything you do in time." The inspector gets in the car and is about to switch on the ignition. "Did he kill Calum?"

"You're jumping a bit ahead of yourself, are you not?"

"A bit of a coincidence, don't you think?"

"What coincidence?"

"An abuser of young boys, a local man; a murder of a young boy, ours, also local; what are the chances of that?"

"We have no evidence to link McDonald, Mr Rooney."

"He was in the area of the school, the beach?"

"We are pursuing a definite line of inquiry. Now, if you'll…"

"The Albanian is a diversion, Inspector. We both know it."

"He is a suspect. Inverbeg McDonald is not, but we will keep an open mind on this as we proceed."

"Inspector?"

"What?"

"Get something for the cold, it could be the death of you."

The inspector looks at him for a second, grins, and gets in the car and pulls away. The father turns to look across the car park towards the sea. He is facing my way and appears to be staring in my direction as if he sees something. Only when I reify, which I do occasionally when required, I am the green dog, otherwise I cannot be seen. Though, a deerhound has been seen around these parts for two hundred years. Some say it is the ghost of a dog left behind by a family which was cleared to Canada, but they are wrong; *I* am the Cù-Sith.

I take to my heels. He is startled and turns. He thinks he sees a large dog make off up the hill. He rubs his eyes. I turn to look back at him. He cannot see me now for I am in the bracken, but I intend following him to wherever he goes. This will take me from the *balach*, however, but it is necessary.

CHAPTER 6

I travel with the father to Glasgow on the morning. It is Saturday, the day of the bonfires, and this man has death in his path, behind and beyond. I will stay with him, to do what I am destined to do, to convey souls. Much more interesting for me here, however, is the potential of another murder. We travel by train, which takes over five hours from the dark of six to the light of eleven.

He will see the man he knows as Bill Bingham, the man who succeeded him as leader of the crime syndicate of the most feared adult gangs in Glasgow. His legacy there was to bring the gangs together to fight a common enemy, a terrorist threat to the city, to the risk of his health and his life; hence, his move north with the boy and the mother. Indeed he would have died here if he hadn't. Just like Davy McGing, the previous Father, had said to him: "You live and you die within the family." The father knew by leaving the Family there was the possibility he could be murdered. This father didn't really believe this though. *He* would escape to the Highlands, but was this far enough from the family to ensure his survival?

The inspector might think otherwise, however. He too is in Glasgow, where he has been summoned by the chief. *Suits me*, the inspector thinks; if the boy's death is attributable to the family, he will know.

"It's good to see you, sir." The inspector eyes the interior of Belle Bar, on the Great Western Road, in particular observing the young female students adorning the place. "Very bohemian sir, not a normal place to conduct business."

The chief gets up from his seat and offers his hand. "It does me, son, less formal."

"Yes, less formal." The inspector takes the chief's hand in a tight grip. He hovers over him, noticing a tub of pistachio nuts. "Sorry, sir, I'm disturbing your snack."

"Lunch, Boyd. Just sit yourself down, you're conspicuous, and we're here not to be."

"Yes sir, indeed." The inspector takes a seat adjacent to the chief at the fire. "Cosy in here, warm fire." He warms his hands.

"I believe you are Lochiel 1200."

The inspector looks around. This chief isn't short in coming forward, he thinks. "Yes, I am, sir, in Lodge Lochiel."

"I am of the craft myself." The inspector is well aware of the Masonic fraternity in the police these days, and of the chief's status in it, notwithstanding the Masonic grip just administered.

"Indeed sir."

"Well, let's get on with it, son. This is my Saturday off."

"Yes, I appreciate this, sir. You wanted to see me." The inspector pulls out a notebook.

"No notebooks."

"No, right." The notebook goes back to his inside pocket. "You will want to discuss the investigation, sir: the boy."

"My grandson."

"Yes, indeed. Must be hard, sir."

The chief looks him hard in the eyes. "You need to find him before I do, Boyd."

"Yes, sir, I understand."

The chief's bulk shuts off the heat of the fire. "What's happening, son?"

"Nothing definitive as yet, sir."

"The Albanian?"

"Victor Temo."

The chief lifts an attaché case from the floor onto his lap and pulls out a buff folder. "I have your initial report."

"Yes, sir. Nothing substantive on him, so far, an iron clad alibi."

"Cast iron, Boyd." The chief reads from the report. "He says he was in the pub?"

"Staff saw him there."

"He had a car, slipped out, picked up the wean, killed him, got back to the pub before anyone noticed him missing." The chief shuts the folder.

"He said he didn't have his car at the hotel."

"Easy to leave out of sight in a place like Lochdarrach, down by the marina for example. I walked myself there just to see. Could have easily hidden the car there between the boats." He sits back.

"Yes, sir, I suppose." The inspector is pleased the heat from the fire is now reaching him.

"The car."

"Sir."

"He set it alight?"

"Nothing to suggest he did, sir."

"If he didn't, who did?"

"An old banger sir, happens."

"You did the car?"

"Burned out, nothing to check."

"Check it. Him?"

"Swabbed, checked it for blood, fibres, fingerprints, DNA: nothing."

"Savvy bastards."

"Sorry, sir."

"The Albanians, they know the score. He was part of the Albanian crew, here in Glasgow."

"He said he had cut all links with them; said he came north to get away from it all."

"Trafficking; he had a part in procuring women, bringing them to Glasgow."

"No form on violence though."

The chief nearly chokes on pistachio nuts. "What? He worked for Lekë Zaharia, a viscous bastard who trafficked under age women. Rooney's guys hit the Zaharia operation. Temo was one of his lieutenants, one of the few left with his kidneys, forty others weren't so lucky."

"Kidneys!"

"Long story, Boyd, let's say the Albanian Mafia was given a serious warning."

"Maybe he was run out of Glasgow, or wanted out of it, ended up in Achfara; coincidence maybe, with Rooney and Jackie moving there."

"Some bloody coincidence. There are links between Zaharia and him, and through him to Rooney. Where is he?"

"We took him in yesterday morning; didn't get anything near enough to charge him. Out this morning, 24 hours. He's back home."

"I just hope he hasn't done a runner, Boyd."

"We're watching him, sir."

The chief leans forward, shutting off the heat. "I want you to get back on him, Boyd. Say we have fresh information tying him to the scene. I want him put through the ringer. I'll check out Zaharia, confirm he was sent there to do a job on our boy." He moves back to rest his back against the seat.

"What if we can't substantiate a charge?" The inspector feels the heat again, even more so as the chief gets to his feet to gain a presence over him.

"Boyd, I don't want to tell you how to do your job. I don't care how you get the information from him. You do the Reid; you beat the truth out of him; you waterboard the bastard; you deploy the good old good cop, bad cop routine; just don't ask me to tell you what to do, just do it." He heads off to the toilet.

"Right, sir," the inspector says, knowing the chief can't hear it from in there.

The chief returns to his seat, point made. "And if that doesn't get a confession, tell him he's an illegal immigrant and I'll personally stick him in a plane and drop him slap bang in a hostile area of the world where he's sure to be fucked."

"Right, sir."

"OK, fine. I want *him*." The chief turns once more towards the fire, talking into the flames. The inspector knows not to argue the point. "What about the CSIs, what are *they* saying?"

"They've released the scene, sir, nothing conclusive."

"Oh, nothing conclusive."

"No, the PM established Calum wasn't killed at the scene. He was strangled and taken there."

"Where was he killed?"

"We don't know sir."

"The Albanian's hut; you taken it apart?"

Like a dog with a bone, the inspector thinks. "Yes, sir."

"He was in the area."

"Everything checked sir, clothes, shoes; he hadn't much."

"Could have cleaned up, changed; they know not to leave anything behind."

"Yes sir, but we have nothing on him."

"Shut up, Boyd; there was the car. Could have been killed anywhere in the vicinity. Couldn't have been very far given the timescales." The chief flicks through the folder. "What are the timescales?"

"The PM estimates the T.O.D to be between four thirty and six, possibly closer to six. The father found him at six. The GP examined him forty-five minutes later, no rigor mortis, though cooling had begun."

"He was in the sea."

"Indeed, but the GP—"

"Algor mortis, I know the stages."

"He left the school at four."

"Picked up by the Albanian then, taken somewhere, the boathouse perhaps, murdered, dumped, all in a timescale of two hours or so." The chief's eyes narrow. "What was he like?"

"Sir?"

"I want to know."

"He was normal."

The chief takes a few seconds to think about this. "The scene?"

"Searched and combed the area: typical rubbish, cigarette butts, also footprints, indentations, anything the waves hadn't cleaned at the water's edge or on the beach where we could take moulds."

"Tracks?"

"Nothing."

"Rubbed out, a brush, a branch?"

"Yes, sir, possibly."

"Not the kind of thing an impulse killer would do, however, he'd be too busy getting the hell out of there."

"The boy's backpack was missing."

"Jackie told me; it wasn't at the Albanian place?"

"No, sir."

"Dogs?"

Oh come on, the inspector thinks. "Sir?"

"The dog unit, Boyd."

"Yes, they covered the beach."

"Tyre marks?"

"Nothing."

"Kept the car on the tarmac; anything else?"

Yes, leave off on the interrogation. "Nothing, so far, sir."

The chief looks into the fire. "Keep digging, son. Take the Albanian apart, you'll find something."

The inspector is almost asleep with the heat. "Sir?" he says, trying to stay awake.

"Yes," comes from the fire, the chief almost inside it.

"I need your advice, your help."

The chief turns to him. "My help, of course. I'll do anything to convict this man."

"No, I mean. Ms Kaminski and Mr Rooney, they have a background in Glasgow."

The chief is back on his feet. "I wondered when you would get round to implicating my daughter." He stands over the inspector.

The inspector looks up like a scared school boy at a headmaster. "No sir, I didn't mean to, sir, not directly. But they led irregular lives."

"What about McDonald then?" The chief realises how much sound carries in there. "And keep your voice down, Boyd."

"Yes, sir, he's also in pathology, an unexplained death as you know."

The chief is now inches from the inspector's face. "I hope he's not in the same room as my grandson," he snarls.

The inspector pushes himself back in the chair as far as he can go without keeling over. "No, sir, Calum is in the mortuary waiting to go home on Monday."

"His form on children, Boyd?"

"Oh, sorry; nothing to link him with the boy, no forensics."

"Forensics, forensics, when did we ever need … forensics?" The chief's voice deepens as he leans into Boyd's face. "Listen, son, the investigation needs to be more assertive, assertive. Do you hear me?"

"Yes, sir, I do."

"Good." The chief sits back down and opens his waistcoat. The inspector looks shaken, but palpably relieved. "Do you need more resources?"

"We have a two dozen DIs, and three times in uniform, sir."

Back to the fire, the chief's words bounce off the fireplace out towards the inspector. "What do you want from me?"

"Rooney and Jackie, sir?"

"I said you were barking up the wrong tree, Boyd."

"Yes, sir, but I feel I need to stress this, they had their enemies."

The chief turns to him. "It comes with the turf, Inspector."

"Your daughter, her operational links with the crime families?"

"Her job, Boyd."

"Mr Rooney, his status in the syndicate?"

"His calling, the Father."

"Yes sir, the Father."

"Sir, I need to ask you this."

"Aye, I suppose you have to."

"Do you think their backgrounds had something to do with Calum's murder? Some killer, psychopath, hood, crazy travelled to Lochdarrach to kill their son. For revenge, a payoff, a contract, whatever. We have to—"

"His, son; not *their* background; why do you think the Albanian is so important?"

"We have to follow all possible leads, sir, obvious lines of inquiry, links to Mr Rooney *and* Ms Kaminski."

The chief takes a big puff out as he does when he tries to bring his blood pressure down. "Look son, I know you are doing your job, but it wouldn't do if you messed up the investigation into the chief's grandson's murder. It wouldn't be very good for the CV, Boyd, eh, now do you get my drift?"

"No sir, I am…"

"You will do what you have to do?"

"Yes, sir, I'll do my best."

"Good, son. You have the Albanian. I'll check out Lekë Zaharia. We put the two together and the case is in the can, eh?"

"Mr Rooney?"

"Aye, go on, him; now you are getting warm."

"He was responsible for the hits of some big team players."

"He sure was, Inspector, none more so than Zaharia. When you play with fire…"

"Have you any information to suggest a link there with the boy's murder, sir. I mean your knowledge of the Glasgow crime families?" Dreamlike, the chief returns to the fire. "Sir?"

The chief snaps back to consciousness. "I said there's Zaharia."

"There may be others." The chief looks up with one of those

looks, as if to say 'don't push it … son.' "It is said Rooney had gang leaders, gang members, killed."

"Killed is a strong word, Boyd."

"Sorry; there was nothing to connect him, he was a figurehead, but it implicated him; can we put it that way?"

"A bit better; name me some of these … implications?"

"The McGings and the Taylors to start; and others, while sorting out the mobs."

"There were no investigations and no charges were made." It is the inspector's turn to stay quiet. "Listen son, the mob killing the mob never concerned me, the mob killing innocent folk always did."

"Right, sir."

"Anyway, had I thought—"

"The McGings and the Taylors?"

"Dead end, son, the indigenous teams don't work like that. If they are going to kill you, they'll kill you; up front to your face, knife in your chest, bullet in your head or up your arse. You concentrate on the Albanian; he's the boy's killer. I'll do Zaharia and together we'll get something substantial."

"Yes sir, but…"

"Inspector?"

"Yes, sir."

The chief leans into him one last time. "Your promotion in the craft will be commensurate with your promotion in the force and your transfer to HQ in Abertay, out of the bloody backwater. Keep your nose clean and do what you are told?"

The inspector's face turns an almost translucent white. "Sir, but it doesn't—"

"For me it does, now leave me to my deliberations." The chief returns to the fire, but not before he gives the inspector a last look going all the way to the back of his head.

There is no more to be said or heard. The inspector knows what he needs to do, whether he agrees with it or not. The chief's head is down as he nods. He gets up and leaves.

Margaret Johnston, Jean Dempsie's old admin officer, makes her way into the office car park on Pacific Quay. She hurries to the car to get out of the rain.

"Hello Margaret." The father steps out from behind her car. "I was sure MI5 staff worked Saturdays, especially you. I thought you might need to get out of there for lunch?" He holds an umbrella over her.

She seems startled and looks around for support. In the car park of CJI she knows security would be there in seconds should she call out.

"Rooney, I thought you left Glasgow, gone to the highlands, after Jea—"

"Aye, I did, Margaret, but not because of Jean."

She pulls out her own umbrella and flicks it open, making some space between them. "No one was convicted of her murder."

"It wasn't me."

"Cold case; the file still open."

"I'll be in there no doubt."

"Can't say, Rooney, if that's what you are looking for." The father shakes his head. "So, what then, why are you here, what do you want of me? I'll call security."

"You could, but you'll hear me out first."

"Why should I?"

"Because you knew Jean better than anyone."

She opens her car and makes to get in. "Excuse me, I can't—"

"I know MI5 protocol, the vow of secrecy."

"Yes, of course, now if you'll…" He is holding the door. She looks up at the security camera. "Rooney."

"Margaret, Jean was a bastard, you know that."

"I…"

"I don't want you to say anything. Just listen, please."

She closes the door of her car. "I'll give you one minute then I get into my car. If you try to stop me, security will come and arrest you."

"OK, one minute."

"One minute." She turns her arm to see her watch.

"Jean was a bastard; she had ambitions and would have killed anyone to get there."

"Forty-five seconds."

"She would have used you to get there. How many times did you cover for her, lie for her, defend her, when all she did was treat you like shite?"

"Thirty seconds."

"What have you been left with, a lot of crap to sort out and a meagre pension to look forward to?"

"Fifteen seconds."

"I need to know something."

"Five!"

"I need some information."

"Time's up. I'm calling security." She takes her mobile from her bag.

"No, you won't."

"Why not?"

"Because you knew about Jean's activities, you knew she tried to kill Jackie, and tried to blackmail her, a senior police officer. Then there were her affairs, me, Alasdair Charlton, the Justice Minister, and many others to further her career. You took the calls, made the appointments, listened to her ravings, and you did nothing about it. While working at the MI5, you were complicit. Do I need to say more?"

"You are quite a bastard, Rooney."

"I know, and all I need to do is to say to the right people and you'll be out of a job. You'll not even have the wee pension to look forward to."

"What kind of information do you want?"

"I need to know if MI5 followed me north, killed my child, are continuing to pursue me; or Jackie, my wife; or both of us."

"So, not much then."

"That's all. You'll be paid well, enough to give this shit up and buy that wee flat overlooking the beach in Marbella to retire in the sun."

She looks at the CCTV camera. "I know I shouldn't do this, but I'll meet you later; the Lis Mor at seven?"

"Suits me."

She gets in her car and drives off. He looks up at the security camera, clearly trained on him. Time to go before the MPs arrive.

The father is pleased Margaret Johnston has offered to meet him in the Lis Mor, a bar close to Partick Cross at the bottom of Byres Road. Her saying she would meet him there meant she had a good awareness of her boss, Jean, and her meetings with him there in the past. It meant her boss confided in her; though, as any good MI5 admin officer, she would have known her boss's whereabouts anyway; where, why, and who. *More the latter*, the father thinks, reassuring himself. He is pleased, however, to have a reason to go to the Byres Road, his old stomping ground; to have a coffee and a wander down the road to the pub excites him. In the past he would have had a 'booze cruise' down one side of Byres Road and up the other side, intending to finish, if he was still on his feet by the time, in Tennent's Bar, something of around ten pubs on the road and another five in the lanes just off. This time, coffee in the Tinderbox would do followed by some shopping.

The *balach's* funeral is coming up and he has arranged to collect the orders of service from the Copy and Print Shop on the Great Western Road. On the way, he passes The Belle, where earlier the chief and the inspector had met. Little did he know the chief was heading along the road towards him.

The chief sees the father before he sees him. The father's head is tucked under his bunnet, his eyes fixed on the pavement, a pet hate for him. "Glasgow pavements are just terrible, just look at them," he murmurs, as he wanders along, until the chief's voice startles him out of his dwam.

"Rooney, I heard you were heading down. Jackie told me. I didn't expect to bump into you here."

"Why not Hubert, where else would I find my son's killer?"

"In Achfara, Rooney. Why don't you leave us to find the man?"

The chief realises the father will keep on walking, to get as far away from him as possible, but he has another destination in his mind. "Fancy a coffee?"

"I'm kinda busy."

"Come on Rooney, we don't get much of a chance to catch up – a coffee?"

"When did you ever want to see me, Hubert? Better watch, you might be seen with a catholic."

"Come on, Rooney, where did you get these hang-ups from; not me. A coffee?"

The father hesitates, but realises this is on his itinerary anyway so he agrees. "OK, the Tinderbox, half an hour. I'll see you there."

The chief nods and the father heads along the Great Western Road to pick up the orders of service. He will also go to Man's World on Byres Road, which is close to the Tinderbox before he meets Hubert. He intended buying a new black tie and a white shirt, but the mother said she wanted bright colours to be worn to reflect the boy's youth and personality. So, after delving into some old stock left over in the shop from the end of summer sale, the father leaves with a Hawaiian shirt.

In a few minutes the father is in the Tinderbox where the chief has taken a seat looking out onto the road, a large cappuccino in front of him. The father joins him and, dropping his bags on his seat, heads off to collect a double espresso and a muffin.

"Been shopping, Rooney?" The father nods. The chief notices the shirt. "Going your holidays?"

The father nods again. "A wee holiday in the highlands to bury my son, Hubert."

"Thank the gods, for one minute I thought you were going high again."

"Here we go again, why you wanted to see me, to check me for mania? Well, you'll be disappointed."

"Don't get paranoid, son. I know Jackie wants colourful clothes."

"What are you wearing?"

"My white suit I guess, last worn in Florida."

"Aye, very good."

"What else are you here for, Rooney? As I said, you're not going to find him here."

"It's none of your business, Hubert."

"Well, it *is* my business, Rooney."

"Oh, head of police business."

"My grandson, Rooney."

"Adopted, Hubert, adopted."

"I was very fond of him, he was my—"

"Adopted grandson."

"You need to back off, son, we'll get him."

"Oh, you will. PC Plod in Stoer and Detective Inspector Jim Taggart from Invernevis."

"If I wasn't confident they could do it, I would bring in the best."

"The best; your … grandson didn't merit the best?"

"They'll get him, son, they're closing in."

"Oh, the Albanian, McDonald, or a local paed?"

"They'll get him."

"I'll fucking get him, Hubert. I'll get him." Rooney's tone turns heads.

"Look son, I know you're hurting, but…"

The 'but' was enough. "But nothing, I've an appointment to keep and a killer to find, so please mind your own business Hubert." The father gets up and heads for the door.

Having also lost his rag, the chief too gets to his feet. "Rooney, this is Glasgow, my patch, just don't cross the fucking line."

"Fuck off, chief of police."

The father is out of the café by the time the chief reaches for his mobile phone.

The father heads down Byres Road and turns off onto Havelock Street, heading towards Partickhill Street and then his destination, the Lis Mor Bar on Dumbarton Road. Then, just as he passes the Old St Peter's school, the inevitable happens. I knew it would, but not enough to concern me; I would not be taking his soul this day.

"Sean Rooney?" The voice comes from behind. He turns to face a short man, with, what I believe is called a beanie hat on his head, and a black overcoat, his hands inside its pockets. He growls from a smoker's throat. "We heard you were in town."

The father turns to him. "Do I know you, pal? I don't recognise you?"

"No, you don't know me, but I know you. We were told you were back in Glasgow."

He thinks for a few seconds as he stands facing the man. "Oh, a wee bird told you?"

Then, as quick as a flash, there is a knife, small but big enough to reach a vital organ. As quick as it is produced, from behind the adversary, an arm wraps around the man's neck dragging him to the ground where another set of arms holds him fast as the knife is wrenched from his grip.

"Bill." The father recognises Bingham as his saviour.

"Just as well we put a tail on you, Rooney. You said you'd be off the half past three train. I knew the second you arrived in Glasgow you could be a dead man. We were watching this bastard following you down Byres Road. He was going to strike when you were out of sight somewhere."

"Who is he?"

"We don't recognise him. But leave him with us; we'll find out who he's working for." The father knows the man's methods of extracting information from hard men, and no one was hard enough to withstand his methods.

The father makes to move away. "Rooney?"

"Bill."

Bingham takes out a canvas bag. "Take this." He slides it into the father's coat pocket. It weighs down the father's pocket. He reaches into it.

"A piece, I don't need… Bill, for fuck's sake."

"Just keep it, you're in hostile territory, Rooney. There are people here who *will* hurt you. You keep it close, you hear me?"

"OK, but not that'll need it."

"It'll be there just the same. I'll see you later, in Tennent's, as arranged. Stay safe, and call me if…"

"Aye right, I will, thanks."

The father moves off and within minutes he is in the Lis Mor Bar in Partick. Despite his disrupted journey, he arrives at seven as arranged; but it is a full ten minutes before Margaret Johnston arrives. "Rooney, you made it." She looks surprised as she approaches the father standing by the bar.

"Aye, Margaret, did you think I wouldn't get here?"

She looks at him as if he had horns. "Are you alright?"

"Aye, why you asking?"

"Nothing."

"Would you like a drink?"

"You not?"

"Controlled drinking."

"So I heard. A medium Pinot Grigio."

"Of course, MI5 hear everything, Margaret."

"I am admin, Rooney, not an officer."

"But you still know, you are still MI5."

"I don't know everything, Rooney."

"A medium Pinot Grigio and a half of Guinness." He gives the order to the barman then turns to her. "You knew Jean and I met here."

"As you said earlier, it was part of my job to know."

They take their drinks to a corner of the bar. "I think you knew a lot about her comings and goings."

"Rooney, you have to believe me, I can't."

"No, the Official Secrets Act, Margaret."

"I..."

"You hated her? She was the quintessential bad bastard and I am not surprised." This prompts a steady but determined stare from her. "She was bad to you."

"You know what she was like."

"Do you know who killed her?"

"Sorry?"

"I asked, do you know who killed her?"

"Well, the safe money was on Alan Taylor, you know he killed her in the taxi."

"Alan Taylor was acting for someone else, we all knew that."

"The inquest was inconclusive on both his motive and any collaboration."

"I know that, Margaret. Doesn't mean MI5 would ever close its case. They don't stop when it's one of their own." She looks around as if to check anyone was eavesdropping. "Interesting; he's now overseas at an undisclosed location."

"Yes, he's at large; got out before the authorities got to him."

"You knew Jean was becoming a bit of a ... liability, an embarrassment, a threat to the agency."

"I can't."

"No, OSA."

Margaret takes a hundred and eighty degree span of the pub. "Rooney, your son, it was regrettable."

"Regrettable?"

"Sorry, regretful."

"Regretful, just like an admin officer of a covert government department would say. MI5 talk."

"Good selection of whiskies in here."

The father gets the message. "Yes, an excellent selection of malts." He moves closer to her. "Tell me?"

She hesitates. "They *are* monitoring you, that's all I can say."

He checks to see if anyone is close enough to pick that up. "Would have been very strange if they hadn't been, given my links."

"They thought you might have been behind Jean's murder."

"Yes, I thought they might. I expected a knock on my door."

"As I said, the inquest was inconclusive."

"Apart from Taylor."

"Yes, apart from Taylor."

"They will find whoever did it."

"I wouldn't expect anything otherwise." The father pauses to take a deliberate mouthful of beer.

"Are you on your medication, Rooney?"

"Margaret, did anyone know I would be heading here to see you?"

"If you are asking if you were seen in the car park with me, you know they would."

The father looks for an indication she knew something about his attack, but he does not see anything; but, before he has a chance to push her on this, his mobile goes off and 'BB' comes up on the screen.

"Please excuse me, Margaret, I need to take this."

"No problem, I need to go anyway."

"No, can you hold on, I—"

"I said I need to go."

"OK, will you let me know if you…?"

"What, Rooney?"

"My file, Margaret, it'll be in my file."

He follows her out and opens the door for her, if anything to see if she is alone. He is disappointed to see her walking along Dumbarton road on her own towards Partick Cross. He returns to the doorway of the pub and opens the mobile.

"I'm here, Rooney, where are you?"

"I'll be there in ten, Bill." He heads off towards Byres Road.

Bill Bingham puts his mobile in his pocket and returns to the bar in Tennent's. As arranged, he is there to meet the father. Since the father moved to Achfara, Bingham had taken over as the head of the crime family syndicate in Glasgow.

"Never thought I would see you back in here, Rooney," Bingham says, as the father arrives at the bar.

The father feels uncomfortable in this place, not just because he is carrying a deadly weapon in his coat pocket. "Never thought I'd be back in the place which destroyed my health, Bill." The father offers his hand. "Thanks for earlier, I owe you, again."

The man accepts it warmly. "That's OK, Rooney; I know you would have done the same for me."

The father takes his coat off and folding it places it carefully on the bar. "Goes without saying, Bill, or should I call you Father?"

"No, your title when you were boss, I find it a bit too …up your arse."

"I know, Johnston coined the title and I continued with it; it kind of fitted at the time."

"I know, your illness."

The father takes a long look around the bar. Feeling a bit conspicuous in the open space, he recommends they move to a seat in a corner. "So what do we call you, now you're in charge?"

They jockey for the corner seat, which Bingham wins. "Well, most of the guys call me Gaffer, and that's OK with me." He is happy he can see the whole of the bar. This comes naturally to both of them and they appear more settled now. Since the early days of the gang wars, positioning themselves in a public space, especially a public house, was an essential part of survival in a place where attacks in public houses were commonplace.

"Gaffer, that's good. I like that, the gaffer."

"You drinking, Rooney?"

"Half of Guinness thanks."

Bingham gets up to go to the bar. "Slumming it?"

The father nods. "Controlled drinking, an alternative."

"Aye, I know. I could do with some of that." The gaffer orders two half pints of Guinness and returns to the table with them. "The journey down?"

"Five hours on the train, no hot drinks for most of the way, nothing to do but think. No chance with the Celtic supporters heading down for the game today."

"Brilliant, welcome back to Glasgow." He hands the father his drink and lifts his own.

"Thanks, slàinte."

"Cheers." Bingham smacks his lips to the taste of the stout. "Sean, I am sorry about the wee man, my sincere condolences."

"I know, thanks again, Bill."

"Here's to the boy. I know he brought you much happiness." The gaffer raises his glass which the father clinks with his own. "I can guess why you are here, Rooney."

"Yes, unfinished business you'll understand. I need your help."

"You want someone killed, the man who killed your son; easy, just point him out and he's a dead man."

My reason for being here is justified.

"Easier said than done, Bill. If I knew who it was … really why I'm here … I need to…"

"You think there was a vendetta, someone from your shady past with a reason to kill your son?"

"Well, it *is* possible."

"There are a few, Rooney, you know that. Where do you want to start?"

"The McGings."

The McGings had more reason than any gang to harm the boy's father or to kill the boy to heighten his pain. The father, as previous head of the Family, in a deadly afternoon in this dark place, had the McGing's wayward leader Mick McGing killed alongside others of the clan. Not something I would have had experience of, but there is more about the dark side of this man I must understand.

"You know the Family rule is not to hit a made man, Rooney. You *are* a made man in Glasgow, by the hand of the father of that team, Davy McGing. To kill you would have brought a vendetta on the McGings, and they are a weakened team, Rooney; without Mick they are leaderless."

Just then there is a loud bang and flashing of lights outside on the street. The father reaches into the pocket for the gun. The gaffer stops him. "Stop, Rooney, It's the fireworks, Guy Fawkes night, just cool it."

"Jesus, thought I was back in the old days."

"No one will touch you in here, Rooney; you are in a safe place." The father nods, knowing that the gaffer would have a few men discreetly and tactfully placed around the bar.

"What about killing a made man's son, does the vendetta rule still apply?"

"Christ, I don't know Rooney, it's not Chicago."

Ha, you could have fooled me!

"You check them out, Bill. For me, there are some other possibilities I need to explore."

The men stop talking for a while, enjoying the feeling of being together in a proper pub atmosphere. They are aware, however, of the heightened tension two crime lords, one current and one past, as well as a number of henchmen, brings to the pub. Most of the locals in there know of these men and avoid their eyes, keeping well away, which gives the men even more space to scan the bar.

The gaffer breaks the silence. "Your man, the attacker, earlier. We know who he was working for."

"Christ that was quick."

"Didn't take much."

"Gun to the head, threatening his children, lots of money?"

"Didn't need to, found something interesting on his phone."

"What?"

"His last phone calls were from the same number. I phoned it."

"Oh aye, who?"

"Listen." The gaffer plays the message and the father puts the phone to his ear to hear 'You've reached call handling for Her Majesty's Security Service.'

"A bit of a coincidence don't you think?"

"Where is he now?"

"We let him go."

"What?"

"Don't worry, we know him, he's ex-SAS, freelance, said he was to give you a fright, to scare you off. Operation failed, aborted, cover blown, doesn't get paid, he'll move on to other work."

"What makes you think he won't have another go?"

"Because we told him we would visit him and his family if he did. He won't."

"Thanks."

The gaffer notices the empty glasses. "You having another?"

"No, I shouldn't. But I'll get you one."

"No, leave it, Rooney. I'm heading home for my tea. I'll have a glass of wine then."

"Right." The father realises the incongruity of two one-time heavy boozers sitting with empty glasses.

"MI5, Rooney. You still caught up in the shit from Jean Dempsie?"

"Who knows?"

"Just watch your back."

"I do."

"I've been ferreting around your enemies down here."

"Thought it would take some time."

"A few calls and a wee think over a cup of tea, simple."

"Jeez, without a drink, you are good, go on."

"Well, apart from the teams who are still sore about you. Well no' you personally, you as Father, when the Family either hit them or caused them grief. But you are right that would take time, there's a right few of them. And no doubt there'll be some rogue bampots with a grudge against you. If you ran into them in a dark alleyway or a pub you should know better not to inhabit, they would take a pop at you."

"Come on, Bill."

"Listen, I think most of them wouldn't have the brains or the balls to follow you up to the highlands and kill your boy. I think we are talking about a serious player with a heavy reason to hurt you, so much so as to plan and execute a hit on your son."

"If they had, why wouldn't they have revealed themselves, gloated in it, enjoyed the kudos of it?"

"Correct, not to bask in the glory of it must mean there is something deep, something more personal. Like a thief who would steal a masterpiece of art and glorify in having it on their wall without anyone knowing about it but themselves. I've a few of them myself." He laughs.

The father has a smile on his face; he too had a few of them.

The gaffer continues. "So, who would enjoy knowing they had killed your son without the enjoyment of you knowing who they were; someone who would rejoice personally in your grief, Rooney?"

"Very profound, Gaffer."

"I know, I surprise myself sometimes."

"And who would that be?"

"Only you would know that, pal."

"Only I would know."

The father looks at him. *The gaffer's face bellies a wise intellect*, he thinks. He had seen this before in this man, who had clearly grown with the job. He pulls out a package from his bag. "This time I give you a package, Bill."

"I've got plenty, Rooney, thanks."

"It's not a gun, Bill."

"What is it?"

"It's Calum's bag and a pair of gloves, mine. I found the gloves in the bag at the scene of his murder. They are my gloves. I didn't put them there. The killer obviously did."

"To implicate you … personally?"

The father stops to think about this. "Exactly, my reason for not handing them in, Bill."

"Sure, get it."

"I wonder if the killer had them on when he did it. I want to see if he left his DNA, apart from mine in them, and if there is anything on the bag?"

The gaffer leans across and takes the package. "Mind, Rooney, only you will know. Now you need to go home."

"Aye, will do; but first I need to explore some possibilities."

"Well, keep your head down, because there are a few hot heids down here who'd like to shoot you just for the fuck of it; and you know what I'm saying."

"I'll be careful."

"Well, we're here if you need haunders."

"Thanks, Gaffer."

The gaffer gets up to leave. "Right, I'm away for my tea."

"Bill?"

"Aye, what?"

"Get rid of my tail. He makes me nervous."

"You sure?"

"Aye, and Bill?"

"Whit?"

"I might need some money."

"How much?"

"Enough to persuade."

"Right."

"You got it; now my turn. Rooney?"

"What?"

"The MI5, you know how they work."

"What you getting at Bill?"

"You know what I'm talking about, Rooney, the thing with Jean, her dying in mysterious circumstances, your lucky escape tonight at St Peters."

"Aye, go on."

"*You* were a suspect, Rooney."

"And so were you, Bill, we all were; all of us who had dealings with her; your gunrunning to Northern Ireland, for example."

"But, it's different with me."

"Sorry?"

"They're still getting something from me, and can still use me, but you…" The father knows MI5 would still be 'associating' with the gangs, obtaining information on their links with Northern Ireland and organised crime groups from the continent. "But I don't think they killed your son, it's not their style, but they may kill you. Fuck's sake, Rooney, you know how they work, their covert operations."

"They've nothing on me."

"Aye, they have. They have something on all of us. It's the way they operate. Just think about it." The father had already thought it about it. "Just watch your back."

"Aye, you too, Bill, sorry Gaffer?"

They embrace and the gaffer leaves him there; his entourage follow him out. The father gets up to look out of the window and catches a sight of an expensive car, a black BMW, not unlike the chauffeur driven type senior politicians use to get around, pulling away from the pub. In the back seat, the gaffer and the tail that had followed him earlier. This is the sign of a rich man, even more so given it is bullet and bomb proofed, befitting a crime boss.

The father moves back to the table and drops into thought, provoked by the conversation with the gaffer, until the friend's voice wakens him from his dwam.

"Hiding in the corner, Rooney." The friend pulls up a chair at the table and puts his pint of real ale on it.

"Shite, Bensallah, where did you crawl from?"

"You indicated you were coming here, Rooney; business you said, on Friday night in the Small Isles."

"Correct; my business, not yours."

"I know your kind of business, Roon; commonly leads to someone getting hurt, not uncommonly you."

"My guardian angel, my own personal social worker, so-called do-gooder, so-called no-gooder more like."

"You know how many times we sat in these seats chewing the rug, you supporting me, me supporting you. Why shouldn't I come here to help you?"

"Why are you here, you've to meet Jackie tomorrow?"

"I drove down today; I'll drive back tomorrow. Come up with me Rooney, before you do something stupid?"

"Oh, give me a break, pal."

"Don't you think the ex-head of the biggest crime syndicate in the country turning up in here may attract a bit of unwelcome attention, create a bit of a commotion, an exodus even?" The father looks around to confirm an unhealthy number of eyes on him, the previous crime boss now on his own without a bodyguard, and an unusual number of empty seats after the gaffer had left. "Apart from that, I was worried about your abstinence. I thought, given your … pain recently, you might fall off the wagon, you might even relapse, needing a bit of moral support." The father looks at him square in the face then gestures to the empty glass cradled in both his hands. "Guess you know the score, I'm pleased."

"Aye, I know, and I don't give a fuck if you are pleased."

"Well, pal, now we've got that out of the way, how does it feel to be back in the big smoke?"

"Don't call me pal, pal, we both lost that title when you fucked my wife."

"It's been over two years."

"Aye, two years sorting out a relationship, bringing up a wee boy, you down here getting on with your life in the big smoke."

The friend takes a large slurp of his ale. "Sure, getting on with my life, in this smelly, shitey, noisy place." Just then, right on cue, the local fireworks display goes off again, making crack, crack, cracking noises from outside the bar. "Noisy will do."

"Aye, a lot quieter at home."

"That's where you should be, Rooney, so go home."

"I'm not planning to be here long, but just long enough."

"Long enough for what, don't you know what this is doing to Jackie?"

"Oh, that's what this is all about, Jackie; now we know."

"No, it's about you, and her, and her—"

"And you?"

"She's burning the candle at both ends, harassing the hell out of Boyd to get something from the investigation, then doing her own thing, ferreting about, you know what she is like."

"Aye, I know."

"And she is wondering about you."

"She doesn't need to worry."

"I said wondering; like what you are up to down here, but she'll be worrying too, no doubt."

"No doubt." The father gets up to look once again out of the windows onto Byres Road, maybe to check the weather, maybe to see the fireworks, maybe to see if there is anyone waiting out there for him. "How you doin', Rooney?"

The father sits back down to face the friend across the table. "Who would rejoice personally at my grief, Ben?"

"Sorry?"

"Something Bill Bingham said."

"You've been talking to the crime lord, the Father elect?"

"Aye; are you spying on me now?"

"I saw you two together, I wasn't going to interrupt."

"Wise."

"Not wise, Rooney, not very wise."

"Where else would I get information?"

"What will you get down here? The wee man was murdered up there. The murderer is up there. That's where they'll find him."

"I'll ask you again, who would want to hurt me that much, pal?"

"I doubt the guy that did it would have had you in mind. You well know from your experience he'll be a horrible, stupid fuckup, a mixed-up pathetic no-life with a need to destroy a wee life, who just happened to come across a wee boy, your wee boy."

"Aye, *my* wee boy."

"Your wee boy."

"I destroyed him."

"Rooney, get a grip."

"No, I took him there. I took my baggage with me. Can you be sure his death had nothing to do with me, with my background?"

"I can't be sure on that, who can? But it's more likely to have been wrong place, wrong time, Rooney. As in many child murders, as you well know, Calum just happened to be in a place where a nutcase just happened to come across him who exercised all his pathological failings on a vulnerable wee boy. You've worked with these guys, you know that, so forget any personal stuff to do with you."

The father drops his head into his hands. "How can I forget the possibility it has everything to do with me? My life, my damaged, crazy, shambles of a life, caused the death of my son."

"At least leave it until they find the bastard, then you'll know one way or the other."

"I can't wait that long; I need to know now."

"And that's why you're here?"

"Aye, and now you've got it. Now, who would rejoice personally at my grief? Who would want to hurt me that much?"

"Deep, Roon, deep."

"Tell me, you're the social worker?"

"You know most of the men who would in any way hurt you, would hurt you without even giving much thought to it. You know what I'm saying. They would just do it. Mindless act, maximum enjoyment."

"The McGings, the Taylors, other players?"

"*You* going to check them out?"

"Me, a weak pathetic shadow of my former self?"

"The man who took on the mob."

"Had people killed."

"Mental illness does things; psychosis, paranoia, delusions, acting on … voices."

"I'm better now. Retribution is always a possibility, however."

"I wasn't going to say that."

"But it's what you were thinking."

"I'm just happy you've changed."

"Indeed, passive man now, can't do it."

The friend allows a pause. "Maybe you need to let it go, let it out on someone, just exorcise the rage before it destroys you inside."

This intrigues me, is this friend taking a different 'tact'?

"I'm scared of letting it go, scared of where it will take me."

"Back to Hairmyres Hospital, that's where it'll take you, or whatever psychiatric hospital they have up in chookterland."

"Oh, here we go, named person. Thought the Order was discharged?"

"It was, two years ago, doesn't stop you cycling up or down to psychiatric crisis."

"My bipolar is stable."

"Losing a son could prompt a relapse."

"Release my rage, prevent a crisis?"

"Cathartic."

'Cathartic' interests me, releasing, letting go, helps people?

"Drink was cathartic."

"But you don't drink anymore?"

"Stay sober and become mentally ill, drink and don't. What would you do?"

"Maybe you should take a drink."

Now, this is dangerously 'facetious'.

"What, my named person, friend, social worker, telling an alcoholic to take a drink. To risk alcohol-related brain damage and his liver giving up, very good that, maybe I'll stick with the pain, the rage, the guilt."

"OK, maybe you should let whatever's going to happen, happen, and I'll stay with you through it if you do."

Is this friend tempting the father into destructive behaviour?

"A real friend, eh, Ben. Even though you know it could kill or section me?"

"Knowing you, maybe it'll kill you if you don't let it go, maybe it's the best way, the only way. I'll look after you."

"Who would want to hurt me so badly, Ben?" The father gets up to look out of the window once more. Then sits down and rests his hand on the coat feeling the shape of the weapon inside. It appears to offer him some sort of comfort.

"That's what we need to find out, Rooney."

"*I'll* find it out, Ben. If it's the last thing I do." He caresses the gun through the fabric of the coat.

"Nothing happening on the investigation front?"

"Nothing, just Temo."

"And Calum's bag, any news?"

"No!"

"I'll get you a pint."

The father is askance; I am intrigued.

"A pint, you're getting me a pint?"

The lack of a dissenting voice encourages the friend to order the father a 'Stella lager'. At '5.5 ABV', I believe it is intended to have the required effect on the father's brain. He takes it, looks into it and drinks it in one long go. Then he hands the empty glass back to the friend who brings another, then another, and then another; and in no time he is returning to a place where he preferred never to return, inside a place in his mind he was determined to avoid.

Drunk, the father stands and holds up his drink. "A toast to my boy, Calum, my son, Calum." No one in the bar takes him up. The friend appears pleased the father had taken a corner booth before he had reached this point: less attention, less likely to attract any sympathisers; though many of the inhabitants of the bar had moved to the door to see the fireworks display.

The friend responds though. "To Calum, Rooney, your boy."

"To Calum, my boy, my wee boy, my wee boy." The father is almost sobbing into his beer.

The father's commotion catches the barman's attention.

Then the drink triggers something inside the father that would have come out at some point, at the funeral, the committal, afterwards, whenever. But is this the time to let it out? He appears to feel it is. The sobs arrive from deep inside, from a place he did not, would not go, would never go. Within this pit of uncertainty holds a cauldron of pain, confusion, anger, guilt, blame, fear and rage, somewhere in his mind, his belly, his heart, his soul. I am aware the soul holds such things; I feel it often enough to know this. It is palpable, like a dangerous biting, clawing, unyielding dog; once unleashed it could destroy him. You can see the sobs threatening to overwhelm him. He gasps for air, his chest heaving, rising and falling in turn with each cycling sob; the deepest taking him down onto the table; the rising whooping sound of the next lifts him out of his chair, like a drowning man grasping for air, wheezing oxygen into his body.

A barman comes over. "You alright, pal."

By this time the father is inconsolable. "He's OK, barman," the friend says. "He's just…"

"Aye, I know he's had bad news, I can see it. Happens to us all. If he needs anything, just come to the bar, let us know."

"Thanks, I think he'll be fine."

"Just go easy on the booze, it helps for a wee while, then…"

"Aye, I know; thanks."

The barman shuffles off, not knowing the full story, but not needing to know much more to understand the pain of the man. The sobs subside and the father stays quiet for a bit, consuming the procession of pints the friend puts in front of him.

Then he hears it. "*You drunken, pathetic excuse for a man, look at you?*" The voice is back, the voice in his head, which was all but gone with the medication, the voice that took him into the mental health unit of the local hospital down here. "*You disgusting example of a human being, you should be ashamed of yourself*," 'it' says.

"Go away, leave me alone … bastard."

"If I didn't know you, Rooney, I would think you are talking to me," the friend says, "but I know your relationship with the voice in your head too well. It's back, isn't it?"

"Yes, I'm back, fuckers."

Now this is intriguing, a dispossessed voice in a man's head, a human condition, I will learn from this.

The father empties the glass of almost a half of a pint and pushes it towards the friend. "I need more, to get this … evil shite out of my head," he says. Again, the friend goes off to the bar, while there hearing the so-recognisable diatribe accompanying the father on a binge. He shouts from the corner, "Just hurry, I need it." Then, as if the friend expects it, "What the fuck are you looking at, you cunt," he growls to others who might have looked his way with concern.

The friend returns with beers. "Just cool it, Roon."

"Don't go there, you bastard."

"You tell 'im, Rooney."

"What do you care; still shagging my woman, my pal, eh?"

"Aye, still shagging Jackie, you fucker."

"Don't go there, Rooney, we sorted all of it out, there's nothing between us."

"Aye, sorted out, my friend."

"I'm still your friend, Rooney, now let's…"

"Watch him, Rooney, he'll stab you in the back."

"Don't worry, I'll get you and I'll get the bastard who killed my son, just see if I don't."

"Just stop it, Rooney, there's no need."

"I'll get whoever did it." The father reveals enough of the gun for the friend to see.

"Jea … sus, Rooney, give me that." The friend tries to reach into the father's pocket to retrieve the gun. "A drunk man with a shooter, a deadly combination." He makes sure no one hears this.

The father pushes his friend back. "You try it and I'll shoot the fucking clock." He puts his hand into the pocket. I almost howl, why would he shoot a clock?

"Don't be a crazy man, Roon." The friend gets up and tries to prompt the father to do the same. "I'll get you to your hotel, come on."

"Go get him, Rooney. Go get the man who killed your wean."

"I need to go to the bog first, then you can get me back."

"Will you get rid of the gun?"

"I'll hide it deep down with the crumbs from the crisps in my pocket."

"I'll go with you."

"I'm capable of going myself, social worker; I don't need you holding my hand, or my cock."

"Right, but I'm getting a taxi."

The father pretends he is going to the toilet and slips out the side door of the pub and up Highbury Road where he calls at a passing taxi.

"Where to, pal?"

"Tradeston … pal." The father keeps his head down as the taxi passes the front of the bar where he sees the friend calling down another one.

CHAPTER 7

The father knows where he is going. The Taylors always drink in the Lord Nelson Bar, a Glasgow Rangers bar south of the river. Earlier, Rangers played out a scrappy draw in Dingwall against Ross County, leaving the hosts bottom of the Premiership and Rangers in third place; not a good day for Rangers supporters most of whom, given the travel to the north of Scotland, stayed at home or in pubs watching the game. There was a sombre mood in the bar when the father falls in the door, not unusual in a bar where men get seriously drunk whenever there is a Rangers match on. He avoids going directly to the bar for a drink for fear of not being served and being asked to leave before he can fulfil his task. He goes to the toilet instead and washes his face with cold water. Lifting his face to the mirror, he sees the man he didn't want to see.

"What do you see, Rooney? A good man doing bad or a bad man doing good?"

He spits into the mirror, "Oh great, the bastard is back."

"A good man ruined, Rooney?"

"A good man ruined, a bad man reborn."

The father reaches inside his coat for the gun. He feels it inside and also feels for his mobile, which he takes it out and is about to call Jackie. He whimpers, "Don't let me do it, Jackie, please stop me?"

"Do it, Rooney. Do it, put your wean to rest. Smite him?"

The father puts the gun away and tries to sober up as much as it would take to do what he needed to do. He pulls himself as straight as he can given his condition.

"John Taylor, remember me?" The father approaches Taylor who is sitting in a group of men discussing the game.

"Fuck's sake, Rooney, the Father." John Taylor laughs and blesses himself. "Where you been, in a monastery?"

"I've been otherwise ... indisposed."

"Aye, so you have; you met my brother, Bob?" He nods to the man next to him.

"We might have crossed paths in the past."

"Aye, I think we might've, Rooney." Bob does not shake hands.

"We go a long way back, Rooney, my dad, George, and Alan, Jim, and the other players."

"Yes, we do."

There's an uncomfortable pause; both parties know pleasantries have passed.

"You and your team killed Jim, and Alan is out of the country *sine die* because of you."

"Sorry about Alan, I liked him," the father says. "He was implicated in the MI5 agent's death."

"I squared Jim with Alan," John says. "He said, 'that's the life we lead and that's the price we pay.'"

"We know, he told us," Bob says. "The main reason you're not pushing up daises, Rooney."

Another pause heralds the next phase in the deteriorating discussion.

"What you doin' in here, Rooney," John barks, "you got a death wish?"

"I hear you have a vendetta on me?"

"Where'd you hear that, Rooney, Godfather Two?"

"Someone killed my son. I want to know if it was you fuckers."

Bob and John look at each other. The father is now in dangerous territory. "Take it this way, Rooney, we killed your son," John says. "There you got it, what you want to hear?"

The father stares them out. "Did you, you bastards?"

"Whether you did or not, take it we did," John says, "because that's the way we want you to remember us – we did your fucking boy."

"Watch your language when you're talking about my son," the father growls. "Did you kill him? Tell me."

"Did you kill our Jim, and did our father die in prison because of you and your lot?" says Bob. "So, did we kill your son?"

The father breenges at them, only succeeding in falling across the table onto the floor. The group descend on him. The next thing he knows he is lying on the pavement outside the pub with heavy hands and knees pinning him down.

"Listen, Rooney," John says, "we have cause to kill you, but you're made. We are businessmen now; we want our place in the syndicate. Killing you or your son would … damage our interests. It wasn't us."

The father reaches into his pocket and clasps his hand around the gun, but the way John Taylor talks makes him believe him. No team who hit a made man or his son would survive in the business. They pick him up. "On your way, Rooney, you're done here." John wipes the puddle water from the father's coat.

"Go home, Rooney," Bob says. "You are in no state."

"I'm going to the McGings; they are next on my list."

John looks at Bob. "You think they had something to do with it?"

"Well, if wasn't you, it could have been them, I know they wanted to hurt me."

"Not much left of the McGings as a team, after you turned on them."

"Aye, we hit them bad, right through Glasgow."

"You, Rooney? You were a shite; it was your family players that did it."

The father reaches into his pocket and wraps his hand around the gun; could he kill someone, he wonders. Perhaps not back then, he thinks, but now?

"There were some very sore players after your men hit them."

"Stupid thing to say, of course they were sore. They were lying all over the pavement."

"Aye," John laughs. "Bloodbath on Ashton Lane – hitting Mick and the other McGing players left them really bealing."

"They were there to kill us."

"Rooney, your guys emptied thirty rounds into Mick and his men. They were left dead and dying on the cobbles of the lane as your guys walked off. Fucking brilliant."

"Correct, all dead."

"Wrong, Rooney." Bob looks at John. "One survived."

"Oh?"

"Aye, Josh Turnbull; the boys didn't have the heart to finish him off, just left him there to bleed to death. I didn't like that."

"No, like I said, Rooney, you're a big shite," says John.

The father tightens his grip on the handle of the gun.

"If you're carrying, Rooney, you'd be a dead man before you managed to pull it out," Bob says.

The father takes his hand out of his coat, clearly acknowledging this. "We did alright by him later, a tidy cash sum, 100K, no hard feelings, etcetera."

"Aye, to stop him talking," John says. "Key witness for the defence; could have sent you fuckers to jail for a very long time." The father's look says he agrees.

"Don't worry, Rooney, he wouldn't have talked anyway," Bob says. "He's freelance, a real player. He could have been working for us; it just so happened he was working for the McGings at the time."

"What about him?"

"He was voicing off, drinking with one of our associates one night, a bit too much to drink."

"Aye, he said he had killed your son."

"Oh." The father thinks about this for a few seconds. "I think he *will* account to God."

"Rooney, you're talking shite again."

"I will smite him, I will."

"Fuck off, Rooney. On your way," John says. "Go find your son's killer."

They straighten him up and escort him out onto the street where he staggers through Tradeston towards the river Clyde. Like a homing pigeon heading to Achfara, he knows where he is going.

The father peers through the window of the Scotia Bar on the Trongate to see Turnbull alone at the bar. He waits. Turnbull is from Castlemilk and the last bus is at 11.31 p.m. Right on cue, at 11.25 p.m, Turnbull leaves the bar, then stops for a minute to hear the remnants of the fireworks going off all over the city. He is disturbed by a voice behind him.

"Josh Turnbull?" To the father this man looks bedraggled, not the fine player he knew him to be.

"Rooney, funny to meet you here, you back to finish the job?"

"You survived last time, Josh, no hard feelings from me. You did well to come out of it."

"Why you here, Rooney?"

The father puts his hand deep in his pocket. Turnbull knows he is carrying.

"We need to explain. Let's go for a walk."

Turnbull understands he must do as he is told. The two men move down to the river just to the side of the Albert Bridge, where they stop and face each other.

"They took four bullets out of me, Rooney." Turnbull leans on the barrier to the river. "Bullets your men pumped into me. I was in surgery for eight hours trying to get the bleeding under control. They hit nothing important; want to see my shattered shoulder, Rooney, the arm that'll never work again? Want me to tell you about the flashbacks, the nightmares, the waking through the night? Want to know about my alcoholism, the drugs, the broken marriage, losing my kids to the state? All down to you, Rooney, you."

"I'm sorry to hear about that, Josh." The father almost sounds sympathetic.

"Aye, I'm sure you are."

"Wrong place, wrong time, pal. You could have been on the other side, the Family rather than the McGings. You play with fire—"

"You get burned." Turnbull takes out a packet of cigarettes, like a condemned man waiting for the noose to be put round his neck. "Do you mind?" The father shakes his head. Turnbull lights up.

"Hold any grudges?"

"Grudges?"

"Against me?"

"Well, you nearly killed me; you fucked up my life, you—"

"You wanted to harm me?"

"And I could kill you right now you bastard." Turnbull moves towards the father who takes out the gun. Turnbull recoils.

"Did you kill my son, Josh?"

"Jesus, put it away." Turnbull has his hands out in front of him as if they could stop a bullet.

"I heard you said you killed my son."

"Who said that?"

"Someone, just someone; did you?"

"Did I say it or did I do it?"

"Did you do it?"

"I wish I had, it would have made it straight, I lost my kids, you lost your boy."

"Did you?"

"Kill him, Rooney, do it, it'll make you feel better."

"Just do it, Rooney, do me a favour. My life is shite anyway."

Turnbull knows he has one chance. He makes a rush towards the father who backs off, just enough for Turnbull to grab the gun from him. "You are a shite, Rooney, not so big without your Family, eh?"

"He's right, you are a shite."

Turnbull grabs the father by the neck and wrestles him to the ground. "I killed your son, Rooney. I killed him."

They get on their knees as the father grabs Turnbull's wrist and the hand with the gun. He turns the gun away from him and squeezes Turnbull's hand, which in turn squeezes the trigger sending a bullet into Turnbull's middle. The gunshot sounds in time with a rocket exploding overhead.

"Ah, you bastard, you did me right now, Rooney, this time I'll bleed to death." Turnbull is holding his side with blood oozing through his fingers, falling in large globules to the ground.

The father gets up and stands over him. "I'll get an ambulance."

"Forget it, it's a good death for a player, beats dying in the gutter choking in my own vomit."

"Did you do it, Josh?"

"I did it, Rooney. I drowned him in the sea."

"You fucking liar, you read it in the papers."

"Aye, well I strangled him then, same as you strangled my weans."

"You, I'll…"

"Kill me, go on, it's easier than suicide, I'm such a shite. You are doing it for me."

"I…"

"You kilt me, Rooney; the Father kills the man who kilt his son. That's how it'll be said. Now get the fuck out of here before the bike cops come along here and find me on the path. Do you want to be arrested for killing an old player? The old Father is back in town. Every ex-player'll be out for you. You'd be a dead man. Now get to fuck."

The father looks down at this dying man. Never before had he killed a man with his own hands. He could stay and try to save him, which would be futile and he would go to jail or he could go and continue his search. He chooses the latter.

The father moves along Clyde Street. Some streets away he finds a doorway and cleans the gun in white spirit he buys from a 24-hour store; he then finds and opens a syver, dropping it in. I stay with the dying man. He will be mine within minutes, his blood dropping down to unsustainable level for life to continue. I wait until hypovolemic shock stops his heart and he dies there on the street. I study him for a moment then give a howl to mark my taking of his soul. I reach deep into him, not physical or concrete – a soul is not a physical thing, but *I* feel it. I suppose the eternal self of the person sums it up, all that encapsulates what the person was, stood for, believed in, as well the good and bad parts of him, his spirit, which carries on. It is not material for humans, but for me it is. It is as if I can feel the person when I take his soul. It does not resist, it knows it can no longer reside in a dead body. It can exist out of it, however. I carry a bag, a soul bag I call it, a place to put it, to strap to my back as I convey it to wherever its destination may be. This man's soul is a sad reflection of his life. There is little to commend him or for which to respect him. He was of his time as have been souls for time immemorial. I get a feeling for the kind of life they led. I feel this man had a hard life, a life of bad knocks, disaffection, and hardship. He is better dead; maybe his soul will have better fortune.

The father returns to his hotel, the Kelvin Hotel on Buckingham Terrace on the Great Western Road, where he falls asleep the instant his head sinks into the pillow. He is not asleep long until the mobile disturbs him. "Hello," he growls.

"I hear Turnbull's been killed, Rooney," the gaffer says. "Did you do it?"

"Are they saying I did?"

"Naw, an undisclosed hit, gangland killing, tit for tat, no one implicated."

"That's good."

"Did you do it?"

"Aye, I shot him. It was a struggle and the gun went off in his hand."

"Why did you do that?"

"The Taylors said he did it, killed my boy, he was spouting off, they heard of it."

"They were lying, Rooney."

"How do you know that?"

"They told me."

"They told you."

"Aye, John Taylor called me. They wanted to square it with me. They want to stay in the syndicate."

"Why did they finger Turnbull?"

"He said they wanted some … payback."

"Payback?"

"Their dad, and Jim, and the other players, Alan not able to come back."

"They wanted something, they couldn't do you. They knew I wouldn't let them in if they had hurt you. And you did them a favour. Turnbull had hit one of theirs in the past. They had planned on hitting him anyway, but you did it for them, a debt paid."

"Used me, they did."

"Sure did, pal. Brings back memories doesn't it?" The father recalls those days, where he used proxies to do his dirty work. "Where are you, Rooney, are you OK?"

"I'm in the dark in the Kelvin, Bill, where I need to be."

"I presume you mean the hotel rather than the river, Rooney?" The father presses his head further into his pillow. "You're getting the fuck out of Glasgow. I'll pick you up. You get yourself on the train north tomorrow for sure. There's one at twelve twenty."

"That's it, Rooney, do a runner, come back to your old stomping ground, do a murder and crawl off to your hideaway up north."

"Aye, I'm going, but not tomorrow, Bill. I'll go on Monday. I've some … soul searching here to do before I go home. It needs doing and I can't do it at home."

"I'm putting two men on you and you'll stay out of sight, and I'll make sure you're on that train on Monday."

The father agrees, knowing the gaffer would not have it any other way. He will try to sleep but he knows his conscience will not allow this. I wonder about this thing, the conscience. Another aspect of the human condition I need to understand. Where is it, in the soul perhaps? I will look for it – next time.

CHAPTER 8

It is the Sunday and the father is organising his day, the day he dreads but believes he has to encounter to exorcise the demons, as they call them. Although I know of these entities, I have no understanding of them being inside people's heads. It is clear, however, this man needs to dispatch whatever is inside him before he returns to the cauldron of Achfara, to his son's funeral, and to his wife. He is aware his life would be destroyed should he return unprepared, burdened with these … demons.

In this hotel, this serial imbiber lays out his requirements for the day. He fills a cross-body messenger satchel with everything he feels he may need for a day with the *deoch làidir*. The *uisge-beatha* has damaged his health, he well knows. He has had ulcers, oesophageal varices, and liver damage, which nearly killed him in past times. Returning to it could kill him for sure, but he is determined to take the risk. Use the alcohol and kill the demons, do not and they kill him in his mind. His choice, his risk, he has to do it. He collects antacids, aspirin, ibuprofen, wet wipes, water, isotonic sports drinks, bananas, B-complex vitamin supplements, and stuffs them into his bag. He lays out all the equipment for the 'expedition'. His mobile, charged overnight, notepad and pen to take notes of his experience to consider later, a large college scarf to wrap him, his bunnet and gloves.

He starts with a big breakfast, a 'full Scottish' with lots of fats and two tumblers of milk to 'put a lining on his stomach'. He takes his vitamins, antacids, and aspirin. At nine of the clock, he heads out of the door and down the stairs, turning to see two heavy made men following behind. He recognises them immediately as his guardian angels from his gang lord days. He nods towards McDuff and O'Hara, who he referred to as James and John, the sons of thunder. They nod back. He knows the gaffer is serious in his determination to protect him this day.

He will start with a seat in the park, read the newspapers, and try to get into a frame of mind for the onslaught of alcohol-induced self-reflection. He knows the Whisky Bar of the Oran Mor opens at the tenth hour and there will do for the start. He is the first through the door as it opens.

The man at the door asks, "You in for breakfast?"

"No, I've had mine."

"Oh, just the Sunday morning cure?"

The father nods. James and John follow him in. Wasting no time, he orders a double Dalmore 12, at £4.40, good value. No water, it hits the mark. By twelve, he has had three more. He heads to the toilet to check his face. He knows when the alcohol starts to take effect his face contorts or his brain changes the way it perceives his face through his eyes; whatever, there is an alteration. People are filtering into the pub for Sunday lunch, which in Glasgow means drinks and something to eat, the something to eat coming last. The face and the voice arrive simultaneously as he looks at himself in the mirror.

"Hello, fuck-head, you on the razz today?"

The voice is back and only he can hear it. His mental illness had been under control for over two years, with no psychotic symptoms, voices in particular; but, with the alcohol hitting his brain, in his case, they came back, or in his case *it* came back.

"Back to haunt me on my day off; just fucking brilliant."

"Why would I let you enjoy your day of indulgence without me, your mental friend, for company?"

I add he also has me in tow, but I worry that may have been too much for his psyche to bear.

He sloshes his face with water. "Fuck off."

"Fuck off yourself," comes from a man relieving himself at a urinal without turning to face him. Then he turns, washes his hands, and faces the father before leaving the toilet. "It's nice to be nice, that's all I can say."

"Sorry, I didn't mean you." I do not think the man believes him.

This was to be the way of it for the rest of the afternoon, the father replying to his voice, others thinking he was talking to them. Talking to oneself in Glasgow normally results in being completely ignored, a sign the man is not worth the bother, or to be punched in the face, a sign he is worth the bother. He manages to get through three pubs on the Byres Road, with six more large whiskies, without getting punched in the face; not worth the bother was getting very close to being worth the bother. James and John, however, knowing this, stay close to him just in case. It is time for the Chip.

The Ubiquitous Chip in Ashton Lane is an obvious target for him. A Sunday afternoon imbibers paradise, indeed some view it to be their weekly vocation. It holds poignant memories for the father, being the mother's and his favourite place for the taking of the *uisge-beatha*, the place of heavy sessions, but also the site of significant events.

Once, back then, he had spent a good part of the day there rejoicing on his part in the demise of the original Father. He had gone up in the world and above Tennent's Bar, which was no longer good enough for him. He had planned the rest of his life. He would have a life fulfilled. He would drink good wine, no more whisky, beer, or any other rotgut, only the best from then on. He left there to take a taxi home. "You're to be a dead man," the driver had said to him. He got the perfume. "Jean Dempsie, the woman who knows things." She said, "You are to be assassinated tonight," but he later discovered the mother had been singled out to be blown up in his stead, to her severe injury.

He met the mother in this place months after she partially recovered. Then he ordered haggis, turnip, and mashed potatoes. "Been a while," he had said to her. "When was the last time you had the DTs, Rooney?" she had replied. The kind of discussion which typified their relationship, led to their respective physical and mental breakdowns, the breakdown of their marriage, where the friend stepped in.

As it happens, back in Achfara, the friend has appeared at the mother's door. "Hi Jackie, it's good to see you. I'm sorry, I'm a wee bit—"

"Aye, fifteen minutes early, Ben." The mother invites him in and takes his coat. "Not to worry, dinner's ready, in the warming oven, hearty stuff, stew and dumplings, potatoes and cabbage." The boy is there keeping close to the mother as she takes Ben through to the kitchen. His demeanour is one of a rabbit at the sight of an eagle.

"Sounds a perfect Sunday lunch." The friend pulls a chair in close to the AGA.

"Dinner."

"Yes, of course, in the afternoon, just like when I was wee."

"Make yourself at home, will you."

"Oh, sorry, I just thought."

"Just don't make yourself too comfortable, I didn't ask you here for any personal reasons."

The friend takes a chair at the other side of the large kitchen table. "No, I didn't think you did. Rooney said it was about 'social work stuff'."

"Yes, social work stuff." The mother pulls an earthenware pot out of the oven and dishes up a portion of stew onto a plate just warmed in the oven. She passes it to the friend. "Just help yourself to veg. I'll get you a glass of wine; red?"

"Perfect." He accepts the plate while pushing over his glass.

"Thanks for coming. I didn't mean to come across as hostile."

"No, I didn't get that. I just want to help as much as I can." The mother also takes a plate and fills their glasses with large amounts of wine.

"Wow, Jackie, go easy, I'm driving."

"Oh, you'll be fine around here; a quick hop along the road to the hotel. You'll be alright."

"There talks an ex police officer. What about the local police?"

"I am not impressed and that's why I want to talk to you."

"Broomlands, Boyd, they seem on the case, Jackie."

"Aye, sure they are, couldn't find a pitchfork if they sat on it."

"You don't have confidence in them finding Calum's killer." The boy coories close to the mother.

"No."

"I see." The friend tucks into the stew. "Nice stew, Jackie."

"Pleased you like it."

"How do you think I can help?"

"I need to narrow down some possibilities around here, in particular if there are any non-convicted abusers around here."

"Why do you think I can help there?"

"Dad checked the register, nothing, no one in the area; one or two in Invernevis, but no links. I'm thinking about non-convicted, not enough evidence, those under the radar. You know who I'm talking about. The keep an eye on them files, the unofficial watching brief ones."

"Jackie, what makes you think, me, a Glasgow social worker, has links with Invernevis social work department, so much so to get access to that information."

"I know how you guys talk, open communication, meeting up at training, conferences, leaving dos, it's a small world social work, so you once told me."

"I remember that conversation. Seemed to recall it was about a gang of men suspected of grooming young girls, investigations but no charges, nothing on the register, not convicted for a sexual offence. This is different, Jackie. Do you have brown sauce?"

She reaches for the overhead cupboard but struggles to balance while gripping the worktop and her stick. "I'll get it, Jackie, sorry I didn't mean to…" She sits down. He chastises himself for forgetting her disability. "Guess these old houses don't have the same … equipment." He refers to her Glasgow flat which had been completely renovated for a disabled person.

"I manage."

"I hope so, Jackie." The friend looks at her: she looks thin, gaunt, tired, but he recognises her typical determination.

"And what's different about it?" He realises she is back to the files. "Same thing, we all know those files exist. I want to know if there are any guys around here we need to know about. Boyd doesn't seem to have the wit or clout to access this information or if he has, he won't tell us about it."

"We are stepping out of our remits, Jackie."

"What, me being a policewoman to my bones, a mother, and you, a friend, saying he wants to help, a social worker who can help? That's well within our remits I would say."

"OK, I'll see what I can do, Jackie; but…"

"What's the 'but', Ben; do you want to fuck me?"

"You know how I feel about you, Jackie, but I want you to confide in me."

"I can confide in my husband, Ben."

"Jackie, I'm worried about Rooney."

"So am I, we're struggling a bit with all of this. You know

Rooney's … vulnerabilities."

She gets up to put the plates in the sink. "I'll do that." He clears the table and tops up their wine. "I know, Jackie, I agree. I met him in Glasgow, last night. I went down, met him in Tennent's."

"How was he? I've been trying to get him by mobile, he's not answering."

"He's not good, Jackie, not good."

"No, I didn't think he would be, not a good idea, but he was determined."

"Determined he is, Jackie, determined to get rat arsed and find Calum's killer."

"Fuck."

"I tried to stop him."

"Killing or getting rat arsed?"

"Both; determined as you say."

"I can't believe he got back on the sauce; he promised, he knows what it will do to him."

"He wouldn't listen to me, Jackie, so bloody minded. I said if he couldn't think of himself to think about you, what you are going through."

"Yeah, a good friend would do that, Ben."

"Aye." The friend hesitates. "You and I both know how he can get … over involved. I don't think his mental health would cope with it. I think you'll need me."

"And what would I need from you, Ben?"

"I helped you, when we were … together."

"We weren't together, Ben, not properly, and I look after myself."

The friend appears stunned at this, as if she had hurt his sensibilities. He is looking at the floor, not knowing the boy has not taken his gaze off him throughout his time in the house. He knows, however, he has reached a time when he has either to leave or make a move.

The last time the father was in the Ubiquitous Chip was during a Hogmanay celebration in 2015 with the new Father, Bill Bingham, when a very drunk Jean Dempsie, the MI5 officer walked in. "Well done, all of you, in particular you, Rooney, the man who likes to get whacked to remind him of his father, the man who likes to be punished. You'll be back. You can't do without your punishment. I'll be waiting for you with my leather belt." She was killed that night and he was back.

Time to mix the whisky with the lager, the father thinks, as he orders up a pint of Furstenberg premium draft. At 5.3 ABV, this is more than enough to reach deep into his head to reach those demons. I will watch this display of human self-destruction. I doubt this would bring him to me soon, but I'll stay around him just in case.

He finds a corner table near the wall where he could observe all at the bar. How they were looking at him would help him determine how far he was on his road to those demons. James and John take up positions at the other side of the bar, just where they could observe him and watch for any potential assailant approaching him.

It is not long, about three more pints, before the signs appear. He has his notebook out and he is writing and talks into it as he does. It is almost like an academic exercise, teasing the beasts in his mind to appear while ready to record the event in his notebook. Then it begins, the fathers appear, his demons.

"You fucked me, Father Healy; you beat me, Thomas Rooney, my father; you destroyed me, Johnston, the Father." Each of these men had abused him in a variety of ways. The priest who sexually abused him; his own father who would beat him senseless with his leather belt; and the arch manipulator, the man who sought to use and abuse him the most, the leader of this largest crime syndicate in Glasgow, Arthur Johnston, the Father.

He looks around and wonders if others can hear the voices he hears. They are looking at him, he thinks, studying him, wondering what is going through his mind.

"Go to the toilet, they won't see you there."

In there, he hangs on the sink as he studies his face in the mirror as each of the faces appear one after the other to assault his mind, the voice in his head playing each of their parts, impersonating their voices.

"You really wanted my willie, boy, you enjoyed it, I know you did."

"The belt was too good for you, boy, always a bad little shite."

"You drunken wreck of a man-shrink, why do you drink, Sean?"

"Shut up you bastards, leave me alone."

"They are in you, up you, on you, Sean; part of you, your sick mind."

A young man pushes in beside him at the sink. "Excuse me, mind if I wash my hands?"

"Leave me alone, bastard," he says, not that the young man would understand he is talking to his voice and yes, he calls it 'bastard'.

"Jesus, att … ti … tude." The young man gets out of there before the Glasgow kiss is applied to the mirror, not knowing how close he came to it being applied to him. The mirror shatters, leaving the faces disjointed like a surrealist painting, the father's blood running down from it into the sink, his head at the brow bleeding from a three-inch cut, a shard of glass still there. The father reaches for it, pulling it from his head, which only manages to open the wound even further. Just then the barman arrives prompted by the young man to 'see to the drunk in the toilet'. The father is then dispatched into Ashton Lane, out onto the hard cobbles. The kindest thing the barman does is to throw him a toilet roll to stem the blood. James and John arrive soon after, having seen him being frogmarched down the stairs. John picks him up and stands him in a doorway as James wraps the toilet roll around his head. It would do until they get him to the Western Infirmary to have it stitched, thereafter to drop him into his bed at the hotel; only an atypical day in the life of the father.

In Achfara, the mother and the friend are looking into empty glasses, after finishing two bottles of wine.

"OK, it's agreed," he says.

I am aware of the wine effect; I have seen it before.

"Good; do you want me, Ben, yes or no?"

"You know I do, but not sure what this is about. After Glasgow, you said it would never happen again, things had changed. What's new now?"

"I want you…" She gets up and has to grab the rail of the AGA to stop herself keeling over.

He helps her back to her seat. "You want me, you want me to do something for you, you need me; what is it?"

"Can you get me the information, yes or no?"

"I just agreed I would help. What then?"

"Wait and see, Ben; you won't be disappointed."

"Jackie?"

"I need to go to the toilet." She gets up. He helps her to the toilet and waits outside until she comes out. She is looking very pale, like the contents of her stomach were now in the big white receptacle. "Right, what is it now, Ben?" He helps her back to her seat. "I don't feel very well," she says.

The friend pulls his seat in besides her. "Jackie, if Rooney wanted to hide something where would he hide it?"

"You think he took the bag, don't you?"

"Well, he was there."

"Why you interested in the bag, Ben?"

"I want it Jackie, as I said, a memento of Calum."

"If he has it, it'll be in his shed, that's where he hides everything."

"Can I look?

"No, you bloody will not, it's his domain. If it's there, I will find it."

"OK."

CHAPTER 9

The following day, the inspector activates the recorder, "We are interviewing Mr Victor Temo. Invernevis Police Station, seventh of November, 2016, 9 a.m." He turns to Temo who is sitting across from him, the constable at his side. "Hello again, Mr Temo, Victor?"

"I do not understand why I am back here?" Temo leans into the recorder. "I am a prisoner. Why have I been arrested, once more arrested?"

"You are here because we wanted to talk to you again, to explore other possibilities, and ask you some more questions. This is a murder investigation. We have powers."

"Possibilities, questions?"

"Mr Zaharia," the inspector replies. "We want to ask you about Mr Zaharia."

The prisoner looks around and looks at the camera in the top corner of the room. "I am back in custody. I have done nothing wrong."

"You have links with an Albanian crime gang in Glasgow, through this Mr Zaharia; we are informed he was your leader there. You lied to us, Victor."

"I have a new life here, I am not…"

"A killer?" The Albanian knows not to respond to this. "You do know the parents, Mr Rooney and Ms Kaminski?"

"I have told you. I have met them … on the beach."

"Did you know them in Glasgow?"

Temo get to his feet. "No sir, I did not."

"Sit down," the constable snaps.

"You are a liar, we know you did," the inspector says. "We have information. Everyone in your … fraternity knew the crime lord and the assistant chief of police."

"I had heard of them, but I didn't know them."

The inspector and the constable take up position at both sides of Temo. "Of course, you knew the boy?" the inspector demands.

"Yes, I told you, he was a friendly child. We shared the same interest of seashells."

"You killed him, Victor, we know you did."

The inspector gets back to his feet.

"I want to see a solicitor."

"Sit down," the constable says. "And I won't tell you again."

"As is your right," the inspector says. "But we believe you did it; we have further information … from Glasgow."

The Albanian looks into the camera once more. "I won't say anymore until…"

"Yes, you see a lawyer, of course you will," the inspector says. "You are an illegal immigrant in this country – your work visa expired months ago."

The prisoner's face is one of trepidation. "I do not take your benefits. I feed myself from the money I make from gathering whelks and mussels. I sell them to the tourists and to the fish merchants in Stoer."

"You are in a lot of trouble, Victor."

"I have done nothing wrong."

"No, but you came here to kill Calum. This is why you are here, in this part of the world."

"I came here because I had heard this was a beautiful place, nice beaches and clean sea."

"You are no tourist, you are a murderer."

"I am not a murderer," the Albanian says. "I arrived here in springtime and decided to stay. I knew I would not be able to get a council house, so I found the boathouse. It was not inhabited, no one was using it, no one seemed to mind when I moved in there."

"You gave your name as Victor Temo," the inspector says. "Yet your visa papers say you come from Durrës. When you applied in the UK, you said you were from there, yet no one of your name has been recorded as having lived there. MI5 was watching you in Glasgow. You had links with ISIS and your role in the Albanian gang was a cover. You had been in Syria?"

The Albanian's voice drops at this point. "Yes, many people had."

"Did you kill anybody in Glasgow?"

"Anybody, sir? You mean anyone. I am learning English. When anyone is used, it is to differentiate one person from many, one person who is killed from many others, as in Syria. Whereas, it is not my English understanding." The prisoner looks up at the camera once more as if he has to impress someone there. "You can see how hard I am working to make myself acceptable here. Anybody is used where from a group there can be many." The inspector and the constable look at each other. "For example, does anybody here have a dog, does anybody see my keys; is there anybody who can drive?"

"Victor, shut up," the constable says.

"Victor," the inspector says. "It is not us you need to impress; it is the jury who will convict you of murder."

"Sir, I must see…"

"Yes, a lawyer." The inspector leans over towards the constable, saying something in his ear, then goes to the prisoner. "Victor, there is Miss Rahman; she works with migrants who get into trouble with the law. She will talk to you and assist us with our questioning of you. Are you happy with this?"

The Albanian nods.

"Then, we will be most grateful for your … help in our enquiries. We need to know who you work for."

"Whom!"

"Victor," the inspector snarls. "The courts attach leniency to those who tell the truth and save court time."

"Sir, I am a truthful man."

"Then tell the truth, sir, confess."

"No, I cannot."

"Then, if we cannot substantiate our case against you, you will be deported."

"If I am sent back, I will be killed for sure." He looks to the camera once more.

"Fifteen to twenty in a cushy UK jail or certain death on your return to Syria, you choose."

"I need to see this lawyer."

As arranged, in his car, the gaffer collects the father from outside the hotel.

"You don't look too good, Rooney," the gaffer says, pulling away from the hotel. "What happened to your head?"

"Cut myself shaving."

The gaffer smiles. "I'll take you for some breakfast and good coffee in a place I know." The father doesn't refuse. They go to the gaffer's favourite coffee house, the Steamie on Argyle Street. I hear them order "sourdough bread with Ayrshire bacon, free range eggs and large flat whites," which are gratefully consumed by both.

"That's a bit better," the father says. "Almost feel human again."

I am in wonder at what this might mean, not ever having known the human condition from a living point of view.

"Aye, it's amazing what a good cup of coffee can do; much better than Iron Brew as a hangover cure."

The father nods, acknowledging this, thinking he could also do with some 'Iron Brew', which he would collect from the nearby store before he goes to the station.

The gaffer reaches into a messenger satchel and pulls out a plastic bag with elastic bands around it. He gives it to Rooney. This is the package he took from the father two days before in Tennent's containing the boy's bag and his gloves. "Here, Rooney, our … lab did the trick. And take this." He also hands him a long brown envelope. "You'll find a breakdown of the findings in there; hope it helps."

"Thanks, Bill, it's appreciated."

They stop talking for a while, as if enjoying each other's company without needing to say so.

Then the gaffer breaks the silence. "You call me in if you need some heavies," he says. "You hear me?"

Of course the father does. "Will do, Bill. I need to catch my train, a bit of a trip ahead."

"Do you want a carryout coffee for the train, better than the Scot Rail pish?"

"No thanks, just get me there and I'll get my head down."

The gaffer accedes and they get into the back seat of the gaffer's black BMW waiting outside.

"This is travelling in style; Bill, I want to thank you."

"Don't think about it, pal, got to salt the money into something. I've another twenty of them for hire. Glasgow City Council uses them for the councillors. Great deal, we take the money from the druggies, we buy the cars, we take the money from the council, we buy more cars. We sell the cars, we buy more drugs and so it goes on. You know the score."

"Aye, I do." The father understands the way of organised crime in the city better than most.

The gaffer drops the father off at the station. He is pleased he has kept him safe, which was his goal. He could not have the previous crime boss killed in his city on his watch, it wouldn't be good business. "I'll, see you soon, Rooney," he says, shaking the father's hand.

"Not if I see you first, Gaffer." The father waves, heading into the station.

The gaffer waits until he sees the father disappear inside then sends James and John in after him. "See he gets on the train safely." They nod at the same time.

Within minutes of the train departing Queen Street Station, the father buys a can of Stella and a miniature bottle of whisky from the trolley. This is not so much for the whisky, which he drinks with gusto, but to procure the plastic glass, which he would use to drink from his own bottle of Glenmorangie, which he keeps in his bag under his seat so as not to draw notice to himself, especially from the train conductor. He did not want to be put off for being intoxicated on a train north, not that this happens on this train well used to imbibers. As it happens, he drinks all the way home and nearly falls off the train at Achfara at five thirty-five. The mother is waiting for him at the station while shaking her head.

"Hi, sweetheart, it's good to see you." He can hardly get the words out.

"Look at you, you're drunk, you can't even stand. And what happened to your head?" She notices the large plaster. "Get in the car."

The father is in no fit state to argue. "I had a few beers on the train. I had a hard time in Glasgow." He gets in the front seat, his messenger bag held tight in his hands.

"Did you not think about phoning, bloody binging again, no doubt; so much for the advice it would kill you if you hit it again?"

"I've been eating well and just on the beer."

"Liar, I can smell it on your breath, and I can see it in your face. You idiot; did you find what you were looking for?"

"I'll give you chapter and verse when we can sit down."

"Before you collapse you mean, you stupid bastard." She takes his cabin bag and throws it into the boot of the car. "And the head, tell me, bottled, butted or bashed as you hit the pavement? No don't, I don't want to know."

"I was chasing up some leads, forgot how rough Glasgow was."

"Aye, you forget why we got out of it." He nods as she pulls away to drive the mile or so along the trunk road from the station. Nothing more is said until they pull onto the coastal road. "Calum's home, he was released by the fiscal this morning."

"That's good, he's home."

"He was taken to the undertakers in Invernevis, where he was embalmed; they brought him home by hearse at three o'clock. Pity you weren't here when he arrived."

"The train doesn't get in until five thirty, you know that; what's the fiscal saying?"

"The cause of death and the means of his murder have been established, but they won't give me any information until the report is released by the police."

"Come on, I know you better than that."

"Why should I trust you, Rooney? I don't know you when you are like this."

"He is my son, tell me."

She looks at him, like she is trying to decide whether to accede to him or create an argument coming anyway. She chooses the former, deciding to defer the latter.

"Bruising around the neck, fractured cricoid cartilage, dark purple marks two centimetres in size; strangulation by two hands depressing his throat and throttling him, death by asphyxiation. By the force of the strangulation the attacker was a man. No DNA found, no sperm or saliva, no bite marks. Lack of diatoms in the body confirms his heart stopped beating before he was placed in the water, ruling out death by drowning." Stunned, the father is gazing at the floor of the car. "Enough for you, can you cope with it or will you run away back to Glasgow and hit the drink again? You're no good to me in this state."

"No good to you at all, sweetheart, in any state."

"You are just a disgrace."

"Not so Ben, Jackie, did you fuck him?"

Again, she takes time to answer this, as if she is teasing him. "Yes, I did, and it did me the world of good to have a man's arms around me comforting me, fucking me out of my … senses."

This has the desired effect, as he opens the door and drops himself onto the tarmac at fifteen miles an hour. Just as well she had not opened up on the trunk road.

The mother brings the car to an abrupt halt and walks back to where the father lies, just where the Achfara river leads to the sea. A car driving in the opposite direction also stops. The driver only happens to be Father Legowski out visiting parishioners. He gets out and walks towards him too. "It's OK, Father," Jackie calls, "I'll get him. He'll be OK; just his silly party trick, thank you."

The priest smiles, waves, and gets in his car and drives off.

The mother applauds as she approaches the crumpled wreck of the father on the road, bruised and bloodied, but doesn't stop him getting to his feet. "I'll walk home," he slurs, collecting his satchel and its contents spilled out onto the road.

"Just get into the car dickhead; I don't have time for this. We have a funeral to arrange and you need to be there."

The father realises he cannot walk the mile or so to the house and agrees to her demands.

The boy is there waiting for them as they drive up the drive to the house. He looks happy like he is about to run to them. Then he sees the father and stops. The mother goes into the house leaving the father to struggle out of the car and up the stairs into the house. The boy is on the path as the father limps past him. It looks as though he is trying to reach him to help. He backs away as I move between them.

The father gets in and pulls himself into a chair at the table.

The mother drops the father's cabin bag onto the floor next to him. "Do you want dinner?"

He looks at her. "Did you?" he asks.

She knows what he means. "Do you think you would be here if I did, Rooney? Not to say I didn't want to. Will that do? Will that get us through the next couple of days? Calum comes home tomorrow and he is to be buried on Wednesday. So you'll get yourself together, right?"

"Right, I'll have something."

The mother takes a plate and spoons stew and potatoes on to it.

"Did you find out anything, like important, in Glasgow? Was your visit there in any way useful?"

"Well, I met Ben." He pulls the plate close and eats like a navvy, not having eaten since he left Glasgow.

"So did I, I mean useful."

The father opens the bag. "I got the orders of service." He pulls out a box and hands them to her.

"I just hope they are OK." The boy looks down at his face on them, then looks at the mother as if to ask what they are for.

"And I got a shirt." He pulls out the Hawaiian shirt he bought in Glasgow." She grins. "I saw your father there; he'll be wearing a white suit." She grins again. "He said they are closing in, and to keep off his patch."

"And did you?"

"Well, not quite."

"I don't want to know, Rooney. I've had enough of your seedy past."

He limps over to the sink with his plate. "I was trying," he says, picking up the electric kettle. "Do you want some tea?"

"Yeah, I can see that." She takes the kettle from him and fills it, taking tea bags and mugs from the cupboard.

"We'll get him, darling, we'll get him."

She puts the tea in front of him and she sits at the other end of the table. "Victor Temo's been arrested, again."

"It's not him, Jackie."

"No? Well Boyd phoned, they interviewed Temo this morning, they've confirmed links between him and Zaharia, and the Albanian gang your lot hit."

He takes a big gulp of the tea. "Fuck."

"Ben said you were in some state."

"Aye, I would expect he would."

He opens the AGA oven door and draws the chair close, then pulls up his sleeves, revealing the grazing on his hands.

The mother goes to the drawer and pulls out the first aid box, putting it in front of him. "Here, and clean them well."

"Thanks."

"Inverbeg."

"Inverbeg?"

"They did the post mortem."

"What did it say?"

"A high level of adrenaline and calcium was found in his heart." She understands this; her experience as a DCI often relied on pathologist reports.

He does not, however. "What does it mean?"

"His heart was flooded with adrenaline." He shakes his head. "Adrenaline from the nervous system gets in the heart muscle cells, the calcium channels in the membranes of those cells open; calcium ions rush into the heart cells causing the heart muscle to contract; a massive storm of adrenaline, the calcium keeps pouring into the cells and the muscle can't relax. And if the heart system—"

"Packs in?"

"Overwhelmed with adrenaline and goes into abnormal rhythms, not compatible with life."

"It packs in."

This interests me, having taken the man's soul from his body. To know what had happened to his heart is interesting.

"He dropped dead."

"Cardiac arrest."

"Brought on by a fright, scared shitless to death."

"Something like that."

Not something I have known before. I will learn from this.

The mother goes to bed. He wants to fall in there too, to sooth his bruised hands, legs, to ease his pained head, stomach, to put the turmoil that is his life to rest, if he could; but the 'demons' troubling him in Glasgow, self-inflicted, still lurk in the crevasses of his mind.

The father goes to his shed; he has much to consider. Settling himself in his old wicker chair he lifts the satchel onto his lap and removes the boy's bag. Then he opens his old filing cabinet, full of old psychology magazines, guidelines for drystane dyking, newspaper cuttings, and puts it in the bottom of the cabinet, covering it with old magazines. Then he takes out the brown envelope with the

DNA report and writes GOD'S RESEARCH on it with a black pen. He takes his old leather-bound King James Bible from the shelf, well-worn from his days in Glasgow. He knows where to open it. "Page 84, Exodus 20:16," he says. "Thou shalt not bear false witness against thy neighbour; thou shalt not covet thy neighbour's house, nor wife, 20:17!" He slides in the envelope between page 84 and page 85 and places the bible back on the shelf.

CHAPTER 10

The day comes and the hearse arrives at the house. It is on time at the tenth hour, having been driven three hours from Abertay. The father and the mother are there to receive it. The boy cowers just behind them as if knows what is to come.

Funeral gets out of the hearse and moves towards them. "Are you sure you want him to be at home?" he asks. "I could take him to the church; Father Legowski says he would prefer it."

"No, he spends the night here, in his home," the mother demands.

"I'll bring him in."

"I'll help you," the father says.

Funeral looks at him and sees his injured face and his grazed hands. "Are you sure? We can manage it. He isn't very—"

"No, I know, he's not very big, but he's my son and I'll help bring him in. OK?"

They know not to argue.

I study Campbell, we have much in common.

The boy's remains are in a white coffin as per the mother's wishes. The top of the coffin is encrusted with seashells and steam train motifs along the sides. The father takes the top and Funeral the bottom.

The assistant takes the trestles ahead to set up in the house. "Where, Mrs?"

"In the bedroom, his bedroom, at the end of the hall."

The father stumbles on the stair causing the mother to reach out to share the weight of the top of the coffin. They take it to the boy's room prepared by her. Nothing had been moved.

"Thank you. Here." She hands Funeral twenty pounds. "I'll get you a pint."

"No," Funeral says, "we—"

"Please," she insists. He takes the money.

The father straightens the coffin on the trestles and drops to his knees. The boy looks on staring, not understanding what is going on; but realising, perhaps for the first time, he no longer inhibits his body, now in the box in front of him. I have been in this situation many times and often wonder what goes through their minds, if indeed anything can or does.

The father and the mother spend some time in there just talking to the boy, reminiscing of a time when there was joy in the house, the sound of the boy's voice filling the home.

After a while, the father moves through to the kitchen, followed shortly after by the mother. The son is there, not willing to face himself in the bedroom.

The father takes the *uisge beatha* from the cupboard and two glasses. "You want some of this?"

She shakes her head. "Can you not leave it for one day?"

"I need it just now. Once I am over this, I'll put it away."

"Sure, Rooney, so you say. I'll be burying you next."

The father looks at her face; he knows she is serious about this, but does not seem to care. "Be the best thing, I destroy myself, having killed my son, and killed … killed, killed, killed."

She offers no crumbs of comfort. "Oh, just wallow in it, Rooney."

The father pours himself a large glass; there would be a few more before he finishes the bottle.

Not so far from them, the young *taibshear* is gazing out of his window. It is still morning and the school remains closed; many of the children remain distressed at the death of their friend.

"It's been one week since Calum died, Angus." His mother, Maggie Stuart, is behind him, putting a jacket over shoulders. "I know you are feeling it." The *taibshear* continues to stare into the distance.

"Mum, I've seen him." He does not take his gaze from the window.

"Who son?"

"Calum, mum."

"Calum is dead, son."

"I know, mum, but I saw him outside the window, just looking at me."

His mother takes his shoulders and turns him towards her. "You have to stop this, Angus. It is not good for you to talk of the dead. You know what the child psychologist said to you."

The *taibshear* looks into her eyes. "I know mum, it is bad for my … mental health."

"You have to try to put these things out of your head, son. It is not good for you."

"But he is following me around, mum."

"You have to try, son."

"Yes, mum." He turns back to the window.

The friend and the chief share a table in the hotel. They think it only right given they are in Lochdarrach for the same reason.

"The wean came home today." The chief does not take his eyes from his Cullen Skink.

"Aye, I know." The friend squeezes a lemon segment over his whitebait. "I was wondering whether I should go over, you know to give them some support."

"I thought the same, but she needs to be in charge."

"She has a strong will."

"Too strong for her own good."

"I agree."

They eat for a few minutes without talking, but each knows what the other is thinking. The chief confirms it for both of them. "She's hiding her feelings, in attack mode, she'll crash."

"And he'll walk away, pissed." They remain quiet for a minute more. "It was good of you to invite me to have lunch with you."

"Well, we are in the same hotel and we are here for the same purpose, to support her."

"Yes, of course, to support her."

"Unless you have an ulterior motive, Ben."

"I don't get you."

The chief takes his gaze from his soup to hold the eyes of the friend. "I know you and my daughter had a fling in Glasgow. I just wondered whether you are burning a candle there."

"How did you know?"

"I'm chief constable, she's my daughter, there's not much I don't know, or can't find out."

"No."

"Well, are you?"

"I can't say I don't still like her, but she's back with him, and she's—"

"I don't think she is." The chief raises his eyes and pushes the remnants of his soup away. "But I don't want her hurt … again."

"Is that why you asked me to join you?" The chief doesn't respond, point made and accepted. It is the friend's turn to face his whitebait. "Food's good here."

"It's alright."

"I'm looking forward to the langoustines."

"Oh, posh nosh, I am looking forward to the fish and chips."

"Yeah, right." There's more of the pause. "Hubert?"

"Aye."

"I'm worried about Rooney."

"Me too."

"I think he's close to the edge."

The fish and chips arrive. "Do you think he'll crack?" The chief tears open the corner of a brown sauce sachet.

"Crack?"

"You're the expert; crack, flip, snap."

The langoustines arrive; the creatures spill over the side of the plate. "He has a mental illness."

"He has that; well?"

The friend struggles with the langoustines. "How do I?"

"You pull the body away from the tail, split the tail, take out the meat of them and dip them in the mayonnaise. Here, I'll show you." The chief demonstrates.

"He could relapse." The friend makes a mess of the process. "Jeez, wish I had the fish and chips."

"Here." The chief hands his plate over and takes the friend's. "If he did, is my daughter at risk?"

I am thinking a friend would say 'no' to this question, but this friend is no friend. "I'm not sure," he says.

"You're not sure?"

"He's harmed people in the past."

"Well, his men have."

"The crime boss pulls the strings, son." The chief looks him straight in the face.

The friend drops his gaze towards the food. "I know what you're saying, Chief." Whereas, a friend would say, 'Just what are you implying?'

"Did you see him in Glasgow?"

"Yes."

"So did I."

"Oh."

"He was in a mess."

"Yes, he was too when I saw him, in Tennent's."

A friend would say 'He was fine, no problem, give him a break, he's just lost his son.'

"Did he hit the sauce in there?"

The friend hesitates. He knows it was him that reintroduced the father to the *uisge*, putting it in front of him. "You could say that."

The chief waves a carcass of a prawn at him. "I won't let him destroy my daughter."

"No, I feel the same."

"I think we are on the same wavelength then." The chief dips his fingers in the water bowl, drying them with his napkin, reminiscent of Pontius Pilate washing his hands of Jesus. "We'll sort him then?"

"We need to protect her. Hubert?"

"What?"

"He had a gun."

"A gun."

"Aye, in Glasgow."

"Thanks son; same page on this?" The chief hesitates in offering the grip but puts out a fist instead.

"Yes, sir." The friend reciprocates with a fist bump.

CHAPTER 11

It is the tenth hour of the Wednesday, the ninth of November, the day of the boy's funeral, eight days since he was removed from the living, and five days following what would have been eight years alive. The parents had disagreed over the location of the funeral, but the father deferred to the mother who demanded a religious ceremony at St Margaret's. The local Catholic Church had a strong relationship with the school. The media circus remains at a respectful distance from the church.

The coffin is carried in by his father, the father's friend, the grandfather, and the chairman, who represents the community. Inside the coffin, his body is surrounded by the shell collection he amassed while living there next to the beach. Assisted by the undertaker, it is laid on two trestles on the centre aisle just before the alter.

The boy's parents sit to the right of the coffin. The mother's father, the chief, and his wife, Deirdre Hamilton-Brown, are there to the mother's right. Ben, the friend, is there sitting at the end of the row.

All the schoolchildren are there sitting together along three front rows to the left, facing the front. Their parents sit in the rows behind.

As is the custom, the practitioners who attended the boy and the parents are there at the back: the doctor, the constable, the inspector, and the forensic doctor who conducted the post mortem.

Religion is important to these people. The thought of eternal life, where they reunite with their loved ones who have moved on, binds them to it. Their beliefs are not important to me; my task is simple, to remove the dead from the living. Where they go afterwards is for them and their 'god'. God is many things to the living, and it is many things to the dead. I do not care; when I usher them from life to death the most I say is 'goodbye'. They turn and say nothing and move on, down a path I have not charted for them. Where they go, I do not know – the other place, which I know something of, or their idea of heaven, or hell. For me to follow them would mean I would move from this place between life and death to death, and I would become one of the dead. I am, however, damned to be an undead and also a nonlife. I do not question it; it is my destiny. It is my calling; fashioned by humans to meet their needs on their deaths. I had a beginning once but now I have no end. Was there something before for me? I suspect so, but I do not know. Is there something before life for these people? I do not know; neither do they. Is there something after death for them? Yes – me. After that, who knows. I don't, do they?

I move down the left side aisle, one step at a time. The young *taibshear* retreats from me, pushing farther along the row towards the central aisle, where the boy is. He is standing and looking on just to the side of his coffin where he rests one of his hands, as if to hold onto his remains. The boy refuses my gaze and looks to his parents, scanning the church in a scared but inquisitive way. The *taibshear* turns to the boy and he, in turn, turns to him. Then the *taibshear* turns around to his own parents as if to look for the security of their presence, to a solid grip on life.

The local people filter in and allow a space of three rows between them and the parents. The mass begins with the priest's welcome to all of this faith, those of other faiths, and those of none.

The mass begins and follows the Roman Catholic rites. The priest offers the mass for the benefit of the boy's soul and to offer comfort for the deceased, exhorting the congregation to pray for the soul of the departed. It is noticeable the father is not comfortable with the proceedings. He fidgets and looks around. I too am not comfortable here, although here is the basis of my existence and where many souls came with me.

I move to just before the alter stair and rest where I can observe the proceedings. I look to the father and I can just see his lips move, only a bit, not to utter a voice but just enough not to be heard by anyone other than me.

"Please Father, I'm a wee boy," he whispers.

"Take the sweets, son, and do what the church expects of you."

"Please don't hurt me Father."

"It will hurt as much as the penance you deserve for having sinned, my boy, now come to me."

"Please Father…"

A tear arrives at the corner of the father's right eye. He looks to the coffin and then to the children beyond it. The boy follows his gaze. He too sees the tear in his eye. Then, the father appears to gird himself for the proceedings he does not want to happen, almost as if he feels it best to go inward. He moves no more throughout the proceedings, not even to kneel at the key events in the mass. He refuses to accept the Eucharist; the children, however, line up to accept it, those who had received their first holy communion, then so do the others. Those who had not remain in their seats. The boy, himself had had his the year before in May. He wore a kilt then, the first and last time he wore it alive. He wears it now in his coffin.

The children move back to take their seats. They show a stoicism known in these parts, until the priest mentions them in the eulogy where he commends them for their bravery. This is too much for one. Mary McNeil is led away sobbing from the church by her parents. Then the funeral ceremony is over and it is time for the boy's body to be taken to his grave.

The men once again move to each side of the coffin then lift it to their shoulders. The boy refuses to follow the coffin from the church, declining the right to go to the grave with his body. He sits in the seat made vacant by the father when he leaves to take his place on the front stave carrying the coffin. Tradition is respected by members of the local community taking turns at a stave, carrying a coffin sometimes quite a distance to the graveyard. In this case, it is taken yards to a far corner of the church graveyard where it is put to the grave following the committal by the priest. The mother declines the burial and retires to the Lochdarrach Hotel for the funeral lunch, the host hotel of the Small Isles Bar. The boy stays close to her side all the way, he too avoids the grave. I do not insist in his moving on, not yet.

I too was interred in this graveyard when the old church was built in 1641, in the north part of the ground near the perimeter wall, incidentally, not far from where they buried the boy. I was a *faire-chlaidh* and they buried me alive, thinking I would protect the church from the devil. I have wandered this place ever since. I have mixed views of these humans. Some were kind to me on the farm, where I worked the sheep, but then others took me from there, put me in a box and then into the ground. My whines could be heard for hours from above, until the air gave out and I succumbed to what I now know as death. I rose that night, as intended to guard the graveyard; until I started to stray and seek out souls. I have no blame or anger for this act upon myself; they were doing what they thought to be their duty, and now I am doing mine.

The parents feel they need to show their thanks to the local community for the support and respect shown them since the boy was removed. A lunch of steak pie, potatoes, and peas is provided in the bar with complimentary drams. The father is from the Irish folk with the food typical of lowlander wake food. An array of whisky bottles illustrates his hope they will enjoy the occasion. Of course, he would want to thank all involved and the community for turning up en masse.

They filter into the restaurant area, picking up a glass of whisky or sherry as they enter, or taking tea or coffee as they arrive. They take up seats at arranged tables, where soup is being delivered by a group of local ladies. I enjoy these occasions, being interested in customs at wakes. Getting the people comfortable, warmed up after the committal with hot soup and refreshments, is well tested and successful. The parents had set aside a corner table for the children to stay together as a group, with pizza and soft drinks available there. A video display shows the boy on the beach and enjoying activities in the area. He stands mesmerised at this, viewing almost a summary of his life there since he came there from Glasgow. As if his earlier days before he arrived with the parents were non-existent; his years before them did not happen. These years remain with him to reflect upon. I wonder if he thinks about his birth parents or has any feelings good or bad towards them. The authorities had deemed them incapable of looking after him; as alcoholics and drug addicts, perhaps they would have no interest in being there. I wonder if they have been advised he is dead. His short life appeared to have improved when he arrived in Achfara, however. Though many there may have wondered, had he remained in Glasgow with failed parents, might he still be alive?

Once all there are settled the father rises to address them. His taking of a half bottle of whisky as he walked from the burial ground to the hotel to steady his nerves has the opposite effect as he struggles to get to his feet. The mother tries to stop his rise, saying it is not necessary for him to say anything, but he is insistent, as is his character.

"Good afternoon everyone, just a few words." He steadies himself by holding on to the table; however, when he removes one of his hands to lift his glass he tilts to the left and almost topples over. The mother grabs his arm to steady him. "Thank you for coming today to honour a lovely boy, our boy," he says, as he looks to the mother. So far so good, I think. "This was supposed to a celebration of the life of our son; I'll see you over the rainbow son. What a load of crap, sure we celebrate his life, his wee life, but this is about his death, his horrible, unnecessary death." The mother sees what is coming and tries to divert him from what she knows he is capable of when in drink. "No, I will not be shushed, Jackie, it needs to be said."

The chairman tries to intervene. "Mr Rooney, we understand."

"No, you don't, sir; no, you don't."

"Rooney." The mother is also on her feet. "Sit down."

The father looks around the room to see the mix of pity and condemnation. "What am I doing here?" he asks himself, then "What are you all about?" he asks them. "Why are you here; are you interested in the life and death of my child or the life and death of your pathetic little community?"

"Rooney." The mother talks over him. "Please forgive my husband, he is … upset."

"Yes, I am upset." The father retakes his seat.

People look to their food, eating and talking to each other in hushed tones. The children are also quiet, until the teacher suggests they remove to the games room to play. The boy has the look of a stranded seal, confused and scared. He needs to move on soon, but I am having sport with him. My tedium with the taking of souls has been eased by him. He will stay for the meantime.

People begin to filter through to the bar from the repast meal. The inspector is there already, favouring a burger and chips. He is aware of the emotion around and was determined not to be at the centre of it.

Dram moves into the bar area, having taken more than his share of the free whisky, and feels compelled to approach the inspector who is sitting alone at a table, eating.

"Terrible thing, Mr Boyd, terrible for them, terrible for us, terrible things happening around here."

"Aye, terrible, not your usual circumstances sir, that's true." The inspector is aware of this man's reputation for talking out of turn.

Dram does not disappoint. "Anything on McDonald, Mr Boyd. You know, his death, his body was taken to Abertay."

The inspector avoids looking him in the face, concentrating on eating his food. "Just procedure, Mr…"

"Findlay, Lachie, but call me Dram, everyone else does."

"Thank you, Dram. All unexplained deaths are the Fiscal's responsibility until the body is released. So please don't concern yourself."

"Do you think it was a murder too, some people are saying that."

"People can say what they like, sir, doesn't mean to say it is correct. Now if you'll…"

"Two murders in a small area like Lochdarrach?"

"Please, Mr Shaw, I'm eating."

"OK, Detective Inspector—"

"Inspector'll do, sir."

"Thanks, Inspector, but I'm only saying what people are thinking."

"Please, Mr Shaw; this is neither the time nor the place."

Dram takes umbrage at the inspector's reluctance to engage him. Like most drunks he feels he can say anything to anyone in a bar, like it is his domain and he owns everyone. He moves to the bar towards the hack who sees him coming and turns his back to focus on Maggie, who is busy pulling pints. "I can't stand drunks," he says to her. Dram finds someone else to annoy.

"No, same here," Maggie says to the hack. "You having another?"

"Aye, go on darlin'."

She blushes at the term of endearment. "Darlin'? Are you being friendly or rude sir?"

"I'm sorry, *very* friendly of course."

"Same again?" He smiles.

"Cromarty Happy Chappy?"

"That's me."

She pulls the beer and puts it in front of him. "Well, that's OK then."

"Thank you, Mrs Stuart." He puts the pint to his mouth and takes a sip.

"I like it, Margaret." She smiles. "Margaret, do *you* think he was murdered?"

"Sorry?" She struggles with the real ale hand pump.

"Inverbeg, do you think he was murdered?"

"I could murder this. How would I know anything about that, Mr Scott?"

"John."

"John?"

"Sorry, not Mr Scott, call me John. Angus?"

"John, Angus." She laughs. "Maggie."

"John, Angus, Maggie?

"Call me Maggie."

"Thanks Maggie. Angus, your son, I hear he … sees things."

"Angus? It is not for me to determine that. Excuse me." She picks up a tray of pints. "I'll be back, as they say." Having delivered the pints she is back pulling more. "Sorry, you were saying?"

"Just wondered, some people are thinking that." He spins around to nod towards the dram.

"Och these people think lots of things, John. I'm sure the inspector'll establish the truth of Inverbeg's death."

Sound carries in the small bar and it is inevitable the inspector would have heard this, but he stays schtum.

"Maggie, can I ask you something?"

"Please, if you like. I'm used to all kind of questions working behind a bar. I just hope you are not going to proposition me. I'm a married woman, married to the owner no less." She laughs.

"You are an attractive woman. I can understand why a man would proposition you." She looks at him. "Your son."

"My son, why would you—"

The hack holds his hand up in mitigation. "Nothing to worry about Maggie, I have heard he is known for … knowing things."

"You like to push it, John." She looks around. "OK, he has the second sight, if that is what you mean. Like his grandmother, my mother, Mary MacLeod, from Lewis, who also had it."

"And you?"

She laughs again. "No, not me, thank god, maybe it misses a generation."

"I just wondered."

"He was born on Samhuinn; he has the gift or maybe it's a curse."

"Oh."

"You just wondered if he saw something."

"Yes."

"I don't know if." She lifts her head to see where her husband is.

"Please, Maggie, you can be assured."

She studies him. "Last night."

"Last night?"

"Yes."

"He saw something."

"Something?"

"A shape of a person in a cloth, like a shroud."

If the hack thinks he is going to get something tangible, he is to be mistaken.

"A shroud?" The hack's face shows disappointment.

"You asked me, he says he saw a person in a shroud."

"In a shroud."

"Look John, he doesn't know who killed Calum. Is that what you are thinking?"

"Are you sure?"

"Mr Scott—"

"John."

"Sorry, John, you are a reporter, and I can understand you are looking for a story, and something to add interest to it, but…"

"I am sorry. I didn't mean to upset you."

"No upset for me, but it is hard for him. It stresses him. He sees things, I know that."

"You know that."

"I believe my son, sir."

"Apologies."

"Accepted. He seems to know things as they are going to happen, but not Calum's murderer."

"Sorry, the shroud."

"Will you promise not to include it any story. Can I trust you?"

"Of course you can, Maggie."

She looks at him over her glasses, like she is not worried either way. "OK, Last night, on the night of McDonald's death, he saw it. It has happened before when people pass." This is true, I know the *taibshear*. "He was in the garden in the dark."

"In the dark?"

"He likes the sky, the stars, and the robins singing."

"Robins singing in the dark?"

"It happens around here, I know it is strange, and he likes the dark."

"When a robin appears, your loved ones are near."

"I like that, John." She smiles. "When he came into the house his face was white as snow."

"Like he'd seen a ghost?"

"Look John, if you don't…"

"Sorry Maggie, his face?"

"We knew he had seen something."

"Yes, this shroud."

Magnus Stuart's bellowing voice eclipses their intimate discussion. "You guys seem to be having a nice chat."

"Just talking, dear. Mr Scott is interested in our local customs."

"I'm sure he is, dear." Her husband's face tells her to get back to serving the customers.

"You'll excuse me, Mr Scott." She moves along the bar.

"Interesting woman, Mr Stuart."

"My wife is of no interest to you, sir, now you'll be busy."

The hack takes one more drink from the pint and puts it down on the bar. "Yes, indeed, writing about a small community and a murderer, Mr Stuart." The owner remains stony faced. "Thank you for your hospitality, sir."

"Good night, Mr Scott."

"Good night."

"And Mr Scott."

"Yes?" The hack halts as he is about to leave the bar to head into the hotel area.

"If there is anything else we can do to make your stay in our hotel … pleasurable, just say, either to myself or my wife." The hack nods with a smile.

A good proportion of the funeral party come through from the restaurant to the bar. I wander among them, between them. They cannot see me nor are they to know I am there, but some suspect I may be; it would be odd if I were not here, at the events of the dead. I hear their fears, there is a pique in their tone, almost a shrill like the crow when alarmed. But more, there is interest, an excitement in what is going on in their boring, pathetic lives. Their contemporaries call it 'Murder in the Machair'; such a human way of expressing a threat to their sad lives. 'Murder in the Machair' has brought the world to this small place, however; perhaps to add salt to their boring lives. For some, it is a god-send, another human term, for others, it is a devil-send.

For those who wish a private life in the remoteness of the heather, they hide behind their lace curtains, peeking out to see who has the temerity to mingle with the 'media' and the 'tourists'. I do not understand these terms, they were not part of my existence, but they are now and to deal with their deaths I must see their lives through their eyes.

There is fear, which is true, there is excitement, which is short-lived. To the day on the street, in the local shops, the pub, where they huddle like sheep penned by the dogs and to the night, when the dark descends sooner these days. Few venture out. I have taken two souls so far, a young and an old one; but inevitably there will be more to come before I can return from whence I came.

There is pain too, however. This place has suffered before, such as in the time of the great hunger and the Black Death, and during and after the great battle of Drumossie Moor which took its sons and fathers, and also their culture, their way of life, their dress, their music, and the old way which protected them for centuries.

They had hardships, it is sure. In the time of the *fuadaichean nan gàidheal*, when their houses were burned to the ground and they were driven to the shore, from places where the reared their cattle and tended their crops to the place where they harvest the kelp. Then the Victorians came, bringing their new authority and their shooting parties.

Murders were plentiful in the old days, such as on one of the islands where one hundred and twenty souls were taken. This was my busiest of days. Clan wars, feuds, and revenge killings were plentiful, but not now. Murder is not commonplace, a child murder, never known; quite different for them, and also for me.

Accepted by the community, as they may well be, the mother and father brought this 'upset' to them. The crime lord and the high-ranking police officer brought their history to this place and to them and also to them; they brought murder, and resentment of this is high. It did not exist before them and it does now; and now they have a second occurrence in the space of two days.

CHAPTER 12

The following day, the man they call Zaharia and the chief meet in Glasgow, in the Tinderbox, a suitable name for such a meeting. It is morning, nine days from the death of the *balach*.

"Thank you for seeing me, Mr Zaharia." The chief gets up momentarily to greet the man.

"Lekë, sir."

"I'm Hubert Kaminski, the chief constable." The chief invites him to sit at the other side of his table.

"I know who you are, sir." Zaharia looks around the place.

"I know, not a normal place to conduct business."

"It suits me, Mr Kaminski. Not for me a police station." He takes his seat and opens his jacket.

"No, I don't think you would be too comfortable there." The chief notices the brightly coloured garment the man wears under his jacket. "I like your waistcoat, Lekë."

"It is a traditional Albanian vest, sir, a xhamadan; it is wool and can be warm, perfectly suited to the Scottish weather."

"Aye, right." The chief looks out of the window onto the rain sodden Byres Road as he goes to the counter and orders coffee for himself. He nods over to Zaharia but he declines anything.

The chief returns with his coffee. "Now, to business."

"*You* wanted to see me sir?"

"I did."

"But you will appreciate we are now leading legitimate lives, since—"

"You were hammered by the Family."

Zaharia pushes back as far as he can to maintain distance from the chief. "We were also…hit by the police, Chief Constable."

"Yes, true, but legitimate, as you say."

"We are business people now, sir, car washing, lucrative it is too; you Scots like clean cars."

"No drug or women trafficking?"

"Not a thing, sir."

"No, I could mention a few things which may point towards illegitimate business, Mr Zaharia. The Albanian Mafia is still very active in Glasgow, we know this."

Zaharia now sat bolt upright in his seat. "Sir, if you asked me here to—"

"If I was interested in your current activities, you would be in Stewart Street; and I would not be conducting your interviews, my officers would."

"Yes, I understand, sir." He relaxes a bit.

"Mr Zaharia?"

"Yes?"

"Victor Temo?"

"Yes."

"I am not going to ask if you know him because I know you do; he was one of your senior soldiers."

"He was."

"And you will remember Mr Rooney, the crime lord of the Family?"

"Indeed I do, they hurt us…"

"So much so you would want to have revenge, an eye for an eye."

"'*Më mirë syri sesa name*', sir, 'Better lose your eye than your honour'."

"Victor Temo?"

"Yes, sir."

"He still working for you?"

"No sir, we had no further use for his services."

"Are you in contact with him?"

"No."

"Was he working for ISIS?"

"He had been in Syria."

"And you took him on?"

"We have given employment to many migrants arriving here from war torn countries."

"I could chase you out of Glasgow."

Zaharia turns to look at the door as if to check his minders are still out there, not that they could offer any protection against the chief.

"Yes, I know this, and it's why we are legitimate."

"I want you to do something for me."

"I do not know what I can do, but of course…"

"If you do, I will ensure you can carry on your businesses without interference."

Zaharia takes a minute to answer. "I would be happy to help, sir."

CHAPTER 13

Later, at the noon, it is time for Inverbeg's funeral. I often wonder why such trouble is taken by the living to dispose of the dead. Although I claimed his soul, Inverbeg's body returned this day for its disposal into the ground. It has been opened, entered, flesh removed for analysis, and then sewn up and cleaned. It is transferred from the mortuary to the church without ever returning to his home. I dispatch his soul to its rightful place for all of his eternity. A churchgoer and supporter of the church, he believed he would go to the place they call Heaven. I can confirm he did not.

His death remains 'uncertain', as is said by humans with such knowledge, but there is no need to detain his body further. It was not uncertain for me, not from the very moment I reached inside him and removed his soul. The physical 'pathology' of his death has been confirmed: he had suffered cardiac arrest; he had a weak heart and his death had been aided by type two diabetes and alcohol-related kidney failure. He would have gone anytime if an affright had not been helped on his way. But for his hands tied behind his back and his lying face down in the Machair this would have been a natural occurrence, but the authorities were in no doubt it was 'man' made. Why and by whom would remain a mystery to them, but not to me.

The man's funeral has been planned with the church, the hotel, and the community. He was a McDonald and his family were of the old ones. They wanted him laid to rest in accordance with their ways, a highland funeral with the old customs. A *moladh-mairbh* will be celebrated which includes the taking of food and drink by all those present.

They come out, but more by community and in solidarity than any liking of McDonald. There is no sadness at the funeral or the committal and the priest says little about his life except he was a good catholic man who supported the church, ran a successful farm, and he looked after 'lost boys'. The priest mentioned his care of boys in a perfunctory way, though all there knew of his 'care', So not much was said of his life or his death there, only the priest fulfilling the funeral mass – and there was nothing else for the living to do than to put his flesh in the ground and say an Ave for his soul.

Inverbeg is from the Clan McDonald, of the ancient ones. His ancestor, my master, John, 12th of the Clanranald, as many here are, was the first. He built the old church and was the first man to be buried there. He put me there before him and I took his soul. I did this out of loyalty to him; he was my master and tended me in my life, but also out of hatred; he buried me there in the graveyard and he let me howl in the ground until I rose and removed his soul. I have taken the souls of these people ever since.

After the mass, his coffin is taken on staves to the church graveyard to be interred in the family plot where his ancestors are. His parents had been put there some sixty years before him. I remember the occasion well. They had died within one week of each other, succumbing from the consumption. I remember him as a five year old, standing over the grave as they were buried together, the father on top of the mother, almost to protect her from the world.

The boy is there. He shows no emotion at McDonald's going to the ground, no fear of the man who has become a suspect in his own death. He appears uninterested in the proceedings in an unsettling kind of way.

Caber is the solitary gravedigger there. He dug the grave when it was known the body would be returning. The soil is sandy and coffins are found intact and untarnished after fifty years. Given the over-occupancy of the grave, with generations of McDonalds, he removed the coffins of his parents, taking the bones and placing them in muslin bags to be put in the side of the grave to make space for McDonald's coffin.

I watch as they dispatch his body into the ground where it will rot. I was happy his soul would too.

A clan piper is there, though in my time bagpipes were condemned as instruments of the devil, no longer the case in these modern days. The tune is *cumha na mairbh*, the *Lament for the Dead*. The community form a procession, passing the open pit where men drop handfuls of sand and some women throw flowers. The boy stands by his parents at the grave. The father refuses to drop in sand, as if to show his doubts over the man.

The procession moves on and towards the hotel where the lunch would be served. Caber girds himself for the shovelling of the earth into the pit when two young men appear. I notice them standing beyond the people behind the metal railing. When they move off they move to the open pit, but instead of dropping in a handful of sand or a flower they drop a birch stick.

The lunch is given by the church as is the singular dram apiece for those who braved the elements on the cold November day. They take the sandwiches and the dram and leave, hurrying along the road to the village. A few move to the pub, as is also the way following a funeral.

Inverbeg was reared by an uncaring grandmother and a brutal grandfather in Inverbeg, the village over the hill, hence his nickname. He felt the lash of the grandmother's tongue and the grandfather's belt through his childhood, normally after a few drams in them. He wasn't allowed to mix with other children and never married.

Later, he moved into Lochdarrach and took a farm. He found funds, however, by taking in young boys, boarded out with him from the lowlands, where he was paid by the head per week. At one time he had four boys. They worked his farm before and after school, getting up at six to tend the sheep and cleaning out the cac on return from school to late. In the school holidays they worked from dawn to dusk. To the outsider they looked fit and healthy, enjoying the company and support of each other. For them, they lived in fear of the belt, the birch stick, his fist, and his boot. Injuries inflicted were confined to the shoulders, the back, the buttocks, the thighs, then the mind, where they could not be seen.

Into this environment arrived the boys from Glasgow where they were neglected by alcoholic parents, to Achfara where they were abused by a brutal McDonald. They survived there for seven and a half years until both reached eighteen, when the order holding them expired. They walked the two and a half miles to the station without a goodbye and boarded the train at Lochdarrach to take them back without a backward glance. Their sorrow was leaving the others too small to leave with them. The promise they made, however, gave them some comfort; one day, they would return.

Friday morn, ten days since the boy's demise, and Andrew Dewar is his solitary self in the playground. He misses the boy, his friend, but he appears more troubled than normal as he paces the perimeter avoiding the other children. The teacher watches him from the window of the school, though waits until all the children have gone in after lunch break before she stops him at the door.

"What is wrong, Andrew?"

"What, Miss?" He pushes against the wall, his hands behind his back, looking at the ground, as if he has done something wrong.

"You seem upset, what is wrong?"

"Nothing, Miss."

"You are very quiet, and have been for weeks."

"It is my way, Miss."

She notices some of the other children looking at him, obviously wondering what is going on. Apprehension rising, she asks him to go into her room. He follows her in. She points to the chair in front of her desk. He climbs on the seat, his feet not touching the floor. She leans across the desk and looking down on him.

"I know you are a quiet boy, Andrew, but not *this* quiet." She waits for a reaction. "Well?"

"It is nothing, Miss." He looks up at her.

"Is it Calum? We have people who can talk to you about that, your feelings, in confidence."

"What is that, Miss?"

"In secret, Andrew."

"It is not to do with Calum."

"Well, if you do not tell me I cannot help you with it and I will have to talk to your mother. I cannot have you—"

"No, Miss, please don't, she will—"

"She will want to know, no doubt; are you like this at home?"

She can see he is thinking about this. "Yes, Miss, I suppose I am."

"We have a child psychologist in Invernevis, would you like to talk to him?"

"No, Miss."

"Well, talk to me then, what is troubling you?" He is fidgeting around on the chair, clearly uncomfortable. She goes around and kneels beside him. "Are you unhappy about something, Andrew?"

"Miss?"

"Your mother says you wet the bed, sometimes."

He retreats from her. "My mother…"

He gets up to leave and she grips him by the shoulders. "Andrew, you can tell me." From her teacher training she knows she should try to balance the right degree of assertiveness with care.

His eyes start to moisten. "Yes, Miss, I do, sometimes."

"It's OK, Andrew, it happens with lots of children."

This reassurance seems to work. "It does, Miss?"

"Yes, all the time. We need to know why that happens, so we can help."

"But, I don't."

"Will I talk to your mother?"

She is aware this may push him back into his shell, but she needs to take the chance.

"No, Miss, please, I will tell you, if you—"

"I won't say anything, Andrew, I'm a teacher, and we have codes."

The boy is slow to answer, as if he is not going to. He looks at the door, as if he was worried about someone walking in. "Even if it is to do with Mr McIsaac, Miss?"

This surprises the teacher. "John, my husband?"

"Yes, Miss."

"What about him?"

He gets up and moves to the window as if he wants to check if the chairman's car is outside.

"Andrew, son." She tries to get the right tone.

The boy knows he has passed the point of no return. "Miss, he … touches me."

"Touches you, like helping you on and off the bus?"

"No, Miss, he tells me to come to sit next to him."

She recognises immediately the significance of this and it is now for her to go to the window to see if her husband is around; though, outwith his picking up the children in the morning for school and dropping them off after, he would be at the garage or taxying in the village.

She treads warily. "Oh, Andrew, that's because you are last off the bus as he takes you down Bótha Dubh, and it is dark; he thinks you would be scared."

He appears emboldened now, as if having gotten it out he has to see it through. His tone deepens as he looks her in the face. "He reaches over to me Miss and touches me."

"It's just to comfort you, son, on your shoulder no doubt."

He would have none of this now. Having come out with it he appears determined to ensure she hears him out fully and maybe even believe him. "On my leg, Miss, up my leg, to my willie."

She just about falls off the chair. "Your willie, come on Andrew, you have a vivid imagination."

He knows this means something he imagines and not something true. "Miss, you have to believe me, he takes my hand, and puts it on his willie." He is aware he has launched himself to a place in the sea where there is no going back to the shore; he needs to keep going until he finds somewhere safe, safer.

"Andrew, what are you watching at home? Are you on the Facebook? You know what we have said to you children about selfies, sharing pictures and things like that. We will need to find out what you are looking at."

"You started this, Miss, you asked me." He pushes over the chair and makes for the door. She stops him.

"I'm sorry, Andrew, it's just—"

"It's just Mr McIsaac is your husband, Miss, so why would you believe me?" He drops his head into his hands. "His willie is hard, Miss. Like Sam our horse sometimes when the mare is on heat."

She takes his hands away from his face. "Andrew, Mr McIsaac is not Sam your horse. I just wish you could put some of this imagination into your compositions, you would do well in English and the creative writing."

"It's true, Miss, he has a big cock."

"Andrew, I'll be telling your mother. I hope she washes your mouth out with soap and water."

"Please Miss, don't tell my mother, she will hit me with her stick." He now has his head back in his hands. "I am sorry, Miss, I shouldn't have told you."

"Well, you will go to Father Legowski and confess to your lies, straight from school tonight you will go to the confession."

"Aye, Miss, I will go and confess."

In the bar, it takes Dram to break the silence on Inverbeg's passing. "Well, I liked him. There, I've said it." No one responds. "He always bought me a whisky." Again, no one bothers. The lack of response exercises him. "I know what you are all thinking." Did he? "Those children." This is enough to prompt a look or two from those around the bar. The hack is in the corner and well within earshot. All the community needed would be a story on *that* incident.

"Just button it, Lachie," Caber moves towards the dram. "You're letting your tongue out of the trap again."

Magnus bookends Dram from the other side of the bar. "Aye, and I'll nail it to the bar floor before it has a chance to trip anybody up."

They all laugh.

Dram gets off his stool. "I'll say what I like. This is my place as much as any man here and I'll have my say."

"What would you like to say, Lachie?" The hack's voice comes from behind a laptop on a corner table. He gets up and moves over. "I will listen to you, Mr Shaw, even although they will not."

Dram notices eyes bearing down on him from the men there. He knows he has said too much even although he has said nothing at all. "Oh, it's nothing, Mr Scott."

The hack packs up his laptop and sidles into the group, pulling in a stool. "You said 'those children'." Dram knows he had best not say anything more.

Dram empties his glass and puts it on the bar. "It is time we were back home, time for our tea, lads." They do the same and get up to leave.

"Don't hurry away on my account." The hack knows the hurrying away is on his account. "I know about the boys." This is enough to halt the exodus.

Caber stops. "What?"

"The boys, I know about the boys."

"Mr Scott—"

"No need, Mr McKinnon. I'll be leaving anyway."

"I think it wise, Mr Scott." Caber towers all of his six three frame over the hack as he gets up.

There is no fear in the man, though. Although well shorter than Caber and most of the men there, this does nothing to quell his candid words, which might ill-fit the ethics of a professional journalist.

He lets rip. "McDonald locked up those boys, beat them up, and whatever else." The collective intake of breath is what he intends. "He got off scot-free, no charges, no one believed the boys who were taken from him." The men look at each other, like they are having a discussion just by their looks. "And you, all of you, this community, were complicit, just as responsible for the abuse suffered by those boys."

It takes Caber, as they expect, to talk on their behalf. "And who are you to say anything about this community?"

"One who has had the opportunity to assess the facts of the case?"

"Well, you don't know anything, sir. Inverbeg McDonald took the boys when no others would, offered them shelter and a life away from the cac of Glasgow. Donald McDonald was one of ours, he just happened to get two bad-ins from the cesspit Glasgow."

"If you don't see an abuser in your midst, Mr McKinnon, what chance do you have to see a killer?"

I know these people as honest, true, and not known to unfairly judge. Just having buried one of their own and this lowlander is saying something very critical of them. Had they not had drams they would have probably turned and left him there to stew in his accusations; with the drams, I doubt if he knows the risk he faces.

"You have outstayed your welcome here." Caber picks up the hack's bag and pushes it into his chest.

The hack pulls his small but bullish frame out of the seat to place it under the man with a face like a stag on steroids looking down on him. "Mr MacKinnon, I have work to do here and I'll leave when I think it is time to leave." He gathers his coat from the corner and lifts the strap of his bag over his head as he makes his way out, but not before he leaves them something to think about. "On my last assignment, ISIS fighters said the same thing to me; I had outstayed my welcome. They said I was about to come to harm if I didn't leave their midst. I left. You are no ISIS fighters."

Andrew Dewar waits for the priest to arrive to take confessions. It is well after school time and he is concerned about going home, but he is relieved the bus has gone. It is Friday after school and the weekend offers him freedom and the chance to go the woods where he can find solitude, but he knows he has to do this.

"Andrew, you are here for confession?" The priest enters the church and walks towards the confessionals. "It could have waited until when all the children come together, during school time."

"The teacher says I have to do it, Father."

He laughs. "Oh, you must have done something very bad,"

"Yes, Father, I have."

"You better come in then." The priest rests his elbow on his side of the confessional window, the curtain concealing him and the boy. No one else is there, but Annie, the *cailleach*, would be there soon; she always arrived at five o'clock. Then he would go for his dinner before evening mass.

Andrew sits and starts. "Please forgive me, Father, for I have sinned." There is no prompting by the priest.

"No need to go through it, son, what have you to say to me?"

"Miss McIsaac sent me to confess, Father."

"Oh." The priest looks at his watch, hoping he could get this over with soon. "Go on son."

"I have sinned, Father."

"And what have you done, my son, to offend the Lord?"

"I lied to the teacher."

"Oh, you did." The priest looks at his watch again, wondering if the housekeeper had put the chicken in the oven. "I am sure lie is a strong term, Andrew, what did you lie about, your homework?"

"I lied about me touching Mr McIsaac's willie and him touching mine."

This shakes the priest out of his dwam, so much so he pulls the curtain back and looks out to the boy. "You have what?"

"Will Jesus forgive me, Father?"

"About your lie, of course he will." The priest thinks about this for a minute; a bit graphic, he thinks. "Can I ask, why did you say this to Miss McIsaac about her husband? It is a very bad thing to say."

"I know, I shouldn't have said he has a big cock like Sam our horse." The priest rarely if ever opens the curtains during confession but this is one of those times. "Will you take me home, Father? I've missed the bus. It is two miles."

"Yes, I'll take you home son. Now go outside and say ten Hail Marys."

"I didn't like it, Father, I promise, I didn't like it."

"OK son, ten Hail Marys. I'll take you home after I see Annie McDonald, she doesn't take long."

The *cailleach* goes in as she does every confession. She has nothing to confess, but likes to talk to the priest in private, to gossip about the young ones in the village, what they are up to, down the pier, drinking and smoking and other things. These 'other things' do not concern me. He listens to her. She has no one else to talk to of the evenings apart from the weekly whist club in the hall where little is said anyway.

The priest takes Andrew home, despite his wish to go to the woods; with a killer around what could he expect? The teacher phones his mother to say he will be home later due to his going to confession.

"Thank you, Father," Mrs Dewar says to the priest as he appears at the door with her son. "Time he went to you; he can be a bad boy, hope he hasn't been telling you I have been giving him a whack." The boy moves beyond her, fearing the priest would tell her. He is relieved he does not.

"He is a good boy, Mrs Dewar, no trouble. You keep him in order."

"Someone has to, Father, since my husband saw fit to…"

The priest is taken back to the time when he was called out to deliver the last rights to Bill Dewar after he broke his neck. An inveterate alcoholic, he had overturned his tractor during a drunken binge. I took his soul. It did not resist leaving his debauched body.

The boy looks out at the priest from behind his mother, glancing to his left to see her walking stick in the coat stand. He hadn't had it for a while. If the priest stays quiet and he keeps out of trouble with the other boys, he will avoid it.

"*Oidhche mhath*, "Father, we will see you on Sunday at mass."

"Yes, Mrs Dewar, at mass."

"*Oidhche mhath*, Father."

"*Oidhche mhath*, Andrew."

The priest returns to the church house and has his dinner in deep thought. He has had children say things in the past for effect, but not like this. It is the sincerity in the boy's voice, if not the adult detail, which disquiets him. He knows the reputation of the church regarding reporting and doing what is right with abuse in its own ranks, and following high profile cases he knows the authorities have to be brought in if a priest hears of child abuse, especially child sexual abuse.

He would need to get advice on this one and thinks about contacting the social work department in Invernevis. But he knows if he does, there could an investigation and with everything else going on he wonders if this would be wise. He is also aware it could be very distressing to the boy if indeed he had been lying, but the chairman's reputation is also at stake. As leader of the community council McIsaac is a respected man. This is very damaging. The boy could be making it up, but as the living say 'mud sticks'.

CHAPTER 14

The next morning the solicitor commissioned to represent the Albanian arrives at Invernevis Police Station where he has been held for five days since he was rearrested and charged with murder. He is due to appear in court the following Monday, from where it is expected he will move to the remand unit of Abertay Prison until his trial.

The inspector invites her in. "Victor, this is Miss Rahman, solicitor from the immigration advice service in Glasgow. She will assist you in our enquiries."

Miss Rahman moves to the side of the Albanian. "You will leave us now, Inspector." "I wish to see my client alone."

"Of course, we will begin the interview at 10.00am."

The inspector leaves.

"Mr Temo, I am here to help you."

"Yes, I think I need help."

The solicitor positions herself in front of him. "Just keep looking at me." He does. "The camera is at the back of me and cannot see my face. I have asked for confidentiality so there is no microphone here. No one can hear us talking. I made the request you remain here until I see you. It would be more difficult in Abertay Prison to … see you. You are to be removed there on Monday."

"Thank you."

"You have been charged with the murder of Calum Rooney."

"I have, but—"

"You don't need to say anything at this point but I am here to give you a way out."

"A way out, what do you mean?"

"The conviction will stick. Mr Zaharia will testify he has information you came here to kill the boy. You were working for ISIS."

"What?"

"Yes, ISIS; Al-Jamal, the leader of the ISIS cell in Glasgow that kidnapped a police officer, Rooney defeated him in Glasgow.

His honour was damaged in Islam and you were sent here to kill Rooney's son to avenge him, which you did."

"But I, I—"

"You will be convicted as a terrorist who has murdered a child and will be sent to prison for the rest of your life, or you will be deported to Syria and you will be killed by ISIS on your arrival. In any case, your family will be shamed and ISIS will destroy them."

He looks to the camera. "You are not here to help me?"

"Yes, I am here to help you, please take this." She passes him a capsule under the table. "Do it and I will arrange for a payment of five million Albanian Lek—"

"Thirty-five thousand pounds sterling."

"Yes it is, and we can make it six million, to be paid to your mother. ISIS will say you died a hero for Islam, your name will be revered."

"I…"

"Just do it, you have no choice."

She gets up and hammers the door. An officer arrives to let her out. "You weren't long."

"I have discussed the case with my client, he has declined my services. I will not be needed."

"Fair enough, as long as he knows it may harm his defence."

"He does, I have told him so."

"OK, thank you Miss—"

"Rahman."

"Yes, I will inform DSU Boyd."

"Thank you. There's one thing. Mr Temo would like some time to compose himself."

"I'll return him to his cell; there he'll have all the time in the world there to compose himself."

The solicitor smiles and leaves.

Two hours later lunch is delivered to Temo in his cell. The officer finds his prostrate body, kneeling over his bed. He thinks he is sleeping at first but when he moves him he falls to the side in a heap. A doctor is called but he is pronounced dead. The empty capsule was found in his hand. It is taken for analysis and confirmed as cyanide. This evening, the inspector calls a meeting in the hall to 'alert the locals of developments surrounding the apprehension of Victor Temo'.

He is introduced by the chairman then turns to those in the hall. "I thank you to you all for coming here today especially on so cold a night."

The drunken father pushes into a seat at the front next to the hack. "I hope you are going to tell us something to warm our hearts, Inspector, like you have our man, dead or alive."

It is more dead, father, I have the man's soul.

"If I could be allowed to report, Mr Rooney; of course I understand your need to receive information on developments, but—"

"Aye, but," Caber says, "we, in this community, have a right to hear what you have to say before anyone else."

The hack cuts in. "And to the outside world?"

"I have asked you all here to update you simultaneously."

"Well, get on with it."

The father murmurs under his breath. "Aye, get on with it. We know you have arrested and charged the Albanian."

The hack has the floor. "The whole country knows the man has been arrested. The copy is done for tomorrow's papers, it's well out, but I would appreciate the scoop, the inside story, given I decide to stay here rather than hightailing it down the road."

Caber takes it from him. "Shut up Scott; let him get on with it. And you too Rooney, let him do what he brought us here to do."

"Yes, fine, thank you." The inspector is fumbling with his papers. "Right, as you know." He looks up. "Five days ago, on Monday seventh of November we arrested and charged Victor Temo for the murder of Calum Rooney." Again, he looks up. "Well, he denies the charge."

Caber shakes his head. "Tell us something new."

"Yes, indeed I will, Mr McKinnon. He asserted his innocence, saying he would plead not guilty to the charge. He was due to appear in court on Monday and to be remanded in HMP Abertay to await trial."

"He was a lackey."

"Please, Mr Rooney."

"Well, we— you and I— know he was."

"Indeed, well earlier today Victor Temo met with his counsel with the intention of briefing her to frame his denial and construct his defence."

Caber quips. "Defence, what defence can he have?"

"Mr McKinnon, he protests his innocence. He affirms he was at the bar during the time it is alleged Calum was killed."

Then he growls, "He's a lying bastard."

Caber's wife is one with him. "Thank god you got him. We can all sleep better in our beds. Let us hope he burns in hell." Indeed, Shelia McKinnon, his soul will know no rest. "I knew it was him."

"And what makes you think you have the right man?" All look at the father. "I mean, there's no smoking gun, nothing."

The inspector replies to this. "We have circumstantial and … corroborating evidence, which alleges Mr Temo left the Small Isles bar between the hours of 4 and 6 p.m. on the evening of the first of November, made his way by car, which he placed out of sight, to Lochdarrach School where he apprehended Calum Rooney and took him to an unknown location, where he murdered him, then placed him on Claigan beach, thereafter to return to the bar. It is further alleged Mr Temo had followed Mr Rooney and his wife and son here to the Highlands to kill."

"Even if he had followed us up here, Calum would never have gone with him. I know he wouldn't."

Dram supports his view. "He was in the bar. I saw him."

The inspector is determined to correct him. "You have been interviewed in that regard, Mr Shaw, as have others who were in the bar that evening, and no one can vouch for Mr Temo being in the bar for a sufficient time between the hours of four and six, to demonstrate he could not have killed the child."

"Funny that."

"Sorry, Mr Rooney."

"Funny no one can vouch for the times he was in the bar."

"You have your man, Rooney," Caber says, "be thankful for that."

"I don't have my man. *They* have their man, you mean. *Their* man, or should I say they have *a* man, *a* man, any man, but not *the* man." He turns to the congregation. "Can you sleep in your beds in the knowledge they have the wrong man? *He* is still out there somewhere."

"Get real, Rooney. The Albanian did it, solid as a rock, and that'll do us. Now, maybe we can get on with our lives."

"Aye," Caber's wife, Shelia adds, "and maybe the media circus will up tent and head back to the lowlands, where it is best suited. The *low*lands are well used to that."

The hack is keen to question this. "Can we ask what evidence you have to suggest he was sent here to kill the boy?"

"I did not say to kill the boy. We have sworn testimony to suggest he arrived here in Lochdarrach to pursue Mr Rooney, to do him harm. We … postulate while here he decided by killing Mr Rooney's son this would harm him most."

"Makes sense," Caber suggests.

The father gets to his feet and moves towards the stage. "It's a lie, it's a set up. I'll sue the fucking life out of Police Scotland if you have fucked this up."

"Please, Rooney," the chairman says. "Please take your seat."

"And why should I?"

"Because, I have an important announcement to make," the inspector says.

"You already made your announcement, Inspector," the hack says. "It is being printed as we speak and will appear as tomorrow's headline news."

"I have more to say."

Shelia McKinnon is becoming impatient. "How long will this go on, Inspector, we want to get home?"

"There is no way to say this other than—"

"To just say it Inspector." Caber is equally impatient. "There's more to this and we want to hear it."

"Victor Temo is dead."

The silence in the hall is deafening.

"Jesus, now there's a scoop." The hack gets on his iPhone.

And the father is back on his feet. "What are you saying?"

"Victor Temo was found dead in his cell earlier this afternoon. We believe he committed suicide."

"Suicide in a secure cell, that's a good one."

"We have begun an investigation to establish the cause and the means of his death. Suffice to say we will keep you informed of this, but we have no reason to think he was not our man nor that he did not kill Calum. All we have, by this latest … event, is a guilty man finding an easy way out, to avoid the shame of appearing in court and of spending the rest of his life in a Scottish prison."

"And you don't smell a rat, Inspector? You are happy with that. He killed my son, then he killed himself. Is that it?"

"Unless the investigation on his death says otherwise, yes, Mr Rooney."

"A stitch up."

"We cannot expect you to think otherwise, Mr Rooney, but suffice to say we will be scaling down the murder investigation."

"Fuck."

The inspector turns to address the congregation. "So, you will all see a noticeable reduction in police numbers in the area, which as you indicate should prompt a diminution in media interest. Let us hope this leads to a return to normal activities in Lochdarrach, Stoer, and Achfara. Thank you for coming and have a good evening."

The slow hand clap starts with Shelia. "Well, done, Inspector Boyd, well done." A few others join in as they filter out.

The father is defiant. "Aye, well done, Inspector, done your job and got your man, case closed, no defence in court, no one to contradict your findings. Temo has been silenced, convenient that."

"Sorry, Mr Rooney?"

"You heard me, this is a stitch up; and what about McDonald? The man has form in harming children. He was in the area when my son was murdered. Why wasn't he a suspect? Why are you putting all your eggs in one basket with Temo? Why was he murdered?"

"We have no evidence to suggest—"

"Oh aye, his hands were tied behind his back and he was found face down in a burn; no evidence?"

"We were informed he died a natural death, Mr Rooney. We have no reason to suggest he was murdered."

"Je-sus!"

Caber pipes up. "Rooney, you have a right cheek to point your finger at anyone in this community, given *your* background."

"We had nothing like this before you came," Shelia McKinnon adds.

"No, and what if the guy who did it is still around, maybe even in here? Do you hear that the people of Lochdarrach, Stoer, and Achfara; he is still out there, or in here!"

The chairman is on his feet. "Mr Rooney, you are out of order."

"Out of order. Well, don't unlock your doors just yet. He's coming to get you. And if he doesn't get you, I will."

The inspector will not allow this. "No threats, Mr Rooney."

"And you, sir, you and your boss in Glasgow will be brought to book. Even if you can't see it, this will finish your career in disgrace. You can forget your pension, sir."

"And I will finish you right here and now." Caber tries to reach the father, but is held back by his wife and others.

The hack is back talking on his phone. "Community meeting, yes, ends in pandemonium, major accusations made by the father of the murdered child against the investigating officer and, do you hear me, the chief constable. Get that out, I'll fill you in later." The hack turns to the father. "What, are you saying, Rooney? What did you say about his boss in Glasgow, the chief constable, will you make a statement?"

"You'll be the first to know, Scott. But, there is something I want to know, Inspector, and perhaps the public too. Why is a detective inspector in charge of this case, when in most cases of such seriousness the length and breadth of the country, it is a detective superintendent, a DSU who would be leading the investigation? Give me an answer to that?"

"I am more than competent and qualified, Mr Rooney."

"A child is dead, another person, McDonald is also murdered. The murder in the machair, does this not warrant a DSU?"

"Well, Inspector?" the hack prompts.

"And whose decision was it, Inspector; none other than the chief constable himself who decides to appoint a DCI to the case?"

"As you will remember, I was allocated to the case from Abertay. I was first on the scene with PC Broomlands and continued with the role throughout; continuity, Mr Rooney, continuity."

"Oh, yes, and the chief constable, my son's grandfather, who could have allocated *the* best policeman, woman, DSU or even higher grade in the country, decides to stay with you a hick from the sticks, to investigate the most controversial case in the highlands, of his grandson, the son of a deputy chief constable. I don't buy it."

"Retired DCC, Mr Rooney."

"She would have done a damn site better job than you, Inspector, believe me."

"Mr Rooney, I formed a sizeable and capable inquiry team to carry out the investigation and am supported by the DSU in Abertay *and* supervised by the chief constable himself."

"So, a puppet of the chief constable; he's pulling your strings, Boyd."

"You are out of order, Mr Rooney. I think you need…"

"Help, support, a caring community, a decent police service, my son."

"I think…" The chairman is trying to bring this meeting to a close.

Until the hack decides to wade in behind the father. "I think Mr Rooney is saying something seriously important here, Mr Boyd. I think he deserves a reply from Police Scotland. I think the public and the people of these communities deserve a reply from Police Scotland."

"I will convey his points to the chief constable. If he has a complaint to make about the probity of this investigation, he should put it to the Scottish Police Authority, where in due course it will be examined and replied to, now…"

"I want a reply from the chief constable. He made the decision not to appoint a qualified investigating officer."

The hack supports him. "Well, Inspector?"

No answer was the loud reply.

"Well, the gloves come off tonight. The father is back. I'll take divine retribution. I've sat back too long and let you … philistines fuck this up. Now I'll take an almighty hand in this sham investigation."

All look the father's way. What is he saying?

"I warn you, Mr Rooney, do not interfere in police matters. I know how you must feel, but you must not take these matters into your own hands. It could only lead one way."

"And what's that, Inspector, my arrest, my suicide in custody, another convenient event?"

"Mr Rooney…"

"You haven't seen anything of me yet … Inspector. God will protect his own and smite the wrongdoers." The father is on his feet and pointing his forefingers towards all there on the stage. "The voice of the Lord will strike with flashes of lightning; beware, beware."

"I think, Mr Rooney, should…" Caber is heading towards the father, but he is up and going towards the door, muttering in an indiscernible language.

He is also pursued by the hack. "Rooney, Mr Rooney. Mr Kaminski, the chief constable?"

The father and the hack end up in the bar. The father pulls up a stool, slams a ten pound note on the bar and demands a double whisky. "Now, woman, dammit."

Maggie scowls at him. "Not with that tone, Rooney. I've seen aggression before in you, and I am not having it."

"I'll look after him, Maggie," the hack says. "I'll keep him right. I'll have the same and one for yourself for later, and maybe I can join you in that."

She throws a smile his way and takes his twenty, to return with two glasses of whisky.

The hack returns the smile, then turns to the father. "If you don't mind me saying so, Rooney. You've been acting a bit … odd since you came back from Glasgow."

"And journalist, what do you know of my going to Glasgow?"

"I saw you in here on the night before you left and saw you when you arrived back, and the picture was like night and day. Rooney, what happened to you down there?"

"Oh, you would love to know Scott, a good story there. And you've landed on your feet with this one." The father downs the whisky in one. "Get me another and maybe you'll loosen my tongue."

The hack gets another. I can see what he is doing, but I doubt if the father cares. I have some idea why the living act in such a way, but those without my knowledge would have no such thoughts on his behaviour. That he has been drinking may be viewed as acceptable; he had lost his son, after all.

The hack possesses the skill to draw it out of him, but I fear it will not be to the father's benefit, but to his. "Many a man goes on the drink on losing a family member." The hack gets close to the father at the bar, both side-by-side, head down, inches from the bar. Not an unusual sight for a highland pub. "It is expected if you lose a son, but it is your behaviour, Rooney, which is, can I say, incongruous."

“Incongruous, Mr Scott, now there is the word. You wouldn’t be trying to sweet-talk me?”

“I hope you don’t mind me saying it, but you appear consumed in yourself, locked in psychobabble, saying strange things. In here I have seen you talking, screaming to yourself, berating yourself, demanding others to order more whisky, beer, or wine. Every day you come in here you head to this corner of the bar, only leaving this spot to go to the toilet. And I’ve heard you in there. ‘Fuck off, bastard, leave me alone,’ is a common cry coming from the cubicle in there.”

Indeed, I have heard it and so have the people of the bar. Far from agreeing with the truth of what the hack says, he springs to his feet and flails his arms above his head as if to shake off a large crow that has settled there, but it is the anger in the man which unsettles everyone.

“‘You are here to punish me,’ is another utterance I hear.”

“Oh, you are the psychologist? No, I am the psychologist, Scott; me, and I was the best.”

“Indeed, sir, I know this. I know about your career in Glasgow, I carried it for the Times.”

“Oh, you did; juicy was it?”

“Why do you think I came here, Mr Rooney? You are a public interest story.”

“Oh, a public interest story. Well, I’ll give you a story, Mr Scott; just pin your ears back and I’ll give you a story which will make your eyes water. Now get me another drink.”

“Indeed I will, sir.”

Over the course of the next two hours, the hack gives the father what he wants to drink and the father gives the hack most of what he wants to hear. For example, how the chief used his fists and bullying to get to the top of Police Scotland; how the mother broke through the glass ceiling of the same organisation using every method possible, including her father to get there; then to the relationship breakdown and the mother’s relationship with the friend. How he, the father, through his crime syndicate was involved in the killing of people in Glasgow; and juiciest of all, his relationship with a head MI5 agent and her eventual murder.

“Enough for you to get on with, Mr Scott?” The father is surprised the hack is not bowled over with this information. “Do you know something?”

"What is that, sir?"

The father shakes his head. "There is something about you just doesn't make sense."

"Indeed sir, not much of any of this makes sense. "For your … assistance, I would like to give you something in return."

"What can *you* give me?"

"McDonald."

"Go on?"

"It was me that drew blood from his nose."

"Didn't kill him, the PM said it didn't."

"I knew what I was doing." *Is this man more than just a journalist*, the father wonders. "I traced the boys," confirms he is.

"The boys he abused?"

"Aye, and wasn't hard. There was coverage at the time. They were sent to and adopted by a couple in Glasgow. Got into big trouble, drugs, violence, gang stuff, both ended up in prison for a time, became hard men in Glasgow. It wasn't difficult to track them down."

"An inevitable career profile for the lads."

"They were at his funeral."

"They killed him?"

"I asked them if they did, in Glasgow. They were noncommittal, but they were here. They saw your son's coverage on TV, and assumed McDonald did it."

"They knew him better than anyone."

"Indeed, they had decided to kill him anyway when the time was right, seemed as good a time as any. Travelled up that night, asked in the pub where he was."

"They were in the pub?"

"They were."

"And no one said a dicky-bird."

"No."

"They were told he would be on his walk and where he would be. They followed him up the path and waited until I was out of sight and then they faced him. They tied his hands, said they were there to shoot him, his face drained of blood, and he keeled over and fell face first into the burn, dead as a post; his heart gave out. They were content with that and left him there."

"The boys were back in town."

"They sure were."

"They were in the pub asking about McDonald, where he was on the night of his death, and no one came forward to say that."

"No."

"Closed ranks, enough bad publicity going on, without opening up another scandal."

"Right."

"And Police Scotland doesn't mount an investigation into his death. His hands were tied behind his back, he had abused children, he was a suspect in the murder of my son and he was in the right place, with the right credentials."

"Though he didn't drive, never did."

"He might have come across Calum on the road." The father puts his head onto his arms on the bar. "Calum gets out of the car, is walking home, McDonald comes across him. No one comes forward; not even to mention the abuse, or the boys."

"Or the potential of him being the killer?"

"No."

"He comes from their community; better the killer from outside."

"And the police don't pursue it; collusion or what?"

"And why I am here talking to you."

"Eh?"

"Why didn't the chief pursue it to the nth degree, his grandson?"

"Step."

"Step grandson."

"He didn't want to?"

"Right, and why not?"

"I have my thoughts on that."

"I am sure you do, Rooney, but the thing I agree with most about what you said in the hall is this goes all the way to the top, to the chief constable."

"To the King of Sodom and Gomorra, Mr Scott. I think more whisky is required."

The hack orders two more as the father goes off to the toilet. On the way he knocks over a table of drinks, sending broken glass and alcohol across the floor. Magnus warns him about his behaviour, saying he would bar him. He would not, however, knowing the pain of the man; but he knows any similar incident outside the pub would bring in the law.

Dram staggers in as the father is about to leave the toilet. Boozers normally get on, sharing the common experience of intoxication, but not this time. "You awright, Rooney?" Dram asks. The father pounces on him and punches him in the face and body, knocking him to the floor.

The father snarls, "You knew about McDonald." Hearing the commotion, the caber arrives and pushes the father back so hard he falls against the toilet wall. "You bastards protect your own." He slides to the floor and moans to himself. "It's the lord's work I have to do." He looks upwards through the window. "Oh lord, give me the power to punish these wicked people." Magnus Stuart calls the constable.

Broomlands arrives and, far from arresting him and sticking him in the solitary police cell in Stoer, through Maggie he contacts the friend who is staying in the hotel. The friend and the constable take the father home. The mother is in bed when the constable opens the door and drops him in a chair next to the kitchen table. "You need to talk to him, Jackie. He is way out of order. He hit Dram in the toilet, left him in a mess, Black is attending to him now."

The mother wanders through the kitchen to the fridge where she extracts a tray of ice. For gin, the constable presumes. She falls as she makes her way back through and out of the room. The friend picks her up as the constable shakes his head in the recognition she too is drunk. "Keep an eye on them, Ben. Do you think I should contact the council to have them supervised until they are back to their senses?"

The friend shakes his head. "I'll look after them," he says.

The inspector phones the chief. "Good evening, sir, I am sorry to call you at home, and so late."

"That's fine Boyd, I told you to. What you got for me?"

"Sir, you would have heard about Temo?"

"Yes, of course, shame that. We will of course state publically our view on the sufficiency of evidence he did it. Good enough for you?"

"Yes sir."

"Good, wrap it up, son."

"Yes sir. Sir?"

"What?"

"Rooney says he is to raise a case with the Scottish Police Authority. He says a proper investigation has not been carried out and you are implicated in this."

"That's fine Boyd, you leave it with me."

"And sir, Jackie and Rooney."

"Yes, Boyd, I know, leave that with me as well."

The chief calls the friend immediately after talking to the inspector. The friend is in the parents' kitchen observing the father lying flat out over the kitchen table, after having just put the mother to bed. "Hello son," the chief says. "I am worried about my daughter."

"Yes sir, me too."

"How is she?"

"She's—"

"Crashed?"

"Let's say she is tired and emotional, sir."

"I want you to act."

"I'll do what I can."

"Thank you. If you need my help let me know."

The friend does not need the chief's help. I follow him along the path and into the father's shed. In there, I observe him searching the place, through the desk, boxes, the files. He is in the filing cabinet, as the father appears at the door. "Can I help you, Ben; looking for something?" he slurs, both hands on the door frame to hold himself up. The friend shakes his head and with the heel of his foot closes the bottom drawer of the filing cabinet then pushes out past the father.

CHAPTER 15

The friend awakens on the morning to the sound of the mother asking, "You alright, want some tea?"

"What's more important is, are you alright?" He pulls himself up on the couch, his bed for the night. "Thanks." He takes the mug of tea.

"Where's Rooney?"

"In the shed with a bottle of whisky."

"I need to talk to you, Jackie."

"You put me to bed last night and brought Rooney home?"

"I did."

She looks at him. *Did he join her*, she wonders. Then she looks towards the outside door. "He's out there, in his man-hut talking to himself. That's where he resides these days, not in here."

"Jackie, I am concerned and so is your father." He swings his legs out of the couch and puts on his shoes. She sits beside him, close.

The boy looks on perplexed. Over the past few days, he has grown older, tired; like a weak, old man. I have been remiss in my duty to escort him away. He will suffer the longer he is here. I question myself. Why am I leaving him here? Am I hoping he would be able to overcome his kind of passing, his murder, to reach a kind of acceptance; to move on in a peaceful way, but it is clear he will not? I know there is more to my decision to leave him. Is it my perverse interest in his type of death, his murder? Is he a part of my study into this human act, even although it grates with my duty to offer a sure transition to the other side? It needs to wait.

The friend is getting closer to the father's wife than would be respectable in this community. He puts his arm around her now and kisses her on her head. This time, contrary to the last time, she does not resist. "He has lost it, Jackie, and you are vulnerable." She does not respond as she would have done to defend her husband.

"You know what I mean; he's off it, psychotic; you know what he is capable of."

It was the 'what he is capable of,' that triggers a response. "Oh, and what is he … capable of, Ben, his friend."

Her tone is enough to create some healthy distance between them. "He has … killed, Jackie, you know that."

She gets to her feet. "Not directly, the Family—"

"No? He has the capacity to harm, you fucking know that."

His swearing marks a change in the tone of their discussion, as he intends.

"And what do you know about his … capacity?"

"Turnbull, Jackie; in Glasgow, when he was down."

"What, who; what are you getting at?"

"Josh Turnbull, a guy who just happened to be found shot after Rooney ran into him in an alley round from the Scotia Bar."

"And how do you know this?"

"Bingham told me. He called me to say he was worried about Rooney."

"Because you and Rooney are friends; right?"

"Right. He met Bingham, the night I met him in Tennent's."

"And he was worried about him?"

"He gave him a gun."

"A gun?"

"Aye, a gun."

"The idiot, why didn't he—"

"I guess he didn't want to upset you, you have enough going on."

"I've got more going on now."

"Here, look, the Evening Times."

The friend reaches into his jacket and pulls out a newspaper. She reads aloud. "Josh Turnbull, hit man for the mob, survives Family shoot out to be found dead in alley next to the Scotia Bar. Jesus."

"Well?"

"How do you know it was him?"

"I don't know him anymore."

"No, and he doesn't know you, and I don't know you. Some friend you are to him."

"I am being the best friend I can be to him and to you. I can't stand by and let this happen."

"Let what happen?"

"He is dangerous, a risk to you."

"He is no risk to me."

"No, and what about Johnston's death; you know he had something to do with that, and the McGings in Ashton Lane, and even Jean perhaps; and what about Calum?"

She gets to her feet. "Calum," she shrieks. "Calum was his son." The boy retreats to the corner by the window to squeeze himself in there between the two walls.

"I need to ask you something, Jackie?"

"Aw, go on, get it out."

"Will you calm down?" She sits and he moves to her side. "But before I do, I need to tell you."

"What do you need to tell me?"

"That, I love you."

She looks at him for a few seconds. "Ben, I don't need to hear it again."

The friend's voice reaches a pitch echoing through the room. "But I do, Jackie," he shouts. "I do." She looks at the door, wondering if her husband can hear this. She is less angry now, as if she is thinking about it. "I am worried about you. How can you be sure he—"

The mother returns to attack mode. "Didn't, didn't, didn't." With each 'didn't', she slaps his face, leaving red, going on purple, marks. "Didn't murder his child, is that what you mean, you bastard?" The 'you bastard', precludes a shove of the friend across the room, almost reaching the boy in the corner. The friend does not reply but straightens himself. He then finds a chair to finish his tea, not looking her way. "You are a disgrace as a friend, Ben. You fuck me, fuck his wife, and now you accuse him of killing his son, such … appalling behaviour."

"Jackie, I don't think Rooney has been completely honest, about Calum."

"Oh?"

"There's just something which doesn't fit … about his story."

"Oh, well tell me about it."

"I can't, Jackie. If I did, it may implicate him and I can't do that."

She drops to her seat and picks up her mug. “How do you know what he said to me?” The friend doesn’t answer. “Why don’t you keep out of our business?”

“Jackie, I am his named person under the Act. I think he needs to go back to hospital, for your safety.”

“Fine, just lock him up.”

The friend reaches across to her and takes her hand. “You need to think of yourself, Jackie. I’ll look after you.”

His mobile phone buzzes in his pocket. “Yes, if you wish, yes,” he says, answering it.

“I need to go, Jackie, but please think about what I said.”

She doesn’t answer as he leaves; she just stares at the door, an empty look in her eyes.

She goes to the shed and pushes the door open. “You fucker.”

A “what?” comes from the dark corner.

“Turnbull?”

“Aye.”

“Calum?

“Aye.”

“Can I trust you?”

“Come in, have a drink.”

“I hope you drown in your … drink.”

I observe human engagement with interest. I appreciate the living condition, the games they play, the way they respond or do not. I observe their human ‘emotion’, but I know not of the condition myself. I appreciate the intensity of the feelings they show in painful times. I have seen them in their depths of misery. I see them in their response to the loss of their own and I know of the thing they call love, but I know nothing of it myself, not having had what they would describe as ‘feelings’. In my work I am not allowed to ‘feel’. How could I, involved in the death and dying of these beings, in such an important task, requiring a clear mind? I must do no more than reach in and remove their soul, pack it off, dispatch it to where it is destined to go, and that is that, no more, no ‘feelings’; though, it doesn’t mean I don’t get … interested.

The priest had telephoned the father’s friend asking if he could come to see him. The friend wonders why but understands he has to go.

"Hello Ben, thank you for seeing me today." The priest invites him to sit in his office. I look around the room; the furniture has not changed in over one hundred years, the mahogany desk has never moved in the same time. I look at the pictures of the dead priests. I knew them all, not that I took them; they have their own being—some call it an angel—no different from me. There are god-like images everywhere, in particular one of the man on the cross they call Jesus.

"Sunday afternoon, Father. Not got a busy day for you?"

There is a picture of the recent pope on the wall behind his desk. I do not know which one; they look all the same to me.

"Always time for a cup of tea, would you like some?" The priest taps the top of a china teapot.

"No, Father, and no problem, I am just not sure why—"

"I should want to see you?"

The friend nods. "Yes, though I presume it is to do with Rooney, me being his friend. Of course he is way out of order and said some serious things about this community last night, got into a fight, thrown out of the pub, taken home by me and the constable. I am worried about him." The friend nearly looks sincere.

The priest pours tea into a china cup. *Very dainty*, the friend thinks; little does he know he also uses it for his drams. The priest adds milk. "Yes, of course you are, and so am I. I have offered pastoral support, guidance, counselling even, but I don't think he appreciates I can help him."

The friend wonders how qualified the priest is to make such offerings, but declines the question. "No offence, Father, but Rooney is not open to spiritual guidance. He has a lot of hang-ups about the church."

"I suspected as such, he never comes to mass."

If only he knew, the friend thinks. "I offer as much support as he would like me to give. We were, are friends."

The priest gives an intended pause. "Yes, indeed."

The pause and the 'yes indeed' convinces the friend the priest is about to say something more, something significant. "Is there something else on your mind, Father?"

"Yes, Ben, something important, a sensitive matter."

"A sensitive matter?"

The friend ponders on the nature of 'sensitive matters' in this community, like who was 'having it off with whom', reaching the priest's ears. Was he about to say anything about Jackie and him, he wonders?

"Yes, about the church."

"The church?" The friend almost sounds relieved.

"It's best I come out and say it."

"Yes, please do?" Intrigue has replaced concern.

"There is a matter with which I need your advice."

"My advice?" This is not what the friend expects to hear.

"You are a social worker." And not what he wants to hear.

"I am, but I am not practising, but a social worker nonetheless of over thirty years' experience." The friend gets up. He has more to do than offer social work to the parishioners. "If it is concerning local authority support you should contact the local office in Invernevis. I am sure they will be only too pleased to help."

"No, I don't want to." The priest is trying hard not to show annoyance. "It's advice of a personal nature."

The friend has heard this before many times, what the social work department may think about personal matters brought to its notice. Although, I also hear people talk about being unhappy about the social services, a care package, the quality of care provided, or funding, always funding.

"OK, go ahead, Father, but you have to realise I cannot talk on behalf of the local authority, it is my professional opinion, *my* opinion, no more, no less."

"Indeed, I understand." The priest pours more tea, as if he is summoning up some 'divine' strength; perhaps he should add his dram?

"Thank you."

"It is about a matter of confidence." The friend knows the priest would develop this point. "In which I am reluctant to divulge elsewhere."

Oh dear, the friend thinks, *time to put the lid on this*. "I cannot promise anything outwith my professional codes, nor anything which would require me, statutorily, to divulge to the authorities."

"What if we speak rhetorically?"

"Rhetorically, like it wasn't real?"

What like god, I wonder.

"Something like that."

"OK, let's see how it goes, but if it crosses the line into reality, I will have to tell you where I stand legally, etcetera."

"OK, Ben."

"Right Father, go ahead."

The games they play.

"Right, there is a boy in a parish who says he is being touched by a significant adult in this community and he has told this to a priest."

"Holy shit!" The friend gets to his feet; not the right thing to say in this place. "Touched?"

"Indeed." The priest turns towards the pope. "Should this priest report this to the authorities, this man's reputation would be destroyed."

Reputation is very important for the living in this place and sometimes the dead, sometimes more important for the dead.

The friend nods. "Go on."

"However, if this priest divulges this, he would break his vow of silence *and* his confessional vow."

I look at this rhetorical priest wondering how often he talks in rhetorical terms to his parishioners.

"Difficult one, Father. Although church policy is clear on child abuse, it has to be reported, it is also the law."

It is clear the priest does not wish to consider the law.

"Even if it destroys a good man?"

The word good is often used to refer to the priest's flock: good people, good Christians; but not all good.

"A good man doesn't abuse children, Father."

I like this, a contradiction, I like contradictions.

"Even if he is innocent?"

Go on, say an innocent man doesn't abuse children? I want to hear what the priest would say to this.

"How would it destroy him if he was innocent?"

Innocence would destroy a good man? The contradiction becomes a puzzle.

"Small communities, Ben."

Now I understand.

"It doesn't matter."

Of course, he is right, why should it, but the priest is about to say it does. "And if it isn't true, it destroys the boy."

"How?"

"By branding him a liar."

A moral dilemma, I think, perhaps irreconcilable; is the boy more important than the man?

"Mmm."

Yes, mmm.

"He would be seen to be a liar in front of his school, his peers, the community, a small community."

He would.

"I see."

"He would also be…"

"Yes?"

"Beaten."

He would.

"Beaten?"

"Yes, his father is dead and his mother is known for her harsh … discipline."

She is. The father died a 'disciplinarian'; this did not stop me taking him. People are no longer 'aggressive' after death.

"Oh."

"The boy is already a solitary figure, he's a sensitive child; I fear it would … harm him, more."

I agree; I know this child.

"And if it continued, would that not harm him even more?"

Ah ha, the horns of the dilemma. Is one harm more harmful than another?

"If it is happening and it continued of course."

"Of course."

"And this is all rhetorical; so I can tell you, indeed, you have a duty to protect a child."

"Yes, but you can't tell me I have a duty, because it is rhetorical."

I cannot keep up with this rhetoric. I prefer facts: fact, he did it, fact, he will account; fact, I will make him account.

"I can tell you, should this not be rhetorical; you need to protect the child by informing the authorities."

The priest stares at him. "Which would betray a good man, potentially harm a child; and, given the sensitivity of a community in the public eye, harm a community."

More harm?

The friend wonders if this is moving into the pit of hyperbole. "You have to do what is right, Father," he says, stepping around it.

"Rhetorically speaking?"

"Real or rhetorical, Father."

A real or rhetorical father or a real or rhetorical god, I wonder. I look at the man on the cross, real or rhetorical, I wonder. Does it matter? Do the people really care?

"Thank you, Ben."

They both get up at the same time. The conversation had become tedious, for them and for me. The priest shows the friend out, I follow him down the stair and past the graves. You will forgive my scepticism, I see these people alive and I see them dead, but in fairness I cannot say where they go. Suffice to say it is neither real nor rhetorical.

The mother needs to get out. She heads for the beach, close to where the boy was found. I walk beside her, he does too. It is close in time to when the boy died. It is as if she wants to walk in his footsteps. It is dark, getting close to the winter solstice. She follows the line of the beach, just to the right of the waves crashing on the shore. Wrapped up well from the cold, she is deep in thought, her woollen hat down over her ears. This day she is destined to die, but I will not allow it, I will refuse to take her.

There is a sound of footsteps behind her making their way towards her; she does not hear this. He is on her before she has a chance to turn, to fight him, to flee. He grabs her by the neck and pulls her to the ground. He holds her in a strangle grip, she cannot breathe. The boy flinches at this, like he is re-dying his own death. Within the next few minutes she should have died. I see Jacqueline Kaminski RIP Dec 2, 1970–Nov 13, 2016, on her gravestone. I see Rooney standing over it crying, her father and the man who attacks her now there too.

But it is not her time. I roar with all my might with a sound which would scare any human witless. It does so this time also. The man releases his grip and flees. The mother gets on her knees and calls after him through the wind. "Bastard," she screams. "Bastard." The boy kneels beside her, while he looks at me confused. Perhaps he would have preferred she had joined him, they would have been together, but even for one so small he realises she is better alive. He appears relieved. "What was that sound?" she says, as she gets to her feet.

The father is on the path outside the shed as she arrives home, as if he heard something too. "Someone tried to kill me, Rooney."

"I'll call Broomlands."

"No, it's my own fault."

"Your fault?"

"Yes, for agreeing to come here with you. Everything that has happened to me is because of you, and it's my fault for getting back with you."

The father does not know how close she was to death and he too. He would have killed himself should it have happened. In his deranged state of mind with the effects of alcohol he would have taken enough tablets to stop his heart and end his life. Then all of this, which started with the boy's death, would have been no more; it would pass into the history of this place. They had come here and died here, to be buried together in the graveyard, in the same place where I lie.

He tries to embrace her. She flinches and coories next to the AGA to warm herself. He wraps a large towel around her. She throws it on the floor and pushes past him as she heads to the bedroom. It is clear she is moving away from him inside too. She has reached the end of her tether.

CHAPTER 16

The priest arranges to see the chairman. It is thirteen days since the boy died. He believes it has a community purpose, a charity tea perhaps, some support for the church renovation, objections to the planning permission for a housing plot near to the old cemetery.

The chairman starts. "You wanted to see me, Father?"

"Yes, John, thank you for coming."

The priest offers tea or coffee, the chairman refuses both. They sit looking over the bay, across the inner sound. The chairman becomes impatient. "If you'll excuse me, I need to get back to my work."

"Yes, of course, the bus."

"Yes, the bus." The chairman waits a few seconds and asks again. "You wanted to see me, Father."

"Yes, I did."

The priest is looking towards the door.

"Father, you wanted to see me."

Just then Caber McKinnon arrives. "I'm sorry I am late."

"Hello Caber, guess this is community business."

"Guess so, John; well, Father?"

"Yes, of course. I asked you both here to discuss a matter of … importance to the community, a serious and confidential matter."

Caber says, "Oh a bit of intrigue, Father, I like it."

"Aye, a bit of intrigue," the chairman adds.

"I don't know how to say this," the priest says.

"The best way to say anything, Father is to say it," Caber says.

"Yes, Father, I need to get back to the bus, the children will be finishing school soon."

The priest gets up and moves a safe distance, not to tackle the chairman face on, then blurts it out. "I don't think you should be doing the bus today, John."

The chairman looks astounded. "What you talking about – I do it every day, every weekday."

The priest glances at the caber, but his words are for the chairman. "After what I have to say I don't think you'll be doing the bus anymore."

"You need to come out with it, Father."

"Yes, get on with it," the chairman says. "I've no time for—"

"Andrew Dewar?"

"Andrew Dewar?" The chairman's face drains of blood. "Andrew Dewar, Father, why would you want to talk about Andrew Dewar?"

"I don't suppose there is any right way of saying this."

"But by saying it, Father?"

"Yes." The priest begins a slow pace from one end of the room to the other, stopping long enough to turn towards the chairman. "I have information the boy has been … abused."

The chairman appears relieved this is not directed at him. "This is terrible; have you told anyone, the authorities?"

"No, I have not."

"This is a police matter, Father," Caber says. "It's a responsibility you know, legal; you have to report suspicions of child abuse."

"I know."

The chairman goes on. "Is it a local man?"

"Yes."

"I see now, I understand, a local man," the chairman says. "The three of us together would deal with such matters. I understand."

"It is why I want to talk to you."

"Of course, and I will help in any way I can, in my civic capacity, and of course again I will treat this in confidence as you would expect."

Caber asks, "Who are we referring to, Father?"

"Indeed, you need to know, Mr McKinnon."

The priest takes a breath, then turns to face the chairman. "It is you, sir." The chairman's bloated face drains of blood once more and he starts to take deep breaths as sweat is profuse on his brow.

"Father, I don't understand, I, me, Andrew Dewar."

"I don't want you to say anymore, John, but it must stop."

"Now, listen, priest."

Aggressive words get the caber to his feet. "John!"

The priest is animated too. "It must stop, John, or else I must…"

The chairman moves towards the priest; the caber sees this and puts his heavy frame between them. "Sit down, John."

The chairman returns to his seat. "This is a bloody serious thing to say, Father. I just hope you know what you are saying. I have friends."

"Please, John, don't make me say anymore, give more detail to a nasty … habit."

Habit, is this a real of rhetorical habit?

The chairman defends himself. "I am being accused, priest, of a heinous thing. I, I will bloody well challenge this nonsense."

In this community one does not call a priest 'priest'. Caber moves closer to him. "Steady, John."

"I don't want you to, John." If the priest was thinking the chairman would leave to give his words careful consideration he was mistaken.

"You, the boy, there is a bloody mistake here, Father. I am the leader of the community council. I have been a respectable figure in this community a lot longer than you have. This is bloody preposterous. I will be taking advice on this matter, consulting my lawyer no less, and I'll thank you to keep your information to yourself, do you know how damaging—"

Caber now takes on the role of the ceilidh bouncer. "Are you listening to him, John McIsaac?" He stands tall over him. "I will limit what I would say to you if there is evidence this is true; but if it is, you are finished in this community."

"I…"

"I believe what the boy has told me."

"You believe what a child says to you over me, the leader of the community council. I…"

"I have to give the child credence."

"You," Caber bellows at the chairman, "you are no more than any other incomer from the south who has inveigled himself into our committee, as you well do."

"I am respected, I am…"

"I know what you are, freemason, and you think that'll give you some protection in this matter. Well, it doesn't wash with me. I'll see you in jail if this is true."

"I don't want that," the priest says.

"What?"

"I don't want the boy dragged through the courts."

"Then it cannot be established," the chairman says.

"It is established here," Caber says. "I'll believe one of ours any day."

"It is my word against the boy's."

Caber grabs the chairman by the neck. "The boy has been through enough at your hands, McIsaac, enough. It stops now."

The chairman wrestles himself free from his grip. "I'll not be condemned by the likes of you," he says to Caber. "And you," he says, turning to the priest. "You'll be hearing from me. This … parish needs reforming."

"It was tried four hundred years ago and failed, sir," the priest says. "Please reflect on my words, Mr McIsaac, you must."

"I must go, I have my bus, the children to pick up."

Caber lunges at him, pinning him to the wall. "The bus, the children or anything to do with the children; no, you will stay away from the children. You will have nothing to do with the children. Do you hear me?"

"I…"

Caber tightens his grip on the chairman's neck. "I will kill you if you go anywhere near them, do you hear me?"

The priest moves between them. "I think he knows, Caber."

"You understand, McIsaac?" The chairman nods his head. "Now take your bus and take yourself from this community. You hear me?" The chairman nods again.

The chairman leaves, cursing. Caber and the priest sit down to discuss this rhetorical situation.

The teacher prepares dinner. There is a heavy atmosphere, even I can sense it.

"You will have had a busy day at the school," the chairman says.

The teacher is cutting onions for the soup. "Much the same as most days, these days." She sniffles from the effects of the onions. "It's hard to get the children going with all that has gone on. What would you like for your tea, I've kippers in the fridge?"

"I suppose; but nothing for me, I've no appetite."

"Why did you get Teenie to taxi the children home today? Did you have problems with the bus again?"

"Aye, bloody wouldn't start again."

"Why didn't you use the car, you've used it before many times."

"Needs an MOT, must get it done soon."

"Yes, you will we need the car." He does not respond. "You have been very quiet."

His eyes too begin to water with the onions. "Do you need to do those bloody things?" He rinses his eyes in the sink.

"And moody."

"I'm OK."

"You have not been very happy. I know your depression can get you, I mean it's a terrible thing."

"I just get on with my work, running the buses, driving the buses, fixing the bloody buses."

She puts the soup on the AGA. "The soup will be ready in half an hour. And the council?"

"What do you mean, you bloody start a sentence about the soup then end it with the council?"

"I know, I am terrible for that. A proper *buaireadair.*"

"And stop the bloody language, I'm no *teuchter.*"

"I need to practice it. What about doing something in the community council, you know to cheer you up, cheer the folk up?"

"It's hard to keep up with you sometimes."

"You could do something, be good for them and for you. You know to lift them out of the doldrums, maybe a dance or something."

"A dance at this time, what with…"

"It's the best time, I think. Be Christmas in a month, a ceilidh, we always do something to raise funds for the old folks' dinner, would help to lift spirits. Raise it at the next meeting."

"Right." He gazes into the open fire.

"I too have been … preoccupied; not so as you noticed. I'll be a lot happier when the inspector gets the man who has brought misery on our community, and he is locked up for good. Then we can get on with our lives."

"It'll never be the same. Might as well bugger off down south again."

"We need to stay here, see it through, for the children's sake. We said we would give it five years."

"Things have changed."

The teacher looks at him. "We've made our home here."

"I might have a kipper after all."

She gets the kippers out of the fridge, wraps them in foil and puts them in the oven. "Potatoes?"

"No."

"I need to ask you something."

"What's that?"

"I don't think…"

"You don't think what?"

"I have known you for thirty years, lived with you for twenty-five. I think I know you."

"What are you saying?"

"I know you have interests."

"For god's sake, what do you mean interests?"

"I've seen the pictures; the internet was open one night; I saw pictures of children."

"Children?"

"Without any clothes."

"Without any clothes?"

"Stop bloody repeating me, you know what I bloody mean: naked children. You have an interest in naked children."

The chairman is on his feet and pacing the kitchen. "I just like the pictures. I get bored around here."

"You liked this kind of pictures way before we came here. I thought getting away from London and the seedy scene there to a quiet place like Achfara would change your … habits."

"The internet doesn't make it any easier."

"It's more than just the internet."

"Doesn't make me a paedophile … anyway it's none of your business."

"You know what that could do, to you, to me. I'm a teacher for god's sake. Do you want veg with your kippers?"

"I said no; anyway it's not an issue."

"There were pictures of Calum."

"Eh?"

"Images, like from the Facebook, on the beach, and some…"

"I have lots of Facebook pictures. Sean Rooney is my friend on Facebook, so are most of the people around here. He posts pictures of Calum on the beach."

"These were in an album, in your pictures folder, he was naked. You aren't eating much?"

"He is always naked on the beach. Appears he likes to go in the sea naked. I am not hungry. God's sake, will you give me a break?"

"Appears to whom?"

"Well, they are on Facebook, so I assume the person who posted them, his father, mother, presumably."

"And what about the ones where his head is put onto other bodies?"

"It's photoshopped."

"Naked boys' bodies?"

"It's just a hobby of mine, there's no harm in it."

"No harm in it."

"Calum?"

"If you thought I had anything to do with Calum, why didn't you tell Inspector Boyd?"

"Because I love you and because I know to implicate you in any way would destroy you. Why won't you take potatoes, and veg?"

"I don't want potatoes or veg. You got it?"

The teacher takes out the kippers. "They are ready. Did you pick up the boy that night?"

"What?"

"Sorry, it's been on my mind and I needed to ask. I didn't mean you did anything. I just wanted…"

"No, and that's all I have to say on the matter. Now, will you get out of my face?" He pushes past her to go into the sitting room. "And stick your kippers."

The teacher puts the kippers back in the AGA high oven and opens the door to the low oven and pulls out an ashet with bread and butter pudding. She places it on the table, takes a large spoon, and fills a bowl to overflowing. "I've bread and butter pudding I know you can't resist, and I've cream to go with it."

He returns and takes it. "Thank you for understanding me."

"You're welcome, darling, shall we watch the news?"

The man they call the chairman is with me now. Fourteen days into the eleventh month, at twenty-seven minutes past the seventh hour, he dispatched his own body from the living. When I got to him, his body and his soul were warm. I reached in and his soul came without a fight. His lifeless body was sitting upright in his car, a hosepipe fed inside, held tight by the driver's window, newspapers stuffed in the gap, the other end fastened by jubilee clips and an arrangement of plumbing joints to the exhaust pipe of the car. He had turned on the ignition, sat back, lit a cigarette, and within fifteen minutes succumbed to carbon monoxide poisoning from the exhaust. He was wearing his Sunday suit, white shirt, and his Harrow High School tie.

The teacher found him, reached in and switched off the engine, then opened the doors to let out the fumes. She fixed his tie and straightened his hair. She did not appear upset at this man's passing. She closed the door and the internal light went off, almost in time with his soul being dispatched. She closed the garage door and went into the house to phone the doctor. Another death certificate is required. The constable called the doctor who pronounced him dead, not difficult to ascertain.

Before he succumbed to cardiac and respiratory failure, he had mental confusion, nausea and vomiting, hallucinations, convulsions, coma, and then me.

The doctor manages to prise a note from his hand.

"Suicide note?" the constable asks.

"I guess."

"What does it say?"

The doctor flattens it out on the bonnet of the car. "It says, 'I have laid down the tools. I regret my actions against those boys. I expect this community to give me due respect.' That's all."

"He said, 'boys', plural."

"Yes, he did."

"What are you going to do?"

"Mrs McIsaac?"

The teacher goes to them. The doctor passes the note to her. She reads it. "My husband was … depressed. I know him."

"He would have been confused as he wrote the note," the doctor says. "Carbon monoxide."

"Yes, confused," the constable says.

The doctor asks the teacher, "Can I get someone to be with you?"

"No, I want to stay with him for a while."

"I'll do the death certificate."

"I don't want suicide on it."

The doctor looks at her. "I'll get in touch with Funeral."

Funeral and I have much in common. We have mutually reliant jobs. He depends on me; I depend on him. He takes the body to its place of rest; I take the soul to its place in eternity.

The doctor and the constable leave her there. They get in their cars and drive off down the coastal road. It is when they reach the road end, the doctor indicates to the constable to look back. What he sees gets him out of his car. They join each other there to look back at the farm where they see flames licking out of the garage containing the chairman's car. They get in their cars and go back to the farm. By the time they get back there, the car and the garage are engulfed in flames. The teacher is standing there, an empty twenty-litre jerry can at her feet, gazing into the flames, like she was looking into a bonfire on the night of the bonfires. There was nothing they could do.

The teacher had taken care of everything, eradicating her husband's body, the suicide note, the car, and any evidence of his suicide. All that's left of him is in my hands.

On the suicide and the suicide note, the doctor says nothing, the teacher says nothing, and the police officer says nothing; and on Andrew Dewar, the priest says nothing, and the social worker says nothing.

The chairman will come with me now, his reputation as father of the community intact. They all know to suspect him of murder would be like suspecting the whole village of murder – best an incomer receives this accolade.

I have no problem with the naturals; as said, the unnatural ones are different. This death interests me. Why? He decided the world was no longer for him but was there more? His touching of Andrew Dewar had a part to play. Was it guilt or was it fear he would do more than touch? Was it something so powerful he could only do what he would do? The boy is here too. Andrew was his friend. Was he here to confirm his death? One day a long time from now he will explain it to his friend, when he comes this way himself, when he consumes a bottle of tablets washed down with a bottle of whisky on the pier by the harbour wall on a cold and wet February night.

CHAPTER 17

This day, the fifteen day of the eleventh month, they come for the father. He is in his shed as usual, conspiring, planning his attack, drinking, talking to himself in religious overtones. The doctor and constable approach the shed. "Mr Rooney, are you in there?"

They know he is. They go to the house and knock the door. Without a reply, they move to the kitchen window then to the sitting room where they see the mother lying on the sofa in her sitting room. They knock the window and she gets up and lets them in.

"We need to see Rooney, Jackie."

She pulls a blanket around her. "He's out there in the shed and you won't get much out of him."

"Thanks Jackie; you OK?"

They know she is not. "Just tikitiboo."

The constable says, "People are worried about you, Jackie, you are not yourself."

"Depressed, fed-up, scared, drunk; take your pick."

They look at her and then to themselves. They are there to help, but best to continue their task.

"Look after yourself, Jackie, we'll come back to see you soon," the doctor says.

She does not answer and heads back to the sofa to pull the blanket over her head.

They go out and along the path to the shed. It is in darkness. "Rooney, are you in there?" The constable shines his torch through the window.

"Leave me alone, I am doing God's work."

"We need to talk to you."

"Is it about divine retribution?"

"Yes." The doctor looks at the constable. "Push it in."

The door gives way easily to the constable's shoulder. He shines his torch inside to see the father slumped in an old tattered armchair, his arms hanging over its sides, an empty glass on a small table by its side, am empty whisky bottle close to it on the table. "Ah, it is the angels of the lord come to take me to heaven. Am I correct?"

"In a sense, Rooney," the doctor says. "We want you to come with us."

"To paradise?"

"Indeed."

"I have heard these words before, the last time I was removed to the crazy ward. I was there forty days and forty nights. They called it a section; a silly word, why didn't they call it incarceration."

"You need treatment, Rooney," the doctor says.

"I need revenge." The father snaps, getting out of the chair.

"You must come with us, friend," the constable demands.

A red rag to a highland bull, the father is up, bag over his shoulder, and, pushing open a door in the back of the shed, he is out and haring down the path, not that the constable has any desire to run after him. "Let him go," he says. "He'll be in the Small Isles later; we'll get him there." The father has no intention of going to the bar this night. He heads up Beinn Mhor to a bothy he and the boy would sometimes visit. He had joined the bothy association and helped renovate the old black-hoose into a fine bothy. He honed his love of drystane dyking there, the boy helping by handing him the smaller stones. The bothy was popular in the summer but less so in the winter; he knows he would have privacy there. A rule there is to ensure bedding, candles, coal, tinned food, and drams are there for people who may arrive. At this time in the winter it would be empty, few visitors call mid-November.

A burn is nearby, a plentiful water supply. He could hide out there for a few days without having to venture out for food. His shed was cold so he was wearing a heavy jacket in there when the constable and the doctor arrived to take him, with force if necessary to hospital, so he was well prepared for a few nights on the hill. It takes him over two hours to get there and he is pleased to look down the hill to see no trace of lights heading his way. He would be safe there. He sets about getting the fire going and after opening some tins sets about making a satisfying meal of stew and potatoes. The bothy is well insulated against the wind and coal, more so than his shed. He gets his notebook and pencil from his jacket pocket and sets about putting his foolish thoughts onto paper. But first he finds a half a bottle of port and sets about it with fervour. Before long *it* is with him once more.

"Hello, Rooney, running away again. They are coming to take you away ha ha."

"Leave me alone to do God's work, bastard."

The voice will ensure he is not alone.

His mobile goes off in his pocket. He thinks about not answering it and wonders if they would be able to trace him there, but he sees 'Jackie' on the screen. He opens it up.

"Where are you, Rooney? They are looking for you."

"It is best you do not know; MI5 will be taping your calls for sure."

"Rooney, I know paranoia when I hear it. You need to come back. You need help, treatment. Just go in, it won't be for long, then you'll be back home and all will be fine.

"They will fry my brain. Anyway I am with God and I will be back to smite the unbelievers."

"Oh, talk sense, Rooney. I know how you can be when you relapse."

"She is taping your call, father, she is working for .... them."

"Yes, I know she is."

"Who are you talking to, Rooney, who is with you?"

"You don't need to know, wife, go back to your duties."

"Your mobile will run out, Rooney. You need to stay in touch with me. Do you hear me?"

"Yes, my dear. Do not conspire with the moneylenders. I will come for you soon and we will leave for a safe place."

"Aye, you do that, Rooney. Are you safe, warm?"

He hears a click and turns off, fearing his call has been picked up, then goes back to his food and his writing.

CHAPTER 18

The next morning the mother has a visitor. On the fourth ring of her doorbell she opens the door, slowly. "Oh, it's you, Mrs McIsaac, I am sorry…"

"No, need, Jackie, but I need to talk to you."

"I'm sorry, Mrs McIsaac, I'm not feeling very well this morning. You would have heard about Rooney, he's gone missing."

The mother tries to close the door, but the teacher is now leaning against it. "I am sorry to hear about this, I…"

"I don't want to talk about it. Now, if you'll…"

The mother can feel the weight of the teacher pressing on the door. "Jackie, this can't wait."

The mother looks down at the rain thumping off the stairs, then to the teacher who is wet through. "We'll, you'd better come in."

"No, I don't want to come in," the teacher says. As the mother opens the door wide, the teacher moves forward, not far, just enough to get out of the rain.

"You better, it's a horrible day."

"You'll be worried about him."

"You'll be going to the school?"

"I've locked the school up, Jackie, I won't be going there." The mother studies her. "Please listen to me, what I have to say won't take long. After I have said it, I doubt you'd want me in your house."

The mother isn't sure what the teacher means about not going to the school but decides to hear her out. "You better say it then."

The teacher looks at her for a while, until the mother starts to feel uncomfortable, running her fingers through her hair, and then she says it. "I think my husband killed your son."

"I am sorry about your husband, though he was a pompous stuck-up… What?"

"You heard me; it's in your face."

The mother steps back, leaning on her stick and wrapping her cardigan around her neck. “Now you really must come in.”

The teacher moves slightly farther inside. The mother can see her plainly now. Her hair is like rat tails, her face smudged with what looks to the mother like soot. Had it been just over a couple of weeks earlier she would have thought her to be guising. “No, but I must tell you. I can’t keep it to myself anymore.” The mother’s mind flashes back to the night of Samhuinn, the night before the boy came with me. She thought of how the children, the boy included, went guising around the doors of Achfara, Lochdarrach, and Stoer, with no worry of their safety. Although she heard the teacher’s words she is in a daze, relieving the night of Samhuinn. The boy had dressed as a pirate and she had taken some soot from the stove to give him a bold moustache and big eyebrows.

“Have you been guising?” The teacher wipes her face realising she had not cleaned it from the fire of her husband’s car the night before. The teacher shakes her head. Strangely, the mother nearly laughs. “Is this not something you should be telling to Inspector Boyd?”

The teacher looks puzzled, but only succeeds in smudging her face even more by wiping her hand over her face. “I am telling you. I cannot live with it.”

“What are you saying?”

“I need to confess to you.”

“Father Legowski is who you confess to, Mrs McIsaac.”

“I doubt if I would find redemption there.”

They both look at each other. The mother is bedraggled by the drink, the teacher is bedraggled by the rain. The mother leans forward, taking the weight on her stick. “Say it.”

“It may have been my husband’s car I saw that night.”

“The night Calum was taken?”

“Yes, it could have been John’s car. I think he took Calum.”

The wind was buffeting both of them and it was possible one of them, if not both of them, would collapse into the hall. The mother reaches for the teacher and grabs her arm. The teacher is unsure whether this is for comfort of support, but she reaches out and holds the mother’s shoulder. The mother does not resist this and pushes closer to her almost in embrace. “I can’t deal with this.” The mother pushes back an arm’s length.

"I am sorry, Jackie; but he had pictures of him, naked."

"Facebook, on the beach. I told Rooney not to post them."

"No, not just the Facebook, here." The teacher reaches into her coat and takes out an envelope, then pulls out some photographs and hands them to the mother."

The mother straightens up at this, to gain a stronger perspective. "Why didn't you come forward with this at the time?"

The teacher drops her head. "I couldn't, I couldn't bring myself to, but now, now he is ... gone, I just had to." She starts to sob.

The mother is not sympathetic. "You may be complicit in murder, do you appreciate this, the murder of my son."

The teacher breaks down. "I know, I know, I am so sorry, I am so sorry."

The mother reaches out to grasp her, this time more to restrain her than to comfort her. "You get in here. I need to telephone Boyd."

"I cannot, I…" The teacher breaks away. "I have to go."

"Fuck you, McIsaac, fuck your husband. I hope he rots in hell. I hope you both rot in hell. You two were complicit. You could have saved my son. You are a murderer," she screams, as the teacher stumbles along the path from the house.

"Please forgive me, Jackie, please forgive me," she calls, as she gets in her car and drives off.

The inspector curses the fact he has two mobiles, one for his occupation and the other for his personal use. He also curses the fact he continually gives out his two numbers to all and sundry. He has just pulled into the Small Isle car park intending a coffee and a hot roll, when the occupational one goes off on his dashboard. 'Father L', appears on the screen. He calls it. "I have important information, Inspector Boyd," the priest says answering.

"I'm in Achfara, Father, give me five and I'll be there." He checks the other mobile, the personal one, and sees 'Jackie K' on the screen.

He phones her on the way from the church car park. "Yes, Jackie, yes, yes, I understand." He returns the mobile to his pocket.

The priest greets the inspector at the door of the vestry and invites him in. "I need to see Eileen McIsaac," Boyd says to the priest.

"Something I can help with?"

"Not in this case, Father, unless you are a police officer."

"Oh."

"It's about her husband; she told Jackie something important. You wanted to see me?"

"Yes, thank you for coming; I also have something to tell you about her husband." He invites the inspector to sit at the coal fire there. He sinks into the sumptuous chair offered to him. "Nice chair, Father."

"Thanks, my reading chair, a gift from the parishioners."

"Her husband, Rooney?" the inspector asks. "He's done a runner."

"No, not Jackie's husband, Inspector, Eileen's, John McIsaac."

"He's dead."

"Yes, I know, but I need to inform you, perhaps the reason why he took his life."

"He killed the boy?"

"What, no, not killed?"

"Jackie Kaminski just informed me it may have been his car Eileen saw on the night outside the school when the boy was picked up."

"No, not that boy, I am talking about Andrew Dewar."

The inspector is beginning to think he should have gone for the coffee in the Small Isles instead of coming here. "Andrew Dewar?"

"Yes, he has disclosed to me, a disclosure, I understand my duties under the child protection legislation. I was about to advise you, then I decided to talk to John McIsaac first; after that, he killed himself."

"You should have..."

"I know."

"The boy, Andrew."

"He revealed John McIsaac touched him. I have reason to believe he was a child abuser. I thought you should know."

The inspector sinks farther back into the seat in thought and would have enjoyed the fire and the comfort of it had he not had another concerning thought. "I need to go, Father."

"Yes, of course, you'll be in touch."

"Yes, we need to discuss this further. It is important. Have you called social services?"

"I have spoken to a social worker."
"Good. I'll be back."

The inspector reaches the house. He moves to the door and raps the door with his knuckles. On the weight of his third knock the door moves open, enough for him to realise it is not locked. *Strange*, he thinks. He moves inside. "Mrs McIsaac, are you in?" She is here, but *she* is not here, *she* is with me. He moves farther inside, reaching for the hall light. He flicks it and the light illuminates the hall and into the kitchen. He remembers the last time he had been there: the warmth of the kitchen, the smell of the food, the chatter of the McIsaacs. This time the house is cold, no smell of food, even although it is not long past tea time. He moves inside the kitchen and reaches for the light switch. Trying it, no light comes on. *Strange*, he thinks, again. Then he sees why the kitchen light does not come on. There, hanging from the ceiling light cord, is the lifeless body of the teacher.

He wonders why the cord had not snapped with the weight of her body until he remembers many of these old houses still had the old tough cabling. *If this house had been brought up to wiring standards she may not have died*, he thought. This is an odd thought for a human, but a practical one, I think. Standing on a chair, he reaches the cord above her head. Cutting it with his penknife he bears her weight until she drops into his arms and he lays her across the kitchen table. He straightens her legs and places her arms at her side. Her limbs bend and her body is still warm, having only been with me less than fifteen minutes.

He looks around the kitchen, and yes, as with many cases there is a note. He unfolds the sheet and reads: "I am sorry for my husband's actions. I am sorry I could have saved Calum and I didn't. Please forgive me."

He pulls out his mobile, the personal one, and calls the mother.

The friend opens the door and walks in. "I need to see you, Jackie."

As usual, the mother is lying on the couch, a half empty bottle of wine on the table next to her, the glass lying on its side on the floor. She is covered with her blanket, her arms on top of it, her mobile in her hand. "Oh, when the cat's away, and don't you know it is polite around here to knock before you go into someone's house." By this time the boy had backed himself into the corner of the sitting room. It is dark in there, but I see his eyes like lights in the night.

"I heard you were attacked and Rooney isn't here." He moves her legs off the couch and sits down. "You need to be careful."

She pulls the blanket around here and sits up. "I can look after myself."

He picks up the glass, puts it next to the bottle. "I need to talk to you, something the priest said to me."

"Well, you were right to come in and sit down then." She pulls her knees up and wraps her arms around them. "Right, speak, I don't have all day."

He runs his finger around the rim of the glass. "No, you've drinking to do."

"None of your business, now what do you want to say?"

The friend puts his hand on her knee. "There's a paed in the community, Jackie."

"And he had pictures of Calum?" The boy's eyes are staring out of the gloom.

"The priest asked my advice, wouldn't say who it was, posed a rhetorical situation of someone significant in the community abusing a kid."

"Someone significant killed himself, Ben."

"Who?"

"McIsaac."

"The chairman?"

"Well, who else is the chairman?"

"When?"

"On Monday; Boyd phoned me this morning."

"The priest was talking, rhetorically you understand, about a boy being touched by a man, a good man as he described; a significant adult in the community."

"McIsaac."

"And he's dead."

"And so is his wife."

"Jesus, when?"

"Boyd found her two hours ago, just phoned me." The boy stares from the gloom.

The friend gets up and moves around the couch. He puts his hands on her neck, like he may strangle her but then he begins massaging it. "You were attacked, Rooney is dangerous, and people are committing suicide. Jackie, it's not safe here, I'll stay with you."

She sits up and pulls away from his hands, then empties the remainder of the wine into the glass, drinks it down, lies down on the couch and pulls the cover over her head. The friend reaches over and tucks her in with the cover. They do not say any more. He moves through the living room into the kitchen. I follow him. He goes to the kitchen window and looks out at the father's shed. I know what he has in his mind, it is apparent. In there, without the father to interrupt him, he will take his time in his search. This is in vain, however; although in pulling out the old bible the brown envelope falls on the desk. He picks it up. "God's Research", he reads. "Bloody delusional fool," he says, putting it back unopened.

I return to the sitting room and look to the boy; maybe he knows his teacher is with me now. Would he want to see her again? I doubt it. I leave him to do my duty to her.

Later that night, the young *taibshear* is unsettled. He tosses in his sleep and cries out.

"The boy is disturbed again; will we get any sleep?"

"He is upset, Magnus," Maggie says. "He is distressed over Mrs McIsaac's death. All the children are very upset. I will go to him."

"He will need the help of a professional I think, his mind is not his own."

"We will see about it later, but for tonight I need to go to him."

"Well go to him, woman. I am getting used to it, being here on my own." Magnus turns over and falls asleep.

"What is it, my child?" His mother reaches out for him in his bed.

"Mother, Mother, please help me."

"Oh Angus, you are upset over Mrs McIsaac, all the children are."

"Mother, they are drowning, they are drowning." He reaches out for her. She tries to console him but he will have none of it.

It is a cold but clear night with no foul weather forecasted. The *Bàta-Iasgaich* left Stoer harbour at noon to fish for sprats, sought after in northern Europe where they are smoked and preserved in oil. With a crew of five, including the skipper, Iain MacDougall, a highly respected local fisherman, they were optimistic about their catch. They would sail into the night and fish at dawn with the sun coming up in the east over the stern of the ship.

Around the witching hour, two of the crew had gone to sleep. MacDougall was on the bridge and the two others were observing the trawling net which was over the side and filling as the boat coursed through the water. He looked out, confident he knew where the shoals of sprats would be found. He would be relieved at four when one of the crew had his sleep. He would not have another sleep however as he felt a sharp tug on the net. It was not unusual for nets to become snagged on the rocky bottoms but this was a fearsome jolt from something moving underneath. He would have been correct had he suspected being snagged by a submarine. It is known rogue Russian submarines had operated in these parts. His instant reaction was to alert the crew, cut the net free, and get the others from below up. It was clear, however, the boat was being drawn under as the crew hacked at the ropes trying to release the net, but it was to no avail. In seconds, the boat was under water and all those up top could do was to grab life preservers and throw themselves into the sea. They watched as the boat was dragged under with their two comrades still in their beds. Two lads, last aged eighteen and nineteen, would come with me this night.

The *taibshear* is inconsolable. "They have drowned, mother, they have drowned, two of them are dead. I saw it."

Mrs Stuart holds him tight against her. "What can I do to help you, son? I am very worried about you."

"Archie MacAndrew and Euan MacBain, mum; they are dead, I saw them."

"How do you know they are dead, Angus?" She pulls the sheet tight around him tucking him in, as a mother would do.

"I see dead people, Mother, they are dead I tell you. Please believe me."

The boy tells the truth.

"I do, my son, I do, but I do not know if it is in your mind."

"It is not in my mind, Mother. I see Calum also, he is dead."

He does, I know he does.

"Not again, your father thinks you, we need to—"

"I try to shut it out Mother, believe me I do, but he follows me, as if he is trying to tell me something. I tell him to go away, to leave me alone, but he persists."

"We must talk to someone, to get you help."

He is talking to you; you are his mother.

"What I say is true, Mother."

"How do you know it is true?"

"He wants me to do something for him, to help him, but I do not know…"

"What does he do, when you see him?"

"I have told you, Mother. He points at the hill."

"He points at the hill, nothing more?"

"No."

"And Archie MacAndrew and Euan MacBain, what makes you think they are drowned?"

"They are looking at me from under the sea, Mother. Their eyes are like stalks standing out of their heads, their faces are like whitewash walls, their tongues are like cattle's bulging out of their mouths, like they have gasped their last breath. They are dead, Mother. I know what dead people look like."

I can vouch for this description.

"All right son, if what you say is true, we will know about it in the morning. I am not going to call out the coastguard for a nightmare of yours. We will see then. Now, please try to go to sleep."

I have a busy time ahead; the teacher, the chairman, the two lads, all in the space of one day. The McIsaac's took their own lives, the boys lost theirs. The McIsaac's would not be mourned, the lads will. This is a troublesome time for these people, as they do, they will question the existence of 'God'. I can tell you, I do too.

CHAPTER 19

It is the morning of the seventeenth day of the eleventh month, and the word is out. Iain MacDougall and two of the crew had been picked up by another fishing boat, but nothing is found of the others. The boat had gone down with them inside. The communities of Achfara and Lochdarrach head towards Stoer to support the community there. The two boys were popular members of the Stoer Shinty team and lived in the village. The MacAndrew and MacBain families are given respect and privacy. The support will be given over the following months, but for now all know they need no more than themselves.

They meet in Stoer health centre to discuss the father: Black, the doctor; Broomlands, the constable; Ben, the friend and named person; and the mother, the nearest relative.

"Before I start," the constable says. "I think we should have a minute for the boys." They all bow their heads for a full minute. "These are sad days for our communities." They all nod. "Thank you. Of course we'll find out what happened in due course; a terrible incident."

"Thank you, Constable," the doctor says, "Now, for our meeting here today. We thought about cancelling under the circumstances, but Mr Bensallah has travelled up from Glasgow."

"I appreciate the opportunity to have this discussion, Constable," the friend says.

The doctor suggests, "We should call it a multidisciplinary meeting."

"I am not a 'discipline', Doctor Black," the mother says. "I am here to discuss my husband. I would prefer to be at home."

"Yes, of course, Jackie, and you'll be happy not to take the minutes this time," the doctor laughs, highlighting how the mother as part-time receptionist in the health centre would always volunteer to take the minutes of meetings there. The mother had taken leave from the job, but she has no intention of returning there, into something of a goldfish bowl. "OK, let us confirm where we are with Mr Rooney." They all look on. "Well, you know, following Ben's advice, after speaking to Doctor Melville in Glasgow, we tried to take Mr Rooney into hospital where he could be reintroduced to the treatment plan which had given him … stability."

"And to get him off the drink, the main reason he relapsed."

"Yes, Ben," the doctor says.

"Although, Doctor Melville also indicated his relapse could have been triggered by the loss of his son, is this correct?"

Ben nods. The doctor turns to the mother to see her drop her head. "Are you OK, Jackie?"

She keeps her head down. "Can we get on with it?"

"Yes, we should," the doctor says. "As we know, we arrived to see him at the house. We hoped to encourage him to come with us, but we were prepared to use the Mental Health Act, should he have refused, under the emergency procedures. We believed he met the criteria, mental disorder, risk to self or others, refusing treatment, and inability to treat him informally."

"Well, guess you had it all worked out."

"Yes, Jackie." The doctor looks at the friend, and then turns to the constable. "Constable, could you bring us up to date on Mr Rooney?"

"Certainly," the constable says. "Thank you. Yes, as we are aware, Mr Rooney refused and before we could apprehend him, he was off out of the back of the shed."

"There was no back door in there."

"No, Jackie, we think he may have prepared it in the event he would have had to use it, for this very purpose."

"He would have expected you. I know him; he knew there was a possibility of being sectioned. It happened to him before; he would have been on his guard."

"Yes, indeed," the constable says. "Well, he was out and—"

"Pretty botched up attempt, Constable," the friend says.

"What?"

"Well, in Glasgow they would have anticipated it, a couple of CPN's outside, and a sufficient number of police officers on hand."

"This is the highlands, Mr Bensallah; we do not have access to such resources as exist in the central belt."

"Yes, of course."

"Anyway, he was off and here we are two days later and he remains at large."

"You'll be worried about him," the constable says to the mother.

"Couldn't give a fuck."

This off-foots the constable. "We have had a search; we don't really know where he is."

"Not much of a search. He didn't have his car, can't have gone far."

"We asked all the haulage contractors, fish transporters, we checked all traffic to and from the ferry. We have his photograph at the ferry ports and on the ferries to the isles, including in all the village halls and shops, and in Invernevis. And, of course, the media has it on the news and the papers."

"Aye, father of murdered son goes missing, good one."

"What happens next?" the friend asks. "Doctor Melville is concerned. Rooney's relapses always include a strong element of paranoia. He'll believe all the government agencies, MI5, etcetera are out to get him. He has religious delusions, believing himself to have divine powers; shown this symptom to me recently."

"He is not all wrong there," the mother says. "You are all indeed out to get him."

"Yes, it could be seen that way," the doctor says.

The friend adds, "He is likely to be a danger to others too."

The mother scowls at him. "Could you explain this, Mr Bensallah, from your knowledge of him?"

The friend looks at the doctor. "He has harmed people in the past." The mother is relieved he did not mention he had a gun in Glasgow and may have killed a man there.

"Yes, I have read the reports from his case file," the doctor says.

"We need to bring him in," the friend says

"So what do we do, Constable Broomlands?"

"Not much we can do until he breaks ground, or…"

"You are his friend, Ben," the doctor says. "Do you have any ideas?"

"I think if he could have managed to get to Invernevis, he would have headed to Glasgow, he could go to ground there, he has many—"

"Friends?" the mother suggests.

"If he is still around here, he could be in difficulty," the constable says.

"It is cold out there. There's a risk of hypothermia."

"His body could be found somewhere in the snow," the constable says. "Or in the spring when the ice melts on the hills, if he is up there. Sorry, Jackie."

"Christ, that's all we would need." All remain quiet for a minute. "I think I can bring him in."

"Sorry, Jackie, what do you mean?"

"I cannot tell you. I think I can get him home."

All look at each other. Has the mother been hiding something, like phone calls with her husband for example?

"No, Jackie, it is too risky. I cannot allow it. He needs to go to hospital. Doctor Melville demands it."

"Look Ben, friend, named person, social worker. I can get him home and if he agrees to treatment, then that's better than him being out there. Better at home where I can … watch him."

"I agree," the doctor says. "And as the responsible medical officer on site I think it should be tried. Informal treatment is always better than compulsion. Minimum intervention under the Act."

"On your heads be it," the friend says.

"Jackie, I believe you have contact with him," the doctor says. "I assume this must be by telephone, which you were reluctant to reveal, but nevertheless I think it should be tried."

"Thank you."

The constable advises, "If there is any risk to health, welfare, or safety, we need to be brought in, Jackie, immediately."

She agrees. "Aye, OK."

"But this worries me," the friend says. "You know what he is capable of doing."

"I know my husband, Ben."

It is agreed and the meeting is over. The mother gets up to leave. "Can I have a word, Jackie, in private?" The friend looks at him as if to suggest he should stay with her. "It's OK, Ben."

The friend and the constable leave. The mother leaves shortly after with a prescription for antidepressants, which she dispatches in a bin outside the surgery. She notices the friend's car in the car park, him waiting for her. Unnoticed, she heads into the village centre.

The mother heads along to the Stoer Coop for 'supplies'. Having loaded up a basket of shopping, she approaches the tills. "And a bottle of Whyte and MacKays, please?" she asks the shop assistant.

Just then, from behind her comes, "Hello, Jackie?" The mother turns to see Morag McAllister behind her in the cue for the tills. "How are you?" Morag asks.

"Oh, not great, Mrs McAllister."

"You would have heard about the boys."

"Yes, I have, just terrible." The mother starts to pass her shopping to the till attendant. "I can't believe it."

"Can I help you?"

"No, thanks, I can manage." The mother is aware of Morag breathing down her neck.

"Life is so hard, hen, so hard."

"Aye, life's a bitch and then you die."

"You've just got to get through it."

"Suppose, not easy."

"Can I give you a word of advice?" Morag is talking into her ear.

"No thanks, Morag, I don't need any advice."

"Just a minute, I'll no' take long."

The mother looks at the till attendant who heads off to help a shopper at the self-serve tills. "Right, if you must."

Mrs McAllister looks around to make sure she isn't being over heard. "Listen, hen." The mother has not heard this term 'hen' since she left Glasgow. Morag is from Glasgow herself, however, having moved here with her husband who worked in the boatyard. "The people here are good people, but they are—"

"Hurting, I know, now—"

"No, they are feart hen, feart."

"Feart, I don't know what you're saying, Morag."

"I'm just saying."

"What are you saying?"

"I am saying, if you want to stay here…"

"I don't know if I do, but I don't know if it is any of your business, now—"

"Well, you did at one time."

"Morag, can you just get on with it, I need to get back. Rooney, you'll appreciate…"

"I know, he's away; just like ma man, always buggering off."

"Look Morag, if you'll…"

"Listen, hen." Here is the hen again. "I was married to an alcoholic tae." Oh here we go, the mother thinks. "He beat me up, before and after we came up here, for years he beat me up. He beat up others in the village too. They were very supportive. Then he crossed the line, hen."

"I don't understand."

"Jackie, he is a bad man, he was involved in crime, you were a good person, a police officer. Get him to leave, let things settle, grieve for your wee boy and start again, here. I'll help you. They all will, they are good people, really. He's the problem here, not you."

Jackie looks at her in the face. This is not the face of an interfering busybody, she thinks, but of a woman who is showing concern, giving her advice. Would she take it, however? "Thanks Morag, I'll think about it, and thanks for the offer of support, I appreciate it."

"Nae problem, hen, just get away before he comes back, you've got a chance, take it." She smiles. The mother sees deep lines on her face. She could have been in her early forties but looks in her sixties. *Is this what I will soon look like if I stay here*? she wonders.

Jackie returns home and spends the rest of the day on her sofa, ably assisted by the bottle of Whyte and MacKays. As it becomes dark she imagines her husband out there, somewhere. She looks out of the window to see a group of men, led by Caber, heading up her path. A supportive gesture, she wonders; the men have been out looking for the father. She opens the door to greet them, to realise very quickly they are not.

"We want to talk to you, Jackie," Caber says at the door.

"Oh aye, what about?"

"You and your husband."

"He's not here."

"No, we know."

"So?"

"He's gone off to Glasgow again?"

"None of your business where he is."

"It's all of our business here."

"Why are you here, McKinnon, and your band of brothers? You, John the post, Billy the boat?" She looks into the darkness and sees a group of locals, more normally found together in the Small Isles Bar.

"Tell her, Caber," Post says. "We agreed it."

Caber looks around and scowls; no one needs to tell him what to do or say. "I can speak for myself, Post." Post looks to the ground. "OK, Jackie, we … in this community," he says, as if he is reading from a statement, looking around, "think things have changed since you arrived here. Today was the last straw."

"You trying to suggest we had anything to do with those boys, the *Bàta-Iasgaich* going down? Get a grip man."

"It's time you left, Jackie."

"No, it's time you left." Jackie taps in the constable's number. "Is it you Broomlands; yes, good. I think you need to come over here, urgently; I have a lynch party at my door led by Caber McKinnon, threatening me. Please come now. No, I don't think you'll need support from Invernevis; it's a group of shites from the Small Isles, who by the smell of them have had too many drams. Thank you, I'll see you soon."

Caber has his back to the mother and is talking to the men, then he turns to her. "OK, we will go, but you need to know you and your husband are not welcome here. Do you hear me?"

"What kind of behaviour is this? All I hear is a fool who has had too much to drink threatening a woman at the door of her house."

"We are not threatening you, we are advising you, for your own safety."

"Oh, like I may be attacked again. Was it you Caber, or you Post, or you Boat?"

"We would not," Boat says.

"No, Jackie," adds Post.

Caber says nothing.

"Now get the fuck off my property, before the constable arrives, you should all be ashamed of yourselves."

Caber turns to the men, who had already starting moving away down the path. "You need to understand, Jackie..."

"No, you understand, McKinnon. Next time you come here—you and your mighty mob—my father will have a SWAT team who will blow your bloody brains out. Now get off my land."

Caber tugs his bunnet and follows the men along the path into the darkness.

The mother waits until they leave and calls the father; he does not answer. "I know you are there and I don't have much battery left, but you need to know I have had a group of men at the door threatening me and you are in hiding. What kind of man are you, what kind of husband are you?"

"I am with the Lord," the father says faintly.

"Rooney, get a grip?"

"I have to go, they'll be tracing all calls."

"Listen idiot, they are looking for you, Caber came to the door today. You—"

"Thank the Lord, now you will believe me. And believe this also, they will feel the wrath of the Lord."

"Rooney, I..."

The line goes dead.

"Fuck," she says, calling him back.

"Yes, my dear?"

"Rooney, listen to me, I can get you home, you can stay here, get treatment."

"No need, Ms Kaminski, I am just tikitiboo—" The line goes dead.

She tries again, no answer, a non-contactable message. "Shite," she says, realising the battery in his telephone has given out. "Fuck!" She throws the phone into the sink.

The young *taibshear* is unsettled once more. He has his headphones on and is positioned no more than one yard away from the television screen in his bedroom.

"You'll hurt your eyes, Angus," his mother says. "Switch off the TV, it is nine o'clock, and it is time for your bed."

"I can't sleep, I see things."

"You won't sleep with your head stuck in the TV."

"It helps. I don't see things when my head is in there."

His mother switches the TV off. "You will go to bed and sleep."

"But, Mo—"

"No buts, you are going to bed." She takes him by the arm and leads him to his bed, whereby she gets him in there.

"I can't help it, Mum."

"I know, son, but you can't live your life seeing things."

"I saw the fishing boys, Mum, I saw them."

"I don't know how you saw those boys, son. But, we need to help you free yourself from this affliction."

"You said you believed me."

"I did, Angus, but we'll need to get you to the doctor in Invernevis, he's a professional. He said he would see you again if the visions didn't stop."

"I will refuse, Mother. I will not go to a sarchiatrist. I will run away if you force me." The boy pulls the covers over his head and wraps his arms around them like rope.

His mother puts the main light off but leaves the bedside light on. "What are we to do?"

The voice comes from under the covers. "Mum, I have seen Calum again, he won't leave me alone."

"Not again, Angus."

"He is following me, Mother; he wants to tell me something."

She pulls the covers from his head. "For god's sake, Angus, he can't talk to you. You can't communicate with the dead, you only see things."

"I know Mum, but he keeps pointing up to the hill."

She pushes in beside him on the bed and lies side by side with him. "And why would he point to the hill? Beinn Mhor has no interest to him now. He cannot ever again climb it with you like he did the last time when the school did it."

He reaches out and grips her arm. "I know Mum, but he won't leave me be."

Maggie releases his grip and puts his arm under the blankets. "You have to try, Angus, this is not good for you, you have to sleep."

He begins to sob. "I have tried, Mother. I can't stop it."

"I know, Angus, but please don't get upset, but will you talk to Mr Rooney?"

"Mr Rooney, Calum's father?" He pulls himself up on the bed.

"Yes."

"He may understand why Calum pursues me?"

"He may, but he has training, he was…"

"Yes, I will see him, maybe Calum will leave me alone then."

"I hope so, I will talk to him."

"Thank you, Mother. Mother?"

"What?"

"Can you put the TV on? It helps."

"OK." She puts it on, "But not on the horror channel. I'll put a DVD on."

"*The Omen*, I like it."

"No." She puts *Toy Story* on.

The mother's phone goes, she thinks it is the father.

"Rooney, Are you OK?" She retrieves it from the sink. "I need—"

"Jackie, it's me, Maggie."

She slides into a seat at the table, lifting a half glass of wine. "Mrs Stuart?"

"I have something to tell you."

Not another paedophile story, she thinks. "I need to go, Maggie."

"It's my son, he sees Calum."

The mother gets to her feet, her stick falling onto the tiled floor. "What!" There is a pause from the other end. "What?"

Maggie Stuart's voice is dim; the mother pushes the earpiece tight to her head. "Calum," Maggie says, faintly.

"Can you speak up, you said Calum."

Maggie Stuart's voice is clearer now as she raises her voice. "I don't want to talk loudly, Jackie, I'm in the conservatory and Magnus is in the next room, I don't want him to—"

"Don't want him to know, hear, stop you talking to me?"

Maggie gets up and pushes the patio door tight into the sitting room. Through the glass door, she waves to her husband as she does. "To hear; Jackie, this is just me to you."

The mother sits down again, picking up her stick. "Right, go on."

"Well, you know he sees things; he saw the boys who went down last night, but he also saw Calum."

"My son is dead, Maggie; do you know how upsetting this is?"

"I know Jackie. I am sorry, but I don't know what to do. I thought you should know."

The mother wraps her cardigan around her as she feels the draft coming through the sashed windows. "What does he say?"

"He says Calum is following him around."

"He needs help, Maggie, now if you'll…"

"This is why I am phoning you."

"Talk to Black, he'll refer Angus to CAMHs."

"He refuses to talk to a professional."

"And why are you phoning me?"

"He says he would talk to your husband."

The mother shakes her head. "My husband, as you will know, as everyone will know in this place, is not here."

Maggie Stuart goes to the window looking out to the hill. "Yes, I know, Jackie, it is terrible, and I am worried about him, we miss him being in the bar, we want him back."

"What does Calum…?"

"Angus says Calum keeps pointing to the hill, Beinn Mhor."

"I can't say I believe him; I don't believe in such things."

If anything is guaranteed to stir an Achfara woman's corraich it is to say their child is not to be believed. "Please don't suggest my child is a liar, Jackie; it isn't very nice. I called you tonight in good faith. I thought you should know."

The mother reaches for the tablets; her head is hurting as it is always these days. "Yes, of course you are worried about your son. He was Calum's friend; he may be grieving like I am sure many of the children at the school are, but Rooney's no good to anyone just now. He's ill himself." She takes a glug of wine.

Maggie Stuart is beginning to wish she had not called the mother. "Angus isn't ill in that way, Jackie; Jesus!"

"OK, calm down. Why do you think Rooney could help?"

"He needs to talk to someone who may have the skill, the training to help him, Rooney was a psychologist."

"I am sure he would help if he was of a … mind."

"Maybe, if, when he gets better." Through the door, she sees her husband Magnus getting up from his chair and moving towards the conservatory.

"Aye, maybe, and soon, when he gets help himself. We're working on it."

"I need to go, Jackie. Just…"

"I can't."

"Just don't say anything, Jackie. My son predicted the death of those boys on the *Bàta-Iasgaich* last night. I believe him and you need to too. He is trying to say something important to you."

Magnus Stuart pushes into the conservatory. "You going to be on the phone all night."

"I need to go," she says to the mother, turning away from her husband. "But, please…"

"Right, of course." The mother is holding her head. "Maybe when Rooney is home and feeling a bit better, then we'll see."

"Thanks, goodnight." Maggie turns back to her husband.

"Who was that?" he asks.

"Jackie. I was just asking about Rooney. Just to say we are worried about him."

"Oh, right, should you not be seeing to Angus?"

"Yes, of course, I think we have another night of it to come."

CHAPTER 20

"Ben?" the chief growls into his hands-free unit from his office in Tulliallan Castle.

"Yes, Chief, I was expecting your call."

"You still there?"

"Breakfast in the Achfara Hotel."

"I hope you are enjoying it."

The friend pushes his toast into an undercooked fried egg. "It's all right. What can I do for you?"

"I hear Rooney's done a runner."

"He sure has." The friend pushes his plate away,

"I thought we were going to get him incarcerated."

"He was to be taken into hospital for treatment, sir, compulsorily."

The chief reaches for the Mental Health Act. "It's what I meant, compulsorily, taken out. What happened?" He flicks it open on the page on Compulsory Treatment Orders. "Thought you could bring him in, under his order?"

"His consultant left it to the GP and the constable."

"They ballsed it up, next time I send in my guys. What happens next?"

The friend gestures to the hotel waitress to take the breakfast away, nodding his head at her 'are you sure?'. He goes back to the chief. "We had a meeting," he says to him. "Jackie wants to try … informal means."

The chief lifts up the Act. "It's not what we want, Ben. Rooney needs to be taken out; he's a danger to my daughter, and to others."

"I agree, but she's his nearest relative, she thinks he'll accept informal treatment."

"Informal treatment, he needs locked up."

"It's the approach in the Act, Chief, the least restrictive approach."

"Social workers!" He slaps the Act on his desk. "I know what it says, but just do the right thing."

"Yes, of course."

The friend grimaces, partly at the undercooked breakfast, but also due to the indigestion from stress related acid hitting his stomach.

The phone has been busy with a pushy newspaper reporter asking about the father: "could you give us a statement please, your husband?"

"Fuck off." The phone returns to the sink.

She takes off, wandering around the house, talking to herself as she does. The boy follows her around.

"Maggie says Calum is there, in touch with Angus." She looks around the sitting room, and the boy looks at her. He looks animated, as if he is getting through to her. "Is he here, are you here, Calum?" He nods and goes so close to her she could, if she could, touch him. "If you are, can you tell me or do something?" He is not a poltergeist, Mother, he is a dead boy in limbo waiting to move on. He cannot 'do' anything. She waits looks around to see if anything has moved, curtains, anything to indicate the boy is near. "Maggie says you keep pointing up the hill, is that where your father is?" The boy is nodding and shaking his head, simultaneously. "Is that what you are trying to tell us? He is shaking his head. "Your father is up there?" The mother moves around the sitting room trying to think this through. "The bothy, the bothy, why didn't I think of that; of course he would go there: the bothy." The boy looks on with a pleased but confused look on his face. But first, Boyd is coming at twelve, then I'll head up. I'll take food, clothing, and talk to him."

Just then, the mainline phone goes again. She lets it ring over twenty times, but the caller is determined. She goes to the sink. "Can you not take no for an answer?" she snaps.

"Jackie, we haven't met, but I know Rooney."

She lifts the phone to her eye line. "Oh, and who are you?"

"We go to the same meeting in Invernevis, I am his … sponsor. Katie, Katie McLeod."

She takes a big breath relieved it is not the newspaper reporter asking for the 'statement'. "Oh, right, he has mentioned you; you introduced him to the group."

"Yes. I hope you don't mind me calling. I heard Rooney has gone missing. I, we in the group are worried about him."

"Oh, that's good."

"We hope nothing has happened to him. He is vulnerable."

The mother only realises her housecoat is open at the front revealing her breasts when John the Post approaches the front door. "Excuse me," she says to Katie. "And you can fuck off, Post," she says through the window to him, the man who last treaded her path as part of the Caber led group. "I'll pick up my letters at the shop." He drops her mail on her doorstep and scurries off down the path. "Yes, what's your name again?" she says, returning to her call.

"Katie McLeod."

"Yes, Katie McLeod, you are worried about him."

"Yes, indeed. If you hear anything would you … get in touch?"

"I will, I'll save your number. I'll get him to call you himself if, when he comes back, or we find him."

"Thank you, Jackie. We … miss him."

"Yes, I'm sure you do, take care, thanks for calling."

The mother sits down pulling her housecoat tight around her. She wonders about the call, why Rooney had not mentioned Katie McLeod by name. She took a note of her number from the phone display before she returns it to the sink, this time throwing a heavy towel over it.

The mother has just dressed by the time the inspector arrives. She shakes her head as she approaches the door. "Thanks for seeing me, Jackie," he says, as she opens it.

"Cut out the crap. McIsaac killed himself on Monday; his wife kills herself on Wednesday, and today's Friday. What else is new?"

"No word on Rooney?"

"Nothing; now about McIsaac, I need to know what you have."

He pulls out a chair and takes his coat and hat off. "Mrs McIsaac has opened up a new aspect to the investigation." He drops them over the chair and sits down.

"Make yourself comfortable, why don't you. Yes, she seemed to think it was her husband's car that pulled away from the school, when Calum went missing."

"I suppose we have to consider—"

"Calum was in the car, Inspector; how many other cars pulled away from the school at that time on that day?"

"There's more."

"I've no doubt, go on."

"Another boy in the village." *What's coming now*, she thinks. "Another boy has said McIsaac touched him."

"Who?"

"We can't reveal, you know, confidentiality."

"Fuck confidentiality, Boyd. It's McIsaac, he did it, is that what you are saying?"

"No, I am not saying anything, but we need to factor it into our investigation, it's circumstantial."

"Oh, here we go, circumstantial he killed my son?"

"Circumstantial he did anything other than pick up your son; if indeed he did; this is not evidence he killed your son." The mother looks vacantly at him. "He's dead, the car is burned out. Mrs McIsaac is dead. The thing we have is he was touching another boy and what his wife said about him and the car. It's not enough."

"Look, Inspector. Calum gets into McIsaac's car, he goes missing, he is found dead, what the fuck more do you need?"

"Please, Jackie, evidence, you know that."

The mother moves around the table to get directly across from him. "Evidence? You want a confession, you can't get it. You want a witness who saw him murder Calum, you can't get it. You want to see blood on his hands, and you can't get it either."

"No, indeed."

"Indeed." She looks despairingly at him. "Time you were away, Inspector."

"Jackie, I wish I could..."

She picks up his coat and hat and hands them to him. "Ms Kaminski, Inspector, do more?"

"Yes, do more." It was in the way he says this, the mother feels *he* knows he really could be doing more. "Caber, the other night?" He appears relieved to be saying something he could *do* something about.

"Yes, the caring community deputation arrived at my door."

"Constable Broomlands told me. It won't happen again. They had been drinking after the boys went down and just got over emotional. I have spoken—"

"Oh, you have; and did you know I was attacked?"

"You were, when, who?"

"I don't know, it was on the beach on Sunday night."

The inspector has his notepad and pencil out. "Sunday night, on the beach. Were you … hurt, injured?"

"No, but it was scary."

He puts his notepad away. "Do you want me to post an officer here?"

"What and imprison me? No thanks, just do your job."

The inspector puts his coat and hat on. "Are you sure?"

"Goodbye, Boyd."

"Pint of Stella, Maggie, please." The hack is leaning over the Small Isles bar. "How are you?"

"Ah, not so bad, John." Maggie has eyes cast down looking at the bar.

"You're not looking very happy, what's happening with you?"

"Oh." She looks around. "Just not sleeping too well."

"Something I can help you with. Sleeping, I mean."

She knows what he means. "Maybe," she says, smirking at him, "I could do with something to help me sleep, John, but it wouldn't sort things."

"Oh, I don't know, it's amazing the power I have over women. I can bore most to sleep." She laughs. "That's better; maybe you need some TLC in that department."

She looks around again to see if her husband is around. "Maybe I do, come upstairs, to room three, on the top floor, at three. Magnus'll be off to Invernevis for supplies then, and we'll see what you can do for me."

Jackie gets to the bothy about three. If she is wrong, or more like if the boy is wrong, she thinks, she would have to turn around and get back down before it got dark. This is not a place to be after dark at this time of the year. She sees embers coming out of the bothy chimney, encouraging her, a fire is on and there is light in the cottage. She creeps up to a window and sees a huddle on the bed pulled close to the fire. She cannot make out the figure covered in blankets but she hopes it is her husband.

She tries the door; it is locked from the inside. "Rooney, you in there?" She calls through it. "Let me in, it's me. There's no one else here with me. I came alone."

The door opens. "What you doing here?" the father says. "I'm not going back. They'll lock me away."

She looks at him: ashen faced, the beard now taking on proportions of a thatched roof, though covered in remnants of baked beans to confirm there is a mouth there, the hair filthy and tousled, not so much fashioned as produced by the circumstances. "Rooney, I had nothing to do with it, you've got to believe me."

"No, I didn't think so. More like Ben, the friend, no doubt." He opens the door and, after having a look outside, locks it tight as soon as she gets in. "How did you know I was here?"

"A wee boy told me."

"What?"

"I'll tell you when you come home."

He looks at the bags she carries. "Did you bring something?"

"Food, clothes."

He opens the bags, pulling out trousers, underpants, and a jumper. "No drink?"

"No drink, how have you managed?"

"There was a half a bottle of port. I had it."

She goes to the open fire, relieved it's well backed up with chopped branches. "I don't mean that, how have you coped?"

She notices he is not talking the rubbish he had earlier. "Five days you've been here, Rooney. You detoxed?"

"Had ants crawling all over me, but the Lord protected me."

She looks into his eyes. *Not quite there yet*, she thinks. "You'll not tell them where I am?" he says.

"No, but they'll work it out for themselves in time."

He ignores it. "Will you bring me drink? I don't want to go down to the Spar. I'll be spotted."

"I won't bring you drink, Rooney, but I'll bring you food." He looks at her warmly. She can see he is coming down, the manic phase is passing, but she knows the black dog will come next. She understands she will need to watch him in case his mood plummets. Not a good place to be suicidal. "I want you to come back down soon. I've agreed it with Black, he'll treat you. You won't need to go to hospital."

"Ben, he did it, he triggered the section."

"I'll talk to him."

"The Huckle brothers, they are coming to take me away, ha ha. I need a drink."

"No bloody drink, Rooney, you'll get juice, soup, sandwiches. I'll be back tomorrow. Give me your phone, I'll charge it." She picks up his bag, not noticing the boy's backpack in there.

He snatches it from her. "God's work, Jackie."

This confirms for her he is 'not there yet'.

"Katie from the group called," she says.

"What did *she* say?" he snarls.

"Easy pal, they are asking for you, they are worried."

"Oh, right." He takes the food, pulls his chair to the fire and eats ravenously.

She looks around the bothy, and notices small wooden crosses he had been carving, evidence of religious delusions, definitely not there yet. She sees there is no more to gain by remaining there and makes her way back down, picking her way through the wood to get home before dark sets in. I follow her, staying by her side. People had fallen in these hills and died with what they call 'hyperthermia', mostly because they ignored advice to clothe and boot properly. She was well shod and wrapped in proper walker's garb. Some of which the husband had bought her at the last Christmas festival.

She would not be convinced the boy had been pointing up the hill, yet she had taken herself up there on that belief. I understand though, although a sceptic by profession and by belief, she, like many mothers who had lost a child, would be tempted by the thought the boy may still be around, in the house, and is even trying to communicate. When she arrives home there follows a kind of game where she talks to him and he talks to her, and whether she believes he does or not, it does not matter, it gives her comfort to believe he does. It gives him comfort as well and he appears happier than of late; so much so, I accept he can stay longer.

"Do you feel better now, Maggie?" The hack says from deep in the bed.

Maggie is at the window making sure the smoke from her cigarette blows outside. "Much better, Mr; you have a way of making a woman … feel better, not like my husband." She stubs the cigarette on the windowsill. "Sorry about the smoking, it does Magnus's head in. He'll know I've been smoking the second he comes in."

"Not for a while, I hope." The hack pulls himself up on the bed.

"Be after five before he's back. He said he'd phone before he left to get the dinner on."

"That's considerate of him. It's Friday – fish no doubt?"

"Aye," she says, on both counts. She pauses, looking out of the window. "But I'll keep my eye on the car park just in case."

"You have a lot on your mind."

"The teacher has killed herself, her husband the leader of the community council has killed himself, two boys drowned, men are being murdered, children are being murdered, my son is seeing ghosts, what else can I have on my mind?"

The hack gets out of the bed and goes to her. "True, but I can help you take your mind off things." He puts his arms around her.

"Sure you can, you're good at that, but if you don't get away from the window the customers will be wondering why a naked man has his arms around the owner's wife. Now, get away with you." She pushes him off.

They both get back into the bed.

"Angus?"

"The school's shut; they're transporting the children to Stoer primary and he hates it there. It doesn't do Gaelic, but they are kind there. They are supporting the children as best they can under the circumstances."

"Well, I'm here to support you."

She pulls the covers around her. "You are here to fuck me, Mr Scott. So don't give me the bullshit. I needed a bit of TLC as you say, that's it."

He takes his sweater from the chair by the bed and slips it on. "Can you close the window?"

"No, I need to get rid of the smell."

The hack understands to enquire more on this would inevitably lead to his expulsion from the room and more importantly the bed. "You are worried." He keeps it genteel. "I know you are."

"Yes, I am."

"Tell me?"

"You breathe a word of this or include it in anything you write and I will find you and I will cut off your balls and stuff them in your mouth; you got it?"

The hack puts on his underpants. "Ok, when put like that. I promise and I keep my promises to my friends. Tell me?"

"Angus sees Calum."

"He sees ghosts, he's the *taibshear*."

"A *taibshear* and yes I believe him. He saw the drowned boys."

"Afterwards?"

"No, before, a premonition; it was true, they drowned."

"Not a coincidence?"

"No coincidence, too close, and he is fixated on Calum; says he is trying to tell him something, keeps pointing to Beinn Mhor."

"The hill?"

"Yes."

The hack gets out of bed and goes to the back of the room, to the window looking towards the hill. "Have you told Jackie?"

"Yes, I have. And come away from the feckin' window."

"I hear she's being given a hard time." He gets into his clothes.

"Not from me and I'll bar any of those bastards if they say a word about her in the pub, you watch." She gets out of bed, wraps herself in the housecoat and heads back for another cigarette.

"I am sure you will, Maggie." He finishes dressing. "What do you think about the McIsaacs?"

She takes a big draw, blowing it out of the window. "I know there was something funny about the man. I've never liked him. There were rumours."

"Oh?"

"He liked … children."

"He took them to school."

"Not my Angus. He would have told me. If he had touched him I would have…"

"I know, cut off his—"

"Balls, like all of you fuckers."

The hack puts his watch on, lifts his jacket and heads towards the door. "I'm here if you need any more … TLC."

"Aye, fine, I'll keep you in mind." She keeps her eyes trained on the car park. "Watch yourself, a lot of people dying around here."

The hack smiles at her. She can't see him, her facing the other way. "I'll see you." He takes his leave.

CHAPTER 21

The following Monday, the inspector calls the chief. "I need to update you, sir; on the investigation, there has been a new development."

"Yes, I know son. McIsaac, I need to talk to you; you need to come here."

"I could talk to you now."

"No, son, you come here, now," the chief demands. "I'll meet you in the Belle, at two."

The inspector looks at his watch: ten fifteen; barring road works, he could make Glasgow by two. The chief doesn't offer much wriggle time.

Boyd arrives on time.

The chief is sitting by his usual seat by the fire. He gets up to greet the inspector. "Good man, Boyd, phone calls are too personal." The inspector takes the same place as last time they met there. "This won't take long, son, you'll be back up the road in time for your dinner."

"Many thanks, Chief."

"No sarcasm, son, it doesn't suit you." The inspector smiles. "Tell me about McIsaac?"

The inspector looks at the bar. "A young local lad came forward to say he had been touching him."

"These euphemisms, he was playing with his cock you mean."

"Well, yes." He looks at the bar again.

"You don't need anything, son. Do we know him?"

The inspector turns his seat in towards the chief. "He was in the craft, sir"

"I know that, Stoer, 1056, I mean otherwise."

"He ran the buses, took the kids to and from school?"

"Calum?"

"Was it him?"

"Sir, he was the leader of the community council."

"Was it him?"

"He'd taken his mark degree, sir."

"Keep your voice down, son. So, it wasn't him."

The inspector lowers his voice. "There is no evidence which linked him to the boy's death."

"Why did he kill himself?"

"The shame, I suspect."

"Yes, you suspect; however, a brother's column has been broken. You will make the necessary arrangements for the brethren to mourn him, Boyd. He had to abandon his project before the temple was built, but he will be revered."

The inspector hesitates. "Yes sir."

"It doesn't change the course of the investigation."

"No sir."

"Good, we already have our man."

"Temo's dead sir."

"So much the better, keep me posted Boyd." The chief is up and going towards the door. "And son, get yourself a pie and tea, you'll need it, it's a long journey back."

The inspector shakes his head and leaves, preferring to stop at the Artisan Cafe on the road up north instead.

CHAPTER 22

The mother is expecting him. For five days, she had taken him food every day, charged his phone every second day, and watched his eyes until she felt he was ready to come home, and now is walking along the path to the house. He looks around, apprehensively, wondering if the Huckle brothers, as he calls them, are waiting for him. She too feels apprehensive, but she will try not to show it. He pushes the door open and there he is, standing there. After nine days in the bothy, he is unshaven, pale, thin, and he looks like he has not had a wash in over a week, which he has not. He looks at her and smiles, and thinks about embracing her but does not feel able to.

"You should take a shower," she says. "There's some food: stew. So go and get changed."

"I will, but first, the deal?"

"You've to go to Black for your depot tomorrow and you've to stay off the drink, you've to act normal, and if there are any outbursts or incidents I've to phone him immediately, and this time you will be in, there'll be no hiding place; you got it?"

"Aye, and Ben?"

She looks at him; has he changed, is he still suspicious? "He is your named person and the link to your consultant. He is to monitor you, and if you slip up they really will come to take you away."

"Aye, indeed; have you and he…"

"Look, I am trying. So please, no more, just no more."

He knows it is time to silence these irrational thoughts. The boy knows it too as he moves closer to his father, pleased to see him back in the house.

"I had time to think up there."

"That's good. I won't take any of your shite anymore."

"I'll try my best."

"You'd better. But there's one thing."

"What's that?"

"Angus, the young *taibshear*, says he sees Calum." The boy perks up at this. "Another sick kid, Maggie wants you to see him." He is looking from him to her and back.

"Do *you* think he is seeing Calum?" The boy is nodding his head.

"Rooney, you need to show you are rational."

"I'll see him."

She moves the stew from the lower oven to the hotter higher one. The boy watches on, like a trainee chef following her every move. "I need to tell you about the McIsaacs, but first the shower, and put your clothes in this." She hands him a bin bag.

He showers, changes, and puts his filthy clothes in the bag. He arrives back in the kitchen pleased to smell that which he has missed for days: hot food. They sit down and eat, and she informs him of the McIsaacs' deaths.

He goes to the pot for more. "Have you seen Ben?"

She reaches for her pills. "I can't lie to you, he's been here."

"You back on them?"

She nods. "Headaches, Rooney inflicted."

"Ben help?"

"You were in your hideout."

"A support?"

"He'll help you too."

"Yeah, sure."

He goes to the bedroom closing the door behind him and empties the laundry basket onto the bed. He finds what he is looking for: the mother's panties. He studies them. He thinks he has found what he is looking for, but he needs to be sure. He returns to the kitchen. "I'm going to the pub to talk to Maggie, about Angus."

"Oh right, any excuse. But, just you remember the deal, and what will happen if you break it."

"I need the walk."

"Just you mind?"

The father stops by the shed on his way down the path. He closes the door behind him and goes to the book shelf where he pulls out the King James Bible opening it to find the brown envelope. He feels relieved it is still there unopened, but notices it is not between page 84 and 85 of the Bible, where he had put it. "Thou will bear false witness against me, but will thou covet my wife?" he says, putting the envelope back between page 84 and 85 and sliding the bible back on the shelf. Then he returns the boy's bag into the filing cabinet, under magazines in the bottom drawer.

"Hello Maggie." The father arrives into the bar, turning a few heads.

"What you doing in here, Rooney?" she asks. "You're barred after your … attack on Dram the last time."

"I'm here to apologise, Maggie, I was out of order. I am better now."

"Well, that's good enough for me, but Magnus may have different thoughts, but I still can't serve you. Jackie and Black say you've to stay off the sauce during your treatment."

He moves to closer to her so as not to be heard by others. "Jackie says you want me to talk to Angus, Maggie." He casts his eyes around the bar. Lunchtime in the bar at this time of the year, outwith the tourist season, would find a few locals there. Dram is at the end of the bar and moves through to the lounge as soon as he sees the father. The terror tourists are also there in their droves and notice the star of the show has just walked in.

Maggie leans over the bar to him. "Yes, Rooney, he needs to see someone and he wants you, but you're still not getting a drink."

"I'm not much of a psychologist these days, Maggie; burned out, washed up, so called shrink I am. Just the one, a pint shandy, I'm dead thirsty."

"I know you Rooney, and I know you care, and I don't give a shit for what they say about you, but you're not getting anything in here."

Hearing his plea for alcohol, the hack sidles up next to him. "Good to see you, Rooney. You OK?"

"I'm OK, but I wasn't after the last time I was here with you. As I remember it, you plied me with drink."

"Well, I promise not to encourage you again."

"Good, you can get me a pint then."

"I said, no," Maggie says.

"Your son?"

"I'll leave you two," the hack says.

"Aye, good idea, Mr Scott." Maggie gives him the look. The father shakes his head as the hack moves away. "You lost your boy and my boy says he is in contact with him, and I believe him," she says.

"I was an adult forensic psychologist, Maggie, not a child psychologist. Your son needs a child psychiatrist, if he is disturbed. Doesn't surprise me though, with all that's going on around here there should be a child and adolescent mental health team in here."

"I stuck by you, Rooney, both Magnus and I, when all the others…"

"Yes, I know, but just one."

"He refuses to see a psychiatrist; he has seen one in the past and says he will run away if we try to force him. No."

"I don't blame him, I would too; my psychiatrist—"

"Your psychiatrist?"

"Nothing, sorry. Anyway, I can't help him."

"You understand the mind, Rooney. Angus says he keeps seeing Calum. He has the *da shealladh*; do you know what that is?"

"I've been up here long enough to know it's the second sight. A pint, Maggie?"

"Angus sees things, he sees Calum. No, Rooney."

"All the children around here are affected … with what has gone on. It could be a hysterical reaction, a kind of … outlet."

"He says Calum has been following him around, like he wants to tell him something. I think if you talk to him it may help him. I am worried about him. "

"I don't think."

"He is your son, Rooney, your son, and it is harming my son. You have to help him."

"I don't know if I can, Maggie, but I suppose if he is fixated on Calum, I have to help."

"Then you'll see him?"

"Yes, I will. Just one pint, Maggie?"

She looks around. "On your head be it, Rooney. If your liver gives out don't blame me; and if you tell Jackie or Black, you're barred from here."

"I'll see him. Bring him to the house, tomorrow, after school. Thanks Maggie, I really appreciate it."

"OK, tomorrow it is." Rooney picks up the pint. "Please, Rooney, this is important."

"Just for tonight; call it a payment up front. I'll do what I can."

"I had nothing to do with it."

"I won't say anything, and Maggie?"

"I won't give you whisky, Rooney. I've seen what you're like on whisky."

"Could you post this for me, it needs to be recorded delivery, signed as received by the recipient, it's very important? I can't go to the Post Office. I want to keep my head down for a bit. Could you do it for me?"

She takes the small package, an A5 Jiffy bag. "Mr B Bingham, Glasgow." She feels it; it is soft, small. "I am not going to ask, Rooney."

"Will you do it? I'll give you the money."

"No you're OK, I'll do it."

CHAPTER 23

This is an interesting situation. I have the father about to talk to the *taibshear*. Ha, but I have the boy, his son, there too. He is animated, as if this is an opportunity he may not have again before I take him away. However, I will allow him this last contact with the living before he joins those on the other side.

Maggie Stuart delivers Angus to the father. "I'll leave Angus with you, Rooney. I'll give you an hour, exactly."

"Thank you, Maggie, I'll see you then."

"I'll be out here in the car, Angus. Are you OK seeing Mr Rooney on your own?"

"Yes, Mother, it is fine," he says, as she leaves.

The father invites him in. "Come in, Angus, would you like some juice, a biscuit?"

The *taibshear* appears uneasy as he is led inside, like he is going to the school nurse for an injection. "No thank you, Mr Rooney, I'll be getting my tea soon." The father invites him to sit at the table.

"Yes, of course you will, you'll be hungry." Angus looks at him and then looks towards the window, as if he is looking out of it. Then he turns and looks towards the son and smiles, appearing more comfortable. "Angus, your mother asked me to talk to you."

"I am pleased to talk to you, sir." He slides his hands across the table palms down.

"She says you have been seeing Calum?"

"Yes, sir, he follows me around. I see him." The *taibshear* is looking at the son as he says this. "He is my friend, I want to help him."

The father is clearly interested. "What does he say? Sorry, you can't … converse with him."

The son looks at him, somewhat confused at the word 'converse'.

"Sorry, talk," the father says.

"I cannot talk to him and I cannot hear him."

"Well, what does he do?"

The son is close to the *taibshear* now, as if he is trying to touch him. "He points at the hill, sir."

"The hill, which hill?"

The son is trying to tell him. "The big hill overlooking the village."

"Beinn Mhor."

The boy nods. "Yes, the big one up there." The *taibshear* points up at the mountain overlooking the village. The boy does too.

"Beinn Mhor?" The boy nods his head at him. "Why do you think he is pointing up there?"

"I don't know, sir." The son appears to be trying to grab his friend, to shake him.

"Did you know I was there, for a few days, I was kind of lost?"

"Yes, my mother told me."

"But I am not there now."

"No."

"When did he last point towards the hill?"

The *taibshear* looks at his friend. "Just now, sir; he is doing it now."

The father looks on askance. "Where, where is he?"

The *taibshear* turns his head. "He is standing right there, sir." He points to the right of the father. The son is so close the father could touch him, if he were alive. The father turns to look at the space where the *taibshear* points. "But there is no one, sorry; I know you can see things, but I find it hard to believe Calum is here."

"Please, Mr Rooney, he is."

"Well then, what is he wearing?"

"His school clothes, sir." The son looks down as if he is surprised at this.

The father, almost out of desperation to make contact with the son, reaches into the space indicated, as if he could touch or even embrace him. "I wish I could believe you, Angus, I so want to see my son again."

"I wish I couldn't see him, Mr Rooney, I don't want to see him dead, I want to see him alive, so we can play together again."

The son drops his head, as if he knows this will never be possible again.

"It must be upsetting for you, seeing the dead?"

"I know they are dead, but they don't seem dead to me, sir."

"No … if it is of any comfort to you, I have also seen things."

This appears to please the *taibshear.* "You have?" He smiles.

"Yes, I have a mental illness, some call it bipolar disorder; when I am very unwell I see and hear things."

"Do you think I have this … bipol…?"

"No, Angus, but I have known some children, in my work, who would see things, some have imaginary friends, but some have an illness."

"What do I have?"

"I don't know, Angus."

"I don't imagine them, they are there. I thought you would believe me, Mr Rooney. Calum is my friend. He is trying to tell you something, through me."

The father casts a steady look at him. "When your mother said you saw Calum pointing to Beinn Mhor, when I was … lost. I thought he may have been trying to show where I was. Calum and I had been to the bothy many times. I thought he may have been trying to help me. But now I am here…"

"He is still pointing to it, sir." The *taibshear* looks to the father's side. "He is doing it now."

"Can you indicate to him, I am confused at this?"

"You can indicate it to him yourself, sir, he is right beside you."

"Right, OK." The father hesitates as he turns to the space indicated. The son looks at his father, almost pleading with him to believe the *taibshear.* "Is there anything else you can tell me, Angus, about Calum?" He turns back to the *taibshear.*

"No sir, that is all."

"How does he look … to you?"

"He looks scared, sir."

"Thanks, Angus. Your mother says you are not sleeping." The father appears relieved to move to a subject he is more comfortable with.

"No, I am not, sir."

"I can help you. I can give you some … advice on how to sleep, some relaxation exercises, or maybe a CD. Also, if necessary, counselling which would help you to take these … things off your mind."

"No, sir. I feel better now. I am pleased I told you, but even more pleased you believe me."

"Good, Angus. If you want to come back at any time to talk it will be OK with me. Will I tell your mother to come for you?"

"Thank you, sir."

The father goes to Maggie Stuart's car. "That's him, Maggie."

"Do you think it helped him, Rooney?"

"Time will tell, Maggie. I didn't do much professionally, but sometimes the catharsis helps. You can let me know."

"Thanks, Rooney."

"No prob, Maggie, see how he goes."

The *taibshear* says no more of seeing the son, as if he had done his duty towards him, as a friend would. The father now knows what the son has been trying to tell the *taibshear* and through him the father.

Three days later, Maggie Stuart is seeking her own form of therapy. She is with the hack; however, he is looking out of the hotel bedroom window. "You are away again, Mr Scott." She is irritated at his lack of attention on her. "Gazing out of the window, have you gone off me so quick, a burgeoning relationship indeed?"

"I'm just thinking about all the stuff, Maggie. Trying to work it all out in my mind, it's what we journalists do. We need to construct hypothesis, give opinions without forcing them down the throats of our readers."

She slips her housecoat on and moves to him, taking him by the hand away from the window. "Away please, naked man at hotel window, with hotelier's wife, while hotelier is at Invernevis, not good." She leads him to the bed, sitting him down on the edge. "So, what have you got?"

"You sure?"

"Aye, go on, I may have some opinions of my own." She switches on the mini-kettle on the bedside table. "Coffee?"

"I would expect as much. Yes please, thanks."

"Just don't you dare put a word of it in print?"

"No, you have editorial control over that one."

She hands him a coffee and a small biscuit. "Right, Calum got into a car, that's all there is."

He smiles at the hospitality tray. "You look after your guests." She smiles back. "The teacher said he did. I doubt if he would have walked home in the dark and if he was on the road someone would have spotted him and picked him up. So, one way or another, yes he was in a car."

"OK, you got a car, but whose car?"

"Well, as much as we know there was Temo or could it have been her husband's?"

"The chairman picked up the kids from the school. Anyway, should we be talking about the McIsaac's the day after they are laid in the ground?"

"Why not? I got some good information from the funeral yesterday. Good lunch, incidentally."

"We try. They were important members of the community."

"I got the feeling the community would be happy to forget how important they were."

"The community has had enough of controversy, Mr Scott; now tell me?"

"Well, according to her statement, there was one car, not another car, if there was she would have mentioned it, and she would have said it was her husband's car."

"Would she, implicate her husband?"

"Well, she said she didn't see the car properly to identify it or the driver."

"Rooney always said Calum would have never got into a car of someone he didn't know. So, what do we have?"

"Well, Inverbeg didn't drive and he didn't own a car."

"This is correct."

"So the possible car drivers we know about include Temo, and Calum knew him, Rooney, of course, and McIsaac. Who else could be in the frame on that regard?"

"An unknown driver Calum knew, to the point he would get into his car."

"John McIsaac seems plausible, given his reputation."

"I said the community has had enough of controversy, Mr Scott. Anyway, why would Calum get into McIsaac's car, given his reputation?"

"McIsaac was a paedophile; he would have groomed him,

offered him something, he would have fabricated something to get a hold over him, it's what they do."

"Ok, let's say he got in, which of course could have been possible. Not that I am saying he did."

"No, of course not, but let's develop the point."

"Go on."

"Right, he got in the car, then got out of the car when whomever stopped, let's say for the present, McIsaac."

"He did a runner?"

"Maybe."

"McIsaac had child locks; he would have had to have."

"OK, he stopped and abused the child in his car, then decides to take him outside, to kill him, dispose of the body, destroy the evidence, ensuring no fingerprints or DNA are in the car, and that is when Calum makes his escape into the dark. McIsaac looks for him but doesn't find him, then heads home to conjure a story that the boy made it all up, he was nowhere near there."

"So, what happened to Calum then?"

"He hides and waits for McIsaac's car to disappear along the road then walks home."

"Then what?"

"Well, here we have another set of scenarios."

"Go on."

"He's killed by Inverbeg who comes across him on the road; or Temo comes across him and kills him; or McIsaac drives back looking for him; finds him and kills him; or he's killed by someone else."

"Someone unknown."

"You should have been a detective inspector."

"I've been ready these kind of true crime stories for many years, you?"

"Well, you develop an interest, make hunches; it makes your copy more real, more plausible."

"True crime?"

"Something like that. So, summing up, as we journalists do."

"Paraphrasing?

"Indeed. The first scenario says, McIsaac picked up Calum and killed him – case closed. The second scenario suggests Calum got into McIsaac's car and managed to escape him; Calum gets out, and is either picked up in another car, for example Temo and was killed by the driver, or someone unknown, or he is killed as he walked home maybe, for example, by Temo, Inverbeg, or McIsaac."

"Or someone unknown."

"Indeed."

"Why you doing this, John?"

"What do you mean?"

"Boyd is the investigating officer, the chief constable is Jackie's father, a large number of detectives are involved."

"Exactly, Maggie, and what do you think about the investigation?"

"They seem to have settled on the Albanian."

"And yet, as we discussed, there are holes in the story."

"So, you are wondering why they are not pursuing other lines of enquiry, McIsaac, Inverbeg, or the other unknown you talked about?"

"Indeed, I am wondering and I intend to find out. In particular, the chief."

"Now you are on dangerous ground," she says. "Go on, why would you want to find out about the chief?"

"Something Rooney said."

"About Hubert?"

"Right."

Maggie looks at her watch on the bedside table. "Right, Mr Journalist, my husband is due back in an hour."

"I get you; you are bored with the hypothesising, time to move from the cerebral to the physical."

"You got it, come here."

Two hours after this, the mother is at home with the father. "There's a package for you, Rooney," she says. "It's on the sideboard, recorded delivery. John the post brought it. I signed for it."

"Jesus, it was mine." He takes the package.

"Don't bloody push it, Rooney; your jacket's on a shaky peg since coming home."

"Jackie, I've been as good as gold since I came back from the hill."

"I meant the Small Isles, last week when you went to talk to Maggie, I smelt it on your breath."

"It was only one."

"Sure, only one. If Black finds out, your feet won't touch the ground and no hiding place the next time."

"I'll be good."

"What's in the package?"

"It's private, Jackie."

"I need to know. If it's something to do with your … thoughts, you'd better tell me."

He smiles and goes to his shed.

He takes his messenger bag, most of his important items are normally in there, and the envelope containing the DNA findings just obtained from the knickers. He places it with the other envelope containing the DNA report of the gloves, and puts them inside the old Bible, making sure they are between pages 84 and 85. He puts the Bible back on the shelf, then he puts the packet containing the knickers alongside the boy's backpack in the bottom drawer of the cabinet, covering them with magazines. He would come back to them later.

It is the Saturday evening. The father has arranged a birthday dinner for the mother, though not much good cheer is to be found in the home.

"Not much of a birthday dinner, Jackie?" He opens a second bottle of wine. "Sorry my efforts at cooking steak were so abysmal."

She has been staring at him through the course of the meal. "You're right, not much of a dinner with you and without my son."

"I guess we have to make the best of it." He holds the bottle over the mother's glass. "Here we are just over a month on and no further forward; you having some more?"

"I've had enough, Rooney."

"Yes, I suppose, I hope you don't mind me topping up though."

"I don't mean …. I've had enough of you."

"Jackie, I know we have problems, but we need to—"

"Stick together, I don't think so. We have nothing any longer to hold us together. Calum was the glue holding us together. Now he's gone…"

"We have each other."

"You no longer have me."

"I've been trying."

"Not hard enough, Rooney; you said you would stop when you went on treatment, you promised; you're drinking again. What about the empty bottles, in the garden, behind your shed."

"Empty bottles?"

"Aye, and in your shed, in your filing cabinet. Your hideout"

This gets the father to his feet. "My filing cabinet, why were you in there?"

"Have you completely lost it, man?"

The father is off out of the house and down the path into the shed, where he pulls out the bottom drawer of the filing cabinet.

"Are you looking for this?" comes from the mother standing behind him at the door holding up the boy's backpack.

"Sorry, I don't know what—"

"You don't know what? It's Calum's bag. You have had it all the time."

"I…"

"And also guess what, I also found my knickers in there and your gloves. You got some perverse interest in my knickers, Rooney, part of your chronic … disabilities?"

"I don't…"

He looks to the Bible, still on the shelf, unopened. She returns to the house, he follows.

She is back to her dinner, trying to cut her steak. "You took evidence from the crime scene, the murder of our son?"

He sits down. "I wanted it."

"You wanted it, but why didn't you tell me?"

"You just happened to find it, looking for my drink?"

"You are a serious fuck up, Rooney." She struggles to cut the steak. "Almost as fucked up as this steak."

He sits quietly for a minute wondering whether he should tell her he sent the knickers away for DNA testing, how he needed to know if it was semen, presumably the friend's, on them. But decides this would be one silly step too many. "Are you fucking Ben?" comes out instead.

"You really are off it, buddy, completely delusional, insanely and pathologically jealous. What wife would put up with that shite, answer me?"

"I need to know."

"You are out of your mind, literarily. This is the last straw, Rooney, final nail in the coffin."

He moves closer to her. "Jackie, we need to get through this, we need to get the bastard, put pressure on Boyd."

"We are no longer a we, Rooney. I can't do us and I can't do you. Ben was right, you are a total fuckup."

"Oh, here we are, Ben. Now I know what's going on. You and Ben just like before."

"He has been supporting me through this, supporting me, rather than doing my head in."

"You don't know him like I do."

"Look at you, a complete mess, killing yourself with the drink, a pathological nut job?"

"I'm—"

"*You* are hearing the voice again." *Is he?* "And can't cope with the investigation, Temo, etcetera."

"It's not him, Jackie, you know that."

"I don't care, Rooney. I just don't care. I just want out. I want a normal life again. I'm going back to Glasgow."

"Oh aye, and where to?"

She opens her phone. "Ben, come and get me?"

"Don't tell me, Ben's?"

"He'll put me up until I get somewhere of my own."

"And you can't go to your dad's?"

"With Deirdre Hamilton-Brown, you joking?"

"Just great, on your birthday, you drop this on me."

"There is no right time." She takes more pills and washes them down with wine.

The boy is looking scared, looking from one of them to the other.

"No, no right time. Well, get to fuck then. I'll manage fine here, on my own." He fills his glass as she gets up and heads to the bedroom. "Give my best to the best friend, and have a lovely birthday; lovely birthday present coming to you." He takes a big gulp of wine. "I hope he fucks you proper, but you tell him I'll be watching him."

"Thanks pal, if I needed any greater justification to go to him that is it. I look forward to him properly fucking me. Aye, a birthday treat, at least he's able to fuck me, not like you, you drunken, pathetic, bastard."

"Get tae…"

The mother gets up and looks down on this man. It could be sympathy, it could be anger, but it is more like pity. "Why didn't you tell Boyd you had the backpack? You didn't tell me you had it. Where was it?"

"I found it on the road at the beach, next to Calum's books. I put it in my car. It didn't seem relevant at the time, I mean to the investigation."

"Not relevant, not relevant. Rooney, there is something in this, all of this; it makes me think I can't be with you."

"Well go away then, but before you do I need to tell you something."

"You don't need to tell me anything."

"No, well what about Angus, about Calum's communicating through him; don't you think he's trying to tell us something?"

"You don't believe what Maggie said to you about her sick son. You are out of it, Rooney; get a grip."

"You just don't know; you just don't know what's going on."

"You should go to your meeting, Rooney, Katie will be missing you."

"At least that's where *I'll* get support."

"Not that you'll need it, eh? You're invincible, the big man, the father, as was on both counts."

"Jackie, I don't need you."

"One more thing, Rooney, before I go?"

"What?"

"It was my birthday yesterday, the second of December. After all these years you still get it wrong."

"Oh right."

"Yeah, oh right, just shows you how much you know or care about me."

She goes to her room and picks up her case, already packed. The father and the son are at the door as she walks past them. "Jackie, we can talk about this, please?"

"Too late, Rooney, too late."

The father and the son look out into the night as the mother gets into the friend's car. The boy appears to cry. I have never known this to happen. The dead do not feel, to my understanding; this boy does though.

"Go. I hope he fucks your brains out."

"Rooney?"

"What?"

"Calum's bag will go to Ben, after I give it as evidence to Boyd. The knickers you can have, pervert." She throws them at him, landing on the table in front of him.

The father looks at her. "You have to do what you have to do," he says, as she leaves.

I look to the boy, a confused and pained look on his face. I move towards him. It is time for him to go, there is no benefit to him or me in him remaining. He recoils from me as I slope past him following the father into the sitting room. In there, he notices two birthday cards lying on the mantelpiece.

He picks them up, wishing he had given her one. He opens the first and reads it. "From Dad and Deirdre, much love on your birthday." He opens the second and reads it too. "To Jackie, from Ben, with best wishes." Then as he is about to put them back a folded note falls out of the friend's card. He picks it up and reads it. "Jackie, Calum's bag is in Rooney's shed, in the bottom drawer of the filing cabinet. Please do the right thing, love you, Ben."

"Bastard!"

CHAPTER 24

It is the winter solstice, the 21st of December, and for the people of this place this marks the shortest day and the longest night. They will soon be celebrating their festival of Christmas, but the solstice predates the arrival of their Christianity by thousands of years. Then they would light bonfires, tell stories, and drink ale; make the occasional sacrifice to the gods to earn blessing on the forthcoming crops. This is the dark night of their souls, where the dark triumphs. From now until the summer solstice the nights grow shorter and the days grow longer, the dark wanes and the sun waxes in strength.

It has been eighteen days since the mother left the father. Throughout this time, the father has fallen deeper into the drams and even deeper into the despair than ever before.

The solstice is the turning point in the year. Would this mark the turning point for the father or will he continue a journey into a dark unknown that can only arrive at my door? He opens another bottle, takes a dram, and vomits blood all over his kitchen table.

"You are going to die, oh master."

Getting on his feet, he staggers into the toilet, where he spews more blood-filled vomit. Would I be taking this man this night, I wonder? He opens his bathroom cabinet, takes omeprazole capsules.

"Fat load of good that'll do you, Rooney, your stomach is fucked."

The father looks at himself in the bathroom cabinet mirror. He cannot believe what he sees. He fills his hands with cold water and splashes his face. It remains the same. The man in the mirror looks like a man he feared, the face, the face of his father; bloody eyes, hair a mess, blood vessels in his cheeks and nose protruding like tributaries of a subterranean red river running just below the skin of his face. This is what he has become. This is the man he fears he would become, the drunk, the father.

He drops to his knees and sobs. "I have become my father."

The father has become 'the father', an unbearable reality. Over the next couple of days, he stays sober, but the DTs return: the rats and other nasties remain for a time. He understands without nutrition he could develop alcohol related brain damage. He drinks copious cartons of milk, most of which is spewed up, and eats omeprazole capsules for his stomach.

The Christmas festival arrives and the father is much improved. He eats a breakfast of scrambled egg and toast and it stays down. He showers and dresses. "Happy Christmas, my boy Calum," he says, talking into the middle of the boy's bedroom. "If you are here, a merry Christmas, son. I wish you were here to share it with me, but I guess, you'll be elsewhere."

You are wrong, father, he is there, right by your side. He is not with me yet, nor with his mother. This is his home and he refuses to come with me. He looks to the father and smiles. He does not see this.

The father appears resolute this day, more than ever before. The voice in his head remains, however, brought about by his lack of medication and his continuing mental illness.

"Lazarus has arisen."

It has bombarded him for days, chastised him through his darkest hours. It still does, but it is less intense now.

"The father has come back from the dead."

He has not been with me.

"The father who became his father, the drunk, the failure, pulls himself together, temporarily, to view life until the next time when it surely will be his last."

On this, I agree.

"OK, bastard; time you helped me for a change?" The boy looks bemused at this.

"Anything to assist, oh master."

The father makes himself comfortable at the kitchen table. He has work to do.

"'Someone who would rejoice personally in my grief?' Bill said. Who would rejoice personally in my grief?" he says to himself, or to his voice.

"'Who would enjoy knowing they had killed your son without the enjoyment of you knowing who they were?' he asked. Who would that be, Rooney, only you would know?"

"Only I would know?"

The father collects the two envelopes from within the Bible. He opens the one containing the DNA report on the gloves. He studies the report. "Who are you, you fucker?" he says to the test. He continues to stare at it for a few minutes then repeats "Who would rejoice in my grief?"

"Bloody DNA reports say nothing, why did I do it?" He thinks for a minute, then says to himself: "I could send it to Boyd to be compared with Temo, presuming they can still get DNA, albeit degraded, and from McIsaac and Inverbeg the same. And what would that do? Could I trust Hubert and Boyd with the results, given they are dead set on convicting Temo? What credence would they give to a DNA analysis provided by Bingham, a crime boss in Glasgow. Would they manipulate the findings to suit their case? No way, I'll do this myself. He's my son and I'll find his killer, because they won't."

He looks at the first report on the gloves and reads: "Evidence submitted for DNA Analysis: a pair of garden gloves. The DNA reference samples obtained are consistent with being a mixture of three male individuals: contributor A, a male; contributor B, a male; and contributor C, a young male. From the methylation, we establish there are two adult males and one child male. Unless DNA matching can be made by obtaining DNA samples from known or suspected individuals a DNA match cannot be definitively provided."

He looks at the DNA report on the knickers and reads: "Evidence submitted for DNA Analysis: Swabs from woman's underwear, panties. The DNA reference samples obtained are consistent with being a mixture of two or more individuals: contributor A, a male and contributor B, a female. The profile can be separated into a major component profile consistent by contributor A, the male, and a possible trace contributor B, the female, both unknown individuals, though presumably B is the owner of the female panties." He has a wry laugh at this and reads on: "Unless DNA matching can be made by obtaining DNA samples from known or suspected individuals a DNA match cannot be definitively provided." He pushes it aside. "A fat lot of good that is, unless I get other samples. Jackie's is the easy one, which really doesn't tell me anything, unless her DNA is from the other test." Does the father really believe his wife, the mother, could have killed the child?

He lays the two reports on the table side by side and brings a table lamp close to study them carefully, going from one to the other. Immediately he sees a similarity in the coding. "A match!" He springs to his feet. "Surely not Jackie; no way?"

"*Would she rejoice personally in your grief, oh master?*

The father looks in more detail to the reports and immediately he sees 'a mixture of two or more "male contributors"' in the second report, presumably himself, given they were his gloves, and the other the killer, given they were worn by the killer at the time of the murder. Then "It's a match," he says. "A male match." He quickly discounts himself as the donor of both DNAs given he hadn't had sex with his wife in the timescale. He quickly concludes the killer of his child was also the lover of his wife.

"Well, who do you think that might be, oh bastard?"

"Caber, John the Post, the Dram, oh master?"

"Shut up. Who is the likely candidate for fucking my wife?"

"And killing your boy?"

"Well the first one is easy," he says.

"Someone who would rejoice personally in your grief."

The father lifts the reports and wanders around the kitchen. "The only definitive way I can prove this one way or the other is to get his DNA. If it matches..."

"Take it to the authorities, let them do it."

"Oh, I take this to the authorities. Excuse me, I have here the DNA of my son's killer from the gloves the killer wore that night and I have a DNA sample taken from my wife's knickers, from the cum of her lover. As you will see, Inspector Boyd, there is every probability that my friend did the nasty deed there too. He fucks my wife and he fucks me too; he kills my son and he kills my marriage."

"And he rejoices personally in your grief?"

"Yes, and yet, if I reveal this for further testing on him to establish if this DNA is indeed his, I let the cat out of the bag he is fucking my wife and I am out to frame him for the murder of my son by contaminating evidence, by using a criminally obtained test, taken from some crusty cum of my wife's lover and putting it in the gloves: a delusional and irrational thing to do. He gets the girl and I get incarcerated. Whatever way, he gets the girl."

"Rejoice, rejoice, rejoice."

"I'll get him myself."

"Then, when you get him and you are locked up for his murder, who will rejoice at your grief then, oh master, except you, for the rest of your miserable life in the State Hospital?"

"Get tae, bastard; I'll do this with you or without you."

"On your head be it."

Not to celebrate the festival of Christmas, more trying to recover from his illnesses, both physical and mental, he makes himself a dinner of chicken and mashed potatoes. He then watches the television set, going from one old Hollywood film to the other: *White Christmas*, his mother's favourite; *It's a Wonderful Life*, his; *Miracle on 34th Street*, his son's.

The boy appears to enjoy the experience of sharing this with his father. I feel more aware that the time for him to move on is arriving, but for this day, he will remain with him.

The investigation of the murder of his son is never far from the father's mind, however, and he spends the rest of the evening writing on his laptop, uttering the same mantra over and over again: "Caplan crisis theory, create crises, create energy, use the energy, make change."

"Once a shrink, always a shrink."

"You have to use what you know, bastard."

The boy looks on bemused, wondering what the father is on about.

"Time to stir it up," he says, striking the keys on the keyboard with gusto.

The man appears obsessed, I think, but this man is prepared to break rules, I have found, and this I must observe.

It is the day after the Christmas Festival. This day the inspector arrives at the parent's home with the constable. They are not bearing gifts, but the father opens the door willingly, like he was expecting them.

"Good morning, Inspector Boyd; you no family to be with on Boxing Day?"

The inspector looks the father up and down as if he is surprised to see he is on his feet, dressed and well kempt. "It couldn't wait, Rooney. We had to see you."

The father notices the constable behind the inspector, "Oh, plus Constable. The last time you came, you were coming to take me away."

"As I remember it, Mr Rooney, after you came back from your hiding place, you were to accept informal treatment, and your wife was to call us in if there was any risk to health, welfare or safety."

"Of self or others, Constable?"

"Yes, of course, Mr Rooney."

"Well, anyway, you'll be coming in then." The father points them to the kitchen where they refuse to take a seat. "Should I pack a bag?"

They look at each other. "Mr Rooney," the inspector says, "we are here because you have made a formal complaint against the chief constable."

"With the SPA," the constable adds.

"I expected you, gentlemen." The father pulls his laptop computer close to himself on the kitchen table. "It must have been the easiest thing I have ever done. I did it last night on the internet, a tick box sheet and the details of my complaint in a box." He opens the laptop. "Worked a treat; want to see it, I downloaded a copy?"

"No, don't worry, we have it here." The constable pulls out an A4 envelope.

The father persists. "Don't you want to hear it? It's why you are here. Funny how intelligence works in this country. You do something one night on your computer, the next day you get a visit from the police, just great."

"We have our own copy here."

"It won't do any harm to reiterate it, so we are all on the same page."

The inspector and the constable look at each and decide to placate the father. "Go on then."

The father brings up the document on his computer. "OK, here it is." He opens a file named *Complaint against the Chief.* "I'll read it to you." They decide to sit down after all. "'I refer to the case of Calum Rooney, my deceased and murdered son. I believe the chief constable has been negligent in his duties in not bringing the person who killed my son to justice. He has influenced the investigation to his own ends, interfered with the course of justice, and he has shown a clear conflict of interest with his role as chief constable and his familial position as grandfather of the murdered child.' How does that sound, clear enough?"

"We have it, Mr Rooney."

"I'll finish it if you don't mind." The inspector's vacant response shows tacit approval. "OK, here goes," the father says. "'Taken together the SPA must consider his position as head of Police Scotland. Under these circumstances I believe it is impossible for him to hold the respect of the force and of the public at large. He must, therefore, be suspended from duties spending a full public inquiry into his conduct. Thank you.' All clear, are we?"

"Yes, Mr Rooney."

"And you are here as the instrument of a corrupt organisation."

"It doesn't do your case any good by insulting us."

"Oh, insulting. I can see the way this is going to go."

The inspector gets up. "The SPA has to carry out a preliminary assessment, to assess whether the conduct amounts to any kind of misconduct."

The father opens a sub file titled *Regulations*. "I know what the regulations say, Inspector."

"We need to say this, Mr Rooney, so you'll understand."

"Well, go ahead, get on with it."

The inspector reads from the script. "Where the authority assesses the conduct would, if proved, amount to neither misconduct nor gross misconduct, it may take no action, it may take improvement action, or it may refer the matter to be dealt with under regulation."

"Yes, disciplinary action against the chief, just what I want."

"However, where the authority assesses that the conduct would, if proved, amount to either misconduct or gross misconduct, it must decide whether the misconduct allegation is to be investigated and if it is to be investigated, it must refer the allegation to the commissioner."

"Or if it is not to be investigated, go on, blah, blah, blah."

"We are to do the information gathering to assist the SPA assessment."

"But you are part of it, Inspector Boyd."

"I am not mentioned in the complaint, Mr Rooney. Otherwise I could not do it."

"By implication, Inspector Boyd, as will be established."

"Can we start with the investigation?"

"Yes, why not?"

The inspector moves to stand over the father. "Are you … able for this, Mr Rooney? You appear slightly haughty."

The father moves to the other side of the table. "Oh, you'll be saying I'm high next; manic, paranoid, wrongful claims against the chief constable."

"Well, you were … ill," the constable says. "You were saying inappropriate things about the investigation."

Fearing confrontation, the constable tries to militate against this remark. "We know you are unhappy with the outcome of the investigation so far. But, in my experience, in time everything comes out. Then you'll appreciate our actions were fine."

"The whole process is, was shite, Constable Broomlands, and you know it."

"I don't know it."

The father faces the inspector. "I want to know where you got the evidence Victor Temo came here to do us harm?"

"I can't…"

"No, you can't, it's subjudice. But I know it was Zaharia, who else would it have been?"

"I can't prejudice third party information, Mr Rooney."

"I believe someone, the chief possibly, leaned on Zaharia."

"These are serious remarks, sir, and we can't comment on police contact with Mr Zaharia."

"No, but I know the chief had his man and that's all that mattered, while my child's murderer was still at large."

"We had other lines of enquiry."

"Rubbish, before you charged Temo you had run out of ideas, leads. You made an arrest, but with no concrete evidence, and then Temo, regrettably, is killed in custody"

"We have no knowledge this is correct; we are investigating his death."

"Oh, another investigation, and in the meantime the trail has gone cold."

"The case remains open until it is concluded, Mr Rooney."

The father sits down and returns to the computer. "Oh, what to 'state publically Police Scotland's view on the sufficiency of evidence' he did it."

"We could not get a conviction, he was dead, Mr Rooney."

"No, the chief made sure of that."

"Careful, Mr Rooney, we can't accept that."

"And what about Inverbeg?"

"We had nothing to link him with the boy."

"He was a serial abuser, Boyd, the boys, and guess what, he is dead as well."

"He was part of our investigations."

"Oh, right, well let's come up to speed with McIsaac."

"There was no evidence."

"You had him, a paedophile; images on his computer, local boy abused, you had his wife saying she thought he had picked Calum up."

"He's dead, Mr Rooney, the car was burned out. Mrs McIsaac is dead. The only thing we had was he was touching a boy and what his wife said about him and the car, but that was not enough."

"So you said to my wife."

"Yes, we did."

"Look Calum gets into his car, he goes missing, he is found dead, what more did you need?"

"Evidence."

"Evidence, you wanted a confession, and you can't always get that from a dead man."

"We do our best."

"Your best isn't good enough."

They pause, as if they are drawing breath. "And why, sir; why do you think the investigation hasn't produced the right outcome?"

"Two reasons, Constable: one, there are outside forces at play, and you know who that is, and two, *he* wanted Temo to be convicted."

"Mr Rooney, why would anyone want Temo to be convicted, other than if he was guilty?"

"To implicate me, that's why. I brought death to my family and to a small highland community. It's all about me."

"And why do you think we could have done better?"

"You know fine, Broomlands."

"I do?"

"Yes, you do; you have not been forensic enough."

"Our forensics were thorough, Mr Rooney. There was no external DNA, no direct evidence, nothing; but there were sufficient grounds to support a conviction of Victor Temo."

The father hesitates at this. Is this an opportunity to discuss his own DNA findings? "I don't mean that," he says, deciding not to.

"What do you mean?"

"Your investigation was shite, Boyd, and you know it, and why, because someone was pulling your strings."

"You are getting seriously close to contempt, sir."

"You know what I mean: a thorough investigation which encompasses a whole range of aspects, including profilers to unpick what you have, narrow the field down, flush out leads, get the man."

They look at each other again. I can see it. They intend defusing the atmosphere, to placate the father. "Forensic profiling, Rooney," the constable says. "What, like *The Silence of the Lambs*? Not the kind of thing we do here in the highlands."

"Oh, you don't have a silence in the hills when the lambs are taken off to slaughter?"

They are laughing at him; I can see it in their eyes. "Yes, of course we do, this is a farming area."

"Starling was horrified by the killing of the lambs. She felt helpless because she was unable to stop the slaughter."

"Oh?" The inspector whispers something in Broomlands's ear. "We are not here to talk about … movies."

"No; how do you feel Constable, with the slaughter going on around here, in your own community, unable to protect them?"

"The constable protects this community, sir."

"Oh, Inspector; you didn't even think about bringing in a profiler."

"We…"

"The chief didn't want a profiler. Why muddy the water and bring in an expert?"

The inspector folds his arms, leans on the AGA, and looks up at the ceiling. "OK, Mr Rooney. We have a profiler: you; so please, give *us* the benefit of *your* experience."

"Veering from your original task, Inspector, are you not?"

"You are making some very strong accusations about our abilities, sir; so, you tell us what we could have done better."

"Jesus, is it worthwhile to try to get through to these tumshies." The father is talking under his breath. "OK, let's do it; right, what have we got, or did we have, Inspector?" He is on his feet and on the move.

The inspector holds his gaze on the ceiling. "Victor Temo remains our prime suspect, he was charged, and he was going to trial."

"The other possibilities, the other suspects?"

"We have exhausted all other lines of enquiry."

"You put all of your eggs in the one basket, and believe me that will come back to haunt you."

"Oh, it will, right. Go on, sir, the forensic profiler." The inspector shakes his head, wondering whether in humouring this man he would reinforce his delusional diatribe.

"Right." The father moves close to him. "Let's get back to basics. According to the old adage what do you need? You need means, motive, and opportunity."

"Yes, indeed Rooney," the constable says.

"And evidence," the father adds.

"Yes," the constable says. "And to prove guilt in a criminal trial, you have to have the what, the how, the why, and the where." The inspector looks on aghast. Should he stop this?

"Correct, and what did you have?"

The inspector intervenes. "Sir, Temo had the means: his hands; the motive: you, equals revenge, you had his friends killed; the opportunity: he left the pub, got in his car killed the boy and got back to the pub to confirm his alibi. That is it, *sir*."

The father looks at him, stunned, as if he is seeking an answer to this attack. He finds, "Ah ha, Inspector, but no evidence. So, don't be so bloody blinkered, Boyd. What did you have?"

"Well, you seem to know, so you tell me?"

Rooney uses his fingers. "OK, you had Temo, but what about Inverbeg, Taylor, McGing … and MI5?"

"Rooney, I believe your belief systems are … under strain just now."

"My systems are under control, Mr Boyd."

"You are drinking, sir, your wife has left you; your illness has re-emerged, I believe as confirmed by—"

"Doctor Black?"

"Medical opinion."

"OK, we'll get back to the MI5 … influence. So what about the Birreli family case? Jackie also had her enemies."

"Police Scotland in Glasgow closed off that line of enquiry."

"Oh, you mean the chief?"

"Mr Rooney?"

Yes, I know he did, and what about the unknown local or incomer paedophile. Let us talk about McIsaac, or someone we don't know about, an opportunist, or someone in our midst with the three elements *and* the evidence?"

"The Albanian met the criteria."

"How long was he out of the pub?"

"He said he left the bar to get bread and ham from the shop, then he went back to the bar; but we think he was out long enough to pick up your son and kill him and then return to the bar."

"Come on, he would have been noticed missing for that length of time, his glass would have been picked up. No evidence, no confession, nothing, and what about Zaharia?"

"Please sir, we exhausted that earlier."

"Oh yes, third party information, etcetera, etcetera; and while you focused on him you missed other possibilities."

"We have been wide ranging." The inspector looks at his watch.

"You don't even know where Calum was killed?"

"The post mortem established he wasn't killed at the scene, sir."

"He could have strangled elsewhere, off the road, in the machair, and taken there. Have you explored that aspect?"

"Oh yes, we believe we did."

"He was picked up in a car? Or was he? Or was killed in it or somewhere the car could have travelled to in the timescale? He was picked up at four and was dead by six, then found by me by seven. He was in the water by six, cooling had occurred, he was in the water. We have four to six p.m., so we have time. Now, to geography: we have one road in and one road out, the same road; one hour to Invernevis, thirty-five miles of windy road. I doubt if he could have been taken there, killed, and brought back in that time, but that's the outside perimeter, the thirty-five miles from here to Invernevis. Did you check any sightings of cars in lay-bys between four p.m. and five p.m., and between here and Invernevis?"

They look more serious now, as if he was commanding some of their respect.

"Not specifically, sir, we asked if there was anything unusual though, throughout the area."

"He got into a car; don't you think it unusual? I know my son."

"Unusual, I agree."

"No indication of distress or assault, he was dressed and tidy?"

"He was assaulted, but not sexually."

"It takes time to do that, to get him to accede to wishes, undress, do the thing, dress."

"There was no DNA, no blood." The father hesitates, thinking about the DNA reports he had recently obtained. "He was dressed when he was killed."

"Why couldn't he have been killed later?"

"He would have been distressed; a distressed, crying kid would have been noticed."

"I keep telling you; Calum would never have got into the car unless—"

"Unless?"

"He knew his attacker or the attacker managed to persuade him to get into the car – 'Your mum and dad asked me to pick you up'. He may have been unknowingly groomed."

"Inverbeg didn't have a car."

"Why are you so sure he got into a car? Inverbeg was out and about for a walk."

"The teacher says he did."

"Did she see him getting into a car? She saw her husband's car pulling away. She didn't see him getting into it."

"No."

"I came across Inverbeg at six. Could he have forced Calum to go to the beach to abuse him, or have killed and carried him there, and got back to Lochdarrach by the time I came across him; and what about McIsaac?"

"What about him?"

"He had form. He could have groomed him, picked him up in his car. Opportunity, means, motive?"

"Sex with wee boys?"

"Right."

"There was no evidence."

"His car was burned out by his wife. Why did she do it?"

"She wanted to destroy everything about him, she said."

"Why wasn't he a suspect?"

"There was nothing to suggest he should be."

"No, not because of his position in the community like him being a mason, perhaps?"

"We refuse to go there, Mr Rooney. Anyway, to all intents he was a respectable—"

"Child abuser, Inspector?"

"He regretted harming the boys, Mr Rooney," the constable says.

"What?"

The inspector stares at the constable who looks back, patently clear he had said something out of turn. "We had a report of a boy, Mr Rooney, a matter which was … addressed by Father Legowski."

"And for which the man killed himself," the constable adds. "There can be no greater justice."

The father is not going to be diverted. "Inspector, the constable said 'he regretted his actions against those boys'; boys, plural, not just the one boy."

"Yes, he did, sir." The inspector scowls at the constable.

"And the chief told you not to reveal it." No answer, but the constable is looking back at the inspector. "But it wasn't him."

The inspector looks relieved. "No, and why not?"

"Because Calum hated him," the father says. "He would have never allowed him anywhere near him."

"How do you know, sir, how can you be convinced?"

"He refused to go in the school bus, Inspector, that's why he was picked up by us. Andrew Dewar was his best pal, of course he would have told him, warned him. It rules him out."

"OK, what else did you have, Mr Rooney? What about McGing and Taylor, the Glasgow element; there were plenty of motives there?"

"I know it wasn't them, believe me, I've checked them out, personally."

"Oh." They look at each other again.

"I know what you mean by your 'oh', Inspector and your looks at each other."

"Do you, Mr Rooney?" the constable says.

"Implication, me, Glasgow, my history, all points to me gentlemen; no local killer for you guys."

"*I* haven't."

"You haven't because the chief wouldn't let you." They decline to answer this. "Anyway, I have and it's not them."

I got bored at this point and sloped off. I hoped I might be called to take a soul. This season appeared to be always a time when some people passed. I do not know why; indulgence was common at this time. I roamed the house looking for the boy. Where would he be? I had no control over where he would go but they always say around their 'environment', their 'home'. There was too much going on in the kitchen for him to remain there, the sitting room too close to it, he would be in his bedroom, and that is where he was. He was sitting on his bed, as if he could not understand why his mother wasn't there or there weren't any presents on the bed as they would normally be at this time of year. Sometimes I wish I could talk to my charges, but what good would that do? I just need to do my job and take them away. I often know what they are thinking anyway. Most are happy to be relieved of the trials of living, especially if they are old or infirm; a blessing, the living would say, a blessing, some of the dead would say too. Some are not happy, the boy is not happy, but would he be any happier if I sent him onwards? I doubt it. I drop down at his feet. He looks at me, as if he has seen an old friend. I am not sure this is right. He needs to respect me, not to like me. But he seems to get some comfort in my being there, as if I can protect him from … the unknown. I would like to comfort him, but I cannot. I would like to tell him his mother and father love him, but I cannot. In feel sorry for him. He never quite reached his eighth year. He spent the majority of his short life in unpleasant circumstances, being taken from his natural parents and given to new parents. He had found some happiness with them, but then is taken from the new world he had grown to enjoy.

I slope back as they are exploring the father's history. He is listening intently as the inspector gives information he thought only he knew. "Josh Turnbull, one of the McGing gang, was killed, after he was mouthing off he killed your son."

"Inspector, how did you know that if the chief didn't tell you?"

"Do you want to tell us anymore about the killing, Mr Rooney?"

"No, but it wasn't him neither."

"So, what's left, sir?"

"The MI5?"

"Back to the delusions?"

"Who's being insulting now, Inspector?"

"Go on."

"The motive, Jean Dempsie; they think I killed her."

"So, where does this leave us; loose ends?"

"It leaves us with an inconclusive investigation, Inspector."

"The investigation is concluded, sir, we had a charge and were confident on a conviction."

"I understand your predicament, Boyd. Your boss holds all the shots."

"The investigation remains open, Mr Rooney, we will continue to pursue new information, should it demand it." The constable looks more comfortable now, like he is on safer ground. "We have 'new' information, Mr Rooney."

"Oh, yeah, and what is it?"

"Jackie gave us Calum's backpack."

"Oh yeah?" he says, as if he was expecting this.

"We found a pair of gloves in it, presumably they were yours. We wondered why they were there, so we have passed them to our forensics unit with the bag, evidence, Mr Rooney, evidence."

"Oh, I guess, Jackie, has been … helpful, Inspector. I guess daughter and father are now working together on this one."

"I can't…"

"No, you can't say."

"The bag, Mr Rooney, why did you remove it from the scene?"

"I told Jackie, I wanted it. It was his."

"There is another possibility, sir."

"Oh, yes, and what is that?"

"You killed your son?" The father does not take kindly to this, something to do with his upending the kitchen table and pushing a chair across the floor. “Please sir, we do not wish to restrain you.”

“Restrain me? You say I killed my son, and you expect me to accept that.”

“Please sit down.”

“OK. So tell me, Inspector, how do you come to the conclusion I killed my son? Unless … external forces are pulling your strings, puppets, Mr Boyd and Mr Broomlands; who is your puppet-master?”

The constable moves around to the door, to bar the escape route.

“Practically,” the inspector says, “you could have killed your son; you were out in your car at the time of his … apprehension; although if you had picked him up, it would not have been an apprehension. He would have got into your car willingly.”

“Do you know how absurd this is?”

The boy is shaking his head.

“But the question I can’t fathom, Mr Rooney, is why. Why would you kill your son? Unless the mental illness you suffer from prompted you.”

“My mental illness is stable, stable.”

“Not according to Doctor Black,” the constable says. “He thinks you are in relapse, and we had information from your wife, about your behaviour, and in the pub…”

“Dram! He knew about Inverbeg and said nothing?”

“‘Oh Father, give me the power to punish these wicked people,’ you said. Rather than taking you home, I should have taken you in,” says Broomlands.

“I am better now.”

“The complaint against the chief says otherwise, Mr Rooney,” the inspector says. “We are informed Mr Bensallah is your named person under the Mental Health Act. And he is very concerned about you.”

“Oh, he’s been in touch too, this man who is out to destroy me?”

They look at each other again.

“Are you hearing any voices,” the inspector says, “Mr Rooney, in your head?”

“No.”

"That is not what we have been told. Mr Bensallah knows you very well."

"Oh great, a conspiracy across all my main antagonists."

"Paranoia, Mr Rooney?"

"OK, open and cut case, nutjob kills his child, case closed, State Hospital for the rest of his life. And what about Temo and what about the real killer who is out there somewhere?"

The inspector says, "Some killers with mental illness say they are commanded by very powerful forces, sometimes driven by voices, to kill."

"This is a stitch up."

"You are now a suspect in the murder of your son, Calum Rooney, Mr Rooney."

"Are you charging me?"

"At this stage, having your son's backpack isn't sufficient evidence you killed your son. We are charging you with removing evidence from a crime scene. But should the gloves show up anything significant..."

"You are not charging me?"

"We are charging you with perverting the course of justice, Mr Rooney; you do not have to say anything. But, it may harm your defence if you do not mention when questioned—"

"I know the rest, I'm being framed."

"We will be seeking an assessment order under the Mental Health Act, to establish your mental state. In the meantime, we are instructed to return you to hospital. Your psychiatrist, Doctor Melville and Doctor Black have signed the documents to have you taken there; we have them here."

"Lovely, you come here to gather information for my complaint with the SPD and you leave with me in your custody. This will look good in the papers. Where is Scott now?"

"Not connected, sir; we had intended raising these matters with you in the course of gathering information for your complaint."

"In Russia you speak up against the authorities you end up in jail. Where are we Boyd?"

"We are only doing our job, Mr Rooney."

"Why me, Boyd, apart from the fact your boss had demanded it?"

The father gets up, but in seconds the handcuffs are on him and he is taken away to the adult mental health unit at Abertay Hospital. The boy comes to the kitchen as they are taking his father away; for the first time he is alone in this house.

CHAPTER 25

"I feel so much better to know you are in Glasgow, Jackie, with Ben." The chief arrives into the living room. "Not much of a house though." He looks around. "Typical social worker's house, bloody untidy."

Ben gets up. "I'll get the coffee."

"I'll have tea, son."

The friend goes off to the kitchen. The chief looks around the sitting room again and shakes his head.

"I'll work on it, Dad; besides, I won't be here long."

"No, I'll help there. You two could do with a bigger house. Once you sell up north, you can restart your life."

"A big step, Dad."

"Rooney and you are finished, darling. He is in hospital, criminally insane, case coming up; could be sent to the state hospital for killing Calum, and look at you, you are … so much better."

"Thanks, and where does that take the Temo conviction?"

"Temo was our best guess at the time." He pauses. "Maybe we'll never know the full story."

"If Rooney is insane, Dad, how can he testify, they can't convict him, insanity at bar?"

"The court can convict based on an examination of facts, where it is beyond reasonable doubt he committed the offence, after which he could be in the State Hospital on a compulsion order with restriction, meaning he could be there without limit of time, meaning for many years. He'll be an old man before he comes out. Burned out, done in, useless."

"I don't want that."

"I know, darling, but he may have killed your son."

"We don't bloody well know that, give him a break."

"Jackie, darling, that chapter in your life is gone, a new one is beginning, a better one, a safe and secure…"

"Away from the alcoholic, crazy dangerous catholic, Dad?"

"You are better off without him, darling."

"He didn't do it, Dad. I know him."

"He had Calum's bag, Jackie; he was out there and first to come across Calum, so he said."

"And you had Temo, sent here to hit Rooney, but who kills Calum instead?"

"We might never know darlin', one thing we do know is Rooney—either by implication, where a hit man arrives and kills Calum, is sent by a man Rooney damaged, or directly in a crazed state of mind—kills his son, believing by doing so he would break the link with his past."

"Oh come on, how do you know that?"

"He had the bag."

"Yes, we know, but where's the evidence?"

"The bag and the gloves, darling."

"You guys having a nice chat?" The friend arrives with the tea and coffee. "Tea for you sir and coffee for you darling."

The chief looks at him, then at her to see if the term of endearment is reciprocated. It is not.

The chief looks at the friend. "Calum's blood was on the outside of the gloves, the killer's DNA, sweat, skin cells in the inside. Rooney's DNA?"

"Oh, come on Dad, his DNA would have been in the gloves anyway, we wore them every day when he was working the dyking."

"The gloves are away for testing, we'll get the report back after the New Year break. We will know then."

The friend sits down and pours the coffee and passes the cup to the mother. "Jackie, he said he squeezed Calum, like he was trying to squeeze the death out of him, maybe he squeezed the life out of him. The boy could have been alive when he came across him."

"You don't know that; don't say that."

The friend pours the tea. "Sorry, darlin'," the chief says, taking the tea. "It is just possible, probable maybe that Temo hadn't … done him in proper. In Rooney's state of mind, distraught, paranoid, he kills him."

"Well, he couldn't have been culpable then, Dad."

"Inadvertently, darling, by connection to Temo or by sick state of mind, he is responsible, darlin', responsible."

"Responsible."

"Yes, Jackie, responsible, and by god I'll make sure he never harms you or anyone else every again."

Thick as thieves, comes to mind as I slope between them.

The following day the father appears in the Abertay Sheriff Court. He appears happy his day has come and has prepared his case well. He will convince the Sheriff that he is well, he is innocent, he should be allowed to go home. He is to be disappointed, however, when he is not even allowed to speak. The Sheriff sends him to the State Hospital on an Assessment Order to be brought back for Examination of Facts.

The father protests, "I am innocent, I am well, I am—"

"You'll have plenty of opportunity to state your case," the Sheriff says, "when you come back for trial, sir. That is all." With this the Sheriff is up and out of the room and the father is left wondering what he needs to do to demonstrate his innocence.

The friend and the mother are at dinner in his house. He had prepared what I believe to be 'pasta'.

"Good pasta, Ben." The mother takes a glass of red wine from him.

"I know, fresh Bolognese sauce; it's good to cook for someone."

"I guess; you've been on your own for a long time, never known you to have been with someone. I used to think you were gay."

"Well, we dispelled that, didn't we?"

"Suppose."

"Anyway, I was always keeping myself for you."

"Oh, so why did you think you would end up with me?"

"I just knew." She looks at him. "I always knew Rooney would mess it up, and when he did I wanted to be there for you."

"You are such a considerate friend; sly bastard some would say." It is his turn to look at her. "Are you still his friend?"

"I supported him through thick and thin, you know that."

"Are you still supporting him?"

"Like more wine?"

"I went to see him today." She spoons more pasta onto her plate.

"Oh, you didn't say you were going."

"No, why should I? They sent him to the State Hospital for god's sake."

"I know, but we are together now, you and I."

"He is still my husband."

"We need to do something about that, Jackie."

"You want me to leave him, divorce him?"

"New life, Jackie, you deserve it."

"I had a new life."

"You have a right to better."

"And you are better; divorce him, marry you, live happy ever after."

"I'll make you happy, Jackie."

"I've already divorced him. Two divorces to the one man in one lifetime is one too many."

"You have grounds for divorce. God, do you have grounds for divorce; he killed your son, Jackie."

"No, we don't know that, he is ill. He has been transferred to the state hospital for god's sake."

"Yes, I know, I was trying to say that, at the time."

"Why do you think he did it?"

"I'm not a consultant, darling, but he was hearing voices, he was paranoid, thinking they were out to get him."

"Well, there was some basis to think that. They *were* out to get him. Christ, they even followed him to Achfara."

"Doctor Melville believes Rooney has been psychotic for years, chronic, delusions of grandeur, narcissism, paranoia over MI5, use of others to harm and kill. He thinks he may have killed Calum, having found him after he had been attacked, to protect him. In his crazed state of mind, he thought by killing Calum he would be removing him from harm's way."

"Jesus, in a crazy way, it makes sense."

"Thank god you're starting to see clearly."

"There's one thing. I don't see how finding Calum's backpack in Rooney's shed can incriminate him."

"No? It ties him to the scene."

"He was there anyway and it isn't conclusive evidence."

"Why didn't he say he found it when he found Calum? Why did he take it from the scene, important evidence?"

"Boyd asked about it in his interview with us. He could have mentioned it then, given it up."

"If he was innocent, he would have had no reason to hold onto it, hiding it away in his shed, important evidence."

"He said he wanted it because it was Calum's."

"Do you believe that? He had lots of Calum's things."

"No, you are right, but I still don't understand why he wanted to hold onto it. Why would it incriminate him? His fingerprints would have been on it anyway."

"What about the gloves, they were on the killer as he strangled Calum, the killer's DNA inside the gloves, sweat, skin cells, and on the outside of the gloves, Calum's skin cells; an indisputable link between Calum and his killer. Rooney stuck them in the bag before Broomlands arrived, then he put the bag in the machair, to pick it up when he was leaving the scene. Broomlands was too busy guarding the boy until Black and Boyd arrived. The gloves were on the killer when he killed Calum, Rooney's gloves. He killed Calum."

"Why don't you wait for the DNA report, Ben, before you say that?"

"It all makes sense, Jackie."

"How does it make sense?"

"Think about it. Narcissists destroy everything they have."

"Jesus, the social work stuff is coming out … again?"

"Come on, Jackie. He couldn't cope with a normal life, look at his life? I've known him for thirty years."

"Aye, a good friend." He looks at her, as if trying to see if she is joking or not. "And I've known him the same."

"We all met together, in university; out to change the world."

"And did we?"

"Did we?"

He reaches across the table to her. "Maybe we can't change the world, Jackie, but we can change our lives." She accepts his hand.

CHAPTER 26

This place gives me the creeps, the hack thinks, as he approaches the seventeen-foot-high green metal fence around the grounds of the State Hospital at Carstairs. As required, he presents himself at the reception area. "I am here to see Sean Rooney, I phoned and arranged it, an hour-long interview, he agreed." He hands over his ID, having submitted a visitor's application form and photograph, stating his relationship with the father and his reasons for wishing to visit.

"Thank you, sir." The receptionist studies the ID, his face, confirming the appointment. "This is your pass." The hack looks at it, smiling at the photo as people do. "We have a group of people going to Lewis Hub, you'll be bused up there. Please read our security arrangement, all visitors must adhere to security procedures; you'll see an officer with a dog, this is for drug detection. You are not allowed to walk in the grounds without an escort. OK?"

The hack nods. "Fine with me." It is well after two of the afternoon when the group is taken through security; all mobiles, car and house keys put in individual lockers; then through body scanning; then transported around one hundred metres from the reception building to the ward in a locked minibus.

The father is passive, albeit impatient as he sits in the patient sitting room in his seat. They all have their own seats.

The hack appears at the ward door with a few others, family members, mainly, valiantly travelling to the depths of Lanarkshire, some from far-flung parts of Scotland, to see loved ones. *How far this is from Achfara*, the hack thinks, *not only geographically but also culturally, socially, physically*. The ward door is opened from the inside and they are in, where he is taken to a sitting area to await the father. He hardly recognises him as he is escorted in to see him. The nurse says to him, "The minibus will be back at three, he is advised. If you need anything just ask. Don't expect too much, Mr Rooney is on admission medication."

He takes him to an open visitors' sitting room, where the hack takes a seat. The father is brought in. They face each other without saying anything. "Hello, Sean," the hack says, eventually. The father doesn't answer. "I was looking forward to seeing you." This isn't going to be easy. "I am sorry I am late, a bit of a hoo-ha getting in." The father looks on impassively. "I need you to confirm you agreed to talk to me." The father nods. The hack can see he is dulled by the medication they put into him. "Just try to respond in any way you can." The father nods again giving an indication he is following the hack. "You know I am doing a story on you and Jackie. I wanted to add your recent circumstances; how you happened to be detained in the State Hospital."

This seems to stir the father's consciousness. "My incarceration, you mean." He looks up gradually. "Don't you smell a rat?"

"I don't."

"You know what I mean, Mr Scott, the investigation, my stirring things up. I get arrested, end up in court, then in here. You don't?"

"They think your mental illness caused you to kill your child." The hack pulls out a notebook, the only thing they allowed him to bring in. "Paranoid psychoses, delusional beliefs, bipolar manic depression, hallucinations, voices telling you to harm others, and a whole host of circumstantial evidence, like being at the scene of your child's death, including your DNA found in the gloves that wrapped themselves around the throat of your child."

The father gets on his feet at this. He holds onto a chair for support. "All lies, all fixed to detract from the real culprits here, the chief of Police Scotland, a rigged investigation, to detract from the actual killer; personal interference, etcetera, etcetera. Will you write about that?"

"People will say this is all part of your persecutory delusions."

"Will you write about it?"

"Yes."

The father goes to the window looking into the nurses' station. "Why?" he asks the hack, his back to him.

The hack gets up and walks to just behind him. "Because I believe you."

The father turns to look the hack full in the face. You can see he wonders if he can trust this man. "OK, let's do it." He accepts the risk.

"You need a good lawyer, a mental health legislation expert. I'll put you in touch…"

"I know the law, but—"

"It is an ass, Sean." The father smiles at him, possibly the only emotion he has shown since being taken there. "Mr Bensallah is your named person; he should be talking for you."

The father's smile changes to a frown. "Him, he's part of the problem, not the solution."

The hack sits and writes this down. "Will you fight the conviction, the detention?"

"I will."

"In what way?"

"I'll get a second opinion on my mental health status, a re-assessment."

"What about your conviction? If they find you sane, and you are convicted, you'll end up in jail."

"That's where you come in."

"Eh?"

The father sits down across from the hack once more. "The investigation; you said you believed me. Why do you believe me?"

"There are aspects of the investigation which didn't ring true." From a dulled half open state to becoming more lucid, the hack realises the father is taking this in. "But for me to help you, you need to help me?"

"And how can I do that from in here?"

"I am an investigative journalist; I need to get to the bottom of this and at the same time do a good exposé, literally to expose them."

"Jesus, you are talking my language." The father becomes animated at this.

"Right, first, the backpack, this is crucial evidence against you; where did you get it?"

"It was left on the road."

"By whom?"

"I don't know, the murderer, obviously?"

"No paranoia, Rooney."

"Reality, Mr Scott."

"You said the investigation was flawed, at the community meeting when you stormed out."

"Yes."

"I need to do some digging, some delving into aspects of the investigation I feel uncomfortable about."

"Start at Zaharia and Al-Jamal, he'll know about Temo."

"Yes, I remember Al-Jamal, Rooney, ISIS. I interviewed you when you ran him out of Glasgow, the kidnapping of John McCourt, the police officer."

Rooney's eyes widen even more. "Now I remember you, Jesus, why didn't I remember that?"

"Because I was operating under another name."

"Oh, you were."

The hack gets up and looks into the nurses' station. "Intelligence."

The father also gets up and looks into the nurses' station. "We can't mention … intelligence in here, they'll say it's part of my delusions."

"Then, we'll keep it to ourselves, will we?"

The father nods, they both sit down.

"Do you think I could be convicted?" the father asks. "I could either stay here or go to prison for the rest of my life?"

"I think that is a certainty if you are convicted, but as for prison—"

"I know what they do to child killers in there."

"What do you want me to do for you?"

"I want you to see Katie McLeod, from the AA meeting in Invernevis. You need to talk to her."

"And Al Jamal, I think I can find him."

The father looks at him and gives a smile.

The hack looks at his watch. "I need to go."

"That wasn't any time."

"I'll be back."

"As Arnie said."

The hack laughs. "Yes, Rooney, as Arnie said."

The following day, the hack is in a café on the Dumbarton Road in Glasgow. He keeps his mobile tight to his ear and his voice hushed for fear of being overheard. "Hello, Mr Zaharia."

The voice on the other end is hesitant. "Yes, who is this?"

"John Scott, investigative journalist, sir, freelance."

"Not the sheriff officers."

"Not sheriff officers, Mr Zaharia, I used that to get you to call me."

"You lied to my office, saying you were coming to take away my goods."

"Zaharia Services Ltd., court decree, failure to submit proper accounts, tax avoidance, easy to find."

"What do you want?"

"I want to talk to you."

"What about?"

"Temo."

"I have already spoken to the police."

"I am doing a story which will prove you perverted the course of justice."

The hack is blagging, of course, and this man falls for it. "Come to my office," Zaharia says.

Scott finishes his coffee and picks up his taxi waiting for him outside. Fifteen minutes later he arrives at the office, no more than a portacabin in the South Side Premier Car Valeting Service. He approaches one of the men with a power washer blasting a BMW. "Mr Zaharia?" He nods to the portacabin. The hack walks towards it, becoming aware of two large men following his path. He turns around. "Mr Zaharia is expecting you," the smaller of the two, says. "We need to search you."

"I don't carry a piece." The hack feigns a New York cop accent.

"Are you wired?" The bigger of the two men frisk him from top to toe and then he uses a detector to cover every inch of his body and clothes. "Give us your mobile?" The hack hands it over. "Follow me." The hack does.

Zaharia is at the other end of a large desk in his office. He gets up to meet him. "I've checked you out, Mr Scott. I know you are very able. You were involved in gangland Glasgow in the past, and covered the ISIS event. You know your stuff, sir."

"Indeed, Mr Zaharia; been around you guys for quite a while."

"We are clean, sir." Zaharia invites the hack to sit at the other side of the table.

"Yes, as you say, sir." The hack takes the seat, turning around to see the heavies block the door behind him.

"You don't have anything on me. Why are you here?"

"Calum Rooney, I am covering the case."

"I have given the police all I have."

"Yes, so I believe, but I believe there is more."

"People can get hurt in your business, Mr Scott."

"Oh, yes, I know, Mr Zaharia. But it's the business I chose. I take the risk, but I always have a safety shield to deflect a bullet."

"Oh, and what do you have here today, to deflect that bullet?" Zaharia looks to his henchmen bookending Scott.

"MI5, Mr Zaharia, they were … monitoring you."

"I cannot help you, Mr Scott."

"You employed Victor Temo; he was one of your lieutenants, an ISIS man. The Glasgow gangs hit the Albanians, your crew. I also did a piece for the Herald on the ISIS kidnapping of John McCourt, the police officer. You gave evidence, in the Temo case, incriminating him, how he was sent to do a job on Rooney."

"I don't recall—"

"The Family hit you guys bad – the Red Hoose we called it in the papers, bloody event that was. Might have been you guys who sent Temo to do a job on Rooney and hit his son instead as it transpired? And he just happened to be linked to ISIS, who Rooney also damaged in Glasgow, got them out as I remember. Temo protested his innocence."

"We didn't send Temo north."

"No, but you linked him to ISIS, which you said did."

"I assisted the police."

"I don't think Temo did it. I don't think Temo was sent to harm Rooney or kill the boy. I think he was set up."

"You have to believe what you believe, Mr Scott."

"I believe you gave wrong information, under duress."

"I told the truth."

"You said Temo was working for ISIS. Al-Jamal Saddam Al-Jamal, the leader of the ISIS fighters in Glasgow. Rooney ran him out. He had a debt to pay and sent Temo to Achfara."

"Regrettably he killed the boy."

"The investigation said that; a very weak investigation that settled on your testimony, the smoking gun, linking Temo with ISIS. Hitman kills son of the father. All sown up, case closed. However, had there been a decent investigation and contact with ISIS, the police would have established no link with ISIS ever existed. ISIS did not contract Temo to follow Rooney north."

"My sources say something different."

"Your sources? And what about Al-Jamal; I have been in touch with him."

Zaharia's face turns white. "He is ... dead, he killed himself after he fled Glasgow."

"No way, sir, not even Rooney believed he would. He took the fifty million the family paid ISIS, or him more like, and is living a playboy life in Dubai. It wasn't hard to find him."

"You are lying."

"Am I?" The hack allows a long pause, sufficient time for the Albanian to try to read his face. "Again, a proper investigation would have tracked him. It wasn't that hard. I did the piece for the Glasgow Herald at the time. I interviewed Rooney; he said Al-Jamal's father lived in his home in Georgia's Pankisi Gorge – Al-Jamal was a Chechnya fighter before he became an ISIS commander. Many of the Chechnya fighters were from the Pankisi Gorge. I used my contacts, traced Al-Jamal to Dubai."

This is where Zaharia is not sure the hack is lying. If he is, he is a very convincing liar.

Zaharia looks to his lieutenants, as if to say 'kill him'. The hack picks this up, like he was expecting it. "Please look out of the window," he says, "across the street." Zaharia gets up and looks out of the window. "Can you see the black cab over there, the one that dropped me off, the one waiting for me?" Zaharia turns to his heavies. "You can't see it, but the driver has a high focus lens on us at the moment, recording us in here. If I am not out," the hack looks at his watch, "in five minutes, he's to take that to the Glasgow Herald, along with my statement saying you perverted the course of justice by giving the police incorrect information on Temo, wrong incriminating information, and a cassette of my interview with Al-Jamal in Dubai."

"What do you want, Mr Scott?"

"I want to know why you gave the police the incorrect information, sir."

Zaharia looks around trying to decide if he can trust his own men. "You don't have to tell me now," the hack says. "That would be … problematic for you, but this is where you will find me." The hack gives Zaharia a card and heads out. The heavies make room for him at the door. He goes to the taxi. "Queen Street Station," he says to the cabby. "I need to be on the 12.20 north." This is a master of the 'blag', I would learn from him.

"No problem, pal," the taxi driver says, as he heads off for the station.

Some five hours later, the hack gets off the train in Invernevis. He walks across to the Bookford Hospital, to a portacabin with a sign: Invernevis Council on Alcohol. In there, he asks for Katie McLeod. "I'm Katie McLeod, we do everything in here," she says, sitting at the only desk arranging the files. "Can I help you?"

"I called you, this morning. You were kind enough to see me today."

"Oh, yes, Mr Scott."

"Do you always work on a Saturday?"

"I am an alcohol counsellor, sir, we are here for people when they need us, and invariably late Saturday is one of those days people fall off the wagon."

"Yes, I understand."

"If you wish to follow the twelve steps, you should go to your doctor or a social worker who will refer you. Once referred, you will be allocated a sponsor who will bring you to the meeting and introduce you."

"I want to talk to you."

"Who referred you to me? It should be social work."

"I may like a drink, but I am not an alcoholic, not yet."

"So why do you want to see me?"

"To talk to you about Sean Rooney, from Achfara."

"Sean didn't mention you to me."

"He goes to the meetings."

"We protect the confidentiality of people who go to the meetings very seriously."

"You are Mr Rooney's sponsor?"

"Yes, and his counsellor. He has told you more than we normally discuss." She gets up, goes to the door and opens it.

"Do you know he is in hospital?"

She closes the door. "Yes, I do."

"Do you know he has been … detained in the State Hospital?"

"Yes, I know." She returns to her desk and looks out of the window. The hack has time to study her. She is attractive, not in beautiful way, but in a handsome, intelligent way, like she would be an interesting woman to be with. He wonders whether he should flirt with her, but his assignment there this day is too important to jeopardize.

He sits on the end of her desk. "I went to see him, he told me about you."

"Oh, he did."

"He said you were friends."

"He is ill."

"I know about you and Rooney, but I don't want to cause you any problems."

The counsellor adjusts her seat to see behind the hack to the door, as if she is fearful someone would enter. "Mr Scott, please, my husband is…"

"I am aware your husband is disabled and you wish for him not to know of your affair with Mr Rooney, but he is in serious trouble."

"What kind of trouble?"

"He has been charged with the murder of his son."

Just then the door bursts open and an extremely inebriated man almost falls in the door. "Hello, Katie, are you able to see me?"

"Not right now, Angus. Come back in half an hour."

"I don't know where I'll be in half an hour, Katie."

"You'll be in the Ben Bar, Angus, that's where you'll be."

"Aye, so I will. I'll come back."

"He needs your assistance."

"Angus just needs to talk and drink and drink and talk, never does anything about his drinking problem, but it makes him feel better about drinking. We are non-judgmental here."

"I understand. Rooney?"

"He hasn't been back to the meeting since the wee boy was killed."

"Indeed, and you need to help him."

"I can't do anything; it would create difficulties for me."

"You care about, for him?"

"I do, but … my husband."

"Mr Rooney's son was killed on the night of the first of November. His wife, Jackie, called him on his mobile at four thirty to say he was missing. He was to be at the meeting in Invernevis that night, which I believe begins at five. He came right home, and arrived in about five fifteen. The boy was picked up about four and killed about five. They are saying he killed the boy."

"He couldn't have; he was with me when he got the call. It takes forty-five minutes to get to Achfara. He left here at four thirty."

"Yes, I thought so."

"I was counselling him privately."

"You were sleeping with him."

"Did he say that?"

"No, I am saying it; there have been rumours."

"No one knows about us. My husband is ill, disabled."

"Are you prepared to testify to save an innocent man, a man who was your lover?"

"It would kill my husband."

"Will you?"

"I can't."

"It's your choice, you let Rooney spend his life in the State Hospital, or you're honest with your husband. He'll understand your needs, you have met his."

He leaves her there to think about it, to await Angus's return, to talk to her husband, to do the right thing.

The hack gets along the road to Achfara, some forty-five miles from Invernevis. He arrives around 5 p.m. and goes straight to the Small Isles bar. He parks the car and heads in. Maggie is there serving as usual. He orders a pint of lager. Maggie delivers without a smile, unusual for her.

"You are quiet, darlin'." He checks to see if Magnus is around. "What's the matter?"

"I don't think I can trust you." She wipes the bar.

He reaches for her hand but she pulls it away. "Oh come on, love, you knew this was platonic, how could it not be?"

"Oh, I know, a good old-fashioned fuck was all to be expected." She goes out from behind the bar and picks up some glasses, to despatch them on the bar in front of the hack, where she sets about washing them in the sink under the bar.

"Did I disappoint?"

"You lied to me, and you used me."

He leans over the bar to ensure no one can hear the conversation. "Men do that, Maggie. You are a mature woman. You know they say things to get women into bed; but you know I like you."

She starts drying the glasses, gaining a perspective over him. "You used me for information, for your story. You saw me as a way into the community, to find out what was going on here, your story, but you are not what you say you are."

"Sorry?"

"You are not an investigative journalist."

"Maggie, all you need to do is to check out my profile online, see the numerous stories I have produced for years."

"I am not sure about that; it could be a cover for something else. Something about you just doesn't fit."

"A cover, a cover for what?"

"I don't know but I heard you talking on your mobile. You thought I was sleeping." She looks around – dangerous words are being spoken.

"Oh aye, and what did I say?"

"You said you needed a warrant to examine police records as they concern the investigation of Calum Rooney."

"Oh, you must have misheard, Maggie. How could I get such a warrant?"

"I'm not stupid, John, there's more to you than an investigative journalist. I think you are involved in some sort of … official capacity."

"Maggie…"

"I'm telling you John, if you don't tell me, I'll be on the phone to Boyd."

"When the time comes, I'll tell you, Maggie, I promise."

The mother is busy painting the sitting room in the friend's house when the phone goes. She would normally let the friend answer it, it is his house after all, but he is not in and the phone will not let up. "OK, OK, I'm coming," she says, taking her paint covered gloves off. She picks up the phone. "Hello, this is Jackie; Ben isn't in at the moment..."

"It's me, darling, your dad."

She knows why he is calling. "Hi Dad, you have the findings, don't you?"

"Yes, I do."

"And?"

"As suspected, Rooney's DNA, skin cells, are inside, and Calum's DNA, blood on the outside. It confirms for me the hands that were in the gloves were the same hands that killed Calum."

"Well, kind of ties it up then?"

"It's part of the overall picture, darling, but pretty incriminating evidence I would say."

"Thanks, Dad." She puts the phone down and goes back to her painting.

"Jackie..."

CHAPTER 27

It is the High Court in Glasgow on 25th January 2017. The mother is there in the public seats as is the friend and the chief. The judge, Lord John Parlow reads out the indictment. "Sean Rooney has been indicted on a charge of murder. The charge is on the first of November 2016 at Claigan beach, near Achfara, he assaulted Calum Rooney, his son, born fourth of November 2008, deceased, and did strangle him and he did murder him."

The advocate depute makes his submissions on behalf of the crown and the case for the prosecution. He calls the consultant psychiatrists with their findings over the father's mental state and his fitness to plead, saying he is not able because of his mental illness to plead. The father looks around at this point. "Me, I am more than able to plead my innocence, what are they saying?"

"Please, Mr Rooney," Rosanne O'Neill, Rooney's advocate says. "Let me deal with this."

The consultants would also provide a view of whether the father could have committed such a crime as murdering his son. The advocate depute prepares to provide the case for the prosecution, detailing the evidence which would confirm the father, beyond reasonable doubt, he murdered the boy.

However, just then O'Neill makes her stab. "My Lord, on behalf of my client Sean Rooney and based on the sworn testimony of Mrs Kathleen McLeod—she was with him during the time of his son's murder—I can confirm he could not have been in the location at the time. He is indeed innocent of the crime with which he is accused."

The mother turns aghast to the chief and the friend. "What, he didn't do it?"

"It is only their defence, darling," the chief says. "It doesn't mean anything yet."

O'Neill presses on, however. "His DNA, found in the gloves, is not sufficient evidence to connect him with the crime; anyone, indeed the actual murderer himself, whomever he or she is, could have worn the gloves."

The chief fidgets uncomfortably in his seat. Judge Parlow casts a sideway glance towards the friend and to the father sitting in the dock.

O'Neill continues: "Additionally and fundamentally, we are advised by Police Scotland, based on its posthumous assessment of the case against Victor Temo, also suspected of the murder of Calum Rooney, there is a sufficiency of evidence Victor Temo is the actual murderer of Calum Rooney. My Lord, it is inconceivable both men can be guilty of this crime."

"What?" The father says, turning to the judge. "I didn't do it and he did?"

The advocate catches the father's eye and gives him a surreptitious glance, as if to say, 'You must let me speak for you, Mr Rooney'. She continues. "My Lord, based on the collective and irrefutable range of circumstances before the Court, and with the greatest of respect, my Lordship can only come to the singular conclusion my client is innocent of the crime before the court. Thank you, My Lord."

"Thank you, Ms O'Neill," Judge Parlow says. "I will now retire to consider my verdict."

The depute advocate looks to the chief, as if to say there is nothing he can do.

The father strikes a lonely figure in the dock. He knows his fate is in the hands of this person. His life is on a pivotal edge between incarceration and freedom to pursue his son's killer. Like a dying man his life to then is all before him, his life in Glasgow, his life in Achfara, his life to come, in—

"All stand," the court official says.

The judge sits down, prepares himself, and begins his pronouncements. "Based on this examination of facts and the evidence put before this court, I conclude there are not sufficient grounds to convict you, Mr Sean Rooney, of the murder of Calum Rooney. Neither alone nor in combination do the pieces of evidence relied on by the Crown convince me beyond reasonable doubt you, the accused, were Calum Rooney's assailant. As it stands, however I can only proceed on the evidence which has been presented to me and discharge my duty on that basis. Accordingly, in terms of the

Criminal Procedure (Scotland) Act 1995 I am able to make a verdict of Not Proven and I acquit the accused."

"What, not proven?" the father utters to the barrister. "What does he mean not proven?"

"Shushed," the advocate says.

"All stand," the court official says, as the judge takes his leave.

Once he does, the advocate goes to the father. "There was insufficient evidence to convict you."

"I know, am I free?"

"You are acquitted."

"A free man?"

"Yes, but not quite free, there are conditions."

"What? I need to find my son's killer."

"Please, Rooney, do not jeopardise your freedom. If you are brought back to the court based on anything which damages today's verdict, detrimentally, it would not go well for you."

"I'll keep it in mind. Thank you for all you have done for me."

The father makes his way out of the court. He is on the steps outside as the mother, the friend, and the chief make their own way out. The mother goes to him. He tries to put his arms around her. She moves back. "No Rooney, we have moved on. I wish you well. I knew you didn't do it, but there has been a lot of damage done to our relationship, so much so we can't go back, we can only go forward."

The friend moves to her side and takes her hand, as does the chief to the other side of her. "You need to stay on the treatment, Rooney, keep out of trouble and off the drink," the friend says. "Only then will you stay out of there." He points back at the courthouse.

"And mind son," the chief adds, "you cause my daughter any more trouble, and I will personally see you back inside."

The father looks at the mother forlornly, crestfallen to see his wife in the midst of these two men who would keep her from him.

"Jackie, I love you," is all that comes out.

"You need to take care of yourself," she says, as her minders usher her along the street and into a waiting car.

The father's first thought is to head for the Scotia Bar, only five minutes from the court. In there, he might find some solace. He resists the temptation, however; he needs to clear his name – to do that he needs a clear head.

“Fancy the Scotia, Rooney?” The father turns to see the hack standing behind him.

“Mr Scott, funny to see you here.”

“Well, I was at the back of the court, keeping my head well down. Journalist’s pass, all part of the story, you understand.”

“Yes, the story, Mr Scott. Let’s go to the Scotia, but not for drink.”

“Not for drink, Rooney, for the truth.”

CHAPTER 28

A banner hangs over the back of the stage in the hall: *Welcome to the Celebration of Calum's Life*, it says. It is the first day of the second month of February, in the year twenty hundred and seventeen.

It is *Imbolc, Là Fhèill Brìghde nan coinnlean* which, albeit the end of the first month, marks the beginning of the true spring. It is a Thursday evening at the seventh hour and the event has been arranged to mark the son's life. For me, *maha*, it is time to mark the boy's death, for his life after death is about to begin.

Everyone who matters to him is there, including his school friends, the father and mother, the grandfather, and members of the local community. The evening begins with school friends singing Gaelic songs, leading to traditional music, and then presentations from those who knew the boy most. The boy appears to enjoy the occasion, mingling amongst his friends.

The mother goes to the front near the stage and takes the microphone. "Thank you for coming tonight, on such a cold night of the year. Calum would be very pleased to see all his friends here and those who played such an important part in his … short life." She tries to hold back the emotions but they are there for all to see. The friend reaches for her and puts his arm around her in a show of oneness with her. The father stands to the side of the stage, which gives her and them prominence. They arranged the evening together after all.

The boy moves to the father's side as if to show defiance of the new partnership her mother has with the friend. She recites a short speech I will not repeat here, suffice to say it covers the boy's arrival and his love of the area, his seashells, the steam train, etcetera. "I hope you all have a lovely time and this will be a happy occasion; that's what we want for Calum, to mark his life with a joyful event. He was a happy boy after all. Thank you." All applaud.

Caber, the new leader of the community council, steps up next, and accepts the microphone from her. She looks at him sternly. He knows she is still angry at his turning up on her doorstep that night. "Thank you, Jackie, for this occasion," he says, "which, I believe, not only marks a celebration as you say of Calum's life but also the moving on of the community from undoubtedly the most difficult of times to happier times ahead. We are grateful to you."

"And if I can say," his wife Sheila adds from the midst of the congregation, "this community sees you as part of it, albeit much has changed for you." In this, everyone knows she is referring to the mother and father's separation and her taking up with the friend. "You are welcome here, dear." The mother nods in approval of her words, the father does not, nor does he take the opportunity to speak. He looks flat in mood, though those there, who know of his recent incarceration, would rightly say this is due to the heavy medication he is required to take to allow his return there this night.

The mother moves to stand with the father and the friend, while the grandfather, the chief, takes the microphone and the opportunity to have his say. "I am pleased you did this, Jackie." He lifts a glass of wine from a long table at the front. "I am proud of you. It can't be easy, but it needed to be done." He proposes a toast. "To you and Ben."

She takes the microphone. "Thank you, Dad, it marks a moving on in many ways, for me, and Ben, for Calum, for Rooney, and for all of us."

"For which we all wish you well," the chief adds.

The mother switches off the microphone to indicate the 'speeches' are over. "All's well that ends well, Dad," she says, going to his side.

"You'll be staying in Glasgow?"

"Aye, at Ben's, until we can find one of our own."

"And you and Rooney?"

"We remain friends. We've had a lot of water under the bridge."

"So true, much of it dirty water."

She looks at him, but resists the temptation of challenging him on his comment; instead, "We are going to do a wee thing at Calum's grave tomorrow, before we head down," she says. "Will you be there?"

"Of, course, he's my grandson. What about Rooney?"

"He's going to stay in the house until we decide what to do with it."

"Do you think he will stay in the area?"

"That'll be up to him. He says he wants stay close to the boy. He'll either move into the village proper and who knows maybe become a local or go back to Glasgow."

"It's for the best, Jackie."

"Aye, Dad, as you say, for the best."

The father is looking over, almost as if trying to determine what they are saying to each other. The hack is there too and sidles over to him. "Nice thing to do, Rooney."

"Aye, my son would be very happy to be here."

"Aye," the hack replies, not understanding the boy is right by the father's side. "We'll talk later, Rooney. I've some stuff to tell you. He moves off towards the back of the room where the food is being served.

I skulk around them and note the inspector and the constable are there too, keeping a low profile right at the back wall. That does not stop the constable from filling his pockets full of sandwiches from the table there. Caber also makes his way back there. The chief sees this and thinks this is a moment to grasp and also goes there.

The chief arrives, just as Caber says, "Well, Inspector, do you think your work here is at an end?"

Just before the inspector has a chance to answer, however, the chief says, "The investigation has reached a conclusion, Mr McKinnon. The sufficiency of evidence points towards Victor Temo, who killed Calum. In our view he was at the scene and he had a good reason to kill the boy, to harm the father."

"So, if Mr Rooney hadn't been here, the murder wouldn't have happened; is that what you are saying?"

"Yes, I am; absolutely sir."

"And John McIsaac and Donald McDonald?"

"Mere diversions from the truth, not to say they were blameless in their behaviour regarding wee boys."

Arriving and hearing this, the hack pitches in. "Both perpetrating abuse of a nature which should have had them arrested and convicted, Chief Constable?"

"Yes, sir," the constable says to the hack. "Had they, prior to their deaths, been brought to justice, with sufficient evidence to convict them."

The chief looks at the constable full in the face, as if to say, 'I'll deal with this.'

"Right," the hack says.

The father moves there to hear what they are saying. Then, as if a trigger has been pulled in his head, he starts. I knew he would. I was watching him scanning the room from the mother to the grandfather, to the friend, to the inspector, to caber, to the members of the community, to the hack. I wondered when it would come out. "I would like to say something," he says in a quiet voice.

The hack hears him but no one else does or, if they do, they do not acknowledge it. "Please everyone," the hack calls out. "Mr Rooney would like to say a few words." Everyone turns to the back of the room to train on the father.

"Thank you, Mr Scott." The father takes a drink of water. "I would just like to say..." All look at him, some in anticipation, some in trepidation, but a faint "thank you," comes out.

"Could you speak up, Rooney?" the *cailleach* says at the front.

The father clears his throat then raises his voice. "Thank you all for coming to commemorate my son's life," he says to a muffled applause. "And I just want to wish my wife, my soon to be ex-wife, I have no doubt, and her new man, soon to be her new husband, no doubt," he says, turning the mother and the friend, "the very best in their new ... relationship."

"Steady, Rooney," the mother says under her voice.

"I would, however, like to ask a question." The father is louder this time, becoming slightly more emboldened after being given the floor.

"Go on son," the *cailleach* prompts.

"Aye, right, thanks." He turns to the overall group. "I just want to ask; do you, as a community, believe you did everything to protect children here, in Achfara and Lochdarrach?"

You could have heard a pin drop is what would be said in such circumstances. But then a "what?" resounds around the room, and a "what did he say?"

"What do you mean, Rooney?" asks Caber. "It was you who brought murder to this place. This was a quiet place before you came here."

"Please everyone," the *cailleach* adds. "Maybe Mr Rooney can elaborate on what he is saying."

He does. "I will," he says. "Calum, his killer; McDonald and the boys from Glasgow; McIsaac and his … predilections; and how many others who have sinned, while this community looked on?"

"You are out of order, Rooney," Caber snaps. "You need to explain your remarks."

"OK, I will," the father says, plunging the room into silence. He takes a breath and lets go. "Well, you protected McIsaac and McDonald, hid their abuse of children, while you knew of their … behaviour."

"And what about your son, Rooney?" the *cailleach* hopes he will divert towards the Albanian incomer.

He does not. "A young boy was picked up in your midst," he says, "by a stranger, right in the middle of your community. Did anyone see anything, hear anything, say anything? See no evil, hear no evil, speak no evil. The three wise monkeys."

They are stunned and it takes Caber to challenge the father. "You are now going just too bloody far, Rooney."

"We are not the police, Rooney," the *cailleach* adds.

I look at these people, into their eyes, their hearts, their souls. They are deeply hurt, ashamed even. He has touched their sensibilities. They have changed, woken up from their complacencies.

"No, you are not," the father says. "Are they, Inspector Boyd?" He turns to the inspector. "Can I ask *you* a question, sir?"

"Yes, go on, Mr Rooney."

"Do you think your investigation into my son's death has been … successful?"

"The investigation has reached a conclusion, sir, you know this," the inspector says.

"Oh," the father says, taking out his notebook. "You are referring to Victor Temo?"

"Yes," the inspector says.

"Right." The father reads from his notebook. "The police have decided no further investigative steps will be taken, but wish to state publicly its view on the sufficiency of evidence – based on corroborating evidence from at least two different and independent sources, Victor Temo travelled to the location to harm the father of the child, Sean Rooney; however, while doing so he killed his child instead, based on his belief this would harm the father even more. We believe the child entered Temo's car, whereby he took him to an unknown location and murdered him before leaving him on Claigan beach. And you are happy with that?"

"We are…" The inspector looks to the chief, though it is clear he is on his own.

"I am asking you, Inspector Boyd, in your professional judgement, are you happy with that?"

"I must stand by the outcome of the investigation." The inspector looks once more the chief's way.

The father turns to the chief: "So, Chief Constable. Do you think you got your man?"

The chief would have been well advised not to say anything but he is determined. "I do, although for a period of time I was persuaded you may have done it."

"Me, Chief Constable?" The father looks to the mother.

"You were a suspect, Rooney; you were ill; you posed risk to others; you were charged and appeared in court."

"I was acquitted. The evidence levied against me was flawed."

"Indeed, sir, the evidence was insufficient to—"

"It was rigged," the father says. "I did not pick up my son that day; I was nowhere near the scene at the time."

"Oh, yes, your alibi. "The chief looks at the mother. "When it was established, proved."

"You were with your fancy woman in Invernevis," the *cailleach* says. "She spoke up for you at your trial."

Once again, there is a hush.

"It wasn't a trial," the father says. "I was deemed unfit to stand trial. It was an examination of facts; and, as far as the evidence was concerned, that was rigged."

The chief is poised to give the official view: "It was established you removed evidence from the scene," he says, "which may yet result in criminal charges; you had removed the gloves which were used by the killer, your gloves."

"As I said, rigged," the father says.

"I resent your assertion, sir."

"And how do you think the investigation into the murder of your … grandson went, Chief?"

"As the inspector says, it reached a conclusion."

"I didn't ask about the outcome of the investigation. I asked about the investigation itself. How do you think it went?"

"Well, it wasn't the smoothest—"

"No, not the smoothest, nor the best investigation known to the police, eh, Chief?"

"Now listen, Rooney, people know you have a grudge against me, which I cannot discuss in public, and which will in due course be examined, but for now…"

"No, you don't want people to hear the full story. Are you a travelling man, Chief Constable?" The chief is stony faced. "You know what I mean, are you a travelling man?"

"I don't know what that—"

"Has to do with the investigation? What about you Inspector Boyd?" The father turns to him. "How old is your grandmother, Inspector, do you celebrate the craft?"

"Most people here know I am a brethren of the local lodge," the inspector says. "We do a lot for the local communities."

"Oh, and was John McIsaac a member of the masons?"

It is his turn to be stony faced.

"We are not here to condemn others, Mr Rooney," Caber says, "especially not the dead who are not here to defend themselves."

"Rooney, this is supposed to be a celebration of your son's life," the chief adds, "not an exercise in your delusions."

"No, of course, this is about my son's life, but also his death," the father spits. "People need to know what has been going on here. They need to know about you bastards." He points towards the inspector and the chief.

"You will mind your manners, sir," the chief says.

"Oh, as you do sir," the father says. "Have you ever throughout this investigation allowed your allegiances to the Masonic order to influence the investigation?"

The chief's voice rises to match the throng. "As said, Rooney, this is part of your complaint, of which will be judged at the time."

"By other masons?"

"As too will be your … inappropriate and delusional rants," the chief says, looking at the friend. "It might be time you returned to hospital."

"Yes, as you would like, get me out of the way like you did when your henchmen arrived to remove me; but OK, let's move away from the ... probity of your investigation; let's look at the outcome of *your* investigation."

"As Inspector Boyd said, we have concluded our inquiries."

"And do you think it was a successful investigation?"

"As said—"

"Successful, Chief, means you got the right man."

"We got our man."

"You got *your* man, Chief, *your* man. The man you settled on for reasons only you can explain."

"I do not understand."

"Temo was *your* man."

"There were others in the frame, McIsaac, McDonald, who knows maybe others here." Rooney looks around the room. "Why did you settle on Temo?"

"As said, we had corroborating evidence."

"Oh, Temo came here to kill me. So says Lekë Zaharia, an Albanian crime boss who held a particular grudge against me from my days in Glasgow?"

"He was one of the informants who came forward with information."

"Why did he give the police incorrect information?"

The father looks to the hack.

"He provided crucial information."

"He was lying and you put him up to it."

"You are going too far. Inspector—"

"Why do you hate me, Chief Constable?"

"This is getting ridiculous."

"Well, you fabricated evidence to suggest Temo came north to harm me, so as to view me responsible for the murder of my child, so as to convince your daughter to get me out of her life, which worked." The father looks around at Jackie. "You influenced an investigation into a clear suspect, a local child abuser because he was ... a brother of the craft, using your Masonic influences over a Masonic underling." The father turns to the inspector. "You, Chief, were happy to accept incomplete evidence I was the killer of my child, flawed evidence. You were behind my incarceration to the State Hospital; hoping, even although I might have been cleared of killing my son, there would be enough to suggest I was a risk to the public to ensure I was locked away for the rest of my life. And, by far the worst for a senior police officer, you ignored crucial evidence which would have pointed to the real killer and that would have done it." The father turns to looks at the friend. "Why Hubert, why?" The chief looks like he is about to explode.

"I'll tell you, Dad," the mother says, intervening, at the same time stunning most there. "Because Rooney was never good enough for you." She looks at the father then to the grandfather. "You never wanted me to get back with him, to come up here with him. He posed a risk to me, but worse, Dad, he was an alcoholic and mentally ill, and even worse … he was a catholic."

"But even more, Jackie, I knew too much," the father says.

"What?"

"I was a risk to you, to him, his career, your career, his life, your life."

"You are a sick man, son," the chief says.

All the time the friend stands, vacant faced, looking on.

"An ill man, he knew too much." The father moves closer to him. "About your Masonic links, corruptive practices, MI5 … associations."

The father turns away from the chief, hoping the constable and the inspector will record these statements and send them to the Scottish Police Authority on the basis that these comments, now in the public domain, would need to be investigated. It is clear the father hopes the chief's days are numbered.

The father turns to face the friend. "But now I come to the most important member of the gang of thieves today," he says. "My friend, Mr Bensallah, or Ben, to his friends."

"Here we go, I'm next for the delusional rant," the friend says.

"Yes, indeed you are, you … murderer of my son."

There is a massive intake of breath throughout the hall only preceding: "Murderer? Did he say the friend was the murderer?"

"Steady, Rooney," says the mother. "Don't move into realms of idiocy; you may be many things, but you are not a stupid man."

CHAPTER 29

"Sharpen your pencil, Inspector Boyd," the father says. "There's more to come." Emboldened, he continues his attack on the credibility of the investigation.

"Now, Inspector, do you know Mr Bensallah planted my gloves, knowing my DNA was in them, at the murder scene in Calum's bag, leaving it to be found as incriminating evidence against me. No, you didn't? Well I took them from the scene, because I knew if I didn't I would be arrested, but more than that because I knew they would have contained the DNA of the real killer, this bastard."

"Aye, very good, Rooney," the friend says.

Jackie looks around to see faces paled by shock. "Rooney, please don't go there, you have said enough."

"I'll continue, if you please, Jackie. So, Inspector, this is the main event. This will conclude your investigation properly and perhaps save your career, after you explain how you were dominated by the chief constable that is." The inspector looks on intently, as if he is taking in the father's words. "Now, sorry to go back to this but it is relevant; back to our supportive community," the father says. "Do you know, Jackie, as others here know, and didn't say or come forward, Ben had been here for weeks leading up to Calum being killed?"

"What?" the inspector asks.

"Well he was, he booked into the hotel; yet, no one saw him and no one noticed him asking questions about us, where and when we came into the village, when we picked up the wee guy. Any investigation would ask people to come forward with any suspicious behaviour. Wasn't that kind of suspicious, folks; no?" The father looks around trying to take in the eyes of those there. "He was here following our every move, working out when we took Calum to school, when we picked him up, where I would be at certain times of the day, week; like being in Invernevis."

"Where you were with—"

"Yes, Jackie, but we can sort that."

"I don't know if we can, Rooney. Why didn't you come forward and say you were with her?" she asks. "It would have proven you couldn't have killed Calum, taken you right out of the loop." She looks at the inspector as she says this, him noting this.

"Because I would have lost you, Jackie; I had just lost my son and I would have lost my wife as well. You always said you would leave me if I failed you again and I knew you meant it."

At this point, I understand what they mean when they talk of love, and I think she does too.

"You were a bastard, Rooney."

"Yes, and so are you, Jackie; you are now with the murderer of our child."

"No, Rooney, he—"

"He played you as he did me, Jackie. He played the psychological game he knows so well. Demean me in your eyes, turn me into a raving lunatic, sick in the heid, a killer of your child, an alcoholic back to his old ways, a danger to you and everyone else, all to get you."

"Me?"

"Yes, you, and he succeeded."

"He succeeded because he protected me from you."

"Oh yeah, he even got the same car as me, so it would have been thought to be me. He killed Calum, Jackie. He picked him up from school in a car the same as mine, hoping it would be seen, to say Calum gets into my car and is killed shortly after. Of course, Calum got into his car, because he knew Ben and he thought he would be taken safely home. Poor wee mite was so wrong."

I can see the boy retreating from all of this. He is suffering.

"He took him off the road somewhere between the school and Claigan beach and strangled him. He decided to wear my gloves at the time, the gloves I used for my drystane dyking, with skin, sweat, blood from numerous injuries from the stones, my DNA. He sneaked into my shed and took them."

"Oh, I am a killer, a liar, *and* a thief," the friend says.

The father is on a roll. "He took Calum's body and laid it on the beach near the sea edge, opened his bag and scattered his stuff, left the bag at the road by the beach to be found by whoever came along, presumably looking for the lost boy. It was a Hogwarts one, only the one given Calum by Ben himself on his previous birthday. How sick is that, Jackie? It had my gloves in it with Calum's torn skin, splattered with blood from Calum's nose, when he hit him to shut him up."

"Don't Rooney, please," the mother pleads.

"Come on, Rooney, this is supposed to be a celebration of Calum's life, not a delusional rant," the friend says. "I'm getting onto Doctor Melville, time you were back in."

"Aye, you do that."

"It doesn't make sense, Rooney," the mother says. "You may have missed Calum on the beach. I remember, it was dark, no moon that night. I remember the night vividly, and Calum was found at the water's edge."

"He left the boy's bag at the side of the road, Jackie, to mark where Calum was. It was light grey, so it would have been seen even in poor light. I came across the bag, then I found Calum."

"And you knew it his bag?"

"Of course, I knew it was his. Harry Potter Hogwarts, the Hufflepuff one, the embroidered patches, the different houses."

The boy peers out from behind the mother.

"Don't Rooney, I can't bear it. I can't listen to anymore."

"Well, you have to Jackie. You need to know what kind of man he is."

"But, do you need to, in public?"

"They all need to hear, Jackie, especially Boyd." The father looks at the inspector, then to the crowd. "I found my dead son," reverberates around the room. He allows a pause for this to sink home. "I found Calum, dead, and he," the father points at the friend, "didn't expect me to find him. When he found out from you, Jackie, the bag and the gloves weren't found at the scene, he knew I had removed them. He tracked them down to my filing cabinet in my shed; then made sure you knew where they were to implicate me in the death of our child. Good one, destroying me and us, our marriage, at the same time, and getting you in the bargain."

"The note in my birthday card?"

"Yup; what he didn't know was I had the gloves forensically

tested in Glasgow and discovered another set of DNA, which I was sure would be there. Very strange the proper investigation did not discover another set of DNA to my own, funny, Chief, don't you think?" The father turns to the chief. "Little did I know at the time the skin cells inside the gloves belonged to Ben."

The mother has to stop him before he says anything more. "Please don't tell them how you got Ben's DNA, Rooney, please don't, not here."

"You know the main sources of forensic DNA, Jackie. I have to make clear how I got his DNA."

"Please tell them it was from his skin or blood or saliva."

"Sorry, Jackie, it was from semen. I got it from his semen. It was on your knickers."

"For fuck's sake, Rooney," she cries.

The father says, "It's evidence, Boyd. I am happy to turn it all over to you."

"Inspector Boyd," the chief says. "Are you going to allow this to continue?"

"Oh dear, oh dear, oh dear," the mother says, dropping her head into her hands, but not before she asks all there, "Well, salacious enough for you?"

"I'm sorry, Jackie," the father says. "I had to."

"So am I, Rooney, and I had to too," she says. "But I need to know why you would have suspected Ben; he was your friend."

"Oh, something the gaffer said."

"Eh?"

"Ben, mind you said the killer would be someone who would personally rejoice in my grief?"

"I said a lot of things to you, Rooney," the friend says. "I was trying to help you, not that you listened to me."

"Who would hate me enough to personally rejoice in my grief, Ben? Well, before I got to you, I had to tick a few boxes on that one." He turns to the mother. "I don't even think your father hated me that much, Jackie, but I did think about it, then I ruled him out, because I didn't think he would hurt you in that way, to kill your son, his grandson. Then there was Inverbeg, but he had nothing on me. I did wonder about, Temo, sent up here by Zaharia, who I had hurt in the past. Maybe he was someone who would have personally rejoiced in my grief. But I knew, I just knew Calum would have never got into Temo's car, no way, not even though he knew him."

"He went to his boathouse, Rooney," the mother says.

"Oh yes," the father says, "but we didn't know about that, and he would have known Calum would have had to tell us he had accepted a lift from someone we didn't know. But also, it wasn't his DNA that was in the gloves, he didn't do it."

"And how did you know that?"

"Because I got his hair from the brush in his house and sent it for DNA testing, compared with the DNA in the gloves and it wasn't him, Jackie."

"And Inverbeg and McIsaac? Did they hate me enough to kill my son? I don't think so. They didn't hate me. Inverbeg didn't have a car and he had his own … background to cope with."

"McIsaac?" asks the inspector.

"Well, his pal Andrew was being abused by him, no way Calum would have gone into his car alone, none of the kids would have. And if McIsaac had killed my son, he would have done so based on his own needs and not to harm me."

"The Glasgow mob?"

"I checked all of the key possibilities in that respect, the Taylors…"

"Oh, yes. Josh Turnbull, Rooney?" the friend says.

"He didn't do it."

"But you did him, Rooney, didn't you?"

The father declines to answer this, preferring to stay on the offensive. "As well as yourself, Ben, they are three possibilities which were never investigated, because the chief constable was happy he had Victor Temo, which would mean I could be held responsible for the death of my, our son, Jackie." He turns to the mother. "A good investigation would have flushed out all and any unknown possible person, someone who had something to gain from the death of our son, getting you, destroying me." He turns back towards the friend. "He, Mr Bensallah, hated me for getting you back. Getting you back and taking you away from me, would not only punish me, destroy me, but also he would be able to enjoy observing me grieving over the death of my son, as the gaffer said."

"Please, Rooney."

"He was your hero, Jackie; he had protected you from me and had taken you away from the man who would harm you, the alcoholic, the madman, the man who was suspected of killing your son."

"He wanted me, he loved me."

"I doubt it, Jackie. He is a classic psychopath. They don't love, they cosset people, he wanted to own you. He wanted what was mine, you, my life, my son. He was prepared to kill your son to get you, because he knew you would leave me, if we were no longer a family or if I had gone off the tracks."

"And what about an alternative, more lucid explanation, Rooney?" the friend says. "That you killed your son."

"I couldn't have, and you know it, Ben."

"Oh, because you were fucking someone in Invernevis at the time?"

"You knew I was having the affair, Ben." This prompts a hush in the room. "You knew I could never reveal it to save my neck because I would lose Jackie, but Katie did reveal it, even at the expense of her own marriage, to save me."

"Rooney, you don't need to say any more about it."

"No, Jackie, but I am happy to. It all needs to come out. How he managed to control both of us." The mother looks at the friend. "But there is something significant; he has been trying to tell us, Jackie."

"What Rooney?"

"Calum has been trying to tell us who his killer was."

"Oh come on, Rooney."

"You really are mad, pal," the friend says.

"Oh, the Taibshear said Calum kept pointing up to Beinn Mhor, Ben More, Big Ben. Who was 'Big Ben', to Calum, Jackie?"

"Big Ben was always Ben to Calum, Rooney." The mother looks at the friend once more and then around the room as if she is trying to see if the boy is there. The boy is square in front of her looking at her as if he has finally got through.

"You are a madman," the friend says to the father. "Your delusions are evident to everyone here today. You are now even implicating your son. Are you seeing him, Rooney, hallucinating perhaps?"

"He's the madman, Jackie, not me. He planned the whole

thing. An antisocial personality disorder in the truest, clinical sense and you know what I mean."

"I am trying hard, Rooney," she says; then, turning to the friend, asks, "Ben, is any of this true?"

The friend looks at her, then to other faces askance there. "He is mad, Jackie, don't believe a word, don't…"

"What he says needs to be explored, Ben, if even to be refuted. You must at least allow that."

"For god's sake, Jackie," the friend says. "Nothing he has said ties me to Calum. Where is his evidence?"

The father persists. "It should be investigated."

"It's him or me, Jackie."

"Don't put ultimatums to me Ben, just don't? What he says *will* be explored. Inspector?"

The inspector is staring at the friend.

"We can work this out, Jackie," the father says. The boy looks at them, as do all there. Is this a sign of togetherness, repentance?

"Would you really have gone to jail for a crime you didn't commit, the murder of our son, rather than lose me?"

"Yes."

This is too much for the friend. The father turns to face him, but he is gone. "Ah, Elvis has left the building," he says. The mother looks to her side askance. "He's done a runner."

"Let him go," she says.

The chief sees what is happening. All his efforts in getting his daughter away from him are crumbling in front of him. He makes a breenge at the father. The hack stands in his way.

Just then, Mary McCourt, the chair of the SPA appears in the hall, her voice cutting through the murmurs like a scythe. "I think it right I should appear here at this time," she says. Everyone spins round in her direction. "I want to thank Sean Rooney for inviting me here today to this momentous event. I did not know Calum, but I did know his parents and Mr Kaminski, the chief, while in Glasgow, during a painful period of time for me when I lost my husband John, a police officer, to ISIS, and whereby I accepted the role of chairwoman of the SPA."

The blood has drained from the chief's face. "Mary, it is good to see you," he says.

"I doubt it, Chief, once I explain why I am here."

"Oh," the chief says.

"You'll know Mr Rooney raised a complaint of misconduct against you with the SPA?"

"I do, all complete drivel."

"Well, not so, Chief, the complaint has been provisionally upheld by the SPA pending a full investigation into your conduct. Meanwhile, the SPA has suspended you."

At this, the congregation start to chant, "Corrupt, corrupt, corrupt."

"I think you should leave, Chief," says the Inspector.

The chief replies, "I am here in a personal capacity; do not challenge me, Inspector, it is not very wise."

The inspector stands firm. "Sir, I am arresting you on suspicion of perverting the course of justice," he says. "Constable?"

"This man hasn't said anything which changes a thing. Nothing in what he says is the truth, nothing," the chief calls, inflaming the crowd even more.

"*Eucoireach*," comes from the *cailleach*.

"You need to go with Constable Broomlands," the inspector says. "Please, sir."

The chief tries to stand firm but the constable has his arm and is pushing him towards the door. "Take your hands from me," he says to the constable. "I'll go, if only to clear my name, which believe me, won't take long. I'll be back."

Words of "rotten, rotten, rotten" follow the constable and chief out.

"And so the chief of Police Scotland makes his exit from the stage," the father says.

The chief scowls at him as he is pushed through the door. The inspector remains. "It is my duty to stay, to record what is being sent here," he says. He looks around the congregation. "You would expect me to."

Mary McCourt nods at the father.

The father says to her, "I just hope you will take my comments seriously and conduct a decent investigation into the murder of my, our child?"

"I have noted everything that has a bearing on this case."

"I am pleased about that, Inspector," the father says.

"And do your job this time, Inspector Boyd," the *cailleach* adds.

The inspector nods.

"This needs to stop now, Rooney," the mother says. "Please, you've got what you want: me."

"I need to face Ben, Jackie. I know he's not going to jail. The chief's right, there's nothing to tie him to Calum. I need to get him to confess."

"Please, Rooney, don't." She tries to deter him. "You'll end up in jail."

Even the inspector tries to stop him. "Rooney, don't, it would only go one way."

"Please, Inspector Boyd, I know the chief has dominated you, drove the investigation, and deterred you from your inquiries, but I don't have the confidence in you getting him. He was right under your nose."

The father heads out of the door. "Do you need any help, Sean?" Caber calls after him. "I'll go with you.

"And so will I," says Post.

Maggie moves closer to the mother. "You OK, Jackie?" she says, putting her arm around her.

"I feel as if my whole life has been laid bare before these people," the mother says. "I guess they all got what they wanted."

"I don't think so, Jackie."

"The inspector got something to work on and Scott got his story; front page news tomorrow."

"I doubt it Jackie." The mother looks at her. "There's more to Mr Scott than you think."

"Rooney said a lot of things there," the mother says. "I'm still trying to take it all in. I feel my life has just exploded in front of me, in front of the whole world."

"I know, Jackie, but maybe, like Rooney says, this will be all to the good, and a proper investigation will reveal the truth."

"What, Ben planned everything, down to the nth degree?"

"You can't believe that?"

"He wanted me, he loved me. He told me."

"And he knew you would never leave Rooney, not as long as you and he were together with Calum; you were a family."

"Yes, we were." She looks to the floor.

"He even tried to kill your love for Rooney, by him destroying what you loved most, your son."

"I can't believe he wanted me so badly he was prepared to kill my son to get me."

"He constructed a plan so perfect it could succeed in getting Rooney locked up and you estranged from him."

"Even to the extent he would kill Calum and put the blame on Rooney. I'm still confused; how the did he do it?"

"What, he followed you both around for weeks establishing your patterns?"

"And nobody saw a thing."

"I booked him in, Jackie. But I didn't know…"

"You didn't know he was up to case the joint to kill my son? He had been here before, you would've seen him with us; we were in the bar for dinner often."

"We had no reason to believe he was here to do anything, other than to see you guys; you don't think."

"You didn't mention it later, as if it was suspicious?"

"We, or at least I, didn't think it was suspicious; how could I? He never asked me any questions about you. He must have asked other people, Inverbeg maybe."

"Jesus, he came up here before, he bought Calum the bag for his birthday; that bag. He built up a relationship with him, even picked up Calum from school for us. He knew Calum would have gone into the car with him."

"Rooney said he bought the same kind of car."

"Guess he wanted the teacher to recognise it as Rooney's. I remember him saying he admired Rooney's car, how he said he wanted one just like it."

"He planned this, darlin'."

"He sure did. He timed his arrival perfectly, exactly ten minutes before I arrived at the school – by that time he was off along the coastal road."

"While knowing your husband was with Katie McLeod."

"Did you know about her?"

"Yes, there were rumours."

"And you didn't tell me?"

"This is not that kind of place, Jackie; we leave people to sort things out themselves. It's the best way."

"The best way, head in sand stuff?"

"Jackie. I need to explain."

"Yes, please."

"These communities have suffered much hardship." I can vouch for this. "They have been cleared from their lands, they have been dragooned into serving foreign kings, they have suffered starvation, poverty, degradation; their language, cultural, music, way of life removed from them."

"I am listening."

"They are protective because they have to be, but they are changing, they are changing, Jackie, and this has been a big learning curve for them." For me, also! "They have endured hundreds of years subjected to the tyranny of land owners, tied houses, unfair rents, hardship, starvation, fighting for causes not of their making, evictions, clearances, being sent away from their lands many thousands of miles, never to return. They have had their customs taken away, nearly lost their religion, their way of life, their culture, and only managed to save it by being protective; then they have the world's attention brought to bear on them: why the hell wouldn't they be protective, Jackie?"

The mother looks at her for a few seconds. "And now they know my lover killed my son."

"For god's sake, Jackie, they know what you have been through. Don't be too hard on yourself, darlin'; lovers often kill for many reasons, revenge, fear of losing that which they love—"

"Possession…"

"Coveting that which they cannot have."

"I need to find Rooney, Maggie."

"Do you want me to go with you?"

"No, I need to see him myself. I'll be all right."

"OK, I'll be here or in the Small Isles, where else."

"Thanks, Maggie."

Maggie puts her arms around the mother, then releases her as the mother heads for the door.

The hack stops the mother in the car park. "Jackie, I need to talk to you."

"I need to find my husband."

"I need to be with you in this. You are at risk. Let me go with you."

"Why, Mr Scott, you have your story."

"There are some things you should know, about you and Rooney."

She looks at him.

"You are not a hack, who are you?"

He takes her arm and pulls her to a bench next to the front door of the hotel. "I am MI5, Jackie, MI5."

She looks at him intently in the eyes. The hack appears in a different light altogether, like a good actor out of role. "Why?"

"We have an open case on Ms Dempsie, remember her?"

"Jeez, how could I forget; Jean, the mad woman?"

"Rooney was a suspect."

"And so, I believe, was I. Is that why you were here?"

"The case had gone cold. Then Calum was murdered, the son of suspects in the murder of an MI5 agent. This triggered a reinvestigation. Was it connected? Was the killer the same person who killed Jean? Kills Jean, kills the son of her lover. Was it the mob, ISIS; whatever, it was back on and I was in charge of it."

"You were here to do that rather than a story on us or to sniff out a story, a poor investigation, as you said."

"Well, it has been my trusty ruse, in a number of my investigations."

"Not one you can use again."

"It gave me the means, as an investigative journalist would."

"As an MI5 agent would?" He stays quiet. "What now?"

"Well, as you can guess, arrests are occurring with more to come."

"My father, perverting the ends of justice?"

"Plus contempt of court and breaking chief constable legal duties."

"As a good—"

"Mason would do?"

"Ben; what happens to him?"

"We need to keep Rooney away from him. He'll kill him."

"He will."

"And we need to keep you out of it, too, Jackie. There's no knowing what Ben will do. He is obsessed with you."

"He wouldn't hurt me."

"No? What about on the beach."

"Him, how do you know it was him?"

"I got … informed of the attack."

"Boyd?"

"As you would expect, I had access to his reports."

"Ben attacked me?"

"It was easy to find the disturbed sand where you were attacked; I took impressions, photographs of the footmarks, even a hand mark in the sand. I compared it with Ben's, easy to do, got him to stand in salt at the bar of the pub, same footprint, very amateurish really, surprised at him."

"The bastard, now I really will get him."

"I don't want you to risk facing him. A high-profile Police Scotland team is on its way from Glasgow; they'll deal with Ben and take charge of the investigation here. Ben will be charged with murder, contaminating evidence, perverting the course of justice, and a few other naughty things."

"Rooney?"

"He'll be exonerated. The finding of not proven will be appealed and overturned."

"His views?"

"His paranoid beliefs and delusions of persecutions are real. He didn't kill his son, the compulsion order will also fall, but there's still the hiding evidence part, perverting the—"

"Course of justice."

"Yes, but we'll take care of that, it was justified under the circumstances."

"Thank god." She gets up. "I need to find Rooney."

Again, he holds her arm. "Jackie?"

"Yes."

"Make a go of it here, with Rooney; you are both needed in this community. They are not—"

"Bad people? No, they are not. I'll maybe get on the community council."

"You could do worse. Jackie?"

"Yes?"

"My job is done here."

"Jean?"

"Ben killed her, proxy killing through Alan Taylor, to pin it on Rooney."

"Jesus, how do you know?"

"Let's say mob, MI5 cooperation."

"Bingham?"

"Yes, through the Taylors. A big demand from them to get back into the syndicate, equal plea from Alan to get us off his back, to allow his sons back into the UK without threat by us."

"Him?"

"Happy to leave him in Pattaya, Thailand."

"You knew where he was?"

"Yup."

"But didn't go for him?"

"Nope, he did us a favour in … dealing with Jean; big embarrassment to the agency, loose cannon, dangerous woman. We wanted who fingered Taylor, however, in the knowledge he or she was more dangerous to us."

"Rooney?"

"We knew it wasn't Rooney, albeit we knew it was a mob hit. We had his mobile monitored twenty-four-seven and we were watching him; besides we knew he wouldn't have been so stupid. No, this was something more devious, personal."

"Personal. Who would rejoice personally in Rooney's grief?"

"Indeed, though we did think about your father, but again we were monitoring him and he would have had too much to lose to take on MI5, but then, when your boy was killed, we wondered if there was a link."

"It's what brought you here – the killer had the same motive here as he had with Jean, to destroy Rooney?"

"Yup."

"Machiavellian bastard."

"Bye Jackie." He pulls her close and embraces her. "Now, go get yourself some happiness, you deserve it."

"*Glè mhath, slàinte mhath* as they say around here, and *oidhche mhath* too, in fact all the *mhaths*to you." He smiles. She wonders if she will ever see this man again. "Maggie?"

"I'll explain to her. It wasn't all a ruse."

"Men!"

He has to move on. I have grown to know and like this boy. Like no other, he has impressed me, this child. Like no adult or older person, he has shown a mature strength, the kind I have seen rarely. He has troubled me, however, also like no other.

Before I dispatch his soul to its inevitable destiny, there is something I must do, something I have never done before. I question myself on the possibility of this; whether I can, whether my powers allow me to, whether my obligation allows me to. I question myself. Why would I do this? Is it for the boy or is it for me?

The friend moves to his car in the knowledge he has one opportunity to run, to disappear before they arrive to question him or at least the father to kill him. He knows, however, as long as those in the community hall are listening to the father's remarks, he has a chance to get away, and he will use the dark to make his escape. He moves through the car park, turning from time to time to see if anyone has noticed his departure from the Achfara hotel. Everyone is at the hall, but his eyes say he is anxious, the sweat on his brow says he is scared. He needs to get away from here.

He looks at the moon, full in the sky, which offers some illumination. A rabbit comes out of the hedge and startles him, itself startled to see a man there, turning and making its way back. Then an owl takes his attention by its hoot. He curses under his breath at the amount of wildlife distraction interfering with his attempts at departure there this night; he did not account for me.

I howl three times, loud enough to be heard in the village hall, enough to herald my task to him this night. He would have heard of me, the *Cù-Sith*, who comes to claim a soul. He may ask himself who in the village I have arrived to take, not thinking for one second it may be him.

I gird myself and prepare to attack. He has the door to his car open, ready to step inside. My reification may be a fantasy in my part for I have not had physical form for many years. I am not convinced if I leap at him my talons will tear his flesh or my teeth will rip his skin. I dispatch souls, I do dispatch physical forms. I reach into them and take their soul from inside their body, buried deep in their chests. It is not of physical form; however, it is a soul. It is not a heart to tear out of a chest or blood to be sucked out of a vein, yet for me it is as physical as any of these things. I just have to believe it. I do, and it happens.

You know how he dies. I explained it to you at the beginning of these events; suffice to know he has 'moved on'.

I slink off into the night, turning only to see the father approach the body of the friend. He stands looking down on the headless corpse, then to the head itself. He smiles. In moments he is joined by the mother and others who heard the scream.

The father holds the mother, turning her away from the sorry sight. "Justice is served," he says.